# THE
# SCRIBE
# TRIBE

## VOLUME TWO

COLLECTED SHORT STORIES
AND POEMS

# THE
# SCRIBE
# TRIBE

## VOLUME TWO

# THE WRITERS OF
# BALLA BALLA

Edited by Diane Brown, Melissa Sayers, Roderic Grigson

Published by Grigson Publishing

ISBN: 978-0-6484190-4-4

Cover design and interior formatting:
Mark Thomas / Coverness.com

# DEDICATION

This book is dedicated to lovers of books and to anyone who has ever dreamt of writing. It is also dedicated to those who have always planned to write and eventually cast aside their self-doubt to emerge from the isolation of their silent potential by activating themselves and embracing the challenge of putting pen to paper.

# APPRECIATION

In this second volume, we owe many people for their help, encouragement, and advice.

We are especially indebted to our writers, editors and reviewers. They have toiled endlessly while proposing improvements for the stories in this publication.

We are also very much indebted to our readers. Some of you have corresponded with us, asking questions that have led to some interesting discussions.

Our original editorial team's enormous and excellent contribution has stood us in good stead for this edition.

We want to thank them again: Melissa Sayers, copy editor; Diane Brown, editor and proof-reader; Lauren McCarthy, proof-reader; Roderic Grigson, developmental editor and publisher.

Our original book designer and ebook conversion provider, Mark Thomas of Coverness.com, who lives in Wales, has done a heroic job of converting our second volume. Thank you, Mark!

We would also like to acknowledge the support and boost we received from the Balla Balla Community Centre. They have provided the platform for us to grow as a writing group. We encourage everyone to support and use the centre's excellent services to this unique community we all enjoy.

# FOREWORD

To describe the last 18 months as a rollercoaster would be an understatement. Lives put on hold, loved ones kept apart, employment disrupted – it certainly has been a difficult time for many people.

Solace has, however, come in many different forms. For me, as someone who lives alone, I have taken comfort in being able to take my dog on daily walks to the dog park. I have enjoyed watching how such a simple activity has been able to bring so many diverse people together. People who were strangers 18 months ago are now friends. People who would pass one another in the streets or the local supermarket aisle are now stopping to say hello. Asking about one another's children and dogs, ensuring they have enough toilet paper and other essentials to last another extended lockdown.

Community is, indeed, an exciting concept. It is often used to denote a shared sense of place within a given geographical area. In some ways, the current pandemic has forced many of us to become more intimately acquainted with our own local neighbourhoods by not travelling. However, there is certainly comfort and familiarity that comes from being able to pop into your local café and order 'the usual'; or knowing which park attracts the best afternoon sun.

The pandemic has, however, also taught us that community can come in a variety of forms. Long-lasting relationships extending beyond immediate geographic and/or genealogical ties can also provide a sense of community.

A sense that we belong. A feeling that we matter. A sense that we are part of something bigger than ourselves.

For some people, that sense of belonging may come from daily trips to the local dog park or their favourite cafe. For others, it may come in the form of late-night online Scrabble sessions with fellow *word nerds* (logophiles) from across the globe.

For the authors in this book, it has clearly come in the form of being able to engage with one another and in being able to share their stories and reflections of living in this time and this place, within the broader context of Covid-19.

Moving forward, I hope that one of the lessons we all take from the pandemic is that life is precious and precarious, and we all need people in our corner who have our backs when the unexpected comes. So invest in relationships. Take the time to really get to know the people that surround you. Say good-morning to strangers at the dog park, because to quote American author and political activist Helen Keller – *"Alone, we can do so little; together, we can do so much"*.

*Nicole Battle*
*CEO, Neighbourhood Houses Victoria*

# INTRODUCTION

The first writer I watched at work was my grandfather. He would close his study door and sit down to write a letter to his long-separated son and youngest daughter, one living in Melbourne and the other in faraway London. He had seen neither since they had left Colombo on their life journeys many years previously.

The task was familiar to him as he wrote, every month, a personal commentary on the news from the country and their siblings, living in a nation going through the growing pains of independence.

The sounds of his typewriter came in hesitant bursts, with long silences in between. Hours went by. Summoned for lunch, he was often silent and preoccupied and soon excused himself to get back on the job. Finally, he would finish, grumbling that he should have done a better job, remembering things he should have included.

This image of my grandfather pecking away at his ancient Remington typewriter left a lasting impression in my mind.

Writers have always created tangible memories for loved ones simply by writing things down. But writing is hard, even for writers who do it all the time. Less frequent practitioners often get stuck with an awkward passage or find a muddle on their screens and then blame themselves. What should be easy and flowing looks tangled and feeble or overblown – not what was intended at all. *What's wrong with me*, each one thinks? *Why can't I get this right?*

Writing is a lifelong process, and the best ones never stop learning or striving to improve their craft. Some stories strike through like lightning, coalescing and coming out fully formed. And when that happens – what a pure gift it can be. But more often than not, they trickle. They drip. There is some grit and tenacity involved in smoothing out the rawness.

The pandemic has made us all stand still and face the constantly breaking news that has changed our lives forever. What does it mean to continually have to respond creatively to what is happening around us?

Now, more than ever is the time to put onto paper all those stories that have accumulated since it all began as a record for the community and for future generations.

As our ancestors once did, recording those bleak days in 1918 as they navigated their way through the Spanish Flu, many lessons hard-learned at that time have undoubtedly helped us in 2020.

It's increasingly difficult to know what stories you will receive when you begin a project of this nature. The day and age of massive organisations taking care of us from beginning to end are over. But that is exciting news. It means that we choose the life we want for ourselves. It's about people reinventing themselves and starting new conversations for their being.

This change is clearly demonstrated by the diversity of the stories in this volume. The key is to be bold right at this moment. Right now! And our eighteen authors have embraced this moment with over 44 stories and poems, accounts of events and families with a deep hope that this book will engender a greater appreciation of the year past and a more respectful approach to the future.

We have brought together these stories from our group, their history, and their life in a panorama of vibrant and imaginative display in one fell swoop. The historical, the economic, the spiritual and familial life all moulded together as one throbbing unit.

As this book has been compiled through the cooperation of many, it is hoped that life will always progress with the collaboration of all.

*Roderic Grigson*
*August 2021*

# TABLE OF CONTENTS

# THE
# SCRIBE
# TRIBE

## VOLUME TWO

# STORIES

# OF THE

# PANDEMIC

# THE YEAR 2020

*DIANE BROWN*

## PROLOGUE

The year 2020 heralded its arrival with the continuation of the unusually intense bushfires. They were raging from as early as July 2019, their intensity giving them the name of the Black Summer Bushfires. Before the CFA eventually extinguished the fires, they had taken 34 lives and caused millions of dollars in damages, especially in Queensland, New South Wales and North-Eastern Victoria. They also wiped out a vast number of our native wildlife and fauna.

During January 2020, the fires continued to rage, and it seemed as if the whole of Australia was on fire. The coverage of the fires took up most of the evening news, with just some added details of an unknown virus, supposedly being traced to a Seafood Wholesale Market in Wuhan, China. Then, on

25th January, the first COVID-19 case was discovered in Victoria, brought into Victoria by an overseas traveller from Wuhan, China.

Initially, this information did not worry most Australians, believing that the virus was just another type of flu in their usual laid back fashion. However, it was not until reports began to filter thru that the virus was rapidly spreading throughout Europe, Asia and the Middle East that the Australian population started to worry.

In March 2020, the cruise liner "Diamond Princess" discovered that COVID-19 had infected their ship, and nearly 4,000 passengers were required to isolate themselves in their cabins until the ship docked in Sydney.

That same month the World Health Organization declared a pandemic. As a result, March 2020 was the month that Victoria experienced its first lockdown. Mask wearing outdoors was mandatory. Bars, cafes, cinemas, casinos and gyms were closed. Outdoor gatherings were limited to only two people. Schools were closed, and people were encouraged to work from home wherever possible.

By April/May 2020, cases began to ease in Victoria, and the nation believed it had defeated the virus. As a result, the government reduced some restrictions, and Victorians again looked forward to returning to their everyday life. However, from the beginning of 2020 until October that year, 820 Victorians had lost their lives to COVID-19.

In June, serious problems began to arise in Victoria. A second wave of the virus hit the Melbourne CBD. It spread rapidly, with several outbreaks occurring in Aged Care facilities and throughout the hotel quarantine systems. Authorities placed all international flights into Melbourne on hold, and in July, up to 3,000 public housing residents were plunged into compulsory lockdown with no notice whatsoever.

The NSW – Victorian Border was closed for the first time in history, and Melbourne was sent back into lockdown. This lockdown lasted until mid-October, a total of 112 days. At the time, it was one of the world's most stringent and longest lockdowns. The restrictions during those 112 days were harsh. Residents were only allowed to leave their homes for essential shopping, medical appointments, caregiving and one hour of exercise each day. A night curfew from 8 pm until 5 am was in place.

These months of lockdown changed the way many Victorian residents lived their lives. Some took the time to practice new skills, some took up new crafts, some complained non-stop, and others lived through months of solitude, gradually slipping into sadness and depression as the death counts continued to rise.

First, people mourned the loss of contact with their family and friends. Second, they became angry that the virus kept spreading despite most people complying with the restrictions. Third, people worried about their loved ones overseas, wondering if they would ever see them again. Finally, Victorians became increasingly angry when they saw how the other States of Australia were almost back to normal. Victorians, however, could not leave their homes for more than an hour a day.

So how did the average Mr and Mrs Melbournian cope through those long, long days, weeks and months of lockdown? To discover that, we spent many hours interviewing Dave and Joan, an elderly couple who live in a small weatherboard cottage in a leafy suburb 15 kilometres from the CBD. Fortunately, Joan kept a diary and has an excellent memory, so their story explains how the second COVID-19 lockdown affected Melbourne residents.

*

"Here we go again," Joan looked up at Dave as she rested her knitting on her lap.

"What's that?" Dave queried, his head peeking over the top of the newspaper.

"Didn't you just hear the news report? We're going into lockdown again. So come on, grab your shoes. We better head off to the supermarket before all the workers get there."

As Dave drove around and around the car park, it appeared that everyone in their neighbourhood had the same idea. Masked shoppers crammed the shops, pushing past others to access the registers, their shopping trolleys filled. Joan shook her head in despair, discovering there was no flour or rice left on the shelves but felt lucky that she was able to grab a bundle of eight toilet rolls.

Joan raised her voice over the endless pop music that blared along the aisles. "By the look of things here, we'd best stock up. It looks as if things are going to get tough for a while."

After arriving home and making a couple of trips to the car to collect the shopping, they staggered into the kitchen. Groceries covered their kitchen bench, many of the items that they would not usually purchase, and a lot of the things, to use Joan's own words, were "just in case we need them."

After storing the groceries away and surveying the bulging shelves and well-stocked freezer, Joan poured a cup of tea with a sigh of relief.

"Well, Dave," Joan looked towards her husband. "This time, we are going to be more active than we were during the last lockdown. No more sitting around doing nothing. We are going to draw up a plan."

The first two weeks of lockdown passed quite swiftly. Joan put her plan into action, cleaning the windows both inside and out, washing and ironing the curtains, and relining and sorting the kitchen drawers. They were both proud of their achievements and decided to give themselves a few days off before tackling other chores on Joan's seemingly endless list. The following two weeks dragged a little, but they kept their spirits high, polishing furniture, sorting through their old clothes and spending time in the garden when the weather permitted. Four and a half weeks passed, and apart from their one hour's exercise outdoors, they had remained in their home. They decided to order their groceries online as their children had suggested that it was a good idea. Joan was relatively a computer literate person, and their son advised her how to place grocery orders.

They both felt lucky to have family members who kept in touch. Their son and daughter regularly telephoned, although their conversations gradually became somewhat stilted, having very little to talk about as the days started to flow into one. Every day seemed like the day before, knowing the following day would be the same as the last. But what they wanted more than anything else was to see their children and grandchildren. They desperately wanted to touch their faces and give them a hug.

Joan managed to keep herself busy. She was always a person who loved reading, enjoyed her knitting and her great love was writing short stories that she emailed to her grandchildren. Dave, however, was quite different. He was used to being active. He missed his bowls, his volunteer work, and his Bingo. As the weeks turned into months, he became increasingly bored and complained about the lack of things to do.

Joan sighed, thinking back to those days when Dave kept himself busy away from the house. She had cherished those quiet days to herself, playing the music on the radio that she liked, not having to cook lunch, and just generally enjoying her own company. Dave always returned home quite energized, and their conversation flowed over the dinner table as he related his day's event to her.

That all seemed like such a long time ago. Now they seem to have run out of conversation, and every day seemed the same.

Every morning, they religiously sat glued in front of their television to listen to the Premier and the Minister for Health, always hoping the restrictions would start to ease. But no, if anything, the limits were becoming more and more severe. The evening news was all about COVID-19. It seemed as if there was no other news in the country. Medical staff were at breaking point, and the elderly in Aged Care were dying at an alarming rate.

Dave felt warm tears flow down his cheeks as they watched rubber gloves clutching old, wrinkled hands that rested on white sheets and compassionate eyes crinkling in smiles hidden behind a masked face covered by a plastic shield. Dave knew that it was the last thing these older people saw before they died. He reached for Joan's hand, realizing that this could happen to one of them.

The winter arrived, and it was too cold for gardening. Dave had managed to keep himself busy with jigsaw puzzles and had even tried reading, but he was becoming more and more restless. He was now wearing tracksuit pants every day, deciding that it was too much trouble to wear his good trousers.

"Who's going to see me?" he queried when Joan complained about his appearance. "And anyway, you must have put my pants in the dryer, as they are getting quite tight."

Joan's eyes rested on the back of Dave's head as he played a lonely game of Solitaire. "We need to find something more interesting for you to do."

Dave turned towards her. "Well, I do have an idea, but it could cost a bit."

"Well, out with it. What do you want to do?"

"Kayo," Dave's face lit up with a smile. "If we had Kayo, I could watch the car racing all the time."

At last, Dave was happy when Kayo was installed within the next couple of days. He spent most afternoons in the back room watching his car racing, and although Joan was relieved to see that Dave was his old self again, she hadn't realized that the mosquito buzzing noise from the cars as they raced around the track would now become part of her day.

There was one particular day that stood out in Joan's mind. It was after their dear friend died. He had been ill for some time, and they always planned to attend his funeral, but now, due to COVID, only ten people could attend. Their son had explained how they could watch the service on the computer, so they decided they would act as if they were in the church. They both dressed in their good clothes, Joan finding her shoes extremely uncomfortable as she wore slippers most of the time and Dave squeezing into his good suit pants, again complaining that all his clothes were too tight. Joan wore her little black hat and Dave his new tie, both solemnly sitting in front of their computer screen, dabbing at their eyes with their white handkerchiefs as they watched their friend's family members all separated, sitting on hard-backed chairs. It broke their hearts to see their friend's wife crying alone with no family member sitting beside her. After the service, they held a wake of their own in the loungeroom, both sitting primly in their best clothes over a cup of tea, eating the scones that Joan had made before the service, both sharing memories of their old friend.

As previously mentioned, Joan had always loved writing. As a result, she regularly attended a writing group meeting at the local community centre. Unfortunately, the centre cancelled all its regular sessions due to the pandemic restrictions in place. However, Joan was delighted to receive an email from the coordinator explaining that the writing group planned to hold a meeting via Zoom. Joan had no idea how to work Zoom, but after an exciting telephone call with her son, who gave her some simple instructions, she decided to join the meeting.

Joan felt quite excited as this was the first time she had ever participated in a Zoom meeting. The coordinator emailed the nominated time and login details earlier, so she sat in front of her computer ten minutes early to not be late for the meeting. As the minutes ticked by, she patiently waited until four minutes before starting time, then taking a deep breath, she whispered to herself, "Well, here we go."

Glued to the screen, she carefully read each instruction as it appeared, until at last, she reached a "Click here for Zoom Meeting" prompt. Feeling just a little apprehensive, she clicked the enter button. Gazing at the screen in awe, Joan noticed a few little boxes with faces inside. There was Marie, her Italian friend and Betty and Irene all smiling from the screen.

Bill, the coordinator, spoke out from the screen, "Welcome, Joan, how are you today?"

"I'm fine," Joan answered, her eyes searching for his little box.

"You have to un-mute, Joan," Bill advised.

*"Un-mute."* Joan thought to herself. *"What on earth is un-mute?"*

After being told to click on the red microphone with the line through it at the bottom of the screen, Joan exclaimed, "Oh, how exciting. Can you hear me now?" Next, Bill explained that Joan should move her screen, that all the others could see only the top of her head. So Joan carefully pushed the screen further away, only to be told again that all they could see was the ceiling and that Joan must pull the screen towards herself.

By the time Joan adjusted the screen, Gladys and Mary had joined the group, creating more little face boxes at the side of the screen. Next, Bill suggested they try a virtual tour of the group, asking each person in turn what they had been doing during the lockdown and what had they been writing. Before long, it was Joan's turn, and as she started to speak, the little boxes slid to one side, and her face loomed large in front of her, taking up the whole screen.

*"My God,"* Joan stared at her face in horror. *"That really can't be me."*

As Joan tried to concentrate on her response to Bill's questions, she could not stop studying the face that peered out at her. When she had freshened up in front of the bathroom mirror that morning, she thought she looked quite nice. But now, she was horrified. She did not recall seeing those neck wrinkles before and her hair. She was mortified at her hair. She had only put a colour in last week, and now, as she looked at her hair on the screen, all she could see were various shades of grey right down through the middle part. And her chin. She never realized that she was starting to develop a double chin, and oh no, it appeared that she had fine droop lines down the side of her mouth.

As the meeting continued, Joan kept glancing at her face, now staring out from the little box on the side of the screen. Finally, she tried shifting in her chair and noticed that the hint of a double chin disappeared when she sat side-on. Also, placing her elbow on the desk and resting her chin on her hand made the neck wrinkles much less noticeable.

The meeting lasted about 45 minutes, and a date was picked for the following week. However, Joan later confessed to Dave that she was so fascinated by her appearance, she did not remember much of the discussion.

While Dave was settled in the back room watching the car racing, Joan spent most of the next day gazing in the mirror, looking for those awful tell-tale signs of ageing that the Zoom meeting had so cruelly shown. The next Zoom meeting soon rolled around, and by now, Joan was feeling a little more positive. Over the last week, she spent considerable time improving her Zoom appearance and was impatient to see the results. Again, she went through the requested procedure, keeping her screen upright and pressing the unmute button.

Marie was the first to comment. "Oh, Joan. I do love your black beret. It looks so very French."

Gladys' face smiled across the screen. "And what a pretty scarf you have wrapped so tightly around your neck. Do you have a sore throat? You do know that if you have a sore throat, you must have a COVID test?"

Joan studied Gladys' face as it took up the whole screen. "No," she replied. "My throat is fine. However, I have always loved this scarf, so I thought I would wear it today."

The virtual tour of the room commenced, and Joan took a glance at herself in the tiny side box, pleased to see how much better she looked. She made sure she was sitting side on and casually placed her elbow on the desk, resting her chin on her hand. Unfortunately, it did become a little uncomfortable when her whole arm started to develop pins and needles, and she hurt herself when she laughed at one of the girls' stories, and her face slipped and bobbed down towards her elbow.

However, Joan persevered, and soon it became her turn to speak. She pivoted her chair towards the screen, but alas, she twisted just a little too quickly, and her beret flopped into her lap. She was left staring at her large screen face with little tufts of hair tightly wrapped in rubber bands sticking up from her head. She had used them to keep her hair hidden under the beret, but now they were clearly on display. Feeling extremely embarrassed, Joan grabbed her beret and quickly popped it back onto her head, remembering to turn slightly side on again before she started to speak. She replaced her elbow on the desk and again rested her chin on her hand as she began to chatter away, but suddenly she noticed with horror that her teeth had turned a reddish colour.

Before the meeting, Joan had discovered some red liquorice at the back of the pantry cupboard and had placed two small slices on the inside of her top lip, which, she noticed, definitely eased out some of those droop lines on either side of her mouth. But as the meeting progressed, the liquorice had started to melt, and its colour had flooded across her teeth. And to make matters worse, the corners of her mouth had become sticky, and it had become challenging to speak clearly.

Mary chipped into Joan's conversation, asking, "Are you OK, Joan? Have you bitten your lip? It looks as if your mouth is bleeding."

"Oh dear," Joan had mumbled through lips stuck together on both corners. "Perhaps I am becoming unwell. It might be best if I leave the meeting early."

Unfortunately, Joan was not sure how to exit a meeting that was still in progress. She started clicking various buttons on her keyboard, but nothing happened, and she grew more and more frustrated and anxious. She was not one to usually swear, but after a couple of agonizing minutes and not realizing that the speaker was still on, she said out loud to herself, "How the bloody hell do I get out of this stupid meeting?"

Bill's voice interrupted her frustrations, and as Joan looked up at the screen, she saw Bill was laughing. "It's OK, Joan, I'll show you what to do," and thank goodness Bill directed Joan through the exit process.

Joan sat utterly still for a few minutes, breathing deeply, trying to calm herself as she stared at the screen, watching its colour fade into black. Her mouth felt sticky and uncomfortable, the scarf around her neck felt as if it was choking her, and the tight rubber bands holding the little tufts of hair were hurting her head.

She walked into her bathroom feeling deflated. She had always loved their bathroom. The lighting is gentle and so soft as she removed all the harsh fluorescent lighting a few years ago, replacing it with light globes named "Soft Blush." Dave complained that he could not see to shave correctly, but she insisted that the soft light was much kinder to their eyes, so Dave had given in.

After such an upsetting morning, Joan was exhausted and disappointed that her Zoom look improvement plan had not worked. After pulling off her beret, she carefully eased out the rubber bands before shaking her hair free as she enjoyed the sensation of her hair sweeping against her face. As her eyes grew accustomed to the dim lighting, Joan gazed in the mirror. She could not see even a hint of grey, and as she unwound her scarf, she gave her neck a rub, wondering why she had wrapped it so tightly. Then using a soft flannel to dab her mouth, the corners became unstuck. Finally, after brushing the red colouring from her teeth, she again moved closer to the mirror, pleased to see she looked like her old self again, not a neck wrinkle or a drooping line to be seen.

Over a much-needed cup of tea with Dave, while they shared a packet of Tim Tams, Joan pondered what else she could have done to enhance her appearance for their next Zoom meeting. Then out of the blue, it came to her. Due to their age, their grandson, a computer whiz, was visiting the following day. He was allowed to do so in his capacity as a caregiver. So, Joan decided to ask him to set up the computer in the bathroom.

Joan felt much more energized afterwards, probably from the sugar fix of the Tim Tams. With the buzzing noise from Dave's car racing in the background, she spread out an armload of her clothes across the bed, feeling confident that she would find something flattering to wear. She was sure that with the soft background lighting of the bathroom and a carefully chosen outfit, she would look quite spectacular at the Zoom meeting the following week.

At long last, Victoria seemed to be winning the battle against COVID, and in late September 2020, some of the restrictions were lifted, although life in Joan and Dave's household drifted along at its usual pace. Joan filled her days with writing, knitting and cooking, while Dave was content playing Solitaire on the computer or watching his car racing. They particularly enjoyed their online grocery shopping and developed a friendship with Hassam, the delivery driver from Woolworths. Joan knitted scarves for Hassam's family during the winter, while Hassam often brought them little treats that his wife had baked.

But then it all changed. COVID-19 still raged throughout Europe, and Dave was heartbroken when car races were placed on hold. Joan managed to keep him occupied for a few days with his garden chores and cleaning out the garage, but he soon became discontent.

A couple of days later, Dave strolled into the kitchen, frowning at Joan. "Well, I've finished all my chores, the garden's weeded and the garage spick and span. We've finished lunch, and we're not allowed to go anywhere, so what are we supposed to do now? "Dave, stop complaining. You still have the jigsaw you've been trying to finish, and there's that James Patterson book that you've meant to read for months."

"I don't feel like reading, and I don't want to work on the jigsaw either. I feel like doing something different." Rummaging through the cupboard in the spare room, Dave called out, "Maybe I'll find something in here to do."

A few minutes later, a loud shout echoed from the spare room, causing Joan to look up from her knitting. "I've found it."

Dave's cheeky grin beamed at her from the doorway. "Looked what I've found. The old PlayStation that James left here last year. "C'mon, let's have a go."

Placing her knitting on the couch, Joan frowned at her smiling husband.

"I have no idea how to play those things, do you?"

"One way to find out," was the reply. "I'll connect it up, and we can try it out."

Mumbled mutterings filled the silence as Dave plugged and unplugged cords, trying to attach the games machine. Finally, after what seemed an age, he let out a loud whoop as the TV screen lit up with several oddly named games on display.

"Here," he said, turning towards Joan as he patted the floor. "Grab some cushions. The chords are too short for us to sit on the couch, so we'll have to sit on the floor."

Joan studied the control that Dave placed in her lap. It was a strange-looking thing, oval-shaped with two wings spread out like a bird, each wing housing a large black button with arrows on the sides. She tentatively placed each thumb on the black buttons and pressed one gently, calling out in surprise as one of the cars on the screen moved forward.

"That's it." Dave's excited voice rang through the room. "You've got the idea. Let's go."

Their cars raced around and around the track, a red one for Dave and the blue one for Joan. As their game skills improved, they started to race against each other, Joan's car at times crashing into Dave's. Their loud bursts of laughter mingled with the almost manic music blasting from the games machine. "Let's get more adventuresome." Dave lent towards Joan, wrapping his arm around her shoulder. "Let's try two cars each and see what happens."

With frowning faces and straightened shoulders, they both leaned forward towards the screen. The game had suddenly become serious, their competitive spirits heightened. Joan's face strained in concentration as her two cars raced around the track, one of them slightly in the lead. Dave's knobbly fingers bounced around his remote, but he was not fast enough as Joan's car was the first to cross the finishing line.

"I did it." She yelled in delight, flopping back onto the floor. "I won."

"God, that was fun." Dave stretched his arms in the air. Do you want to try another game?"

"Goodness no," Joan replied, looking at her watch. It's 5 o'clock already. I'd better hop up and start cooking dinner. Do you want a coffee?"

Dave smiled into her eyes. "No, let's break our rules and have a glass of wine instead."

Joan returned his smile, but as she rolled onto her knees and tried to push herself upwards from the floor, she called out, "Oh hell. I can't get up."

"Try crawling over to the couch," Dave suggested. "I can give you a push from there."

Crawling on all fours towards the couch, Joan suddenly realized how ridiculous she must look. She collapsed in a heap, her whole body shaking with peals of laughter.

"Keep crawling." Joan heard Dave's voice over the laughter. "Just get to the couch, and I'll give you a shove."

Laughing and crawling, Joan eventually made it, and as she carefully placed her elbows on the seat, Dave knelt behind her and heaved hard with both hands on her bottom.

"Oh, my knee." Dave yelled, "I've strained my sore knee," and as he fell against Joan's back, she lost her balance, falling sideways onto the floor, with Dave tumbling down beside her. At first, they looked at each other in shock, but when they realized that neither of them was hurt, they again burst into fits of laughter. Then, holding onto each other, Joan managed to pull herself up onto the couch before pulling Dave towards her to sit down.

"I haven't laughed so much in years." Dave wiped the tears from his eyes as he cautiously straightened his leg. "This has been so much fun. But, hey, I've got a great idea. As it's a warm night, let's forget about watching TV and have a BBQ. We could eat out on the patio."

After preparing the salad and popping the potatoes into the oven, Joan decided to freshen up. After her shower, she reached for her usual grey slacks and pink jumper but then thought. *No,* as she stretched for one of her prettiest dresses. *I'll wear this instead.* As she dabbed perfume behind her ears, she was surprised to see her reflection smiling back at her from the mirror. Her cheeks were flushed, and her eyes shone brightly. "Why I think I look a little younger," she whispered to herself.

After dinner, the evening shadows crept across the sky, and as the gentle perfume from the gardenias wafted through the patio's open doors, the light from the candles flickered onto the wine glasses and the room was bathed in a warm glow. As Joan sipped her wine, her gaze rested on her husband, taking in the blueness of his eyes, the deep character lines in his face and his silver-grey hair. She suddenly realized that although she saw him every day, it had been a long time since she had looked closely at him. He was growing older, and his appearance was changing, but he was still the same Dave, her Dave, the man she had loved for so many years. Reaching across the table, Joan took his hand, feeling the roughened skin, noticing the age spots and the bumpy joints of his fingers, now so bent from arthritis.

"It's hard to believe we are 76." She smiled gently at him. "It was so much fun today, and what a wonderful life we have had so far. It's been a long-time since we laughed like that together."

"So true," Dave held her hand to his lips. "Life goes by so quickly, but we must never forget to have some fun."

Joan chuckled to herself. "Remember all the tricks we played on the kids when they were teenagers." Can you remember when we returned from Canada where we had bought the same T-shirts and jeans? Remember how we stood together arm-in-arm right outside the movie theatre doorway, wearing our identical clothes, waiting for them to come outside?"

"Oh yes," Dave laughed out loud as the shocked look on their children's faces flooded his memory. "And what about the time you met them after the Blue Light Disco. After parking right near the front entrance, which they hated, you did not let the clutch out properly as you drove off, so you bunny-hopped the car down the driveway, with the kids sitting in the back seat hiding their faces."

"And the time we waited to collect them from a party," Joan continued, "when we parked outside the front door, and I played my Julio Iglesias CD as loudly as I could with all the car windows wound down."

Dave's eyes softened as he studied Joan's face. "Do you still have that CD?"

"Why yes," Joan answered. "I haven't played it for years."

"Well, let's put it on."

As the soft, romantic sounds of Iglesias floated around the patio, Dave held out his hand. Joan drifted into his arms, and on slightly stiffened legs, they slowly danced around the table and chairs, with Dave humming just a little off tune. Then, holding Joan close, he whispered, "this has been the best lockdown day so far."

As the Spring weather crept closer to Summer, the COVID restrictions eased. Children returned to school, Victorian residents could once again travel inside their State and hospitality venues opened. After 112 days, Melbourne was coming back to life.

Over breakfast, Dave placed his toast on his plate as he smiled at Joan. "Well, at last, we can go for a drive. Would you like to go out for the day and perhaps grab a coffee somewhere?"

"Well, actually," Joan replied. "I am quite happy to stay at home. The sun is warming the patio, and I do want to finish that jumper I am knitting."

"Sounds like a good idea., Dave returned to his toast. "I might even try and get into that James Patterson book that I have meant to read. Would you pass the jam, please, dear?"

# A WHITE SCARF
# ON THE DOOR

*........*

## *RODERIC GRIGSON*

*........*

In 1918, a white scarf tied to the door alerted the community to a deadly virus residing within. At that time, one-third of the planet's population got infected with what came to be known as Spanish influenza, which killed an estimated 50 million people.

There are debates even today about the true origin of the 'Spanish' flu. However, the strain was likely named because a lack of wartime media censorship in Spain meant that country's media was reporting on the epidemic much sooner and more frequently than the rest of Europe, the UK, and the US. This media coverage created the impression the cases had begun and were higher in that country.

Patients were quarantined in their rooms, unable to communicate with the outside world. Parents and siblings stayed in their homes and apartments heeding city-wide warnings to avoid exposing others in their community to the disease.

Survivors could later recall the isolation and the fear with eerie detail, and the image burned into their brain of coffins passing by their windows. Countless stories circulated of healthy individuals who went to work in the morning and never came home. Neighbours who were healthy one day were dead the next.

These survivor stories could have ended differently. But, instead, some survived to live an incredibly long and whole life because they were clever. As the flu swept through cities and towns, they practised the kind of social distancing and quarantine that is today being actively sanctioned but inadequately implemented. These survivors, because of their white scarf warnings and caution, saved each other, their neighbours, friends, and colleagues, as well as their doctors.

In an irony that could never have been predicted 100 years ago, while scarves were placed on doorknobs, we were asked to repurpose bandanas and scarves into homemade masks.

When this extremely deadly strain of influenza appeared in early 1918, very little was done to stop its spread. The study of viruses was in its infancy. The first scientific study showing evidence of a viral disease in human beings took place in 1900, when it became known that mosquitoes transmitted yellow fever. But no one knew what viruses were or how they worked.

At this time, influenza was commonly thought to be transmitted by bacteria, as the bacterial infections that often accompany the illness were mistaken for the cause. Vaccines for the flu were decades away. Worse than that, no one imagined that the flu could take on forms that were so deadly. The movement of people worldwide during and after the war meant that the disease could not be easily contained.

Anyone who has paid the slightest attention to history knows that pandemics don't muck around. The bubonic plague, for instance, began in

THE SCRIBE TRIBE - VOLUME TWO

Egypt and travelled with rats on ships to Constantinople in AD 541, where it became known as the Plague of Justinian. "From there, it seemed to spread all over the world; this catastrophe was so overwhelming that the human race appeared close to annihilation," wrote Procopius, a legal adviser to Emperor Justinian's most important general. It is thought to have reduced Europe's population by half over the next 150 years.

Eight hundred years later, the plague returned as The Black Death and killed an estimated 75 million people in Asia and Europe between 1331 and 1353. It dispatched an estimated 20-30 million Europeans in six years, reducing Europe's people by a third.

But there was nothing straightforward about the flu that year: it would prove much deadlier than the war itself. Around 20 million people, half of them civilians, had died in World War I. But more than 50 million people - and some estimates say 100 million - would die from what became known as Spanish influenza during 1918 and 1919. It remains one of the deadliest pandemics known to human history.

Given how quickly this influenza developed into pneumonia, it is not surprising that some people thought it had to be something other than the flu. However, recent DNA research on the virus has shown that it was indeed influenza, an H1N1 variety similar to the one that caused a pandemic in 2009.

It is not known with certainty where this flu originated, but a widely accepted theory is that it developed in the Midwestern United States in about January 1918. Influenza was causing illness in military troops preparing to go to war who likely carried it to Europe. Thus, it was called the "Spanish flu," but it seems that the Spanish newspapers were first to report it to the public only because they were less affected by wartime censorship of information.

An account in The Federal Writers' Project: Folklore Project Histories, Dr Curtis Atkinson of Wichita Falls, Texas, and collected by Ethel Dulaney provides a physician's description of the disease. The doctor was the Post

Surgeon at the hospital at a US military airfield and training facility during the war. He remembered the day that the severe form of influenza arrived. He described how quickly the illness developed and explained how he and the staff responded:

*"When the 'flu' epidemic struck, the boys began to come down very rapidly—a football game was in progress. The commanding officer immediately ordered the game stopped and sentinels posted at the gate of the field with orders that no one was to be admitted. It was extremely hard for the citizens to learn that a military quarantine could not be evaded. Within an hour, the two ambulances were terribly busy taking men from the different parts of the camp to the hospital, and by the next day, the hospital was filled to its capacity. All enlisted men of the medical department were placed in tents and barracks used for hospital purposes. Other barracks were available and immediately transferred into an emergency hospital. After we began using this emergency hospital, the sick men were sent there first, and those that became extremely ill or developed pneumonia were moved to the hospital proper, and the convalescents from the hospital proper were moved to the emergency hospital. One ambulance was kept busy at this work. There were so many men stricken with the 'flu' that the regular routine of the flying instruction was nearly at a standstill. On account of this arrangement, no soldier at the camp suffered from the lack of medical attention, and the death rate from the 'flu' epidemic was next to the lowest of any field or camp in the United States."*

This story shows that this doctor understood the importance of outbreak containment by this time in the epidemic and identifying the sickest patients quickly. Of course, it was unwise to hold a football game, but such measures were used unevenly in 1918.

An Army nurse, Alice, [Alice L. Mikel Duffield Collection, Veterans History Project, Library of Congress] recounting her experience of dealing with the virus, told what it was like to be in a hospital overwhelmed by severely ill patients and deal with death daily. She learned not to dwell on the dying too much but to get on and take care of the patients in front of her.

Like all the other young ladies living in the US in the early 1900s, Alice was expected to marry and be a stay-at-home mother or remain single and get a job as a servant, telegraph operator or store clerk. If you were fortunate enough to have completed at least the eighth grade, you could work as a schoolteacher. Those were pretty much all the available opportunities. Although she found the first option of marriage and motherhood initially appealing, Alice discovered that not only did her beau give her a fake sapphire engagement ring, but he was also unfaithful. So, she sent the ring back, called it off and swore off marriage forever.

Four years later, Alice connected through a friend, which opened the door to nursing training. While still in training, the Great War broke out. Franklin Roosevelt's sister came to town recruiting nurses to help with the war effort, and Alice decided to do her part. As time went on, she found herself assigned to a pneumonia ward in which all the patients were African American soldiers—an uncommon assignment for a white nurse in those days. Nonetheless, Alice carried out her duties with compassion each day, sometimes to a fault. Once, a charge nurse caught her in tears over a dying patient and quickly reprimanded her.

*Now, listen here. People are born here. And they die here. We can't do anything about it. If you spend your life crying about everybody that dies, you'll never get any work done.*

The flu pandemic of 1918 was vicious. Deaths during Alice's daily shift were quite common and too numerous for the nurses to count. Questioned later, she said, *"We didn't pay any attention...we didn't have time! It was published in the paper, every day, who died."*

Alice also recounted a gruesome incident, which caused one of the orderlies to have a breakdown on the job

*And finally, the black orderly and a white orderly took a patient to the morgue, and when they opened the door, the morgue was so full that one dead body fell on the floor and the black orderly came back, and he said, 'Just can't take it any longer! Just can't take it any longer!'*

*Unfortunately, the orderlies were unable to squeeze the body back inside the morgue. After hearing that, I needed some fresh air. The story became too much for me. I know I won't always be this way, but for now...*

As we sit inside our homes teleworking by day and glued to the breaking news reports by night, we teeter between trepidation and hope. As people of faith, we passionately believe this too shall pass, and we will be okay—the majority of us will be okay. Yet, at the same time, it's hard not to experience a bit of angst when our lives have been turned upside down and feel like they have come to a screeching halt with little time to brace for impact.

If you were to ask most people how they are feeling in this climate, you'd likely get responses like "uncertain," "triggered", and "afraid." You'd probably also hear "inspired," "motivated", and "determined." You'll often run the gamut in 24 hours. Alice must have experienced all of these feelings at some point in that hospital ward. Unlike nurses today, she didn't have the privilege of taking a break; she had to push through and do her job to the best of her ability. There was no time for tears or fresh air. We are grateful for her service and that she lived to tell her story.

Although people did not understand much about the disease that caused the pandemic, and citizens without medical training often had a limited understanding of disease prevention, many people used their common sense, sometimes combined with folk remedies, to survive the crisis. In addition, some local governments used measures such as closing schools and discouraging large gatherings, actions that made a difference when implemented.

Today we are using some of the same basic knowledge to get through the current crisis. Instruction followed instruction – assume you could carry the disease without knowing it, practice social distancing, help other people while avoiding direct contact with them. Support health care workers and wear a cloth mask when going out and about, and, of course, wash your hands.

Australia remained free of Spanish flu throughout 1918 thanks to our strong quarantine measures. Ships arriving from infected countries had to quarantine for seven days, with patients subject to 'daily thermometer parades and daily inhalation with steam plus two per cent zinc sulphate solution'.

However, disagreements between state and federal governments marked Australia's response to the virus. The first cases of Spanish flu were detected in Melbourne in mid-January 1919. But the Victorian health department didn't report these cases to the Commonwealth for about a week. By the time Victoria was declared an infected area on January 28, there were 350 infections in the state, and the virus had already spread by train to Sydney.

The border between Victoria and NSW was sealed. No trains, cars or pedestrians could cross. At the main interstate crossing, Albury-Wodonga, newly arrived soldiers desperate to see their families tried swimming the Murray River, only to find themselves pursued by police boats and interned in isolation tents.

With the virus in Australia's two most populous states, gatherings were discouraged, and theatres, hotels, dance halls, and churches closed. People began regularly inhaling antiseptic fumes and wearing masks in public –

even though the Commonwealth Director of Quarantine thought that wearing masks were useless and even dangerous.

There were too few doctors and nurses to deal with the crisis – many were still with the armed forces overseas, and others caught the flu. Health facilities were overrun. In Melbourne, the Exhibition Building was turned into a large hospital, as were some schools. Tent hospitals sprang up at sporting grounds and parks across the state.

Those playing cricket or tennis or performing in an outdoor band were permitted only if they stayed six feet from each other. Spectators had to be masked. Church services were held outdoors. Schools, hotels, and public buildings were shuttered.

Queensland closed its southern border to everyone, even people living inside the 10-mile buffer zone implemented with NSW. Queensland police were stationed at crossings along the border to enforce mandatory examinations and detain and isolate anyone who might be infected.

This was a clear breach of a Commonwealth agreement between the states, and a few days later, the Commonwealth renounced the deal, leaving the states to handle their quarantine and restrictions at land borders. Yet, at the same time, the Commonwealth continued to control quarantine at ports.

From an account written about that period, a young Australian soldier who fought on the battlefields of France contracted the virus in Europe and was nursed back to health in England. He married his nurse and came home to an Australia captured by determined hysteria. He was from a Protestant family. However, his new bride was an Irish Catholic. It caused great resentment within the family in Australia and wariness among neighbours in the overwhelmingly Protestant farming district.

But when influenza broke out in the district, fear of the disease proved greater than bigotry. His English bride, pregnant, clambered aboard a horse-drawn gig and rode through the night to answer the calls of neighbours for assistance. She was presumably immune to the disease after long exposure while nursing in a military hospital in Birmingham. She brought soup and soap, clean towels and sheets, and a natural gentleness to the district homesteads. She saved them all. Malice melted and she became loved for who she was, not judged through ignorance.

Many welcome-home parades for the troops were cancelled. Returning soldiers were forced into quarantine before they could be reunited with families and sweethearts.

The wildest case of quarantine shock led to almost 1000 troops staging a mutiny on February 10, 1919, after being isolated in a snake-infested camp at Sydney's North Head Quarantine Station.

Fortunately, the global population developed a natural immunity to the virus. As a result, the flu pandemic was over by the end of 1919, but not before it claimed the lives of around 13,000 Australians.

Does any of this sound familiar to you?

# I SAW HER DIE ON FACETIME

*BRUCE HEWETT*

We supposedly study to help avoid repeating the failings of past generations. However, when it comes to human conflict and epidemics, we continue to commit the sins of our ancestors. In my lifetime, there have been wars in Korea, Vietnam, Israel, Lebanon, East Africa, the Gulf States, Iraq and Afghanistan, to name just a few. With disease, we have seen outbreaks in recent years with Ebola, SARS and Coronaviruses, taking countless lives worldwide and impacting our day to day lives.

With a history in mind, I was most sceptical of the protestations of the various politicians that all was well with the outbreaks reported from Wuhan in China back in January 2020. However, as more and more information came to light, it became apparent that there would be a problem given my training as a pharmacist. It also seemed that the situation could get more severe given the mobility of the global population in our modern world.

Consequently, I started to prepare to cancel a much-looked forward trip to Morocco. There was no way I wanted my wife Beverley and I to be trapped in a foreign land, uncertain if and when we could get home in the event of an outbreak of disease. Initial feedback stated that we would lose our money if we cancelled, but it was only money to us, and we made our minds up not to take the risk to undertake the tour, albeit at the cost of thousands of dollars.

At the same time, I received regular calls from a very concerned sister Jewells in Sydney that my 90-year-old Mum was not doing well health-wise. She was diagnosed with inoperable abscesses in her bowels. Medical advice indicated she was unlikely to survive the complex surgery required to remove the growths, so the development of the infections was kept in check by high doses of antibiotics. Unfortunately, the medicines were impacting her quality of life while slowing the progress of the disease. Side effects such as nausea and vomiting were common, even eating became an unpleasant task rather than a joy.

With news coming through that the outbreaks were worsening in Australia, we decided to fly to Sydney in late February 2020 to see my Mum if the situation worsened. Internal travel restrictions came into place. However, despite warnings from my sister, nothing could have prepared me for the deterioration I saw in my Mum when entering her room at her aged-care facility.

Only six months earlier, I had been in Sydney to celebrate Mum's 90th birthday. For her birthday, she was her usual cheeky self, expressing a great zest for life. You could see the joy in her face as she basked in the adoration and love bestowed upon her by family and friends from all over Australia, some of whom arrived in Sydney to celebrate her big day.

Despite her not feeling well, our arrival from Melbourne boosted her spirits, and we enjoyed a wonderful visit, getting her out of bed and into the sunshine. We were blissfully unaware that it would be the last time we would see Mum alive in person and be able to do that very human thing of giving her a kiss and a hug. We took her for lunch at her favourite place, Frankie's Restaurant at the Flower Power Centre in Glenhaven, in Sydney's North-West. A visit to the restaurant always brought a tear to her eye, as it brought memories of her great-grandson called Frankie.

It was a teary farewell as we shared our last hugs and kisses before heading back to Melbourne with promises of coming back to Sydney to see her soon. The carrot dangled in front of Mum to attend her grandson Sean's wedding was announced later in 2020, and we presented her with her formal invitation. Participating in the wedding, we hoped, would boost her to keep going and see her grandson wed. She loved her grandson, Sean.

Returning to Melbourne, reports were coming through in early March of the deterioration of the situation with the COVID virus, and health systems worldwide swamped with patients and a rapidly mounting death toll. However, from a personal financial perspective, the good news came that the organisers had cancelled the tour to Morocco. As such, we were able to claim the monies paid via travel insurance, apart from a nominal policy excess fee.

The joy at being able to claim the cost of the tour was short-lived, with continual reports coming through from my sister that my Mum's condition was continuing to deteriorate. With the help of a cousin whose husband was diagnosed with cancer, my sister was carrying the burden of attending to Mum needs. We knew we needed to head back to Sydney as soon as possible to see her, but those plans came to nought with the announcement of nationwide travel lockdowns. This announcement precluded us from escaping the "ring of steel" encircling Melbourne, which was fast becoming the COVID capital of Australia.

My Mum's mental well-being was further compromised when my sister and cousin, both nurses working in aged care, were denied entry into Mum's nursing home. The situation was devastating for my sister, who could not provide Mum with reassuring hugs and kisses.

To an extent, technology came to the rescue and via the cooperation of the nursing staff at my Mum's nursing home, we were able to arrange for regular sessions on FaceTime to speak with Mum.

Various times got scheduled to include grandchildren and great-grandchildren, which always perked Mum up. We were forever trying to get her to hold the mobile phone so that we could see her face rather than the ceiling in her room. She was not a gifted user of technology. Also, the mail was still getting through, and we were able to send photographs regularly of what we were up to, and the great-grandkids were always ready to send a drawing or two.

Mum's condition continued to worsen as she was restricting her food intake slowly, and the feeling was that she was resigned to preparing to meet her maker with the continual pain. Being a woman of strong Christian beliefs, this was not an outcome she feared, confident about where she was going at the end of her days. However, the continued inability of my sister to gain physical access to her dampened her morale. Jewells worked as a nurse in aged care, where there had been many COVID related deaths in Sydney.

Given Mum's condition continuing to worsen, the nursing home finally agreed to give my sister access to Mum via a Perspex screen which meant a physical barrier between Mum, a very tactile, 'huggie' type person and my sister Jewells. Mum could not understand denied access to her daughter, and with the distress caused, one could question if the visits only worsened her condition.

With me unable to travel to Sydney due to lockdown and my sister not being physically close to Mum, it was evident in the regular Facetime sessions that her health was rapidly declining. You could see a yellow pallor in Mum's skin, and in discussions with my sister, we knew that with a deep, productive cough that pneumonia was lurking to attack Mum's lungs. This development, combined with a significant bodyweight loss due to not eating, did not bode well. It was hard for my sister and me to try and maintain a realistic medical view given our professional healthcare backgrounds, and at the same time, not be emotionally impacted.

We know Mum was preparing for the end of her time, and during our regular FaceTime sessions, she kept asking me when I would be coming to see her. She could not grasp why I wasn't there to be with her, her only son. The inability to leave Melbourne's "ring of steel" became a source of guilt and anguish.

Finally, while Bev and I were watching a footy match, Jewells called on FaceTime. My teary, upset sister advised us that she received a call from the nursing home to say that Mum's condition was severe. Despite being denied access, my sister was now allowed to be bedside with our Mum, a strong signal that all was not well.

It was a very emotional call as we knew Mum would not be with us much longer. But, unfortunately, even if she could survive long enough for me to complete 14-days in quarantine, the nursing home policy precluded access to the facility because we would be coming from Melbourne.

The tears were flowing as we spoke to Mum and told her we loved her and tried to make her understand why I was not allowed to come to be with her in her semi-conscious state. Then, still calling for me, a tired Mum drifted off to sleep, and my troubled sister made her way home and promised to contact us again with any news.

A couple of hours later, another FaceTime call from my sister from Mum's bedside, which I knew could not be good news. Jewells had just been called from the nursing home and advised that the end was near, so could she come quickly.

When Jewells arrived, a shot of morphine had helped to ease her pain, and her eyes were closed. Her breath was shallow, with little movement in her chest. With tears rolling down my sister's cheeks, she held the phone close to Mum's ear while I read her the 23rd Psalm. It was Mum's favourite reading from The Bible, and we sang her much loved hymn, "How Great Thou Art".

At the end of the melody, my sister placed her head next to Mum's on her pillow and held the phone, enabling us to see Mum take one final gasp and then she was gone.

How can I ever forgive the inaction of various politicians that delayed taking action against an invisible enemy and did not heed lessons learnt from history, which allowed the dreaded COVID to do its evil in the community?

All of them put me in this position to say, '*I Saw Her Die on FaceTime*'.

# THE SILENT KILLERS

## *DALE WALKLEY*

I sit at my desk with a brand-new calendar and a pen to begin writing in the critical dates for 2020. First in goes our granddaughter Rhiannon's twenty-first in the latter part of April, then Bernadette's seventieth birthday party in early April, and last but by no means least, Jenny's seventieth in September.

Bernie, as she prefers to be known and I have been friends for over ten years. We were work colleagues, but our friendship blossomed once we both retired. Jenny, I met at a social gathering at Balla Balla, and we became friends. Together with another friend, Mary, the three of us attend many outings together, including Morning Melodies at Hamer Hall in Melbourne.

I have been ticking the days off until our friends Janet and Brian arrive from England for their holiday. Neither Janet nor I can wait as it has been three years since we saw each other. We have been friends for over forty years and greatly value our time together. They are due to arrive here in March. July sees us heading to the Gold Coast for our winter break.

But unbeknown to us, the Silent Killers were getting ready to take over our world as we know it. It would bring changes that haven't been seen since the Spanish flu epidemic of the 1920s and the Great Depression of the 1930s. We were ignorant about what was waiting for us in 2020, and boy, were we in for a shock.

With its severe heat over parts of Australia and the United States, the summer saw a Silent Killer in the form of heat, impart its devastation in the fires that swept the world. Many areas suffered the severe destruction of property, livestock and nature. The fires burned up the Australian Eastern Seaboard and Kangaroo Island off the coast of South Australia, amongst many other places. The Navy evacuated hundreds from Merimbula enjoying their summer vacation when the Federal Government sent the Armed Services to help. Not this year, folks.

Janet and Brian were beginning to worry about whether they would be able to drive from Brisbane down through Bathurst and on to Victoria. I kept a regular ear to news programs to find out what roads were closed. At least they had an idea of how big Australia was, having been here before. Other English friends and family, particularly Max's brother and sister and his other children, constantly texted to ensure that we were safe as they had no idea how near or far from the fires we were. So, we had to continually keep them informed and up to date on our location.

Before coming to Australia, Janet and Brian were travelling to New Zealand to visit members of Brian's family living there. While they were there, another Silent Killer launched itself onto the world in the form of COVID 19. Unbeknown to us, this Killer was to upset all the activities we had planned to do. There was also a genuine possibility that Janet and Brian might not get home and find themselves stranded in Australia. The borders shut to all incomings and outgoing flights the day they left New Zealand. Phew, they made it to Australia, when three days later, the local borders also closed.

This new Silent Killer had quickly spread worldwide because people travelled, not knowing they were sick. According to my research, some likened it to the Spanish Flu of 1918-1920. At that time, over five hundred million of the world's population got infected, and between twenty and fifty million lost their lives. Was this pandemic to reap a similar number of people either by infection or death? At least today, we have antibiotics that the doctors of the time didn't have. And after the First World War, with the Spanish Flu, many hospitals were still overcrowded with patients malnourished due to a poorer standard of living.

Janet and Brian did all they planned to do before driving to Victoria. The roads they planned to travel were no longer affected by the fires, but they could see evidence of the devastation on their journey. The two of them were delighted to arrive in Cranbourne even though they had received a message from Qantas advising them to cancel their flights to the United Kingdom. They had genuine worries for their families back home, as apart from COVID, the United Kingdom was also exiting the Common Market. The country's people were unsure how it would affect their daily lives, which caused some unrest in the UK.

How quickly the world shut itself down, hoping the measure taken would prevent the spread of this Silent Killer. It couldn't be done in 1918 because there was no internet or social media, so countries didn't know what was happening to their neighbours. We all hoped that this Killer would not take such a massive toll on the world's population. In the meantime, our social outings became very limited. We did manage one or two-day trips before the real effects of being in isolation hit. Janet and Brian soon knew Cranbourne almost as well as I do with the daily walks we had.

Getting them back home to England was now the goal, even if it meant shortening their stay. But, despite everyone in the house on the phone to Qantas, it was all to no avail. In the end, Brian was able to get flights out with another airline five days after they should have returned home.

I was sad to see them go, as we hadn't been able to do any of our planned activities, but they needed to be home in Wotton Under Edge with their children and grandchildren. So, I just prayed they would be safe from this unknown virus.

Disappointment comes in many forms, and ours seem to get worse after having to cancel our granddaughter's twenty-first, then Bernie's party and our trip in July. Because we couldn't go anywhere, I suppose breaking my left arm in April was a highlight of lockdown as I did manage to go out, albeit in an ambulance. I spent two days in the hospital.

Waiting until I was sixty-eight years old to break a bone is not anything to smile about, especially as I broke my right wrist in September. Coming home, I couldn't do much, but I had help from my daughters Naomi and Kirsty living in the same house. Unfortunately, this situation didn't help my other daughter Fiona and my grandchildren Rhiannon and Jacob as they couldn't visit living in Karingal.

We were fortunate as Naomi was able to continue teaching via computer. Not the most ideal of circumstances, but at least she was still teaching. It just meant we had to be very quiet. Rhiannon works in childcare, so she was considered a frontline and an essential worker.

Fiona, Kirsty and Jacob all work in retail and their store Kmart was considered an essential service. So, Max and I just pottered about in between medical appointments. No one had any need for government help, unlike many others. Max had the blessing of knowing that he was finally to have his right knee replaced in October. Unfortunately, he was diagnosed with small cell lung cancer during this stay in the hospital, and the next few months were all about hospitals and doctors' appointments. As I write, he's in remission.

Many of us looked forward to the Olympics, only to cancel them like many other major sporting events. Not just here in Australia but the world over. I sincerely hope that once this virus is over, the like of it will never be seen again, at least not in my lifetime.

While COVID ran rampant throughout the world, other Silent

Killers were rearing their ugly heads. The Democratic Republic of Congo experienced another outbreak of Ebola. The World Health Organisation advising that there were 3195 cases. I hoped it wouldn't take off across the African continent and COVID.

An enormous explosion in the port of Beirut due to poorly stored dangerous materials killed hundreds and destroying the area adjacent to the harbour. Turmoil still reared its ugly head in the Middle East, and the United States of America seem to think that if you couldn't see the Silent Killer, it didn't exist, although many were infected and dying. There has always been a silent undertone in the United States of America where the coloured population is the underdog and the white man superior. This situation escalated when a white policeman killed George Floyd, a black man, in the execution of an arrest. Would the white murderer be let off or found guilty? Tension continued to simmer for months, with African Americans demanding equal rights in the eyes of the law.

When COVID is over, I believe the biggest Silent Killer will be those suffering from mental health issues due to the isolation, fear and uncertainty in their work and social life. So many thousands of people worldwide have no interaction with others. It is not normal for most people to isolate themselves for twenty-three hours a day with only one hour for exercise. It is like an extreme prison sentence, and some people will not have coped.

Death has been the heartbreaking tally every day on the news, and one has sympathy for those who have lost a loved one without saying a proper goodbye. However, my family can stand with these people like my wonderful friend Andrea, my daughter Kirsty's Godmother, who succumbed to this dreadful Killer. Although we had the means to travel to England for her funeral, we could not say our goodbyes as all borders were closed. We were gutted!

2020 was a disastrous year for many mom-and-pop store owners who found they had to fold because of not being open to the public. The big conglomerates would survive even if it meant more of their staff working from home. To a certain extent, they could absorb most losses, but those who will sink into oblivion will be those. The world economy will have taken a direct hit, and the Silent Killers roaming the world might put the economies of many countries into a similar position to that of the Great Depression. Countries came out of this with another War. I certainly hope that is not the case, although you can watch the news and find all manner of unrests simmering away in the world.

2020 was very much looked forward to in this household, but the reality was that we were not prepared. We made the best of things. Many unfinished projects got completed, and finally, the pile of photographs had homes in albums, which meant stronger family bonding to me.

The Silent Killer is still creeping around the world in different mutations, but I hope that with all the vaccines now available due to a large amount of cash these companies have received from their respective governments, we will see it come to a silent end.

# MELBOURNE
# CUP DAY 2020

## *NORMA SAVIGE*

Oh boy! A sunny day on Melbourne Cup Day.

I don't like horse racing, but I do like a day off. It means my husband, David, is home with me, and my day will be very different from my regular weekdays.

For example, after breakfast today, we went out for a lovely walk around Casey Fields behind our village. There, we spotted two white-faced herons preening each other on a fence. We also came across a clutch of ducklings that were almost full-grown. This mother duck has done a magnificent job over the weeks raising ten ducklings to the adolescent stage. It is quite a rare achievement as many predators usually manage to pick off one or two babies. Well done, Mum!

We are currently living through the terrible Covid-19 pandemic of

2020 in Melbourne. Our lives are very different as we follow government directives such as no group gatherings and the compulsory wearing of masks in public. While these requirements are sometimes inconvenient, they are undeniably worthwhile. In our state, we have been very fortunate regarding this highly infectious virus, and these constraints are a small price to pay to keep ourselves and the rest of the community safe and well.

Of course, as usual, there were a couple of people at the park breaching the rule about compulsory mask-wearing. This arrogance and lack of consideration for others amaze me. If they don't care about their own health, that's fine, their choice, but what about other people? It could be their Grandmother whose life they protect by wearing a mask.

In passing, I commented to David that not wearing a mask says a lot to me about a person's lack of empathy or caring for others and I also wonder what it says about their mental capacity. Not being able to understand the science of COVID-19 and its management seems a little unintelligent to me.

Anyway, whilst I am often tempted to speak out and remind the rule-breakers of their responsibilities, I bit my tongue as we continued on our walk. Discretion is the better part of valour, as they say. Plus, I didn't want to ruin a beautiful stroll around the lake by being abused by a stranger. I could see the relief in David's eyes each time I kept my mouth shut. We just stepped off the path, held our breath, let them pass, and then we walked on.

Home for some toasted raisin bread with a cuppa, and we are ready for the next part of our day. How exciting it is too!

We are going to Bunnings – the Mecca at some time or another for many of the people I know. I have been to Bunnings just a couple of times during this Corona Virus Lockdown period, but it's different today because I have company. David is much stronger than I am and can lift and carry more and reach a lot higher than I can.

Feeling nostalgic for our garden back in Berwick, we purchased a beautiful Japanese Maple at the Squatting Frog Nursery the previous weekend to plant in a specific spot in our back courtyard. However, after a night's reflection, I decided that spot would be too hot for the maple, so we need to buy a heavy tub to contain it in a more suitable position. The container must be solid as we live in a wind tunnel, and lighter pots blow over with great ease.

Woo-hoo off we go!

The car park is quite crowded. There is only one entry and one exit into the store, serving to direct customers more safely, avoiding bottlenecks and keeping everyone separated. Unfortunately, we needed to park at the Garden Centre exit but walk all the way around to the general entrance to get in. But rules are rules, so I prepare my knees for a long walk on the hard concrete. Quite a few people are walking towards the entry door, but I am not concerned as they are all wearing their masks and keeping their distance.

The sun is blazing down as I step from the car. David always takes much longer to get out of the car than I do. First, he needs to turn the car off, find and put on his sunnies, put his spectacles in a pocket, find his wallet and find the car keys. Then he needs to put on a cap or hat if it's sunny or cold or raining and decide whether he needs to put on a coat or take off or put on his vest. After that, he must find his phone or both his phones if he has his work phone with him and decides which pocket to use for them. Last but not least, of course, David must find and put on his mask then check his hair in the mirror.

I usually choose to stay in the car while all this happens, but Cup Day was stinking hot, and I decide to pick up my handbag and make a seventy-five-metre dash for the entry to get out of the heat.

'I'll see you there,' I say as I stride off purposefully.

David knows I hate standing in the sun and replies, 'OK,' and off I go.

At the entry, I am confronted by a large container of hand sanitiser, big Covid-safety signs, arrows on the floor directing traffic and four or five staff members greeting customers. I sanitise my hands, smile at the nearest staff member and continue in to wait inside the foyer for David.

While I wait, a lovely staff member asks me how I am, and I reply, 'I'm well, thanks. How are you?' She smiles and tells me she is fine too. A nice, friendly greeting indeed. I tell her what a great job they are doing keeping us all safe.

I see David arrive at the outer door, and I enter the huge, cool inner space of Bunnings ahead of him. What fun! I swear *everyone* there looks happy. Mums, Dads, Kids, together or alone all enjoying an outing to their favourite place. Us included.

I take off searching for someone to point me in the right direction to find what we want.

I spot a young assistant halfway along an aisle, and as I approach, I ask her, 'Excuse me. Can you tell me where I can find the trolley stands for plant-pots, please?'

She frowns, and I realise she probably couldn't hear me clearly through my mask. I move closer and repeat my question more loudly this time. She steps back again.

Taken aback by her behaviour, I wonder what's wrong? I step forward again, and as I do, I sense a creeping suspicion. Can it be? I wouldn't. Would I?

I put my hand to my face and gasp out loud. 'Oh my God! My mask! I've left it in the car.' I put a hand to each side of my face and stand rooted to the spot. What do I do?

David arrives and bursts out laughing, 'I'll go and get it from the car,' he says as he rushes off.

There I am, trapped with this poor young girl. I think she is as baffled as I am. What to do?

She seems to shake herself out of a frozen state and says, 'It's alright. I'll get you one.'

I am blabbing on about being so sorry, and I can't believe it, and I feel so stupid. 'Will I come with you?' I offer.

'Yes. Over here.' She rushes off, still keeping her distance.

We walk quickly through the store as I cover my face with both of my hands doing the Walk of Shame. People step away—some stop and stare. Two mothers pull their children away, and a couple actually scowls at me.

I cringe and try hard to disappear. At last, the shop assistant hands me a packet with a mask in it.

'Thank you so much. I can't believe I did this. I'm so sorry.' Blabber, blabber, blabber. I am shaking and cannot open the packet. She does it for me as David arrives with my mask.

'I'll take the rubbish for you,' says the shop assistant.

'Won't I need it to pay for the mask?' Trying hard to make amends any way I could.

'Nope. You're good. It's free.' She smiled but still stayed away.

David is still laughing, and I am still blabbing on. I want to go home. He wants to do what we came to do.

I try to deflect the blame from me, 'Why did they even let me in? Why didn't they stop me and ask me why I wasn't wearing a mask? Why were they all standing around the entrance if they don't care who just strolls on in?'

David takes my arm and steers me towards the back wall of the garden centre, still laughing. Then, finally, I calm down and get on with it. I feel sick, but we do our shopping and as we leave a police car drives very slowly through the car park with two officers in it.

'They're looking for you,' laughs David as we walk to the car.

Not funny! 'Just get me out of here,' I snap and raced to the car, climb in and wait, perspiring. David goes through the process of loading our shopping in the boot, returning the shopping trolley to the bay and reverses all of the exit processes he follows as he prepares to get into the car.

The drive home seems to take forever. One of us laughed all the way, and the other felt mortified and tried to find an excuse for her behaviour.

Now I know I don't need to say anything to you about hypocrisy or the fact that my judgemental attitude well and truly bit me on the backside or that it was a good lesson hard-learned.

So I'll just leave it here with you. A cautionary tale indeed accompanied with a large serving of very humble pie served cold.

# A LITTLE BIT OF MISCHIEF

## JUDY NEARY

My husband walked into the house, a look of astonishment and a little bit of merriment on his face. He had returned from having a COVID-19 test.

"Why are you looking like the cat that got the cream," I said, grinning.

Then, he began to relate his story to me.

First, I need to update you on events leading up to this day.

2020 was a year like no other. A new virus had hit the world, and everything seemed to have gone mad.

We had welcomed in a New Year as usual and had begun planning holidays. The first time we heard about COVID-19 was when we heard from our travel agent our cruise was cancelled. All cruising came to a stop worldwide, and the World Health Organisation declared a global pandemic. International borders were closed, and people began wearing masks covering their noses and mouth.

On the news, people were talking about nothing else. Here in Australia, we thought we were safe because of our isolation. I first became aware of how crazy times had become when I received a message from my husband telling me to try and buy some toilet paper while at the supermarket. He had heard that people were emptying shelves at the shops with panic buying going on everywhere. I could not believe this was happening. Seeing the panic firsthand was something of a surprise. Not only were they fighting for toilet paper, but essentials, like rice, flour, tissues and many other items.

People were talking about a lockdown. Then the Victorian Government, in consultation with the Health Department, ordered a lockdown with strict rules in place.

Only go out for four reasons, the news blared. For health or care for others. For work. For education and essential shopping only. If you had any symptoms, you must get tested and isolate at home until you received your result.

This was all well and good, but the results took several days to come back, and people became frustrated.

My husband and I, being retired, life went on as usual. My daughter visited, delivering face masks, and told us sternly that we must wear them when we went out. Being elderly, not old, but having some health issues, we were considered vulnerable.

Although Victoria had a few cases, we came through the first wave reasonably well. With hotel quarantine in place for returning travellers, all seemed good, but schools were closed, and children were learning from home. Only essential businesses remained open, and all workers worked from home if able.

Our daily routine was sitting in front of the television and waiting for Premier Andrews to come on with the numbers for the past twenty-four hours and what restrictions were in place.

Children had not been to school for the whole of term two and hoping to get back in term three, but this did not happen as a second wave of the virus hit Victoria.

Security guards at a quarantined hotel with cases of the virus somehow caught the virus and carried it out into the community. Then, family members, extended family members and friends all carried the virus into the community.

Victoria lost over eight hundred residents over the months that followed. It was horrible as a lot of these were vulnerable people in aged care facilities. But, of course, many countries worldwide had suffered much more, with millions catching the virus and hundreds of thousands dying. Around the world, hospitals went into crisis. Health workers and some doctors and nurses, all contracted the virus and this compounded the problem. None were immune to COVID-19.

When the second wave hit Victoria, Federal Government and the States played the blame game, pointing fingers at each other. Children never went back to school, so they spent all of term three remote learning. Other Australian states closed their borders to Victorians.

From July to November, we went into the tightest lockdown. We were not allowed to visit other family members living in different households. Only one person was allowed out to shop for essentials. We were only allowed out for one hour for exercise and not going more than five kilometres from home. Masks were mandatory at all times when outside the home.

Now my husband is a very fidgety person, always on the move and looking to keep busy. So these restrictions were exceedingly difficult for both of us. Not being able to see any of our five granddaughters was really hard, of course, we had Facetime and Zoom, but not at all the same as a cuddle.

We advanced to September. Springtime is a lovely season in Melbourne. Some nice sunny days, but we could not even go for a drive anywhere. No sport 's complexes were open, not even gyms. So our routine had become quite dull. When it was sunny, we had taken to putting our fold-up chairs out the front in the sun and sitting there, watching the world go by.

Whenever we awoke to a bright sunny morning, I sent my husband to the shop for some supplies.

One day after finishing lunch, the sun still shining down, he said to me. "I'm going for a test, just to get out in the sunshine." He had complained of a dry throat, but still, I thought it a bit strange.

"I'm okay. I just want to get into the sun and feel the warmth on my face, "he declared with a twinkle in his eye.

And so, his little tale began.

"I drove around to the testing site," he stated, grinning like a Cheshire cat. "I followed the signs and arrows, eventually coming across a lady who I presumed would take my details. Stopping and winding down my car window, I waited for her to speak."

He watched me as he continued his story.

"She began by asking, do you have any symptoms?"

"Well, I said. When I started, today, I woke up with a dry, sore throat and a runny nose, slight headache, which seems to have dissipated now. The throat seems a lot better but still quite dry. So I thought I should still come for a test."

"Looking a bit naughty, she slowly put her hand to the opening at the top of her jacket and began to peel the jacket open. I didn't know what to expect. Then, pointing to the badge that I could now see on her shirt beneath the coat she said, see this badge. It says traffic. I just needed a yes or no answer, not your whole medical history."

My husband chuckled. "Sheepishly I said, maybe you should wear that badge on the outside of your jacket. The lady stared at me like a naughty child who a parent has just scolded. I quickly drove in the direction of her pointing finger, feeling intimidated and very foolish. Finally, I came to a stop where a masked woman in PPE took my details, and soon after, I had the test, given all the required information, like, stay home until you get your results, and so on. Then, still feeling a bit confused by the entire process, I headed home.

Arriving home and telling me his tale made us both smile and lifted our spirits.

There would still be many dark days to come. Here in Victoria, we stayed in strict lockdown for two more months. I remember hearing double doughnuts, 0 new cases and 0 deaths for thirteen days in a row on the 12th of November, and for many days this continued.

But my husband's need to get a bit of sunshine will always make me smile. We often relate his story to others, and it always has the desired effect, making people smile.

So, I believe the moral of this story is. You can lift someone's spirits with a little bit of mischief.

# CINNAMON'S VIEW

## *ANNA ROBERTS*

Hmm, Michael's in the shower, so this gives me some alone time with Olivia, and hopefully, she'll shower me with some sweet kisses. Well, here I go! One paw, two paw, three paw, four.

While Olivia is sleeping, I feel compelled to climb onto the right side of their large bed and snuggle up. Blue Wedgewood coloured walls makes the room cosy, while the exquisitely soft doona gives my back instant comfort. It's like resting on a cloud.

The handcrafted bedhead with a swan head on each post makes me feel like I'm outside. I so love to chase birds when I can, but these birds never move, so they're no fun. Above the bed is a picture of an elegant woman smelling roses hanging over a brick wall. Now that's a lady after my own heart, and I can almost imagine the sweet perfume.

Olivia's long black hair frames her pillow with is its shiny, soft curls. She looks so peaceful; it's almost a sin to wake her. But the alarm went off at six, so it's time she got up anyway to feed me.

Putting my cold nose on Olivia's cheek, I will slide it across to lick her nose, starting from the tip of her nostrils and finishing up to the space between her perfectly shaped eyebrows. Waking up, she might scold me but will soon relax, gently hugging me.

She talks to me while placing her hand over my nose and kissing her hand over and over. I can't help but think that she is embarrassed by her stale breath in the morning, which would explain placing her hand over my snout. I'll roll onto my back slowly during my morning ritual, then Olivia will begin to rub my chest, all the while humming to herself. Finally, I'll encircle her wrist with my paws and place my cold nose on the back of her hand before licking it to thank her for my soothing massage.

Olivia often complains that Michael's method of massage is like having a vice squeezing her flesh. Yet, I have seen her give the most relaxing massages to Michael while mumbling about Venus and Mars. I've wondered how you can blame planets for not being able to provide a simple back rub. Instead, I'm more worried about a full moon. That seems to set off all the dogs in our neighbourhood. All that howling and barking makes it hard for me to sleep.

As a German shepherd, not being vertically challenged gives me an advantage when getting onto the bed. Not like my friend Schnitzel, the wiener dog, who lives at number 13. Schnitzel is my best friend, but he and his master make for an odd couple. Douglas is 6 foot 6 on the old scale, making Schnitzel look like he's not standing up, and from side on he looks much like a baguette. Douglas even made a ramp for Schnitzel to enable him to reach the top of the bed at night to get a cuddle.

Like clockwork, Michael will soon join us, wandering out in his underpants, displaying his six-pack - *that's what humans call it*, kneeling and kissing Olivia on the lips, running his hand over her hair, and removing a stray hair from her eye. Then, finally, Michael will pat and talk to me in a low husky voice, telling me that I'm a naughty girl for getting on the bed and hugging me just for being so lovable.

No one can stay mad at me for long; even my name Cinnamon conjures up the smell of something sweet. Being together with my human pals is just heavenly.

They have both been working from home lately due to COVID, and although I love being with them, as I'm never bored now, having no alone time to myself means I haven't got time to work in the garden, which Olivia calls digging.

Michael has rearranged the garden next to the veranda by planting a row of standard Blackberry nip roses. The roses are a deep purple, and the scent Olivia says is to die for. I like to smell everything, yet I want to go on living, so I'll pass on smelling those roses.

It's been hard lately for my humans as they don't have people over for dinner and drinks anymore. They seem to be cut off and restricted in their movements. I hear them talk about coronavirus, which makes Olivia cry a lot—telling Michael how worried she is about her parents.

I go with Michael to visit Olivia's parents, Jim, and Ruby, deliver supplies and cooked food, leaving the items on their doorstep. Michael rings the bell, speaks to them from about three feet away, blows them a kiss and tells them Olivia sends her love.

It's hard not to see them hug each other as before. Ruby is a short lady with white hair tied in a bun. Her hands are crippled due to arthritis, her back slightly bent, but she always has a smile for me. She blows some kisses our way, and I know they're all meant just for me, but I won't disappoint Michael by letting our secret out. As a former soldier, Jim is tall and straight, and he is sure to be a German shepherd when reincarnated. Ruby, on the other hand, will most likely come back as a corgi.

Olivia is not allowed to visit her parents due to her weak immune system. Last year she ended up in hospital with pneumonia which started at first with the flu. Michael has often expressed his concerns, not wanting to lose Olivia to this terrible virus. While Olivia was in the hospital, Michael was ever so sad, and the two of us fretted over what might happen.

While in lockdown, they have tried many new recipes, and the kitchen is often abuzz with activity. Some of the baking failures go to the neighbour who has chickens. Word is the chickens love the food offerings.

I hope I get to visit awhile with Jim and Ruby soon. They fuss over me, making me feel extra special. Ruby loves to pat me endlessly, saying it helps warm her hands, and I'm happy to oblige. Jim even built a giant ottoman, placing it at the foot of their bed. Ruby sewed a wool blanket to keep me warm; what a darling she is. They make me feel like I'm their baby.

Olivia has managed to declutter the sewing room, wardrobes, linen cupboards, donating the items to the op shop. Michael wanted to keep some of his old jumpers, but Olivia pointed out that they don't fit any longer, and others need them more.

As usual, Olivia, Michael and I go for our daily walk around the park, then back for breakfast. Our local park looks so lovely now with its emerald-green grass and plenty of trees to smell. But I do miss Autumn when I can go ploughing through the piles of leaves and hear that rustling sound they make. There will be no stopping to talk or play with my friends. No chasing my four-legged buddies, barking at any slow old dogs. Barking makes the oldies move so we young ones can run amuck.

Sniffing the grass, the air and each other is non-existent now. Those earthy smells would get me so excited, especially when I have pinpointed a feline. It would have me sniffing all over, trying to track it down.

Back home, my breakfast will come in a metal bowl with fresh water served in a ceramic bowl decorated with tiny bones. What will I have today? Chicken, lamb, or beef with veg. or maybe some sardines. I have noticed that Olivia and Michael tend to avoid bringing their faces near my mouth after having sardines. I can't think why? Although they rub my coat and declare that the fish is making it soft and shiny.

Later, I will run around the back garden past the roses and magnolias then stop at the grevillea, trying to catch some bees. Next, I will drink from the fishpond while tapping the koi on their heads - I think of it as patting the koi. Finally, scare the bejesus out of that fluff ball they call Mitzi, the cat who lives next door.

I will tear around as though I have been stung by a wasp till I'm tired and then drop down in front of Olivia, looking for pity. I am hoping for, by looking up, hinting to get a snack - *I like smackos best*. I will then search for an inconspicuous spot to do a number two. Finally, I wag my tail to alert Olivia that it's her turn for yard duty.

After all, you can't leave dog doo-do lying around as I might get some under my nails, and that would be shocking as I'll be sniffing my toes all day. Olivia, I've trained you well, but funny how you never tell Michael he's a good boy when he has done his business. I appreciate what the two of you do for me, and that makes you irreplaceable.

I miss my friends as we are not allowed to meet up at the park for now. We often raced around in the park, and sometimes I would go slow so that Schnitzel would think he had won. He always looked so excited and happy, so I hadn't had the heart to tell him that I let him win. He would always brag to Max, the bulldog, about winning on the way home, but Max is deaf as a doorknob; and he nods like an older man waiting for the bus and trying to avoid trouble.

It used to be quite a canine crew that met in the park. There's Smug, the Pug who always manages to fart just when he gets to the punch line of his jokes—making it hard to know if the others were laughing at his jokes or his passing wind. Booby, the Boxer, always looks sad and complains that his mistress insists on putting perfume on his coat. I smell like a sissy. It's just not fair!

All the guys like Lola, the Poodle, cause she's so elegant. Her legs, so slender, go right up to her throat; her soft curly white fur always trimmed to perfection. I caught a glimpse of Lola the other day, and I wondered what the others would think if they could see her now.

Unable to get her beauty treatments has turned her into a bear-like creature. So much fur and from behind, her furry legs chaff together; it's not a pretty sight. Molly, the Corgi, whimpers when she sees me at the park; she would dearly love to press her nose against mine, which is impossible for the time being. Molly's coat is a lovely caramel shade, but keeping her white chest clean is challenging due to her height.

Prescott, an Airedale, manages to slip his neck out of his collar daily to run and greet Vanilla the Collie. He is so in love with her. Prescott will twirl around like a circus clown getting everyone's attention. Humans laugh at him while his owner Anne tries to reign him in but not before he kisses Vanilla's cute little nose. It's hard for Anne to control her lovesick pup.

Hunter the Doberman has an air about him that makes you think he will bite your paw off. His dead straight ears and lean muscle are quite threatening even though he can be quite a softy. Hunter nicknamed me Pollyanna cause I am always happy and try hard to get the others to look on the bright side. I don't mind the nickname; I think we need to consider that mental well-being is essential for all.

The crew discussed how funny it is, seeing people wear masks as they go about their daily chores. *Why are they trying to go incognito?* Even if they wore sacks over their heads, we would still be able to pick them out. We can smell them and know who they are straight away.

Our cousin, the bloodhounds, have been used for generations to find the lost or trapped dogs. Have also been used to find land mines, drugs, and criminals all over the world. Our noses give us essential skills that humans value so much.

Previously, it was always so annoying to see the male dogs drooling over Lola; but I decided to get over it. Yes, I am a little jealous cause they treat me like one of the guys. I'm a bit of a tomboy and like to play ball with them. I'm also pretty athletic, and my coat is so smooth; Why can't they drool over me for once?

I don't interrupt the news while Olivia and Michael sit transfixed to the numbers on TV. At first, I thought they were taking some maths class on steroids. But, no, it's the alarming figures of people in other countries affected by the Corona Virus.

We used to take road trips before to the mountain or the sea. I miss the beach so much; —sand between my toes and running into the salty ocean to fetch a ball. Chasing seagulls with the other dogs on the beach and seeing Olivia smile and wave to Michael as he headed off to surf the waves. What fantastic fun we had. Olivia would wipe my back and toes with a towel before we got in the car.

I hope and pray that soon this Corona Virus surge will vanish and that all my friends, humans, and canines will remain safe. Eventually, with luck, our lives will return to normal.

So, to all my animal friends, including Mitzi, enjoy each day, try to bring some joy to your human companions. We all need each other now more than ever. But I do worry that I may forget how to dig, I mean garden!

Gee Michael, what's for dinner tonight? My stomach is rumbling, louder than Schnitzel's bark.

# YES, I AM OLD

## *AN ODE TO TS ELIOT*

### *MELISSA SAYERS*

I am old. Old as the trees, the mountains, and the rivers that meander their way carving their mark in the world. Old as the winds that whisper my name.

Yes, I am old. My body is weak, and my bones are weary. They creak and groan when I move. If I sit for too long, they freeze up. That is why I bought the Ezy chair that tilts forward.

I feel the cold more acutely these days, and my internal barometer forebodes the coming of a storm. My body tenses up and aches. There was a time when I loved nothing more than the pounding of the rain and the peal of thunder. Now that I am old, I dread the wet season.

Yes, I am old. The years show on my face. But, while my eye sockets are dark and hollow, my eyes are still the bright green they were in my youth, the same colour as the British Racing Green MGB I once drove, wind in my hair, with the top down. I missed those days when I didn't have a care in the world.

My cheeks are sunken in too. The skin on my face seems far too big and saggy, particularly around my jowls and under my chin. Over the years, I have tried many treatments, but gravity will not be defeated. My whole face gets sucked in when I take my dentures out, which still extracts squeals of mock terror from my grandchildren.

Yes, I am old. I wear my clothes too big now, grandma-style, loose and not very flattering. But comfortable. My body is bent over, and my skin is merely a covering for my bones. And an ill-fitting covering, that is.I shuffle heavily when I walk. My feet don't leave the floor. I merely slide across the surface of my home. My slippers wear through quickly, and my socks show through the holes.

Yes, I am old. But given the trauma it has seen, this body has been good to me and has survived its nine lives. Yet, at times it holds me to ransom and frustrates me. I have had so many surgeries in my time, most painfully the removal of both breasts, riddled with cancer. I wish I could say I have fought bravely, but I have moaned and whined most of the way through it.

At the moment, though, save the aches and pains of age, all is surprisingly satisfactory. But, of course, sometimes the shakes and trembles impede the simplest of tasks, and just holding a cup of coffee is a challenge. But drink my coffee I shall, until I can no longer, albeit in half-full cups.

After too many beers, I lost my parents early when my father drove himself and my mother into a tree, killing them both instantly. There were no seatbelts back then. I was fifteen and the oldest of the family with two brothers to look after. Life was hard, but with the help of my grandmother, old though she was, we got by.

Yes, I am old, and there have been times that have been sad and dark in my life. At 19, I married, but only because I was pregnant, and it was a marriage without love, producing only one child. My husband was a vicious man and manifested this with bouts of screaming and violence. I stopped leaving the house. The bruises were too shameful. I took to the bottle to quiet the ghosts of my dead parents and the coldness of my husband. Some days I did not even get out of bed but stayed under the covers and cried. I could not be there for my daughter Belinda; I did not know how.

Miraculously, though, she has walked her own path, despite me, and turned out to be a fine adult, putting herself through university to become a kind and skilful nurse. My heart swells to bursting with pride when I think of what she has achieved.

After Belinda left home, I left my husband and the bottle behind and moved to the mountains. The serenity eased the voices in my head, and the fresh air cleared my pickled mind. One day a man came to the door, offering to chop wood and maintain the house for somewhere to stay and three-square meals a day. Occasionally we made love, but mostly we just sat quietly in each other's company and listened to old jazz music on the record player. It was nice to have a hand to hold. He made me feel safe and looked after me well. I think he was my true love. Unfortunately, he died last year of the Corona Virus that gripped our state for what seemed to be the longest time. At no time did I feel the crushing weight of my age more.

It struck swiftly. He went into town for supplies one day and a few days later developed flu-like symptoms. His lungs were weak from years of smoking a pipe, and it took a stranglehold on him quickly. After we received the positive test results, we knew he would not survive it. I nursed him as lovingly as I could, with soup and warm tea, and we did not seek treatment. He wanted to stay at home where he was comfortable, and we knew we would not be together in the hospital.

"All I need is you, my darling," he would say, stroking my wrinkled hand as I cried into his chest. "There is nothing they can do." I do not know whether I cried for him or myself.

The isolation after he passed was palpable like a thick, heavy cloud engulfed the cabin. It was so empty and cold.

I do not see my daughter or grandchildren very often. However, a few times a year, they would make the trip up to see me, although it is a long journey, and I suspect that deep down, Belinda finds it hard to be around me, harbouring a deep resentment for her upbringing.

During COVID, the girls were not allowed to visit at all. No-one was. It felt that the sunshine had been sucked out of my life, even though their visits were infrequent. We had no choice, and I did not like that helplessness. In brighter times, Alyssa, 19, cooked with me. Emily, 17, did puzzles with me. And I loved watching Bailey, twenty-two, ride her horse. But there was simply nothingness during the pandemic, for many, many months. Nothing but the daily news conference and the oppressive numbers each day which just seemed to climb and climb. At times it felt like we would all go mad with the loneliness. I would sit and listen to my jazz and cry, wishing the virus has taken me too.

But take me, it didn't. And now I am very old. These hands are old, too. Twisted and gnarled like an old ghost gum, with veins exposed and skin like crepe paper that bruises at the slightest knock. Hands that tenderly nursed the only man who ever truly loved me. It is almost time for them to hang up their crochet needles and pass down their secrets to a worthy apprentice. Surely one of my three beautiful granddaughters will show an interest.

So now that you can be here, my sweet girls, and I can see you and speak to you, please sit at my feet and listen. Although I am old, my mind has a child-like quality - still sharp and bright. My wit is still intact, though my jokes are silly and corny. So, when it is my time, remember that I loved and was loved as much as one person can. Remember me as funny. Remember the cooking and the jigsaw puddles and the long walks on misty mornings. I do not remember this. It is not me. This is a mere shell of who I used to be.

Yes, I am so very old now. But do not look on me with pity. One day my time will come, and when it does, I do not fear the darkness of the end. I will join my love. I will leave this world fulfilled, shapeless dress and worn-out slippers, with a hollow face and a subtle smile. And people will say to my daughter, "my, you have your mother's eyes."

# I CHOOSE…?

## *REBECCA KENNA*

*Relationships are hard. Sometimes it is all about one person's stuff, and other times the opposite is true. It's about balance.*

*Adding a pandemic to the mix is like unexpectedly finding a chilli in your sauce. Like a Jalapeno, not one of those glossy green ones that are all look and no substance; Very disappointing! But I digress.*

*So, do you embrace it and make a spicy dish? Or do you focus on the familiar ingredients and worry about the heat later?*

*And what happens when you don't make the same choice?*

## *MARCH 2021*

Who the hell was knocking on the door at ten o'clock on a Sunday night? Claire flicked the porch light on and snapped back the deadlock.

"Hi, any vacancies at hotel Thomas?"

Claire took in Sarah's mascara-streaked face and the overnight bag, "Sure, if you don't mind sharing with Hermione. She's decided that she needs her very own dog-free room. Cats! Such attitude!" Hanging Sarah's coat on the hook, she raised an eyebrow, "Tea or wine?"

"I think tea."

Mark looked up as they walked in, "Hey Sars, what are you doing here?" He caught Claire's warning shake of her head, "Right, I might go and watch the game in the other room."

"No, Mark, don't leave on my account."

He winked, "It's okay, I get to watch the game in peace!" Then, he paused, "You, okay?"

He gathered her in a hug and kissed the top of her head, "No, but I will be," she smiled ruefully, "Now that I've had one of your hugs."

It was an accepted fact that Mark gave the best hugs. He reminded Sarah of a teddy bear - floppy, brown hair that never looked styled, and lovely, soft brown eyes. Mark was the principal at the local primary school, loved by students and parents alike. He was the calm voice of reason among their group of friends.

Grabbing a chunky throw, Sarah flopped onto their deep sofa, tucked her legs underneath her and leant back into the cushions. Coming here had been a no-brainer. Claire had been her best friend since the first day of high school. They had laughed and cried together and shared everything from blue eyeshadow to their darkest days. Even when Claire moved to university to study medicine, they visited each other frequently. She closed her eyes and took some deep breaths, feeling her shoulders drop and her neck loosen.

"Chamomile." Claire handed her a mug and sat cross-legged at the other end of the sofa.

"Thanks". Sarah took a sip, then looked at Claire, "I've left him. I can't do it anymore, Claire." She closed her eyes, "It's not supposed to be this hard!"

"It's been a bizarre year; some time out is probably a good idea."

"Mmm, I'm not sure time out is going to cut it," Sarah said, her eyes downcast. "I think I'm done!"

Claire schooled her face, "That's a big call. Don't you love him anymore?"

"I think I will always love him," Sarah wiped the tear that escaped and sighed. "But we have nothing in common anymore. I know that I've changed too, but it's like he's a completely different person. We are strangers living in the same house. We don't even talk, only argue."

"Do the girls know?" Claire asked, still in the dark as to what had happened today.

At the mention of her daughters, Sarah looked deflated, and she shook her head. Even though they were adults and no longer lived at home, she knew Lily and Evie would be shocked and upset that it had come to this.

"Oh, Sars. Take your time to work through it. Either way, I think being apart might give you some clarity. And maybe a wake-up call for Peter! You have a room here for as long as you need, you know that?"

"Thanks, Claire Bear." Sarah's hug was fierce. "Hey, do you mind if I head off to bed, it's been a big day?"

"Of course not. You know where everything is." Then, laughing, she added, "There's my stash of hotel toiletries in the bathroom cupboard if you need anything!"

## JANUARY 2020

Juggling a cheese board, a present and her bag, Sarah called, "Peter, did you grab the wine?" She heard a faint "Yes" as the garage door went up.

Peter had already backed the car out by the time she locked the door, and she jumped into the passenger seat after securing the food in the back. He smiled at her, but she knew he was tense as they were running a little late.

"Relax," she put her hand on his thigh, "Mark and Claire aren't expecting us dead on one o'clock!"

He put his hand on top of hers and smiled, "I know, but you know I hate being late."

"You should have married Lisa!" she laughed. "She's the punctual one!"

"No, too many lists! Some things are better unplanned!" he replied, turning to give her a cheeky wink.

"Oh really! You could pull over, and we could be really late?" she said, only half-joking.

Peter pulled into their friends' driveway and came around to open Sarah's door, "Remind me, who's going to be here today?"

"Just Rowan and Lisa, Michael and Jo, and Andy." Not waiting to see his reaction to Andy's name, she marched up the path and onto the verandah. She thought it funny that he was still jealous of her old boyfriend, even though they had recently celebrated twenty-six years of marriage. Sarah had dated Andy in high school, and Claire had dated his brother Mark. Claire and Mark had a similar easygoing relationship back then as they did now, whereas she and Andy were far more volatile. Mark used to joke that they were on and off like a light switch.

When Andy left to work overseas after they finished school, they called it quits for good. Claire's brother Michael also attended the school but being a few years older, he didn't hang out with them often as teenagers. However, when he met Jo at around the same time Sarah met Peter, they became a regular group of six.

Peter introduced them to Rowan, a fellow accountant he had met at university, and together with Lisa, they had become a group of eight. For over twenty years, they had socialised, celebrated, commiserated, and holidayed together.

Knocking, then calling out, "It's just us!" she opened the front door, knowing Claire would have left it unlocked.

"We're out the back!" Looking down the panelled hallway, Sarah could see Claire waving from the deck. Claire and Mark bought the weatherboard cottage just after they were married. The house had been a dive but was on a massive block in their ideal area. Over the years, they renovated and extended, adding a large, open plan living and kitchen area that ran the width of the house. Claire had a knack for interiors, able to create beautiful, livable spaces on a limited budget. She found it relaxing, something completely different to her work life.

"Bubbles?" Claire offered, waving a bottle of prosecco. Not waiting for an answer, she handed Sarah a glass and clinked it with her own, "Cheers!"

"Cheers! Where's the birthday boy?"

"I'm here!"

She jumped at the voice in her ear and laughingly turned around. "Happy Birthday, Mark!" planting a kiss on his cheek, she handed him the gift.

"Oh, you shouldn't have. But I'm glad you did!" He put the gift on the table and reached to shake hands with Peter, who also wished him a happy birthday. "Beer, mate?"

"That would be great," Peter answered as he followed Mark over to the BBQ where Michael and Andy were chatting.

Sarah watched the dogs, Charlie and Fred, chase each other as she walked towards Claire. Claire named all her animals after Harry Potter characters. "Where's Lisa and Rowan?"

"Oh, they can't make it until later. But, hey, did you bring the Bali brochures?"

"Yep, in my bag." Sarah clapped her hands, "I love the planning bit!"

"I love the lying on a sun-lounger with a cocktail bit!" Jo laughed as she joined them.

Claire headed to the kitchen, "Right, let's eat! Then plan!"

# *FEBRUARY 2020*

"This is beautiful! I cannot believe I've never noticed this place!" Sarah returned to the table and topped up the glasses. As she sat down, she leant back, enjoying the feel of the sun warming her face. The local winery was small and casual, and they had been seated at one of the outdoor, weather-worn tables resting on gravel. The surrounding vines created a courtyard, the lush green leaves and umbrellas lowering the temperature slightly on this dry, hot Sunday typical of this time of year in Melbourne. Sipping the chilled Pinot Gris, gazing out at the vines, Sarah drifted into thought.

The hum of conversation flowed around her. Snippets of a discussion about this new super-bug, Claire's calm doctor's voice answering Michael's and Lisa's questions, Rowan and Peter animatedly debating the performance of their football teams, peppered with laughter from Jo as Mark entertained her with an anecdote from his grade-three students. Pleasantly daydreaming, she suddenly snapped back to the present realising someone was saying her name. Jo giggled, making the beads on her braids clack together as they swayed, "Hello, earth to Sarah?"

"Sorry, off in my little world! What were you saying?"

Lisa repeated, "That the consensus is a few days in Nusa Dua to begin, then Sanur and to then return to the place in Ubud for a week, this time, at the end. Thoughts?"

"Sounds like heaven. Where do I sign?"

"Great, I'll give them a call this week. Let me know if you want to do any tours or activities, and I'll get them added. I'll email the quote to you all when I get it." Sarah and Lisa usually took care of the pre-holiday organising. Both working in administration, Sarah at a wellness centre and Lisa at a fashion magazine, it was easier for them to deal with the emails and calls.

Aromas of fresh bread and garlic wafted over the table as the waiter arrived, and the conversation turned to the delicious dishes. Good-natured banter accompanied lunch as they updated each other about work and family, chatting until the last of the plates were cleared.

"Anyone wants to come back for a swim?" Rowan asked as they walked to their cars.

"We're in!" Michael gave a thumbs up at Jo's nod.

"Sounds lovely," Mark said. "But the dogs need to be fed, and I've got to get organised for tomorrow."

"We still have to pack." Peter made a groaning sound, and Sarah laughed.

"You mean I still have to pack? You just put out the clothes you want to take!"

"What? They don't make their own way into the suitcase?" he feigned a look of surprise.

"Enjoy your week away! I wish we were coming!" Claire blew them a kiss.

As they drove home, Sarah turned on the radio and sang along. Peter smiled at her, "You're very happy."

"What's not to love? Great day out and then a week away at the beach relaxing. The most strenuous things I intend to do are walking and yoga. So, no working while we're away; I'm sure they can manage for a week without you!"

"I'll have to take the laptop, just in case, but I promise it's only for an emergency!" he compromised.

## MARCH 2020

Sarah sipped her drink, enjoying the late afternoon sun and appreciating their efforts in the garden. Peter had turned the football on, angling the family room television so he could watch it from where they sat on the deck.

Ping! "Is that your phone again?" Peter glanced away from the television momentarily.

"Yes, it's the girl's group about lunch on Friday." Sarah smiled as she typed a response then flicked the phone to silent, so it didn't continue to ping while she read the messages in the chat.

"Did you invite Anna?"

"No," she frowned. "It's just a birthday lunch, pretty low-key. But, of course, it's only forty-nine this year."

"Yep, the big one is next year!" Peter laughed. She and Claire were the youngest, the rest of the group having already turned fifty. "Anna is a girl, you know," he added.

"Huh?"

"I said, Anna's a girl."

"Yes, and?"

"You said it's a girls' lunch, and Anna is a girl, so I was wondering why you didn't invite her?"

Sarah looked up in confusion, "She's your work colleague's wife. I mean, she's nice enough, but this is just our group."

"Doug's not just a work colleague. We've known him for twenty years! Anna's been at other social events. What about the golf weekend away, and you all went off to the spa?"

"That was part of your fiftieth birthday celebrations. Anna and the other 'work wives' were there because you invited the guys." Sarah hesitated slightly, "But she's really not a friend."

Peter stared at her, "You don't like her?"

Sarah was unsure if it was a statement or question.

"It's not a case of liking, or not liking. She's just more of an acquaintance. I don't see what the big deal is. Unless it's a big birthday, we always do something casual with just friends." They used to socialise with Doug more often, but that was years ago when he was married to his second wife, Di. Sarah had remained friends with Di, who went on to find her happily ever after, while Doug moved on to a third, and now a fourth wife.

"Okay. I just thought it would be nice to include her." Peter shrugged, turning up the volume on the TV.

*

"Sorry, I'm late!" Rushing into the restaurant, Jo kissed Sarah's cheek and handed her a gift bag. Garabelli was a favourite lunch choice for their get-togethers; by the beach, it was beautiful on the deck in the warm weather, but the open fire and cosy décor made it just as appealing in winter. "Happy birthday! It is totally unimaginative and clearly not wrapped to Lisa's standard!" she hooted.

Pulling out a bottle of her favourite bubbly, Sarah laughed, "Never apologise for champagne! Thank you!" She placed it beside her with the other gifts, "Thank you, everyone, I've been so spoilt."

They enjoyed a long seafood lunch, during which the conversation bounced from disbelief at the handling of Ruby Princess Cruise ship debacle to a robust debate about quarantine procedures, from diet fads to fashion, and inevitably, the inexplicable obsession with hoarding toilet paper. It was followed by cake, with candles and singing. Just Claire and Sarah remained at four o'clock, enjoying a quiet cup of coffee.

"Good day?" Claire asked.

"Lovely day. You all made me feel incredibly special, and it was great catching up with everyone. I hadn't seen some of the girls since before Christmas."

"I know, a nearly four-hour lunch, and we never run out of things to talk about. I love our catchups!"

"A lot is going on to talk about at the moment, but I know what you mean. And me too." Sarah took a sip of coffee, "Hey," she hesitated. "Peter asked me if I had invited Anna – do you think that's weird?"

"Yes, it is a bit. You don't really socialise with them, do you?"

"Only occasionally, mainly for work things. I think Peter would like to do a bit more like we used to, but it's not the same."

"Because you are still friends with Di?" Claire asked.

"No, she wouldn't care. You know Doug – likes the high life. Dinners, drinks, corporate Boxes, marquees at the races…" Sarah waved her hand. "I prefer a quiet night in with a book or a chick flick."

## APRIL 2020

"Okay, I've put in the meeting ID and the password, but nothing happened!" Sarah leaned forward, peering at the laptop on the coffee table. "Oh wait, ha-ha, there they are!" She waved and grinned at the screen as Peter joined her on the couch.

"Hi!" Claire and Mark, the organiser of this catchup Zoom session, waved back.

Soon other squares appeared, Lisa and Rowan in one, and Michael and Jo in another. An expert at guiding novices after setting up remote learning sessions, Mark patiently sorted out the initial teething problems with volume and too many people talking at once. There was much hilarity. Jo leaned closely into the camera every time she spoke, Charlie the dog sat between Claire and Mark, determined to be part of the meeting, and Hermione, the cat, showed the camera rather too much when she stretched, "It's true what they say; don't work with kids or animals!" Claire wiped away tears. The conversation turned to how much had changed in such a short space of time.

Jo leaned in, "Not even a month ago, we were at your birthday lunch!"

"I know, I feel so sorry for restaurants and cafes. Really, all of the businesses who have had to close." Lisa asked, "How are you going with Sars, being a wellness centre?"

"Not too bad. We're lucky that some of our services are medical, so they continue. The yoga, Pilates and meditation classes and training have all gone online, so I've been busier than normal trying to coordinate all of that."

Lisa again, "Can you go into the office?"

"I did at first, just to get set up, but our IT company have been great so that I can do everything from here."

"Where's Peter gone?" Rowan interrupted.

"Oh, his phone rang. Hang on. I'll get him." Sarah stood up and disappeared from the screen.

*

Knowing he would be in the front room, which performed dual purpose as a quiet sitting room and a study, she pushed open the door and saw Peter relaxing in a chair by the fireplace, glass of wine in hand, and his feet on the ottoman. He was laughing and looked up when he saw Sarah. She gestured toward the deserted Zoom session in the family room and mouthed, "Who is it?"

Covering the microphone, "It's Doug. Bit of an issue with one of the jobs."

"Can't you ring him back?" she hissed.

"Won't be much longer. You carry on." Returning to his call, "Sorry about that…." "No, no, all good, it was just Sarah."

Exhaling forcefully through her nose, she mimicked "Just Sarah!" as she walked back down the hall to re-join the Zoom. She took a breath and relaxed her face before sitting down.

*

Sarah continued chopping vegetables, not looking up when Peter sat at the island bench.

"Wine?" he asked.

She stopped momentarily, "That was really rude!"

"What was?"

Returning to chopping, slightly more forcefully, "You, bailing on the Zoom!"

"It was a work thing, Sarah, couldn't be helped. We have people working weekends, so I need to be available."

Rolling her eyes, "It was a couple of hours for a Zoom with friends. You're in finance. It's not exactly life or death. Surely it wasn't that urgent?"

"I don't expect you to understand. Just be a bit more supportive," Peter said in a low voice.

"Don't be so bloody patronising! My work is open on weekends too. Your conversation with Doug sounded more like a social chat!"

"Yes, but I hardly think a yoga class needs urgent attention!" he waved his hand dismissively.

"You can be a real arse sometimes!" Sarah stomped toward the bedroom, "I'm going for a walk."

"You have already been out walking today," Peter called after her.

"Thank you 'exercise police'. I'm going for another one. To get away from you!"

"Don't be childish!"

The door slammed on the end of his comment.

## MAY 2020

Sarah lit the candles, wiped the wine glasses, and gave the table a final once-over. She smiled, running her hand along its slightly rough edge. Inherited from her grandmother, it was one of several furniture items that had travelled with them to each of their homes. Sarah loved the old wood and blending it with modern pieces had created her own eclectic, comfortable style.

Delicious aromas of spices lingered from her afternoon of cooking, mingling with the fresh scent of the herbs she had chopped. It had been a glorious autumn day, crisp and cold this morning, then sunny and bright, but in the last half an hour, the sun and the temperature had dropped. She closed the patio doors and pulled the curtains across, turned the heating on low and clicked the remote to the gas fire. With an hour until everyone was due to arrive, she had plenty of time for a quick shower, makeup, and dress.

"Argh, I'm not going to be ready!" Sarah wailed. It was ten minutes to seven, and she was still in her robe, applying her makeup. "This is all your fault Peter Davis!" she was laughing and trying to apply mascara at the same time.

"It was worth it." He wrapped his arms around her and kissed her neck, "You don't need that. You're gorgeous. Forget makeup. Let's have a quick round two." He waggled his eyebrows at her.

"Go and put some clothes on so at least one of us can answer the door!" she swatted his behind and shooed him out of the bathroom.

*

Michael groaned, rubbing his ample stomach, "That was sensational, Sars. If I die tonight, I'll die a happy man."

"No dessert for you then?" she raised her eyebrow at him.

He sat up and winked, "Give me ten minutes."

"You've got at least half an hour; us girls need to organise our weekend away. So, go! Give us some peace." Jo softened her request with a kiss on his cheek. Sarah was sure that they were the couple who would still be holding hands at ninety. Their marriage had weathered a lot; initial resistance from Michael's family due to Jo's South African heritage and her son from a previous relationship, then their inability to have a child together. But they were a happy family of three, and Michael raised Luan as his own, Luan's biological father never in the picture.

Peter led Michael, Rowan and Mark to the other room after Sarah promised to call them when dessert was ready. Then, after the finalised plans and an accommodation request for the agreed dates in early July were sent almost an hour later, Sarah called the men back for the apple pie and ice cream.

*

After waving off Mark and Claire, who were, as usual, the last to leave,

Peter latched the front door. He walked back into the kitchen where Sarah was rinsing the last of the dishes, "That was a good night! It felt normal." he declared. "Not even 'COVID-normal'; just normal!" As she shut the dishwasher door and turned it on, he snaked his arms around her waist and whispered in her ear, "I'm ready for round two!"

She giggled and took off toward the bedroom, calling, "You have to catch me first!"

# JUNE 2020

Abandoned dresses and tops covered the bed, and half a dozen shoeboxes littered the floor. Sarah stood in her underwear holding a black, sequined top and a white, chiffon blouse over a pair of narrow legged, black trousers. Sarah usually enjoyed getting ready here; they had sacrificed an extra bedroom to accommodate a large master suite, including a dressing room and ensuite bathroom. She had not regretted the decision, loving the luxury of the deep bath and the bespoke wardrobe. Tonight, however, the space failed to calm her.

"How many outfits are you wearing?" Peter chuckled as he stood in the doorway.

"Shut up!" she ducked under his arm as she snatched a pair of strappy, black sandals from the floor.

"It's only dinner. Why are you so stressed?" He lifted the two hangers with his trousers and shirt and took them into the bedroom to get dressed.

Sarah surveyed the all-black ensemble in the mirror from every angle, "I am not going to explain the nuances of women's fashion to you again!" she said through gritted teeth. Striding to the dresser, , she added chunky silver earrings and an onyx-set cuff, sprayed a mist of perfume, and grabbed her black clutch, "Right, I'm as ready as I'll ever be."

"You're not going to a funeral!"

Her eyes widened, "I am not changing again!" she shouted.

"I meant your face, not your outfit," he clarified. "What's wrong?"

"Nothing," she hesitated. "I just don't know these people, and..." she trailed off.

"You will be fine; you know Doug and Anna, and I'm sure you met Chris and Jill at the Christmas party. You look gorgeous. What's not to love?" He placed a kiss on her forehead and drew her into a hug.

*

The chandelier above the dining table skittered light patterns up the walls and onto the soaring raked ceiling. The house was stunning. Vast and cleverly designed with exquisite finishes and décor. *It is beautiful*, Sarah thought admiringly *but lacking soul.*

Hearing raucous laughter, she glanced up and noted the number of empty wine bottles at the other end of the table, wishing she could pour herself a large glass. But she would not risk it. One with dinner was her limit when she was driving. So instead, she sipped sparkling water, turning back to the woman beside her, prattling on about a cruise she wanted to take. *Good luck with that*, Sarah thought. *A cruise ship is the last place anyone would want to be. It would be like taking a holiday in a floating petri dish!* Thankfully, Anna had just served coffee, so Sarah hoped they could leave soon.

"Thanks again," Sarah waved as she buckled her seatbelt. She closed the window and turned the heater to the max as she pulled out of the drive.

"What was the hurry? We didn't need to go so early."

"Peter, I've been up since six. I worked until four, and then I had to pick up the flowers and get ready; I'm exhausted."

"We had only just finished dinner. We were just about to have a game of snooker!"

Sarah tried to ignore the peevish tone, "It's eleven-thirty. I'll turn into a pumpkin soon," she joked.

"I thought you would have had loads to chat. I know Cherie and Jill do Yoga or Pilates."

She took a deep breath, "Mmm, yes, they do."

He stared straight ahead, "It would have been nice if you had made a little more effort."

She snapped, the combination of tiredness and his belligerent tone eroding the last of her patience, "My conversations tonight were Oscar-worthy! Gail wants to take a cruise! A cruise, for God's sake! Cherie thinks she needs a career change from the makeup counter, so she is looking to do an injectables course! And Jill and Anna were discussing the merits of a five-thousand-dollar Chanel handbag! Trust me – I made a bloody effort!"

"Oh, so sorry my friends aren't highbrow enough for you! Not everyone wants to discuss important world events all of the time."

"Wow, so many things to unpack. *Your friends?* They are work colleagues. *Our friends* are not highbrow. We talk about what is important to us! To you!" Biting her lip, "You know what? You've had a few drinks. Let's park this before we say something we don't mean."

"Right, so I drink too much now?" Peter turned in his seat, and Sarah could feel his gaze on the side of her face. "I *meant* what I said. You work at a wellness centre, Sarah – it's not the United Nations! Since this COVID thing, you act like you're saving the world. Sometimes people just want to talk about the footy. Or cruises. Or handbags. Everything doesn't have to be earnest. Just lighten up!" He laid back in the seat and closed his eyes.

The conversation was clearly over, and Sarah didn't know if she was relieved or annoyed. It was probably both if she was honest. Long before Sarah pulled into their garage, Peter was snoring. For the first time in their marriage, she left him in the car. She could not deal with it anymore tonight, but she did put a blanket over him before she went to bed.

# *JULY 2020*

Sarah's mobile buzzed, and she swiped immediately, seeing Claire's name appear. "I rang to check on Evie?" Claire asked, wasting no time on chit-chat. Evie was Sarah's youngest daughter, and her job as a nurse at the Royal Melbourne Hospital meant that she was in the thick of the latest outbreak. She was currently in one of the teams testing the residents of the public housing towers, and her suburb was now back in lockdown.

"I spoke to her yesterday. She's okay. It is hard on her not being able to see anyone, but as she said, she doesn't have time either. So they eat, sleep and breathe it," Sarah's voice cracked, knowing she was talking to someone who understood. "I worry about her. I know she's strong, but it is taking a toll."

"I know. Gem said the same thing when I spoke to her. She goes from the hospital to home and back again. I think they have been messaging each other to vent." Claire's daughter Gemma was an intern at another city hospital. "I know they were planning to meet us next weekend, but they won't be able to now. I'm getting worried *we* might not be able to go on the girl's trip if they can't get this under control!"

"Don't say that!" Sarah groaned. "I really need this break."

"Things haven't improved?" Claire asked.

Sarah had confided that Peter was spending long hours at work, and there was residual tension since their argument.

*

Sarah was at work when she heard the announcement that Victoria was going back into lockdown three days before they were due to leave. She swore out loud, causing the receptionist to look at her in astonishment. She had been relying on a few days away as a circuit breaker to the atmosphere in the house. Returning to working from home was going to be interesting.

Sarah wondered how people survived if they didn't have friends like hers. Knowing that it would be a tough time for everyone, Claire scheduled a virtual Friday evening 'book club' telling them to bring a wine label to discuss, and Lisa organised a walking roster. A group of them also decided to cook meals for the frontline workers. Having several doctors and nurses in their intimate circle gave a sense of pitching in and giving back. But importantly, it gave them regular contact with people who cared and understood what each one of them was going through.

Peter had set up his virtual office in the front lounge on their home, only going into work when necessary, unlike the last lockdown. After a week working at the dining table, Sarah realised she would need daily physio to continue like this. Two days, a paint job, and an online shopping spree later, she stood back and admired her new office in the previously unused bedroom. The sage green walls were soothing, paired with crisp white trims to match the furniture and desk. A squashy navy armchair offered somewhere to read, throws, cushions, and plants provided colour, and some of her favourite things added personality. The space had a lovely, Zen feeling, and she found herself spending more and more time there.

## AUGUST 2020

Sarah swatted away the fly, but the buzzing continued. Then, finally, she realised that she had dozed off on the couch and the noise was her phone. The husband of one of the yoga teachers at the centre explained that his wife had begun early labour and asked if she could organise a replacement teacher for her classes.

The yoga classes were covered easily with a few texts, but the morning meditation classes proved to be an issue. The classes had started in July to help members adjust to another lockdown, and they had been immensely popular. Tomorrow was the beginning of the August series, but Sarah could not secure a replacement instructor due to the early time slot, home-schooling, and other commitments. So she headed to her office to call the Centre manager and draft cancellation notifications.

Tom answered on the first ring, "Hey, Sarah. What's up?"

Sarah explained the issue and concluded, "…so unless you know someone, I'll send out apology texts and emails."

Bemused, she stared at her phone after hanging up. How had she agreed to run the series? It *seemed* like a good idea when Tom explained how easy it was to run via Zoom, reminding her that she had done the July series, and expressing complete faith in her abilities. *Crap*, she thought, staring at her screen, *what have I done?*

I cannot believe I did that! Rubbing her eyes, a couple of hours later, she stood up, stretched, and did a little dance. She would only know for sure tomorrow if it resonated with the participants, but her gut told her it was good. Or maybe that was hunger or nerves!

*

The meditations received rave reviews. They had already scheduled a September series and received numerous subscription requests for the current videos. Tom's 'I told you so' text made her smile.

Bouncing out of bed before the alarm went off this Friday, "Good morning, Sarah" she smiled at her reflection in the bathroom mirror. Putting on some light makeup after her shower, she marvelled at the boost this new role had given her. While she had enjoyed her admin role, she realised it no longer presented a challenge. Her friends had noticed the difference, too, Claire asking if things had improved between her and Peter.

Unfortunately, the opposite was true. The stage four restrictions meant Peter could not go into the office at all and his attitude had deteriorated. He seemed stressed, edgy and she was worried he was drinking too much, judging by the wine bottles in the recycling bin. His central, almost only interaction was with Doug and his work colleagues. This filled Sarah with dismay, knowing that Doug's life was littered with ex-wives and children with whom he had little or no contact. However, Peter brushed off her concern whenever she attempted to bring it up. Separately, Mark, Rowan, and Claire had all reached out, but he had stonewalled them too.

For Sarah, starting at six on Monday, Wednesday and Friday mornings meant she was getting up at five to be set up and video ready. At first, so as not to disturb Peter, who was now starting later and working later still, she began sleeping in the spare room the night before her meditations and using the family bathroom rather than their ensuite. However, before long, the early mornings became a habit. She was on a schedule of bed by nine, and Peter's late-night discussions kept her awake. When she mentioned it, he suggested sleep in the spare room while they had to work at home.

She agreed, knowing it was somewhat avoiding their issues but finding relief from the pressure cooker their home had become.

# SEPTEMBER 2020

The screen came alive as faces appeared, "Book Club is in session!" Claire declared, raising her glass. "This is a Yarra Valley Pinot; it is vibrant and juicy with wild strawberries and luscious cherries. Sounds quite sexy!" she giggled.

"How much of that have you had?" Jo laughed.

Mark's face appeared next to Claire as he topped up her glass. "This is only her second, but she's had a long week, and she's been hanging out for a session with you girls. Look after her." He kissed her head and disappeared from camera view, but Sarah caught his tender look at his wife as he left and knew he was concerned about her. Being a doctor during a pandemic was no easy feat.

The following two hours flew by as they exchanged news from the week. They cried with Lisa, desperate for the South Australian border to open so she could visit her mum, who had been unwell, and then laughed with her as she showed off her chin-ups in the gym that she and Rowan had set up in their garage.

"Trust you, Rowan," Claire laughed as he came into view. "You were never going to lose your supermodel physique, and now you've got Lisa hooked too!" He took their teasing well. Food was an essential part of his Indian family's traditions. His mother was an excellent cook, but he had been a chubby child and endured teasing at school, so he became dedicated to his fitness regime as a teenager. Now, he made them laugh with stories of his mum constantly trying to feed him, believing him to be too thin.

Mark popped back in later, and Michael stopped to say hello. They hijacked the discussion for a few minutes until Claire and Jo told them to make their wine club. "I thought you said it was a book club?" Mark laughingly pointed out as he left.

"Potato, 'Potarto'!" she said. Then, turning back to the screen, "Our new doctor is one of your meditation students, Sarah. He has been singing your praises and was very impressed when he found out I knew you. But unfortunately, he was not as impressed when I told him I didn't meditate!"

Sarah laughed, "I told you! So now you have heard it from an expert." She had been trying to get Claire to meditate for years, but Claire insisted she could not sit still for that long and preferred gardening as a mindful activity. *Whatever floats your boat*, Sarah thought; *Yoga, meditation, mindfulness, call it what you like, but people doing it seemed to be coping a lot better than those who were not.*

The Zoom session made her feel better and worse. The laughter, silliness, and comfort she received from those she loved most made her more aware of what was lacking in her relationship.

# OCTOBER 2020 – FEBRUARY 2021

The last three months of the year brought with it the easing of restrictions, a return to work and some pre-COVID activities, but Sarah found herself unable to slot back into life as it was before. Although Peter seemed happier, returning to the gym, golf and work, there was a disconnect. It felt odd, like putting on a suit that no longer fitted, familiar but not quite right.

On the upside, work was fantastic. Experiencing and coming out of lockdown had been challenging for so many people and as a result, there was more awareness and focus on mental health. The Wellness Centre was busier than ever and had branched out, taking the mindfulness and meditation programs into many workplaces. Sarah was heavily involved in this aspect, so Tom created a new role. She now coordinated all of their wellness programs after handing over some of her previous administration tasks. He had been accommodating and generous with his time, and Sarah appreciated his knowledge and support.

Work and friends were Sarah's saving grace. Lisa and Rowan had hosted a small party to celebrate all the birthdays and achievements they had missed during the lockdown, the walking roster continued, and the Zoom book club was now fortnightly and no longer virtual. For a short time, Sarah even thought that she and Peter might be getting back on track.

Christmas felt familiar. Lily and Evie came to stay for a few days, bunking in together as Sarah kept her office set up. The festivities and camaraderie took a front seat and pushed day-to-day life and any niggles to the back. They shared breakfast and presents together as a family before heading to Claire's for lunch. For many years Claire and Mark had hosted Christmas dinner. They had an open house policy, growing or shrinking when necessary to accommodate boyfriends and girlfriends, family, friends and colleagues. Sarah, Peter, Evie and Lily were firmly on the permanent fixture list and always arrived early, with their contributions, to lend a hand. The celebrations continued well into the night, concluding as always, with games selected by the younger generation, Gemma, and her brother Alex, Evie and Lily. It had evolved from snap and monopoly when they were younger to drinking games and trivia as they got older, but it was always the cause of much hilarity and a few fights when they were young.

Michael and Jo spent their Christmas with Luan and his partner, who announced they were expecting their first child. They were over the moon about becoming grandparents. Rowan and Lisa travelled to South Australia to be with Lisa's family, who they had not seen for almost a year. They changed their plans while they were there and decided to stay for New Year, which would break a long-standing tradition of the eight of them spending New Year's Eve together. Booking, particularly now, was essential, so there were two spare tickets to their booked function. Rowan suggested they invite another couple to save them going to waste. Peter immediately suggested Doug and Anna, offering to text straight away.

Awkward was the politest way to describe the disaster that was New Year's Eve. It was like mixing oil and water; it just did not work. Despite an admirable effort to engage Anna, she was polite but appeared uninterested in much of what Jo, Claire, and Sarah discussed. Doug was in sales mode, brash, holding court, and plying the table with wine. He flirted outrageously with a waitress, and his jokes bordered on inappropriate, only Peter laughing as if to justify why he had invited them. It was a relief when midnight came; nobody was too keen to continue the party.

Sarah's optimism for the state of their relationship plummeted during the summer. They were both busy with work, their hours mismatched once again. Peter went to the gym more often and played golf on the weekend. Sarah was still doing yoga, Pilates and walking. Even the limited time they did spend together could hardly be described as quality. What began as a cosy night in, with a movie, ended with Sarah watching most of it alone while Peter took a call in the other room. At one point, she wondered if he was having an affair, but she soon realised that Doug was the only candidate.

One Friday evening at the end of February, Sarah dropped in to see Claire. The book club had dwindled with the return of normal catchups.

"So, things have improved lately? Peter seems to be much more his old self." Claire asked as they took advantage of the balmy evening on the deck.

Sarah stared into her wine as if looking for the answer, "I wish I could say yes, Claire, but unfortunately, you only see the 'public' Peter." She got up and paced to the edge of the deck.

Claire waited, knowing Sarah had more to say, giving her time to collect her thoughts.

"I wish you saw the Peter I have to deal with at home."

Claire walked over and put her arm around Sarah's shoulders, "Talk to me. What's happening?"

Sarah shrugged her off, needing movement to get out the words, "When we're out, he's social, happy, and conversation is no issue. But, at home, he's moody, withdrawn, even angry over the slightest things. It's like Jekyll and Hyde. I've tried to talk to him. I know you and Mark both tried to talk to him last time too. But I feel like it's worse this time. Last time, we could blame lockdown. This time, I don't know why!" As the tears fell, she felt Claire's arms around her and gave into the outpouring of long pent-up emotions, "I don't know what to do?" she sobbed.

Claire let her cry it all out, "Well, you're not driving home, so how about you sleep here, and we make a plan in the morning with clear heads?"

After a good sleep, coffee, breakfast and an open and honest chat with Mark and Claire, Sarah felt much better. However, they were shocked at how bad the situation had become, and Claire was direct in her opinion that Peter needed professional help.

They agreed that Mark was the best person to talk to Peter without appearing to be an ambush. Although she wasn't sure that it would work, it felt good to be doing something. She knew she couldn't continue the way things were.

# MARCH 2021

Sarah padded out to the kitchen and made a coffee, intending to take it back to bed and read her book. *Ahh, a lazy morning is what I need.*

It had been a long day and a late night celebrating her fiftieth yesterday. She had enjoyed the day in the city with her girlfriends, followed by dinner with their regular group of eight.

*But not what I'm going to get apparently*, hearing footsteps on the porch. A loud knock preceded her daughters bursting through the door, partially hidden by flowers and balloons, "Surprise!"

"I thought you weren't coming until this afternoon?" Sarah gathered them in a hug.

"Change of plans!" they exchanged a conspiring look. "But first, presents!" putting a beautifully wrapped box on the bench. Their thoughtful words in the card and the charms they had each chosen made Sarah cry. Taking a second envelope out of the box, she raised her eyebrows at them. "That's the best bit!" Evie clapped her hands. The day spa voucher had no date, "You have forty-five minutes. Go, get ready!"

"We're going now?"

"Yes, chop, chop!" Lily pushed her toward the bedroom.

Peter shuffled out, looking a little worse for wear, "Hey, you two!"

While Sarah was in the shower, they told him about the surprise, adding that they had also organised to cook dinner this evening. "We should be back by five at the latest."

*

The three of them enjoyed manicures and pedicures before having a light lunch. Then the girls went off to the pools, leaving Sarah to enjoy the treatments they had booked. Meeting her later in the lounge, they each selected herbal teas and sat beside her, "Feel good?" Evie asked.

"You are going to have to pour me into a bucket to take me home! That was bliss, but I don't think I can move," she said, snuggling into the chair.

"I don't think they let you move in." Lily laughed, shaking her head.

The car trip home was full of chatter and laughter, sharing anecdotes from the day, "I am so glad we are staying in," Sarah sighed.

"We figured as much. We knew if we went out, you would shower and get ready. But, of course, that totally defeats the purpose. You want to enjoy those creams, oils and smells for as long as possible." Lily sniffed her arm.

"And definitely, no makeup after a facial!" Evie added.

The house was quiet when they walked in. After placing their bags on the wooden hall table, Lily updated as she continued to the kitchen, "Dad texted, he went to play golf but said he would be back by five." Taking out the champagne bottle they had left in the fridge earlier, she poured three glasses, "Cheers, Mum! Happy Fiftieth!"

Sarah was only allowed to watch from the other side of the bench while the girls prepared a family favourite dish of salmon, soba noodles and Asian vegetables. Preparation complete, the food just awaiting cooking.

Lily glanced at her watch at six o'clock. "I might just call Dad..." she started to say when they heard the front door open. Lily leaned around the corner to look down the hall.

Sarah realised something was wrong by the look on her face.

"We've got a few extras!" Peter announced, brandishing a bottle of champagne. "And we won this!"

Plastering a smile on her face, Sarah accepted congratulations from Doug, Anna, Chris and Jill and handed around drinks.

"It's your birthday dinner, Mum!" Evie growled.

Assuring the girls that she was okay, Sarah excused herself momentarily. Heading to the bedroom, she changed flip-flops for sandals and applied some mascara and lip-gloss, more to give herself time to collect her thoughts than a need to make herself presentable.

Between them, Sarah, Evie and Lily managed to supplement the meal to feed eight rather than four. Sarah dismissed the girls' offer to help clean up before they headed off, knowing they both had early starts. Their hugs goodbye felt extra tight, and although Lily smiled and waved on her way to the car, Sarah could tell by Evie's strut that she was not impressed.

Returning inside, she closed the door and leant back against it, straightening her shirt. Using the walk down the hall to restore her face to a pleasant mask, she returned to the living room where her husband and four of his friends were having a great time celebrating her birthday. Collecting bowls, cutlery and glasses, she began rinsing and stacking the dishwasher.

Peter called from the couch, "Leave that. We'll do it in the morning. Come have a drink!"

"It's fine. You carry on. I'll just finish up here." Hoping the sarcasm didn't come through in her voice.

She heard him laugh, "Sarah always has to have everything pristine!" However, his tone had a bite that wasn't humour. She elected to ignore his hints for dessert as 'the meal had been small'. What did he expect, bringing home four unexpected guests! She was furious with him for ruining the night and crushed for her daughters, who had done such a wonderful job. On top of that, he had not lifted a finger to help. The guests excused themselves soon after, Peter seeing them out, while Sarah was past caring if they picked up on her less than gracious vibe.

"What the hell was that about?" Sarah jumped in reaction to his roar. "That was embarrassing! You were so rude to our guests. And they will probably have to stop for MacDonald's on the way home!"

It took every ounce of self-control she had not to throw the bowl she held at him, dropping it with a thud into the sink instead. There were countless thoughts, words and feelings whirling around inside her, but she was mute. Looking over at him, taking in his self-righteous stance, flushed face and red wine staining the corner of his mouth, she said, "You know what? I'm done!"

"Fine! Go to bed. I'm staying here!" he poured another wine and flicked on the sports channel, flopping onto the couch.

"No. I meant I am done!" She whispered as she packed an overnight bag. The tears came in the car. Peter, already snoring, didn't hear her go.

Rapping the knocker on Claire's front door, the last of the adrenaline that had got her here left, and she just felt numb.

# SEPTEMBER 2021

Sarah let herself in, kicked off her flip-flops, hung her hat on the hall stand, refreshed after her walk. It had left her a little short of time to get ready, but it was worth it.

Having the beach opposite was the best part of this unit. Sarah could not believe she had lived here for nearly six months. At first, it had been a welcome space of her own. Somewhere to retreat and come to terms with all that had happened, but now it felt like home.

After a couple of weeks with Claire and Mark, she knew that she and Peter needed time apart to work things out. This place was a lucky find through a connection at work. Friends and family had pitched in to help her move and provide some necessities, as she had taken only the essentials, the spare bed, her desk and personal items. It was sparse, to begin with, and she didn't have a television for the first six weeks, but it didn't bother her, she had enjoyed the tranquillity. Only having herself to consider was a novel experience, and it was entirely different to the last time she had been on her own. Although it had its challenges, it was just what she needed.

Tension had been high on moving day, Peter practically snarling at Andy, who had arrived with Mark to lend a hand. She was sure if the others had not been there, it would have turned ugly. However, having Andy back in Melbourne permanently had been good. She had caught up with him a few times when he was visiting Mark, and the two of them fell into a comfortable friendship. They met for coffee or lunch when he was working out this way. Andy had always been good company, and they found themselves talking for hours. Apart from Claire, he became her closest confidante. She could say things to him that she didn't feel comfortable telling their other friends, not wishing to make them uncomfortable after they had been so supportive of both her and Peter.

It took Peter the better part of two months to get his act together. Lily, Evie, and their friends listening, cajoling, and even threatening as they grew frustrated with his tears, anger and drunken binges. Eventually, Evie, Mark and Claire staged an intervention. Not holding back, the three outlined where Peter was heading in the most graphic terms unless he straightened himself out.

Sarah was sad that it had come to this but could not help. Their relationship was barely civil at that time, only corresponding about the house or essential matters. She even blocked his number at one point, following several unpleasant late-night calls. But to his credit, he started counselling and was making excellent progress. Things between them had greatly improved in the last months. They had met a few times, and Peter had brought over some of her favourite furniture and items from the house, filling the little unit, so it felt like hers. He reminded her of the Peter of old.

Her work life had gone ahead in leaps and bounds; she had adapted the workplace programs to take them into schools, proving so successful that she now had a staff of ten delivering them. She regularly collaborated with Tom, improving their existing programs and working on new projects. She liked that he challenged her, both at work and as friends. Tom enjoyed active sports and took her rollerblading, indoor rock climbing and kayaking; if laughter was the measure of success, she passed with flying colours! She loved work, not thinking of it as a job. It combined all that she was passionate about and gave her the confidence and zest she realised she had lacked in the last few years.

*

Applying the final touches to her makeup, she surveyed the result. Not bad, she winked at herself in the mirror. Butterflies flapped in her stomach as she slid on her sandals and picked up her bag. Getting ready for a date was something she had not done for an exceptionally long time! She started as a knock sounded on the door. Taking a deep breath, she opened it and smiled.

Eyes widening and a whistle escaping his lips, he held out his hand. Taking it, Sarah walked through the door and into the next chapter of her life.

# 70ᵀᴴ BIRTHDAY – DURING LOCKDOWN

## *BERNADETTE WEISS*

It was the end of April 2020. Monica and Klaas were in their eighth week of voluntary isolation. She was wearing stone-washed jeans, the hues of her floral blouse matched that of faded jeans, and she wore white runners. She moved the garden recliner to the edge of the patio to benefit from the sun while at the same time avoiding its glare as she read this months book club novel. The blurb on the book's jacket promised Chris Womersley had excelled in his latest novel.

The story set in 1986 was about stealing an original Picasso painting, *The Weeping*

*Woman*, from the National Gallery of Victoria. The story was told from the perspective of an 18-year-old teenager 'Tom Button'. His relocation to the flat inherited from his maiden-aunt in a heritage-listed building named

Cairo in Fitzroy would provide accommodation during his undergraduate studies at nearby Melbourne University.

However, the boy from the country missed the cut-off date for student enrolment. The first 150-pages alluded to Tom's part-time job as a dishwasher in a nearby restaurant and the various bohemian tenants at the Cairo. These artists and writers waited for their 'big break' while drunk, high on drugs, or both.

The book mentioned the planned heist of *The Weeping Woman* painting on a handful of pages halfway through the 320-page epistle. Monica had been attempting to read the book for three weeks, rarely getting far before the words began to dissolve and slither around the page. The combination of sun, breeze, and lack of interest in the tiresome prose, tempted her to close her eyes, sit back and relax. Instead, as she reminisced on the weeks they lived in quarantine, the book fell from her liver-spotted hands.

It wasn't that they had a communicable disease. Instead, the choice to *self-quarantine* was to avoid exposure to a new strain of virus called COVID-19. China reported the respiratory illness caused by this virus to the World Health Organization (WHO) on the cusp of 2019/2020. The symptoms included fever, coughing, sore throat, and shortness of breath.

The WHO website indicated nigh on three million cases documented globally on April 20.

Moreover, the site advised almost two million cases remained *open*, with over 800thousand described as *recovered*, with an excess of 200-thousand ending in death.

Reports compared these numbers to the Spanish Flu pandemic of 1918-1920, which affected a third of the global population, with three per cent of the recorded cases (50 million) resulting in death. She'd *Googled* these figures and dates on a website provided by an American government agency, known as the Centre for Disease Control and Prevention (CDC), last updated on April 20.

There was no vaccine to counter this virus, so life in the second millennium drastically altered. Unilateral action by governments worldwide prescribed measures to slow the spread of the potentially killer virus, thereby ensuring the survival of each country's population until a serum became readily available. However, the medical research process to develop such a vaccine was forecast as an 18-month process, amongst the raft of recommended procedures was strict attention to health and hygiene. In addition, *social distancing* was part and parcel of everyday life. The term referred to the mandated distance of one and a half meters between persons in public places, not persons within the same household. Also, the wearing of face masks in public places was recommended by March 21. These changes to daily life came to mind as Monica slipped into a deep sleep, dreaming of the residual effect on her family life.

Klaas and Monica increased their time and theoretical distance covered by pedalling away on their home trainers. They developed a 15-minute exercise regime which they worked through religiously daily. Their two-kilometre walk around the block increased by adding a lap around the adjacent football oval. They realised this might become less attractive in the cold, wet winter months ahead. Staying indoors was not a problem as both had several indoor hobby activities. With the arrival of the colder autumn nights, they enjoyed the cosy warmth of the Braemar gas heater in the lounge. However, they often found themselves waking up staring at the ceiling instead of the television, or retrieving fallen crossword puzzles.

Monica surmised that people would ask each other in 20-30 years, 'what were you doing when the COVID-19 pandemic hit in 2020?' Often the answers would no doubt be linked to the events occurring in the respondents' personal lives.

Monica's silent expectation was a celebration of her 70th birthday with a group of forty friends and family. Try as her husband and two sons might, their plans for the surprise party were leaked. She was aware something was afoot about 6-weeks after Christmas. During a weekend visit to Melbourne by the family from Cobram, some 300-kilometres away, she was reading a bedtime story to her grandchildren on the Saturday evening when Madelaine asked in evident excitement,

'Oma, are you coming to the surprise party too?' Not to be left out, her brother Larry enthusiastically shouted,

'Daddy says eating birthday cake is healthy! The more you eat them, the older you get!

So we are going to have a sleepover at Uncle Mark's after the party!'

Monica did her best to play along with the deception spun around her big seven-oh.

However, early in March, the Victorian State Government introduced Stage-3 of the COVID-19 restrictions, 1.5-meter rule and NO large gatherings. And so, by extension, the planned celebrations were delayed by at least 6-months.

Thoughts of the creative efforts undertaken to celebrate the *Big 70* parading through Monica's mind brought a smile to her sun-dappled face. The day began with an audio-visual chat via the social platform *Zoom*. After that, she rarely raised her head from the bamboo memory foam pillow before 8 am.

However, a plan to put an iPad on the double bed pillow next to her at 6 in the morning while she was still asleep, was cooked up between Klaas and elder son Les. Then with the sleeping Oma visible on the screen, at the count of three, four voices sang in faraway Cobram.

"Happy Birthday to you "...... Les and his wife Trixie immediately disappeared from the screen at the final refrain. However, their giggling was still audible in the background.

The children's gleaming faces did not hide the fact that Larry was upset.

'What's the matter, mate?' the birthday girl asked.

'Daddy said we're not going to be a sleepover at Uncle Mark's!' No one could say the lad did not have his priorities in order!

After the early morning reveille, Monica was able to shower, dress, brush her hair and remember her dentures, glasses, and hearing aids before 7.30 am, when another audiovisual communication, this time via *Skype*, came from the Netherlands. Mary, now in her eighties, maintained close contact with her little brother Klaas over the 30-years since he and Monica migrated to Australia. Boris had insisted they call before going to bed as it was almost midnight their time.

'Happy birthday, we have been drinking to your health, join us', Boris suggested.

'I will. Tonight. It is only seven in the morning here.'

After a ten-minute chat, the daily routine set in. Breakfast and washing the dishes preceded a 4-kilometres stroll around the adjacent footy fields. Later, as they settled in the kitchen for coffee and biscuits, a loud banging on the front door disrupted their quiet reading time. Monica answered the door to see a couple of one-meter-high helium balloons formed the number 70 through the security door.

'Happy birthday!'

Kay, a former colleague at the customer service centre Monica once worked in, and her second husband, Arthur, shouted from the public footpath. Both had dressed in matching grey Adidas tracksuits and black non-descript runners.

'We won't come in! Instead, we will celebrate together on the flip-side of the pandemic,' they promised, jogging back to the waiting Saturn Blue Toyota RAV4. Bringing the balloons and the package anchored inside, Monica found a gift box of Praline chocolates and a 750ml bottle of her favourite Australian Chardonnay. She laughed when Klaas looked up from his online newspapers and asked:

'Where did those come from?' Proving he hadn't yet put in his hearing aids.

Both Monica and Klaas were chocoholics, so the saucer of dry biscuits was substituted by several chocolates as the second cup of coffee was enjoyed. The mailbox brought a dozen or so birthday cards, some with gift vouchers arriving during the preceding days. Logging into her e-mail account after coffee-time, she found several friends and distant family around Australia hadn't relied on the Post Office *snail mail* to deliver their birthday cards. Some created personalised cards, while others provided funny quotes, adding wishes for a great day in Lockdown. Several others sent SMS texts adding emoji figures via their mobiles.

Towards lunchtime, Jenny rang to ask if they had connected to *What's App*, yet another form of visual-audio media platform. Having established that the oldies had connected to the app, she hung up. The *What's App* signal emanated from Klaas's iPad. Mark, the younger son, and his wife Jenny worked from home and decided the lunch break was ideal for wishing *the old girl* a wonderful day.

Finally, the 15-minute chat between the two parties in Malvern and Cranbourne came to a reluctant end.

'Got to go, mum,' Mark said. 'Unfortunately, some of us have to work for a living!'

Minutes before 2 pm, there was another knock at the front door. Upon answering it, Monica found more balloons tied to a gift box sitting on the doormat. Looking past the gaggle of five helium blimps, she noticed Annie and Otto standing out on the footpath as they sang Happy Birthday. Otto was their best man 46-years ago and had dressed to the nines in his business suit even though he hadn't worked in twenty-two years since his heart attack. Annie, his second wife, a wealthy woman in her own right, dressed to please the teddy boy who was her junior by five years. These octogenarians held each other as they carefully walked back to their powder blue 2020 series-2 BMW coming with a price tag of $52,000. Turning to carry the gifts inside, Monica became emotional. She joined Klaas in the lounge room as she burst her bubble.

'What is wrong?'

'I'm so happy! Everyone remembered', she replied as he put his arm around her.

Then an exasperated Klaas commented, 'Women! Cry when they are sad, cry even more when they are happy!'

During the four o'clock news program on channel seven, the landline announced another call. It was Eve, telling the day's septuagenarian to walk around to the back-gate in 15-minutes time before she hung up. Then, slipping into their cardigans, they strolled around to the driveway, arriving as the roll-a-door opened.

Eve, Wally, their daughters Kitty and Nellie, and their guests from Britain formed a straight line and pulled out a banner bearing the greeting *Happy Birthday*. Together they sang the obligatory birthday song before shouting three hip pip hoorays! The gifts were deposited halfway up the drive to conform to the one-and-a-half-meter distance between themselves and the crying birthday girl.

It wasn't a great way to introduce the British guests, Joy and Bryce, whom Eve often mentioned. It wasn't a great way to spend their Australian holiday, having to comply with the compulsory stage-three lockdown constraints.

So, chatting and taking happy snaps for the next twenty minutes, it was time for the wanderers to leave. As they strolled back inside, another knock at the front door. A colourful box of flowers in autumn hues was left on the doormat by the courier.

'All good?' queried the delivery lady from Whoops-A-Daisy in High Street, who was standing on the footpath.

'Yes, thanks,' Monica replied, picking up the flowers as she read the card to find these were from Mark and Jenny. 'So sweet,' she thought, 'a live chat and now flowers to boot!'

Coming back inside, she found her partner ordering a take-out meal for tea. It was his *workaround* because going to a restaurant for dinner was not possible during the Lockdown. In addition, food and drink outlets were closed by government directive, without indicating when they would return to *normal*.

With a population nearing 26-million, there were only 2,000 Intensive Care Units (ICU) in hospitals around Australia. In normal circumstances, this was all needed to guarantee effective care for anyone needing help to breathe. However, with the unprecedented dangers imposed by the infectious COVID virus, the aim was to slow the spread of the virus by reining society's social interaction. At the same time, the Health Department took steps to double or triple the nations ICU capacity. These measures would not stop the virus but would reduce the spread of the virus, thereby saving lives.

In the meantime, businesses facing closure were in the process of adjusting their service strategies. For instance, local eateries now offered take-away and home-delivered meals.

Hence, Klaas was ringing through an order for a five-course banquet from the local *Hoyling* Chinese Restaurant in High Street, pre-paying it by *Paypal*. Half an hour later, the courier rang, announcing the delivery sitting on the front doormat. As she picked up the meal,

Monica looked up in time to see the courier waving as he pulled away from the curbside.

Coming inside, she found that the lights were switched off and could hear the strains of soft inspirational background music coming from the stereo. Entering the kitchen, she found a candlelight setting for two, complete with linen napkins and wine goblets. The Chardonnay delivered earlier in the day was now chilled and decanted.

The man who tended to live in shorts and polos for eight months each year wore black trousers and a colourful Hawaiian shirt, completing a quasi evening out atmosphere. So it was background music, candles, wine, and a well-cooked meal leading to an enjoyable break at the table, with neither party wanting to rush away? Bring married almost fifty years, there was much to talk about, as long as wine remained in the bottle.

Going to the cinema for a movie was not possible because of the lockdown restrictions.

However, their cable provider provided free access to the movie channel until the end of June. Thus, several movies were sitting in their recorded playlist. Finally, with coffee and after-dinner mints, the heater turned up, they settled down for the evening. The film chosen was '*The Mule*': directed by and starring Clint Eastwood, was one they'd enjoyed months earlier at the cinema. Klaas assured Monica that he would stay awake in choosing it, and they would enjoy the movie together.

The final birthday surprise came at 10 pm when the landline rang, announcing another long-distance call from Holland. Rita, second oldest Klaas's sister and Leo timed it to coincide with their lunchtime, knowing bedtime for the Australian couple to be around 11 pm. Despite a distance of some 15,000 kilometres and an 8-hour time difference, they conveyed their birthday wishes on the day itself.

Such a memorable day! Stretching and waking from her nano-nap, Monica brushed her hair away from her face, realising she was cold. A drizzle was pre-empting the showers forecast in the news broadcasts. Jumping up from the garden recliner, she ran into the laundry, beating Klaas as he came running in from the garage.

As they took tea, Monica thought, life was good. We are healthy and still together. She would remember the year she turned 70 because of its inspired creativity. She recalled an apt saying by contemporary artist, author, and speaker Bruce Garrabrandt.

*"Creativity doesn't wait for that perfect moment. Instead, it fashions its own perfect moments out of ordinary ones."*

# TOMORROW'S PROMISED TO NO ONE

## *MARYANN GRIGSON*

We were a happy-go-lucky nation living in Australia when all of a sudden, COVID-19 descended into our lives with a bang and shook the entire world. The unfolding of uncertainty every day proved to be challenging times for everybody. The pandemic happened suddenly, the virus spreading its tentacles rapidly and creating a roller-coaster of emotions amongst every country. Daily news broadcasts grew intense as the situation escalated and nation upon nation started to experience unprecedented and unsettled times.

Depression crept in like a thief in the night. Freedom of movement was curtailed by governments enforcing curfews and lockdowns. Mental health became a grave concern, especially among the elderly, who handled these alarming issues differently. The Universe transformed into a world of the unknown.

Sheila is a middle-aged lady who has Parkinson's disease and lives in a townhouse by herself. She is tall, has a medium build with a lovely smile. Sheila always dresses in dark coloured pants and long-sleeved jumpers. She wears a hearing aid with her curly grey hair styled in a bob. Sheila has a host of friends who drop by regularly for a cuppa and a chat. She enjoys their lively company.

She is passionate about her little garden and spends the entire morning tending it. She manages to lift the watering can so she can water the plants and her beautiful flowers. She also loves visiting the shops on sunny days when her friend collects her, and they spend time together browsing various items of interest.

Because of the pandemic, Sheila is now homebound and misses out on things that made her day. Fear and anxiety are now overwhelming factors in her life, and she has become too scared to leave her home. However, Sheila doesn't realise that she is not alone, as thousands of others are affected by these same emotions.

One person Sheila trusts is Edith, who is a social worker who visits Sheila during the week. She is a friendly and compassionate woman and relays all the happenings outside Sheila's small little world.

Three times a week, Edith opens the gate and strides up the driveway. Sheila always stands by the front door and greets her with a smile. 'Hello Edith, I've been waiting for you, please come in.'

'How have you been?' Edith always asks.

'I have been very lonely, and I miss my friends. They don't visit anymore.'

'You know they cannot do that Sheila', Edit responds.

It's always the same every time she visits.

The two women chatter for a while, and Edith conveys everything that she witnessed on the way as she drove to Sheila's house. An ambulance had raced past with its siren screaming, probably carrying a patient to the Emergency. She had also driven past a line of people wearing masks outside the grocery store, waiting their turn to enter the store. Further on, Edith said, she saw a road sign that directed the traffic on a different route due to an accident. Finally, just before she entered the turn off to Sheila's, Edith had seen a couple of teenagers jogging in the park nearby.

The two of them always sat at the table when they had a cuppa and shared some biscuits. Edith's news always brightened the day for Sheila, as she flashes her beautiful smile, making sure that Edith always promises to visit again.

*

Sheila locked the front door and sat on her favourite chair before switching on the television just in time to hear the latest news. The newsreader relayed the number of COVID cases detected and how many deaths, especially in old people homes. An extension to the lockdown was expected later in the day, and people were only permitted to leave their homes for five reasons. First, to get groceries and necessities, second for exercising for only one hour, third for caring and caregiving, fourth to leave home to do essential work, and the fifth reason was to get the COVID vaccine now that it was finally available. The news depressed Sheila, so she switched off the television.

She picked up the telephone and called her friend Martha. 'Hello Martha, how are you doing? Have you got any new plants in your garden?'

Martha wasn't feeling the best as her little dog had scratched up her best purple rose bush. Nevertheless, they chatted for a while on things of common interest and wished each other well before she replaced the telephone.

Sheila was overwhelmed with loneliness every day. It seemed to be getting worse. She had lost the joy of tending her little flower garden and was impatient for the restrictions and lockdowns to come to an end.

She had never felt so isolated, and each day felt so empty. She did not realise that this was a daily pattern amongst many others who lived alone who also longed for company and the fleeting moments when they could enjoy whatever made them happy.

Recently Sheila had been thinking about her husband David, whom she missed desperately. She remembered those days when they were a happy-go-lucky couple who had migrated to Australia many years ago and settled in Melbourne.

Sheila had a job as an office assistant at a school in Springvale. She enjoyed her work and interacted happily with her workmates. David was a serious man, an accountant who worked in a bank in the city. He was extremely tall, with bushy eyebrows, intelligent eyes and wore large round spectacles that made him look like a professor. Sheila was a beautiful woman, fair and robust, with shoulder-length hair styled in the latest fashion. She liked to dress in trendy clothes and stiletto heels. She was also deeply passionate about music and loved to play the piano.

David was always concerned about their future, with his greatest wish being to buy a property. One day she remembered he said, 'Sheila, my dear, we must look for a house in a safe, convenient area, close to public transport and the shops where we can settle down.'

'Yes, David, that is a brilliant idea,' she remembered replying. She had always longed for her own home and hoped they could afford it one day. The two of them spent weeks searching and inspecting a range of houses before they finally settled on their dream home.

Sheila was ecstatic when they bought and furnished the two-level townhouse, with two bathrooms and two toilets. David spent Saturday mornings at home attending to the household chores. At the same time, Sheila browsed around the shops, searching for cushions, vases, ornaments, and eye-catching trinkets to decorate their home.

Sheila had always loved cooking and was adventurous in the well-equipped kitchen, cooking healthy, wholesome food. David often complimented her whenever she prepared something special.

'Oh, darling, that pasta dish was delicious, and the roast pork you made yesterday was exceptional too,' David would say. Sheila was always delighted with the compliments as she hugged her husband and smiled contentedly to herself.

Sheila and David shared an active social life and had a large circle of friends who often met up for dinner and sometimes even joined them on weekend trips to the country. The cinema was another favourite venue, and the couple looked forward to the latest movies in town. David was delighted when he was promoted to the bank's managerial level the following year. A company car came with the promotion, and the couple decided to celebrate by inviting a few friends to dine at an exclusive restaurant in Richmond. Everybody enjoyed the wine, the food and the company. They clinked glasses, their friends wishing them the absolute best.

Sheila loved David and would do anything to please her husband. They were a loving couple and the envy of all their friends. They never uttered a harsh word to each other and remained happy together. Unfortunately, they had no children. The only relatives they had were Sheila's sister and two cousins who lived out in the country.

They dined early each evening when they returned from work before Sheila played the piano and entertained her husband with her beautiful voice. David would close the book he was reading as he reclined on the sofa and listened to his wife singing her favourite songs.

Sheila had plans to hold a surprise party to celebrate David's 60th birthday. So without a word to David, she invited a few friends for dinner and took the day off work. She ordered food from an exclusive Thai restaurant and decided to make a three-tiered ribbon cake, one of David's favourites. She went into the kitchen after David left for work to prepare his birthday cake, taking flour, eggs, sugar, and a host of other ingredients from the cupboard. Once the cake had baked and cooled, she covered it with blue icing humming a tune as she drew the figures 6 and 0 in white icing on the top layer.

Completely satisfied with the result, she placed it on a tray and went upstairs, where she showered and dressed in a black linen skirt and a yellow and green floral long-sleeved blouse. She brushed her shoulder-length hair before applying bright red lipstick, and hey-presto, she was ready to surprise her husband. Sheila had reminded her guests to arrive before the birthday boy got home.

David opened the front door as a chorus of voices. 'Hello, David, happy birthday. Welcome to your birthday surprise.' He was utterly surprised. He looked at his wife, saying, 'Thank you, Sheila, I know it was all your idea, and I am happy that you asked our friends to celebrate this milestone in our lives.'

Everybody enjoyed the wine and the delicious food as they chattered happily together until Sheila tinkled a little bell and said, 'Hey everybody, it is time for David to cut the cake'. As she brought the cake on the table everybody sang 'Happy birthday David, cheers to your 60th.'

David thanked his friends for remembering adding a special thank you to Sheila for arranging the party. The guests handed David their gifts and wished the couple a good night before climbing into their cars to drive home.

Together David and Sheila cleaned and tidied the kitchen and the sitting room, then went upstairs. They changed into nightclothes and snuggled into bed. David kissed his wife good night and drifted off into slumber.

The following day, quite suddenly and without any warning, David passed away in his sleep. The autopsy results revealed that David had died from a heart attack.

Sheila was devastated and refused to accept the fact that her beloved David was no more. Friends dropped in over the following days to see and comfort her, but she was beyond any form of consolation. So instead, Sheila just wept and cried for her husband. She could hardly sleep missing David and all the happy times they shared.

*

Edith, the social worker, had always been concerned about Sheila and worried about her mental state. So she picked up the telephone and dialled

Sheila's number. She planned to visit the next day and usually warned Sheila that she would be calling on her.

The phone rang on and on, but there was no answer. So Edith waited for ten minutes and tried again.

This time Sheila answered, 'Hello, who is this?'

'It's me,' Edith replied, 'Are you alright?'

'Who is it?'

'It's Edith, Sheila.'

'Oh yes, Edith, I'm all right. I just woke up after a snooze. Nice to hear your voice.'

Edith informed Sheila that she would visit the following day.

It was a cold frosty morning. Edith woke up early and had a shower. She dressed in warm clothing, snuggling into her jacket and draping a knitted scarf around her neck. It was a twenty-minute drive to Sheila's house. She started the car, switched on the headlights and drove along the wet road. Edith parked in the garage and walked to the gate. She opened the gate and rang the doorbell, but Sheila did not open the door, so she rang the doorbell again. When she did not hear or see her friend, she began to panic.

Edith became troubled and had a suspicion that something was wrong. She tried banging on the door without any success. She shivered as she dialled 000 from her phone. In fifteen minutes, a Police car and an ambulance sped along the road with sirens screaming.

Edith was standing outside the locked door when the Police arrived, and she told them of her dilemma and received no response from Sheila. Within the space of a few minutes, the two policemen decided to break open the front door. Edith trembled before running into the house with the policemen close on her heels. She opened the bedroom door and let out a cry when she found Sheila lying very still in bed, looking ashen and as pale as death.

The paramedics took hold of Sheila's hand, but they found no pulse at all. She had passed away sometime during the night. Edith sobbed as they placed Sheila's body on a stretcher covering her entirely with a sheet before transporting her to the ambulance.

One of the policemen asked Edith if she knew of any relatives they could inform of the tragedy. During past conversations with her friend Edith had learned that Sheila had a sister named Maureen and distant cousins who lived in the country town of Bairnsdale. So she wrote Maureen's address on a piece of paper and handed it over to the policemen requesting that they break the sad news to Sheila's sister and cousins.

The policemen fastened the front door and locked the screen door. They gave Edith a comforting pat on her shoulder and bid her goodbye.

Edith was traumatised by her friend's death; she had grown very fond of Sheila and became good friends. Every visit was a living memory, and Edith remembered Sheila's lovely smile and her loneliness after David had passed away.

It is a bitter lesson to be learned. But life is so uncertain. So, enjoy every moment and live for today, for tomorrow is promised to no one.

# THE HAPPENINGS
# AT THE LAKE

........

## *GRACE DE VISSER*

........

The last golden rays filtered through the leaves of the tall gumtrees, creating dappled patterns on the wooden bench and the sparse grass-covered earth. A group of four sat slightly apart, heads somewhat bowed, each appearing to be deep in their thoughts. A heady fragrance drifting through the air from the belladonna lilies caught on the light afternoon breeze, a multitude of bright pink trumpet-shaped flowers on top of the slightly bent naked stems stood out against the group, mostly dressed in black and white.

Willie, Maggie, Lovey and Duckie often met in this familiar spot near the weeping willows after their busy days. It was a great place to escape from their demanding lives, just sitting, chatting and looking out onto the changing beauty of the lake.

If they had been watching, they would have seen the ripples moving slowly as the shiny blue-black waterfowl glided past, disturbing the brownish water that looked painted in greens and yellows of the willow trees and blue from the sky with cotton wool white clouds. Whitewashed gumtree stumps appearing in and out of the lake made it all look just like a Monet painting.

But no one was watching as they all appeared lost in their little world, perhaps thinking of how the day had unfolded and what it meant for each of them.

Overhead the swiftly darting dragonflies were creating their magical dance in the air, skimming above the water and reeds. Buzzing of bees in the nearby bushes could be heard, and the wafting fragrance of honey drifted through the air, but the group of four did not appear to notice. They could have easily be mistaken for life-like statues of stone.

*

Just an hour earlier, they were busy chatting, just four friends happy to catch up and watch the world pass by. So naturally, they loved nothing better than to listen to snippets of other peoples' conversations.

"Have you noticed how many people walking past keep their distance from each other?" Willie spoke more to himself than anyone in particular.

"I overheard the cute redhead say it's a deadly virus," Ducky added.

"What's a virus?" Queried Willy, putting his head to one side.

"I heard someone say they remembered when the bird flu was around, and they had to kill millions of chickens!" Maggie spat out the last sentence in disgust.

"That's a lot of chickens, poor things." Lovey directed her gaze downward.

"Lookout, here comes that horrible grey-haired man with his dog, the most disgusting pair I have ever seen." Maggie glared at the pair as they lumbered by. "He rarely has that brown beast on a lead!'

Lovey looked away, shaking her head until the pair passed by. "Rule breakers, don't care for them at all."

"Dogs! Can't say I like them. One chased me when I was a youngster."

"That was a bit of bad luck for you, Willy" Maggie reaching out but not touching him.

"Good, now he's going the other way" Lovey nodded as the man and his dog headed down the path away from them towards the open parkland.

"I could listen to Maggie's voice all day. It is so melodic."

Ducky turned his head towards the group and chuckled. "I bet her husband doesn't say that."

"Hey, Lovey, you do know she is a popular member of the morning choir down at the local church," chipped in Willy, trying to ignore Ducky.

"Well, I never!" said Ducky shaking his head.

"I am not surprised at all", Lovey cooed.

"Hey, Maggie, sing us a song," cajoled Willy as he watched Lovey's proud silver-grey head bop along to some imaginary song in her head.

Maggie stretched out her neck and limbs, nodding towards the path.

"Here comes that kind family with the chatty children, never get a word in when they are around."

"Watching others is so interesting, but it can be tiring." Lovey sighed. As she stretched her body from her toes to her head, wriggling her shoulders and settling back into the seat. "Has anyone seen Percy today?"

Everyone shook their heads except Willy.

"Saw him yesterday fishing over near the old pier."

Moving from his position on the bench, Willy straightened himself and, with a quick wave, "Must dash, the wife will be expecting me home. See you tomorrow."

"Off you go. I will sit here a little longer."

Duckie nodded, his dark features looking even darker in the late afternoon shade.

"Me too," said Maggie watching her friend's pert slim body as he waltzed away, thinking to herself how well he carries himself, a tiny glint in her eyes.

"It's so peaceful and cool here. I will stay a while too," Lovey murmured, looking across the lake. "I was admiring the mass of green leaves of the water lilies over there that stretch towards the old wooden pier far off in the distance. The buds are just emerging from the murky depths below. The white buds look ready to burst open and show themselves for the glorious flowers they are. What do you think, Maggie?"

Before Maggie could reply, the shape of their friend appeared through the shadows approaching them.

"Hey, look whose back", they chorused together.

"Thought you had gone home" Maggie looked up, moving her gaze from the waterlilies to Willy. "What are you doing back?"

Willie hopped from one leg to the other with building impatience, "I just heard about the murder on the other side of the lake."

"What are you saying? A murder?" screeched Maggie wide-eyed and shaking her head.

"When did it happen?" Duckie queried, adjusting his position on the wooden seat.

"Oh dear", Was all Lovey could say, her head and shoulders drooping. "I don't know, just heard they found the body in the water, a shot straight through the heart. Over near the basket willows, they found him partly submerged in the water under the wooden pier. The culprits tried to hide the body with drooping branches."

"Lookout, here comes Peewee." Called out Duckie as Peewee swiftly joined the group. "I wonder if he has heard anything."

"It's bedlam over there." Peewee shook his head from side to side, his body twitching. "The Place is swarming with people in uniform and vehicles."

"I wonder who it is?" Duckie queried. "Hope it's not anyone we know?" Lovey spoke softly.

"Stop butting in, and I will tell you" Willy's whole body was shaking with indignity. "It was Percy" A chorus of "oh no" "Poor Percy" tangled in with the sound of mournful groans that floated in the now still air.

"Poor Percy as large as life itself, he was always putting his big beak into others people's business," Duckie added.

"Poor Percy", Lovey replied, hanging her head in sorrow. "Duckie, don't be so unkind. He was harmless. A bit curious, but he wouldn't harm anyone."

"Well, he did harass those little children one day." Added Maggie turning her head away.

"That! That's just a little misunderstanding; they were fishing in his lake." Peewee protested.

"Why kill him? He was a great mate, never did anyone any harm." Duckie's head drooped.

"There have been some nasty young types hanging about," Maggie commented. Willy, unable to stand still any longer and bursting with more news, was anxious to calm his friends. "On my way back here, I heard some people saying that the R S P C A officers have caught the hoodlums that shot the arrow into poor Percy."

Suddenly, the grieving group realized they were being watched and moved slightly, shrinking deep into the shadows. The grey-haired man, who this time had the brown beast on a lead, was standing a short distance away. He stepped back quietly to give them more space.

"Sorry, Lovey, to hear about Percy. I know how much your feathered friends mean to you."

Lovey adjusted her glasses. Maybe he was not so horrible after all.

# THE OUTBREAK OF CORONA

## A CHOOSE YOUR OWN ADVENTURE STORY

*BY ZOE SKJELLERUP*

It all starts with a big BANG! Shortly after the 2020 bushfires, you are introduced to COVID – a pandemic which is spreading fast across the globe. It remains with you, even into the New Year. You are powerless to stop it.

You are issued with direct orders from the government to stay at home. The lockdowns have just begun. You must:

1. Socially distance yourself from everyone, including those who you love dearly.

2. You must wear a mask in the community unless you are exempt for medical reasons.

3. You or your child must learn remotely for school, university, or college.

4. Purchase takeaway from restaurants and cafes, or order online if shops can remain open.

5. Work from home or temporarily close your business unless you are an essential worker.

You quickly scramble towards your television, switching on the NEWS program. You cannot believe what you're seeing. You're trying your best to make sense of everything.

*

Choose your adventurer ...

**Natasha:** *My hands immediately fly towards my mouth. I'm struck frozen with fear, just staring at the television screen. Oh my God! What is happening to our world? It used to be peaceful but now, everything's turned upside down. People are collapsing dead on the streets... It feels like a zombie apocalypse. They are going crazy, rushing to the grocery store, including me- buying everything and anything that comes into sight. I'm a young teacher at a university in Melbourne. I have been teaching here for 7 years, ever since I arrived from Russia. It's a small class in creative writing. I love every moment that I spend with my students. Life has been great until... I was forced to teach from home. It just isn't the same without my students, face-to-face. It's so hard to share my content and relate with them over a computer screen. I just want to see them in-person, hear their stories, and see their faces brighten when they walk through the classroom door. Everyone is locked down and spending time in the house. I'm really stressed out. I can't return to my homeland because Australia has closed their international borders. Nothing is the same as it was before.*

**Levi:** *I don't really give a damn about it. I have been isolated long before COVID hit, so that doesn't bother me much. I have my own problem to deal with - this rare genetic disability. Congenital disorders of glycosylation (CDG) causes me to walk with crutches for support and have difficulties with speech. I also have an eye condition - Retinitis pigmentosa - which means I am legally blind. I face my own challenges already, and I'm trying my best to improve in* *every way possible. I don't need another issue on top of this to stress about right now. My friends from school all abandoned me anyway. It's not like I have the ability to sprint and keep up with them. I've got my sticks! And I'm not afraid to use them. So, I grew up feeling this way- isolated and enjoying my alone time. This is life for me. I have carers to assist me with daily tasks. I can clear my head and just forget about the outside world. I'm just gonna hibernate in my warm and cozy bedroom. Switch on some Bluetooth music and do workouts at home. I keep a stash of salt and vinegar crackers, and Humbug lollies in a jar - in case of an emergency. So don't worry about me. I'll be just fine!*

**Mason:** *I hold my forehead with confusion and plop myself onto the leather couch. My head's spinning wildly, trying to process what exactly is happening. I'm a married man with two children- Hannah and Brandon. I am barely holding onto my marriage at the moment. My wife is under stress, as she lost her job when the lockdown began. The kids are stuck at home, struggling with remote learning. I just want us to get through this together. Oh, hell no! What is this shit anyway? This pandemic is doin' my head in. I mean, none of this research is makin' any sense to me. I'm just trying to make the right decision for the family. I want to provide safety and supplies for everyone. I work overnight at a factory, packaging and delivering toilet paper to help the community. I know it's a difficult time, not only for me but for everyone out there.*

*

As soon as you hear about these restrictions, your eyes widen, and your jaw hits the floor. How do you respond?

**Natasha:** *Oh Shit. We're all gonna die because of this COVID. What about my family back in Russia? I just want to make sure they are coping during this time.*

**Levi:** *Yay! More time around the house. More time for exercising and improving myself. The shops are still open. That's a good start! I can order my shopping online. It's no big deal, just use the internet.*

**Mason:** *These lockdowns are causing people to lose their jobs. Fall behind in* schooling. *Marriages are strained and fallin' apart, trying to make ends meet. It's ridiculous and unfair, but the law is still the law. There's nothin' we can do about it. I guess, it's one way or another- either stay at home, or more people will become sick.*

*

After a couple days, you hear that there are new restrictions being introduced. You're urged to obey more COVID rules:

1. You may only leave your house for 4 reasons...
   - Grocery shopping
   - Exercise outside
   - Medical care
   - Essential work
2. Nobody travels further than 5-kilometres, and only one person from each household at a time.
3. Curfew from 8pm to 5am.

Anger bubbles violently inside your stomach, and you don't believe it. You just want to get out there, be free from COVID and live your normal life. But instead, you feel like you're stuck in prison every day, and every direction you face, there's no escape. You think:

**Natasha**: *Oh my god! Oh my God! Oh my god! These restrictions are becoming worse! A curfew, and a 5-kilometre limit has suddenly come into play. Why do people have to make it so difficult? Life is pretty much stopping us from doing the things we love at the moment.*

**Levi**: *Four reasons to leave home? Seems alright. Who needs to access the community, am I correct? We have everything we need anyway- the internet, online shopping, chatting with your friends, working from home...*

**Mason**: *Gotta seriously get off my butt and do some shoppin'. I have a family to take care of! But how are those people who can't work supposed to afford everything? I must admit, I'm a real couch potato these days! Life's pretty hectic and it's a very strange time. When will this ever go away?*

\*

You make your way towards the garage door and enter the driver's seat of your car. You key the ignition, hearing the engine roar to life. You slip your mask over your face and buckle yourself up. You think:

**Natasha:** *Oh great! I must hurry to the store. What if everything's sold out, and people have no idea? We never know what to expect these days! People are losing their jobs and can't cope with life. It's horrible to watch. We shouldn't be living life this way. What happened to the days before? The time when people didn't go nuts...*

**Levi:** *Seriously? I'm finding myself strapped up in a vehicle, unable to drive because of my vision! How am I supposed to shop now? My internet died, so now I have no choice but to head out. Do you really think a legally blind person can drive safely? Well, let's find out. Shall we? Do you dare me? I would if I could! Luckily, I've brought a carer along with me. We're still kinda obeying the COVID rules at least.*

**Mason:** *Oh jeez! People say that online shoppin' is easy, but I just can't seem to get my head around it, ya' know! Ah, technology. It's a real pain these days! Better off goin' to the grocery store, and actually buyin' stuff for the family. I must prepare for the upcomin' days. Nobody can be sure what will happen.*

\*

You begin your journey, travelling to the store. It's difficult just finding a park. However, you finally spot one and turn into it. You exit the car and head towards the automatic doors.

You think:

**Natasha:** *This doesn't seem like it's gonna go well! It's fully packed here, and shoppers just keep coming from every direction. How are we supposed to socially distance now? I better hurry up before everything flies off the shelves.*

**Levi:** *I don't normally shop much because of other people. They constantly get in the way all the time, like ants on their daily mission. So, this is exactly why I choose to stay home.*

**Mason**: *People everywhere heading my way, towards the grocery store? And we all need to social distance? How exactly is that gonna happen? Ah well! I'll do the best I can.*

*

You spray hand sanitiser onto your palms before heading further into the building.

You think:

**Natasha**: *Hand sanitizer! This is exactly what customers need in every store. It's perfectly healthy and helps stop germs. I'll go crazy over bottles! I've been told that vegetables, anything could have COVID on them. So, better wash before moving on.*

**Levi**: *Who needs hand sanitiser anyway? I mean, I understand why people want it so badly at the moment. But what about those with crutches? If some were to fall on the ground, and a person with low vision can't see where the spill is, then my sticks would more likely slip out from underneath me. So, I'll pass thanks. It's not me grabbing the groceries anyway. It's the carer pushing the shopping cart! My hands are obviously full!*

**Mason**: *Ya' know what? I actually don't mind the squirts of hand sanitiser! The texture feels refreshing and it smells so good! I am used to using hand sanitizer every day at work, when I'm packaging. I want to keep the community safe. I'm concerned about other people's health. What they are going through in this hard time. Surely this won't go on forever!*

*

You glance up after cleaning your hands. The grocery store is packed with bustling people, and they are quickly becoming sold out of food and other essentials. You think:

**Natasha**: *Oh Shit! There is almost nothing on the supermarket shelves. I need to hurry up and purchase my groceries. I have become addicted to shopping and can't help myself but to purchase everything these days, just in case. Now, what exactly do I have on my list? Let's see...*

- Toilet paper
- Loaf of bread
- Coffee and milk
- Caesar salad
- vegetables
- Wheat bix
- Carrots

**Levi**: *I'm not too fussed about my shopping list. Usually, I am quite happy just chilling in my room eating simple snacks, like salt and vinegar crackers and my Humbug lollies. But I guess since I'm out in the community, I may as well treat myself! I have a problem with digestion. Certain foods can cause me to have acid reflux, so I have to be careful with what I choose. I've got an odd shopping list compared to others...*

- Vanilla slice
- Cheesecake
- Big M iced coffee
- Chicken nuggets
- Strawberries
- Cherry tomatoes
- A large water bottle

**Mason**: *Let's see what I've written on my shopping list. Well, I don't really need toilet paper now that I deliver it. Someone has to make and package it! It might as well be me! Ha! What other products do I have on there? Gimme a minute...*

- Spaghetti
- Rice
- Chicken
- Tomatoes
- Frozen Pizza
- Sausages

- *Potatoes*
- *Mushrooms*

*

As you head through the supermarket aisles, you feel like you're in an awkward position. These masks make you feel like you're robbing a bank.

You think:

**Natasha**: *Everyone wearing masks now? What's happening? We never did anything like this before! I understand that it has to be done through. But wearing a mask seems to become a little annoying after a while, and you become hot in it. I just can't wait to get home and rip it off...*

**Levi**: *Oh great! They want me to what now? Wear a mask outside? Even with my legally blind eyesight? You've got to be kidding me! I can barely see out of it. How am I supposed to walk through the supermarket aisles, and find what I need? I'm more likely to plummet to the ground and have an emergency hospital trip. Or keep accidentally bumping into the back of others. Oh, stuff this! The doctors say it's legal not to wear a mask if you have a medical condition. That means I'm exempt. I'm just gonna rip it off then! I would totally give it a go if I had better vision, but it just isn't worth the risk.*

**Mason**: *People want a mask upon my face? OK! Let's do this thing! As a child, I've always loved masks, scarves and other things around the neck or face. Besides, I have to wear masks at work for hygiene anyway! That doesn't bother me one bit. I haven't really changed. I don't find them annoying at all. I am just happy. It's like I had a strong feeling that this day would arrive. To be honest, I don't really like it when people recognise me in public. I like being able to disguise myself. This face mask idea is my favourite part of COVID restrictions! Haha! :-)*

*

As you continue scanning for the products on your shopping list, you notice the aisle becoming crowded. People are just throwing everything and anything in their shopping trolley.

**Natasha**: *I glance upwards over my trolley, stashed with toilet paper and other groceries. A boy using sticks begins making his way down the same aisle as me, and has another person behind him, possibly a carer or his mum. He seems to be in his mid-twenties. He doesn't have a mask. He's just scanning the shelves. I gasp. Why doesn't he have a mask upon his face? He could become sick and spread the virus to others. He needs to be tested! I grip the handle of my trolley tightly. I look around for the best direction to exit the aisle, but both ways are crowded with shoppers. My only option is to pass the anti-masker! I burst past the boy, holding my breath. As I rush off, I hear a clatter of plastic and metal fall onto the ground. Mortified, I realise that I have accidentally knocked him off balance...*

**Levi**: *I feel myself falling backwards before I realise that I have let go of my sticks. My blonde carer Chandra, quickly rushes in to catch me, steadying me to my feet again as my sticks tumble loudly onto the ground. ... I notice a man bend over near the shelf to retrieve my sticks. He rushes towards me. As he comes closer, I take the chance to have a better look. He seems to be in his early forties, with olive skin. He is wearing a tracksuit. He stops in front of me, passing my sticks over. "Are you alright?" He asks. Even behind his mask, I can see concern in his brown eyes... I knew it! I should've stayed home. This happens to me way more often than it should. It's not me that's the problem. It's other careless people creating obstacles! I'm just tryn do the best that I can.*

**Mason**: *As I pass the boy his sticks back, I watch the rude red-headed lady dash away with her packed trolley. She looks to be in her late thirties, with pale skin. I heave a deep sigh, feeling quite pissed off. People... they can be extremely rude, and some don't even respect others. She's kinda attractive, but I must admit she doesn't seem that nice now. Why didn't she apologise? Stress over this COVID, perhaps? Or maybe she's just rude...*

I glance back at the disabled boy, and the blonde woman beside him. It isn't long until I remember the most important COVID rule- to socially distance yourself from others. My eyes widened with fear, as I began to step backwards. I can't believe it! I broke one of the rules! I'm so used to helping other people! I kinda forget about the lockdowns, and all these new rules. Must get it ingrained into my head!

*

You grab the rest of your groceries off the shelves and chuck them inside your trolley. You make your way towards the cash register and place your items on the counter. After making the purchase, you head towards the automatic doors. You think:

**Natasha**: *Oh great! What if the world doesn't ever go back to normal, and people have suffered life this way? It's really sad for those going through tough times. Homelessness, unemployment, divorces, and those who have medical conditions... not only them! But for everyone. Life sucks at the moment. It should never have turned out this way! What about my fellow students? How are they coping?*

**Levi**: *This whole COVID thing is nothing new to me. I don't care if the world's gone crazy at the moment. Should I, really? I mean, don't I have enough to deal with right now? I'm more than happy just locking my door and enjoying my workouts. Both before and after the pandemic began, the safest option for me is to avoid those who make life harder.*

**Mason**: *Oh, what the heck! Maybe the world is gonna be like this for a while. Who knows what tomorrow will bring, ey? All I can do is prepare, and care for my family today! I have a strong feeling that there may be more upcoming restrictions. But at least I have what I need for now.*

*

You head back to your vehicle, enter the driver's seat, and make the journey home. You think:

**Natasha**: *That poor disabled boy that I accidentally knocked over. That young man rushing to catch him, and I didn't have the words to apologise... I need to show more respect to others. COVID has been difficult for me to come to terms with, but it is hard for everyone in different ways. It's been a most* *horrible year but certainly, one we won't forget.*

**Levi:** *Obey, or don't obey? Be considerate of others, or just think about yourself? This is your choice to make. You aren't in control of the world, but you are in control of yourself and your actions. One way or another, your choices affect the people around you.*

**Mason:** *COVID is overwhelming to everyone, but all I can do is take care of the people around me. One step at a time and we'll get there. Let me ask you this question... What is more important to you - catching up with some friends and putting yourself and others at risk, or staying home and looking after your own health?*

*

After a long day at the shops, you start unpacking and relax in the house. You feel overwhelmed by all the many shoppers, and the COVID rules. It blows your mind, just how exhausting it is to accomplish your daily tasks in a COVID world!

**Natasha:** *Ah! It feels so good to be home! So good to finally be free from that mask. Now, I can relax in my warm and cozy house, read a book and do some writing. But I must admit, I feel so bloody terrible for not apologising to that boy. I regret being rude. I live in a small apartment in the city, not far from the university. It's just me and my affectionate puppy, Teidi - a black Labrador! I adopted him when the lockdowns began.*

**Levi:** *Finally, I can stay hidden in my bedroom again. My workouts are the main thing that I'm concentrating on right now! My decision is made, I'm not leaving the house again unless I absolutely have to. I'm better off at home! In my own space, where nobody out there can make life harder for me. Back at the supermarket, I could've broken a bone - I could've gone to the hospital! People... they have no fuckin idea what it's like! I cover my face with my hands, hoping that my carer doesn't see the tears. They don't go through the shit I deal with every day. Why should I risk it?*

**Mason:** *OK! I'm back home from purchasin' groceries, and once again, I* *find myself stuck in the hollow of the couch! It's been a big coupla days. I'm exhausted from all the long hours on nightshift. Plus, my COVID research, ya know what I mean? I dunno what to believe anymore! But I must do whatever I can. I'm concerned about the people around me, and what will happen in the near future. I just wanna make sure that everyone out there is safe.*

\*

As the days pass, you flick on the news once again. To your surprise, restrictions have started to ease. You are now allowed to access the community, visit shops freely and invite visitors to your home again. A smile breaks across your face. You think:

**Natasha:** *This has been one hell of an awful year. However, I'm so glad to know restrictions are lifting. Victoria's a nice place! However, I am still stressed about international travel restrictions. When will I be able to go home to Russia? And what if the lockdowns happen again?*

**Levi:** *How is life any different for me now? I don't want to access the community at the moment. My internet is back, and I'm happy doing my own thing! Let's just hide in my room and see how the world plays out, shall we? I don't believe that it's anywhere near safe just yet! There's really no point in me leaving the house. People's carelessness has made life harder for me. Besides, nobody can be sure that COVID is gone for good.*

**Mason:** *Has COVID finally eased up? Or is it just messin' with my head? This world has definitely been turned upside down, and people can't be trusted nowadays! But if this pandemic continues, and we get thrown into lockdown again, at least we'll know exactly what to do! Life is tough. It's hard for families to stay together and keep safe during this difficult time. Nobody can say what will happen in the near future, but I have done everything I can.*

# IT WAS SUCH
# A UNIQUE YEAR

*CORINNE KING*

2020 was dawning just like any other New Year's Day. All the fun, frolic and merriment in the celebration of the beginning of another year was upon us. For some, the New Year met with trepidation and uncertainty as to what the ensuing three hundred and sixty-five days would reveal. We were in the middle of our summer, typically an arid season in Australia,

By the end of January, news came over the airways of many bushfires raging around the country. Ferocious forest fires, fanned by strong winds, were burning out of control all over the southeast. These fires threatened entire towns, some even evacuated by sea as the uncontrollable fires brought devastation right down to the water's edge.

The entire country, in fact and the whole world responded with emergency personnel and water-bombing aircraft used in times of intense bushfires. Foreign nations gifted medical supplies to help with the processes undertaken by the Australian Red Cross and other notable charities. The nightly statistics on news coverage was devastating to hear.

The Victorian State Emergency Service was out in force, helping combat those stricken in remote areas where bushfires had ravaged personal property, stock, and wildlife. They are highly skilled, well equipped, and trained comprehensively in a wide range of emergency environments. Today, they comprise more than 5,000 volunteers and 200 employees across the state of Victoria.

Both individuals and various groups were organising charitable events early in the year to help farmers and families that had been victims of utter devastation. My husband Ian and I were involved in two significant charity events advertised on our weekly radio program broadcast on a community-based radio station 97.7FM in the Shire of Casey.

One event in February was organised by Derrek Junkeer, a Ceylonese-born Melbourne entrepreneur who devoted his time and energies to inviting many interstate entertainers to perform. Many travelled from far and wide and did so as a personal gift for the cause. All of these entertainers were professionals. Some were 'Tribute Artists' of world-renowned entertainers, some with us and some passed on.

Peter Triantis organised the first event in conjunction with Derrek Junkeer, both music and entertainment industry entrepreneurs. Greg Evans, a well-known media presenter, was the Master of Ceremonies for the first charity concert called the 'Night of Nights'. In addition, there were entertainers such as Dennis Walter, OAM of 3AW night-radio reputation. Others on the night included Tony Pantano, Martin Penrose of 'Big O' Tribute distinction, Andrea Marr and John McNamara, who sing Rhythm and Blues. Then, David Gould, known for his ability to hit the baritone notes with ease, sang one of his speciality songs, 'Ole Man River'. Another performer was multi-talented Geir Borholm, who hailed from Adelaide, an artiste who could sing like Elvis Presley, Tom Jones and Frank Sinatra. Many more entertainers gave their very best talents and time for a great cause in Victoria - The Black Summer Bushfire Appeal.

Ian and I offered our services to help on the day at 'The Grand' in Wantirna South, an elegant function venue. Venue management was highly generous in waiving many of the overhead costs involved with hiring its premises. We also assisted in bringing together many friends and family members to participate in the event by purchasing tickets and attending.

Ian filmed the entire event. I took photos of every entertainer and helped with detailed coverage in order to explain its purpose and how it came together successfully for bushfire relief. My coverage of the event was posted on Facebook.

The next was yet another charity event for the exact cause of collecting funds for the Black Summer Bushfire Appeal, also organised by Derrek Junkeer. This event was held on Valentine's Night at the elegant 'The Grand' at Wantirna South. It featured the legendary international entertainer Sir John Rowles OBE, who hailed from New Zealand and and was Knighted in 2018. He sang for three hours all the songs he was known for in the late '60s, the '70s and early '80s. He had a rich voice and is similar to the singing styles of Matt Munro, Des O'Connor, Frankie Vaughan, Max Bygrave's and Engelbert Humperdinck, to name but a few.

This majestic event at 'The Grand' was a dinner and a show event, with the venue turning on their culinary expertise in presenting a lavish three-course menu for their guests. We were happy to broadcast the entire event with full-length coverage by video and Facebook. In addition, my 'Black Summer Bushfire Appeal' appeared in many overseas newsletters and newspapers, making me immensely proud.

When all the bushfire charity events had subsided in the first three months of 2020, the World Health Organization announced that we were all facing a mystery disease originating in the District of Wuhan in China. A global public health worldwide alert announced a deadly coronavirus called COVID-19, resulting in many preventive measures at airports of major cities worldwide. Australia closed its borders to all non-residents as early as mid-March 2020 as a precautionary measure. All arrivals into the country had to be quarantined in hotels for two weeks under strict medical disciplinary rules of social distancing and the wearing of masks.

An announcement that a worldwide pandemic was imminent prompted panic buying by the Australian public who stocked up on many essential items including toilet paper. As a result, Australia announced its first State of Emergency on March 16th, 2020. The strict State Government moved to enforce the free movement of people within Victoria to stop the virus from spreading by enforcing a curfew and 5km distance from home ruling. People who defied the State of Emergency had warrants executed on them with heavy penalties.

We were all plunged into an unknown lifestyle of staying indoors without any social activities unless caring for family, banking and shopping for essential items. We felt like 'prisoners' within the walls of our own homes.

Adjusting to this lifestyle was hard. It meant a great deal of mindful discipline and thought about how one would engage in various hobbies, reading and writing activities, painting, and other artwork methods. Some went into home renovations and refurbishing. It was also time for many to get into decluttering, a job many keep shelving for a 'rainy day'.

Those working had to follow a 'Work from Home' policy which was new to many. Schools closed, and teachers introduced a remote home learning system. It was challenging as parents needed to become students themselves to cope with the demands the school syllabus relevant to the student's grade year.

I read several different books during this time. I started the lockdown by reading 'Dalai Lama, My Son – A Mother's Story' by Diki Tsering. It certainly was a compelling narrative written by the mother of the present Dalai Lama, a Spiritual Leader I am passionate about indeed. He is the fourteenth Dalai Lama who was born to humble but prosperous peasant parents. Diki Tsering, the Dalai Lama's mother, had a traditional Tibetan upbringing and was married at sixteen. When her son was approximately one year old, she found out that her son was the fourteenth Dalai Lama, and this announcement turned her world upside down. The book was a fascinating read about the personal account of a mother's true love.

The next book I read was 'Four Paws and a Heart of Gold' by Molly Oliver Sasson. The late Dr Graeme Smith, the Managing Director of The Lost Dogs' Home in North Melbourne, wrote its foreword. Molly's story accounts her life and that of her husband with their dog Jessie and cat Maxi who were not just pets but affectionate co-residents of their home. It was a very warming story, just when the news of COVID was starting to become sad and depressing.

The third book was 'A Street Cat Named Bob' by James Bowen. This book was released as a successful movie a few years ago by the same title. The desire to read the book arose from the passing away of Bob, the famous Ginger Cat at a mature age. He was seen daily with his master James Bowen and subsequently became an icon. James was a busker, playing his old black guitar and lived by himself in sheltered accommodation. Still, when he befriended the stray ginger cat and took him into his warm abode, a mutual friendship started that was more than just a love of a pet and likewise a pet's love for their master.

The fourth book was one which absorbed me from cover to cover. The title of the book was 'The Forgotten Islands' by Michael Veitch. It was an entertaining and comprehensive voyage of a single man into a little known and truly 'gothic' Australia. I was fascinated to read about the many islands in the Bass Strait between the mainland and Tasmania. The author covered the many nights he spent in the Bass Strait under cold, dark and treacherous weather conditions, fulfilling his ambition to visit Deal Island, following a fascinating story of a fisherman that had disappeared many years ago.

Well, I was on a roll, and my fifth book was a combination of true short stories of some of the hardest-working dogs in the world, a bit of light reading. It was a collection of such inspirational tales of hard-working dogs who knew they were on a mission. The title of the Book was 'Dogs with Jobs' by Laura Greaves. The stories were a heartwarming tale of dogs with various fascinating jobs including a blind guide dog, a diabetes and mental health support dog and a Border Force detector dog.

My second last book, 'A Mother's Story by Rosie Batty with Bryce Corbett', was a book of heartache, grief, passion and purpose. A gripping story about a single mum who had everything in her power to give her only son Luke the very best of life. She had her world turned upside down when her ex-partner and father of Luke killed their son in the act of atrocious family violence at the Tyabb Cricket Grounds in February 2014. He had met with his son at cricket practice and murdered him in one villainous act of horror..

When the Police arrived, they found Luke's father armed with a knife, and when he defied Police orders, they fired a single bullet into his chest. The victim died of his gunshot wound later in the Emergency Department of the Frankston Hospital. This story was a gripping story of heartbreak and has been the reason for Luke's mum, Rose Batty, establishing the 'Luke Batty Foundation – Never Alone' and becoming a crusader against family violence. This book had me in tears.

My last book for 2020 was again a very light read. I picked it up at the local Post Office, where one could find many bargain books on sale. This book was titled 'Great Australian Railway Stories' by Bill 'Swampy' Marsh. Again, a collection of short stories brought together by a riveting collection of first-hand accounts from the tracks and railway sidings, the engines and the guard boxes, the pubs, and the carriages. The short stories were funny and dramatic at times, an enjoyable light read.

While all this was going on, a request came to me from an author based overseas seeking information from material that I had in books stored in my keeping relevant to the subject matter that he was basing his fifth book on. So, I did correspond with him and sent him the material he wanted to complete his book and made him very glad, a project that took me three months to fulfil.

I ended the year much like everyone else, glad that we were out of lockdown but unsure of what was in store for us in 2021.

# SOMETHING LURKS
# OUT THERE

## *RODERIC GRIGSON*

The old man sat alone in his house. He had been alone for months and was beginning to wonder whether or not he was losing his mind. Since he was in his mid-eighties, he realised that it was highly possible. Yet he could still do the crossword and remember what he did yesterday, and although he no longer had anyone to play with, he still enjoyed the bridge column in the newspaper, which he read on the internet. Moreover, he could remember all the books he had read recently, of which there were many, and could remember the Premier's name, which was one thing he would gladly have forgotten.

He had never imagined that it could ever be like this, sitting on his own, day after day with not even a dog for company. After his last dog Angus died, he had not wanted another, for who would look after it when he died?

What, he ceaselessly asked himself, what was he supposed to do in the event of getting ill – should he go and lie on his bed and patiently wait there alone, to die?

At this stage of his life, what a waste of time when he still had his faculties about him. Not to go back to where he had been born as he planned, although the old man did not know how it would feel when he visited his parents grave. Not to go to the theatre or the cinema, or just to the park. Even the supermarket with those half-empty shelves would be a distraction.

He had lived alone for over 20 years, but he had never been lonely, bored, or depressed about it. *What a waste of time, when after all, you don't have much of that precious commodity of time left,* he thought.

Sitting at home all day, listening to the preachy self-satisfied voices of the radio – to endless repetition and gloomy prognosis of the pandemic did not sit well with him. These reporters are supposed to give us the news, but they only want to spread their own opinions, rumours, and innuendo in the name of breaking news.

He was glad that he was financially secure and could live at home. He couldn't imagine what it would be like to be locked up in one of those Old People's homes. At least he could wander around his house and spend time in his garden. He always enjoyed gardening, although it was getting more difficult to cut the grass in his backyard.

The endless silence was almost the worst thing, a silence that seemed capable of drowning out the music he often played in an attempt to mask it. And to also hide his thoughts. Thoughts which grew bleaker every day, however hard he tried to remind himself that he was not the only one. Thousands of old people like himself were condemned to this purgatory all around the country – all in the name of saving their lives. The old man rather wished he could have caught the disease at an early stage since, being in good health, he felt sure he would have survived and then he would have been free again. Free to stretch his wings and to feel alive. Free to go to the bloody supermarket, free to sit on a bench in the park and talk to a stranger. Free to go for a proper walk.

Since Emily died, he had always been accustomed to taking exercise. He supposed that housework counted as some exercise, but during the last interminable months, he had taken to walking up and down his narrow stairs ten or twenty times a day until the carpet began to wear thin.

The old man supposed that once the lockdown was lifted, old people in every town and village, in every home up and down the country would swarm out into the streets, frail and pale and mad from their incarceration, wild-eyed with excitement and amazement at the sight of the world the virus had left in its wake. Then, of course, one by one, they would succumb. But unfortunately, someone hadn't thought it through.

Who imagined that the arbitrary locking away of over twenty per cent of the population might be a good idea? He knew that being lonely and isolated could affect his mental health. Nevertheless, there was something amiss about the thinking and something singularly unpleasant about having the groceries left anonymously outside the front door as if he were some pariah or leper. However, he was perfectly healthy – so far.

Even his neighbours were not around for him to talk to. Next to him, John and Grace, who lived in the townhouse, moved to Queensland, leaving their home empty. Two nurses who worked at night lived on the other side. He would occasionally see them coming home in the early hours of the morning if he were awake and looking out of his bedroom window.

Every day, one or other of his nieces telephoned, which was always a pleasure, but Claire said she wouldn't dare call on him for fear of infecting him. You never knew, she said. Claire worked in the city, travelling back and forth on the train every day. She could easily be carrying the virus, she said. Justine, his other niece, lived in Bendigo.

He would have loved to see Claire in person. Just as he would have loved to see any member of his family, even those he used to find annoying. He began to worry that he would never see any of them again or, for that matter, any human being ever and so took to ringing people he hadn't bothered to ring before, to say hello - or was it good-bye?

The voice of a brother-in-law for whom he had never particularly cared was suddenly music to his ears. Being only sixty-five, his youngest sister was at liberty to go out and about, pick up the virus, and bring it home to him, whereas he was not allowed to do so for himself.

He rang old friends from the past, all, like him, cooped up, isolated, exiled from society - all feeling as though they were going mad - and younger ones who said it was all for his safety.

But it's only to keep you safe, they said.

Let me get the bloody disease and risk it, he thought.

Remember to wash your hands for at least twenty seconds, they said. Or for the time it takes to sing the first verse in the National Anthem. Wash your hands. Wash your hands. Why did he have to keep washing his hands when he had been nowhere? Had he picked up germs from Amazon's cardboard wrapping? Had he touched his face after picking up the package of books from the library? He found himself checking on the internet to find out which surfaces were most porous or most likely to carry germs.

Wash your mobile, they said.

Wash my mobile? I must be mad. No one but he had touched his mobile. It had been nowhere. Could he pick up his own germs and give them back to himself?

Wear rubber gloves. Wear rubber gloves. What for? Rubber gloves can pick up germs as quickly as your hands.

Don't touch your face. Don't touch your face. We feel our faces on average sixteen times an hour, he thought. Who worked that one out? But don't touch your face. His face began to itch - his nose, his lips, his cheeks, his chin - but do try not to touch your face.

None of it made any sense. So, what were they not telling us about this disease?

He found himself putting on rubber gloves to do the meanest household task. He found himself washing his mobile again and again. He found himself frantically trying not to touch his face. He must be going mad. He wondered whether he should go somewhere and get tested for the virus, but no one had given him any direction and how would he have contacted it anyway.

He had read somewhere that human beings lose their individuality in isolation. That made him wonder if he and all the other lonely, isolated people shut up in their houses and flats the length and breadth of the country were somehow becoming indistinguishable one from another.

There could be no doubt that living alone and seeing no one was conducive to selfishness. Before all this happened, he used to go out a good deal. He had things to do, various classes to attend at the local community centre where he helped out. He had people to see, and if he hadn't seen anyone for a day or two, he would go to the corner shop or the park where he would pass the time of day with anyone willing to chat. He liked other people and was always interested in their lives. Now he had only himself to think about. He could barely remember how long it was since anyone came for a meal, and he had grown tired of cooking for himself even though he once loved to cook. Being amongst the rich aromas when he was cooking made him happy, and he had always enjoyed the taste of what he had created. Nowadays, he was tempted to drink too much.

The days stretched into weeks and the weeks into months without there ever being any real let up to his interminable boredom. He had fought it quite cheerfully, to begin with, but it was becoming increasingly difficult. He thought of the extraordinary courage of those people kidnapped by cruel men or cruel regimes, who, kept in solitary confinement in the dark, managed to make marks on their cell walls to measure the passage of time. Some of them survived to tell the tale, and yet here was he in a comfortable little townhouse with music and books, a television, a radio, a telephone, the internet, and, it seemed, about to go mad.

He'd wondered about horses alone in fields. Could they go mad? They who, like humans, were herd animals. And alpacas. Alpacas he knew could quite simply die of loneliness. He felt tears of pity streaming down his cheeks. Yet, when all the world was in turmoil, here he was, sitting at home, weeping for theoretical horses and alpacas.

He could no longer count the days since it had all begun and wished that he, too, had made marks on his wall for every day since he last saw a living human being.

Why he repeatedly asked himself, did he so blindly obey the injunction to isolate himself? He was not especially afraid of dying, not even terrified of the virus. Yet, again and again, he reached the same conclusion. Despite himself, he had succumbed to the mass hysteria.

During the months of isolation, he had read, among other things, many of the Wilbur Smith novels which he had in his library. He enjoyed Smith's stories which always set in Africa. In addition, he had just about watched everything he could on the telly, including sixteen seasons of Grey's Anatomy, which he immensely enjoyed. But not even *the reruns of Fawlty Towers* provided light relief anymore.

For a while, the old man daydreamed about all the places he had been in his lifetime, the countries, and cities he had visited, the food he had eaten but quickly got tired of doing that.

He was glad when the local library was able to deliver books he wanted to read. He read an awfully long book called *Shantaram* set in India, written by an Australian who had escaped from Pentridge prison. What a life that man had led. He also read the entire George Martin *Game of Thrones* series, several modern thrillers, and even tried one of the *Harry Potter books to see what the fuss was about. He had great admiration for writers who could create magical places in their minds and wished he could do it himself.*

Reading had always been such a pleasure for him, but now he had begun to hate some of the characters. He'd had enough of fictional characters, imaginary creatures who mysteriously had the power to wind themselves around one's heart but who were no substitute for the real thing. *He* was sick of the lot of them.

Eventually, there came a day when he knew he could bear it no longer. He didn't tell his nieces that he intended to go out since they insisted that he should take every precaution, stay in, bear up. It couldn't last forever. Living in a city, you could never be sure of keeping a proper distance from a passer-by in the street, they said, or even in the park. And what if that passer-by were to sneeze?

It was a fine day in early spring. There would be roses and agapanthus in the park and dogs and people. People, people, people, how he longed for people. He was trembling a little as he stepped out of his front door - it seemed so strange after all this time. Then off he went, briskly, head in the air with a tremendous sense of relief and freedom.

It was a short walk to the park, which, as he had foreseen, looked clean and shining in its fresh spring colours. He strolled, thrilled at seeing people, at last, not many but a few, some walking their dogs, a woman pushing a baby in a buggy. A runner dressed in slimy lycra ran past a group of schoolchildren elbowing each other and giggling. A man about his age, leaning on a stick, spitting angrily at the ground: he loved them all.

Rejoicing this newfound freedom, he decided to look for a bench where he might sit and watch the world go by.

He hadn't been sitting for long when to his amazement, a woman came and sat down beside him. Had she not heard of the social distancing rule? The distance between them on the bench was barely a metre.

He looked at her and saw that she wore a faded green parka with the hood pulled down over her forehead so that he could hardly see her face. A good-looking face as far as he could see. Not old. Not young, but tired looking.

He turned to address her, having, he supposed, felt her gaze upon him, and so they fell into conversation.

They talked for a long time. Or rather, the woman spoke for a long time, telling him that she was homeless, that she had been sleeping rough since all this began. She was glad to be able to talk to someone these days. People were only too ready to turn their backs, to keep you at arms' length. She felt shunned even by some of her fellow rough sleepers, and the one thing she missed was human company. There were charities around trying to help get people to get off the streets – the woman could get a hot meal most days – but she had reached the point where she felt she deserved to be where she was. It was hard at times, especially in the winter, but she had grown accustomed to her lot.

The woman talked and talked and talked about her life, childhood, and circumstances that led to her being homeless. And he, forgetting everything else, listened avidly. He almost felt he shouldn't leave her, but he did have to go home at some stage.

As he stood up to go, she turned and thanked him for listening with a faint smile.

'I'll be in the park again tomorrow,' she said.

Walking home, he felt extraordinarily light-hearted – even happy. She was a decent woman who had fallen on hard times, he thought, and he was glad that she had chosen to talk to him. He would ask her name tomorrow. He didn't for one minute think about the virus.

Then all of a sudden, just as he was about to cross the road, he felt dizzy. He put his hand to his head, *don't touch your face, don't touch your face*, he heard an inner voice say as a wave of nausea engulfed him. Before he knew anything more, he had collapsed onto the road. Paramedics did their best to revive him, but he was pronounced dead on arrival at the hospital.

'Cardiac arrest,' Claire told her sister later. 'Just like that, with no warning, and he'd never had a day's illness in his life.'

# NO MORE ANGELS

........................

*MELISSA SAYERS*

........................

I'm scared.
This pernicious disease
has me in its grasp.
Again.
One parent gone
a loss so tragic,
so painful,
that it hurts me still.
And now,
again,
it holds me to ransom,
and renders me lost and powerless,
just like before.
I'm scared
of the not knowing,

of what could be,

of the pain that once crippled me.

I'm not ready for this,

can't go through this

Again.

I'm scared.

So scared

that my feet won't move,

and my mind won't stop.

I can't lose him too.

The agony would be

insurmountable for me.

One angel is enough.

Please don't take him too.

# MY FAVOURITE PLACE

## *MELISSA SAYERS*

The stage is her home.
When she dances
she is grace and beauty and poise.
Each movement flawless,
toes pointed,
hands soft.
Each step one with the music.
Peace is her own
when she dances.
She is calm and single-minded,
she is her pure self,
 full of light,
rhythm personified.
Each subtle movement has a reason,
executed perfectly.

My eyes fill with tears,

and I see her as she is.

My heart swells with overwhelming joy

when she dances.

# THE JOURNEY

*MELISSA SAYERS*

Shall I pen this random thought?
This fleeting sensation
of a journey long sought.
Homewards –
Inwards –
Upwards.
Shall I attempt to capture
this newly racing heartbeat
sending pulses
from a seemingly new heart?
Comfortable with looking back,
yet moving on.
Can I capture this momentum
with a pencil
and a few mere words?

# THE NEED FOR SPACE

*MELISSA SAYERS*

Space.
It's a tangible commodity
when it comes to
you and I.
Bargained –
bartered over.
Like squawking chickens
in a crowded marketplace.
Most times I can see
the space you want –
the wall around you.
Then you drag me in,
screaming and bleeding.
To reinforce the space between you
and the world outside.

But in four or five cold words
and an icy stare
I'm set adrift again.
Conflicted,
but out of the danger zone.

# FLYING

*MELISSA SAYERS*

I am rising,
flying towards the sun,
embraced by her warmth.
I am soaring through the heavens.
I am weightless,
above the clouds,
far from the worries of the world.
I am lost.
No-one can find me here.
No-one knows my name,
my past, my future.
Now I am descending,
I can see the ground approaching fast.
Although I feel the crash,
for a moment

I rose above it all
and I was free.

# GUILT WITHOUT SHAME

*MELISSA SAYERS*

Vulnerable.
Standing naked,
armoury down,
all my imperfections exposed
for all to see.
But I am not afraid of them.
I own them.
Guilt without shame.
I am worthy
of love, of joy, of respect.
I am enough for me.
Strength through weakness,
and as a result
power beyond measure
to map my destiny.

You may cast your eyes away in fear,

but I stand firm.

And I am whole.

A shining light

unafraid of the dark.

# THE BREVITY
# OF YOUR LOVE

*MELISSA SAYERS*

This is the place
where all is dark
and moonbeams hide in fear.
Yet I can see so clearly.
I am dragged again
Into this blackest place.
You wait for me there
with your black woollen blanket
to wrap me in its warmth
to tease and taunt me
with the love woven into it.
I know how briefly

I will feel it's loving comfort
(a brief respite
from your winter chill)
and how swiftly you will steal it
from me and let me freeze.
Yet I stand here still
Desperately longing for your solace
Hopelessly craving your light.
Just one tiny beam will be sufficient
in the darkness of the night.

# THE MOON

*MELISSA SAYERS*

I come home for the moon
and the way it's light embraces me
in its tenderness.
I am saved from the dark
and in its shadows, I can hide.
For just a few nights
I am precious
and the stars dance for me alone.

# A TEENAGE DAUGHTER

## *MELISSA SAYERS*

Defiant and stubborn
determined to a fault.
Yet lofty and whimsical and wild.
A great mystery to me,
this complex, crazy creature
Who sings with the beauty of a bird
and screams like a banshee.
And never, ever lets me in.
What I would give for some piece of her.
Although overbearing and uncontrollable
she is emotionally inside-out.
Even in her silences,
even in her moments of inexplicable calm
something brews below the surface.
I am unable to reach her.

Her frequent fluctuations
leave me reeling and beguiled.
Merciless rejections mixed with
love without bounds.
The beauty and facets of a stained-glass window
reflected in the eyes
of a twisted, tangled woman-child.

# SONGBIRD

*MELISSA SAYERS*

It's so still.
The calm is palpable.
Then a sonic white light
bursts through the silence.
The song of a bird
in perfect pitch and tone.
A reassuring sound
that all is well
and peace is in her heart.
She is content,
my bluebird.
And her dulcet tones
Set me soul free.

# HOPE

*MELISSA SAYERS*

Two pounds, two ounces,
16 weeks early.
We named you Hope
but held little.
Your hands were the size of my thumbnail
(that I had filed to nothing for fear of hurting you)
and your body was sustained by machines.
Too easily broken to hold.
For 4 days we squashed
In a lifetime of love.
I whispered to you through my tears.
I clung to you in desperation.
I ached for you to be
still inside me.
And then you were gone,

I felt your soul fly.
The world stopped
and there was nothing.

# THE SAFETY OF ANGER

*MELISSA SAYERS*

The great poet called it
the "witching hour"
wherein to drink hot blood.
But my anger seems to fade at night,
A curious entity requiring light.
And I become scared,
like a child in the darkness
afraid of the monsters and hobgoblins
that hide within my closet
and under my bed.
I long to feel soothed, reassured
and lulled like a babe to gentlest rest.
So I hide, in your arms from my loneliness,
But still I am stalked by sorrowful emotions.
Your arms ease me not.

A counterfeit hoax.
So I hold fast to the notion
that soon the soft dawn
will bring the safety of my anger
and the cocks crow will dissolve my sombre plight.
But in these hours of darkness,
for now,
I helplessly cling to you
and pray for matins light.

# INSOMNIA

*MELISSA SAYERS*

Sleep alludes me
and this wakeful state
pushes me to the brink
maddens me.
My mind races,
my muscles spasm,
my eyes twitch and sting.
My vision is a blur.
I yawn incessantly.
Time passes
1am, then 2, 3, 4
and yet I am still awake.
Sheer exhaustion overwhelms me.
My body feels inside out.
I am agonisingly tired

but my mind won't shut off.

Come words, come poems,

come all types of tale.

Completely depleted of energy

Sad and tired and pale.

Whilst I take ease in the dark

this desperate insomnia comforts me not.

Open eyes behind veiled lids, for now,

for sleep, albeit dark, can find me not.

# THE LAST GOODBYE?

*MELISSA SAYERS*

Every time I leave
I fear that this will be our last goodbye
and that the darkness will come
before I return.
I have watched the
fading of that beautiful face,
now gaunt and grey,
that soothed me as a child
and counselled me in adulthood.
Those piercing pale blue eyes
which oceans themselves would covet.
Those eyes that have looked into my soul
And know my darkest secrets.
Once you were my rock,
those eyes, my moral compass.

Now your body is weak and trembling
and your feet shuffle across the floor.
I know that you will go soon
and those eyes will look upon me no more.
But when death comes to take you
Shall it sneak it through the back door
and take you by surprise?
For you will not go freely or quietly
or slink silently into the darkness.
You will do what you have always done,
and you will fight
against the coming of the darkness,
against the coming of the night.
But for now, give me those eyes,
fixed on me and open wide.
See the love I have for you.
Feel the love you have for me.
And hold on until I see you next
Even though your life may now be
a raging tempest, like the sea.

# 2020

# SHORT STORY

# COMPETITION

# ENTRIES

# EMILY'S HOUSE

## *DIANE BROWN*

I felt awkward, standing tall on the bare ground, nothing but a concrete path from the street to my front door with wooden fences enclosing me on either side. I was new, the fresh smell of timber from my veranda and windowsills wafting through the air as I glanced both right and left. We stood like erect soldiers, all different shapes and sizes, patiently waiting to be claimed, waiting to be owned.

The warm sunshine reflected from my windows as the first group of buyers arrived. Mostly young couples, some with little ones, some alone, but all wearing the same anxious look as they scanned the row of houses. Hand in hand, they strolled along the street, heads leaning together as they spoke, as if afraid to be overheard by the now thickening crowd.

Three or four couples entered my front door, and as their voices echoed around my empty rooms, I strained to hear their conversations. Mutters of "No, I don't like this room." "This kitchen is too small." "I don't like bay windows," bounced through the empty spaces. With each cutting comment,

I felt my walls shrink inwards, my rooms feeling smaller and smaller.

Late afternoon and the crowds began to thin, many couples clutching purchase papers, huge smiles now covering their faces. Again, I felt raw, cold, unwanted, afraid I was the only one in the street not to have been chosen. Once again, footsteps sounded on my front path as yet another couple arrived. I steeled myself for more cruel comments. The afternoon was drawing to a close, and as the sun eased downwards towards the ground, it filled my front rooms with a gentle pink glow. I hoped it offered a welcome to yet another young couple as they entered my front door.

The young woman gasped, her golden hair bouncing around her shoulders as she opened her arms to encircle my space.

"Oh John, this is it. This is exactly what I have been looking for."

I watched them closely as they moved from room to room, their voices becoming louder as their excitement grew. The young man walked with a limp, leaning on a cane for support. A pretty little girl stayed at his side, her face tilted towards his, not quite understanding but sharing the happiness that beamed from her parents' faces.

The young woman wrapped her arms around him. "John, can we please?"

John held her close, his gentle, smiling eyes crinkling in his tanned face. "Yes, Emily, yes we can."

The little girl clapped her hands with glee. "Is this going to be our house, Mummy?"

"Yes, Susan," Emily replied. "This is where we are going to live for a long, long time."

I stood empty for a while, a couple of weeks, I guess, but I didn't mind. There was so much to see. The street was a buzz of excitement, large trucks unloading furniture, lawns being sown, garden beds dug. Then, finally, it was my turn. One warm, sunny morning just after daylight, my front door eased open, and from that moment, movement filled the day. Furniture was placed, beds assembled, kitchen cupboards filled. By nightfall, you were all exhausted, but I felt warm and secure. At last, I had my family.

I watched you closely over the years, Emily, transforming me from an empty shell into a beautiful home. You were always so content with life as you tended to your family, sewing, knitting, cooking, gardening, usually singing quietly to yourself as you carried out your chores.

Susan's little brother, Bobby, joined us within the first year, and four years later, we added Banjo, a black, scruffy puppy.

Warm afternoons usually found you outdoors, weeding the garden beds or planting flowers, and as their soft perfume floated through my open windows, their delicate fragrance lingered in every room. John planted an oak tree outside Susan's window, just a thin stick at first, but it spread its wings over the years. Large spreading branches arched so gracefully over the lawn, allowing flickering sunlight to peep through the leaves, casting shadows on Susan's bedroom wall. What wonderful times the two of you shared as you huddled together on Susan's bed. The sound of Susan's tinkling laughter filling the room as you created images from those shadows, watching their everchanging shapes dance through the leaves and onto the bedroom wall.

Your home was such a happy place, but Emily, how the Vietnam war had left its mark on John. Those terrible nightmares that never left him as he thrashed about in bed, you are holding him in your arms, your voice soft, soothing until he awakened and calmed down. After those nightmares, he was always so cold, shivering, as if his body would never be warm again. So those were the times I turned up the heating, just a little, hoping to make him more comfortable. Did you notice?

My kitchen was the heart of the house, and the kitchen table was the lifeblood. Children's birthday parties, homework, dinner parties, Sunday lunches, evening meals, the table hosted them all. The evening meal was always my favourite time when laughter reverberated around the room as you all discussed your day. However, after Susan entered University, some of the discussions became quite heated. Susan had such strong views on politics and women's rights and loudly voiced her opinions. John always listened so patiently, sometimes adding his views or nodding, occasionally raising his eyebrows as he looked towards you. And you, Emily, you sat there so quietly, watching your family, such pride and love on your beautiful face.

Young Bobby was a special boy, quietly spoken, so different from his clever sister. As a small child, he loved to play on my back veranda, lining up his matchbox cars, drawing, painting, playing marbles, always with Banjo at his side. I also watched him over the years as he grew from a young boy into a fine young man. How proud we all were when he was accepted into university to study engineering. But then, Emily, that terrible, terrible night. The loud knock on my front door, two policemen entering; your sobs, John's sobs, Susan's sobs. Harsh rasping sobs that resounded through every room. Our beautiful young man was gone. A car accident had taken him away from us. So sudden, so unexpected. No time to say goodbye. The wind sighed and muttered as it caught its breath in the branches of the oak tree. My rusty tears flowed from my rooftop, streaming down the glass panes of my windows to blend with the rain until they saturated the garden below.

Did you know I let Banjo into the house that night? He had never been an inside dog, always content to sleep outdoors in his kennel, but that night he knew something was wrong. He scratched and scratched at the back door until I eased it open, allowing him to come inside. I watched him hobble in on his old, aged legs, wandering up the hall until he reached Bobby's room, where he stayed all night, resting his head on his front paws, his dark brown eyes never closing.

Susan grew into a fine young woman, very independent and so talented. Such a special day when she graduated from University with a Bachelor of Laws. You and John were so proud, not realizing at that time that she would soon move into her own apartment, leaving the two of you to now live alone. I saw the hurt on your face and felt your pain the day she left. From your many telephone conversations I'd overheard through the years, I knew you always thought she would leave her family home as a young bride. But sadly, that was not to be.

As John grew older, his health deteriorated rapidly, his war injuries taking their toll. And so, Emily, another sad night. A wet, windy night where the sky looked damaged with angry, dark clouds rumbling overhead. Yet, I knew what had happened the moment you walked through my front door; Susan walking beside you, her arm around your shoulders. Life for you had now changed and would never be the same again.

Day after day, you sat at my bay window, gazing at the garden, as if you were waiting for someone, but no one ever came. You carried out all your usual morning chores, silent now, no more threads of soft singing drifting through my rooms. You'd lost your sparkle; sadness surrounded you, loneliness seeped from your whole being. There were so many times Susan promised to visit, only to change her mind at the last moment. Always too busy, work always coming first, but you never chastised her or let her know that you'd baked her favourite cake or prepared her favourite meal. Instead, after her phone calls, you'd wander into her old room, sitting on the bed as you gazed at the dancing shadows casting images on the bedroom wall. You sat there, so still, not moving until the night's darkness gathered the last glimmers of the day. Had you hoped that one day you would share the shadow game with your own little grandchild?

Months passed, each day identical to the last. I watched as you grew older, your golden hair now grey and fine lines etching your face. I felt your frustration when the pain in your arthritic fingers made it impossible to knit or sew your embroidery and the difficulty you had when kneeling to weed your much-loved flower garden. Most of all I worried about your disinterest in cooking. Some days you hardly ate at all.

One cold winter's night, I suddenly felt on edge, uneasy, as I sensed a change in your breathing. Short, shallow breaths, a soft moan, then nothing but silence. I gazed at your face as it seemed to soften, the age lines fading away, the faintest hint of a smile, flooding my memory with the image of that young woman who first walked through my front door all those years ago. As I watched over you, a beautiful sight gently floated into my vision. Your soul rose from your body, and your face was smiling its gentle smile as John appeared, one hand resting on his cane, the other reaching out towards you. I held myself perfectly still, not allowing a window to rattle or a door to groan as you quietly drifted away together, through the open window and into eternity, leaving your perfume of rosemary, sage and roses floating behind you.

Months passed. I stood alone, empty for such a long time, saddened as removalists took away your furniture, suffering the insult of cleaners with their harsh chemicals scrubbing my floors, washing my windows and hosing my veranda. A board was placed in my front garden, but I could not read what it said. What was to become of me?

One cold afternoon my front door was roughly pushed open with a loud bang as three young men bounded inside, struggling with overflowing boxes. Oh, Emily, how things changed after that day. These boys treated me so badly, breaking my cupboard doors, leaving stains on my carpet, rubbish on my veranda and even leaving empty pizza boxes on the bookshelves that John had so lovingly made. Your favourite chair in the book nook was covered in grubby clothing, and smelly sneakers lay scattered around the floor. Ugly posters were stuck on my walls, and loud music vibrated through my rooms whenever they were at home. Your flower garden became overgrown with weeds. Even the oak tree looked tired and neglected, its green leaves dropping like raindrops, so out of season. I tried to pay them back, banging my doors loudly when they were sleeping, causing my walls to moan when the wind was strong, blinking the lights, leaving my taps dripping and allowing the windowsills to rattle and creak.

"This old dump is haunted." A voice sounded loudly above the vibrating music.

But eventually, Spring arrived, and as your flowering bulbs struggled to surface through the long weeds, the vivid colours of daffodils, freesias and tulips helped to brighten my day. So I sighed with relief when at long last, the terrible three packed up their boxes, jamming them into the boot of their old car. The sound of screeching tyres broke the morning silence as they rounded the corner and left my street.

Susan arrived a few days later, looking so corporate in her tailored suit and smart shoes.

"Sell it for whatever you can get." She turned towards the tall man holding a clipboard. "I will never live here again."

How hurt would you have felt hearing that remark, Emily? I could almost see your saddened face. Her comment made me feel so neglected, so unwanted, and so bruised.

A few days passed before another group of cleaners arrived, this group far more caring than the last. As they cleaned and polished, their voices echoed around my empty rooms. "This one will need a lot of work to bring it back to scratch." "I hope whoever buys it is handy with a hammer."

Lawns were mowed, garden beds weeded, and the oak tree given a trim as another notice board was placed in my front garden. As each person arrived with the tall man, I anxiously searched their faces, wondering if they would be the ones who wanted me for their home. Young people, middle aged people, small families, single people. They all came and left. Some were checking all my rooms, nodding and talking together, others going within minutes of arriving. Many weeks passed, and there were days when no one came until late one afternoon, the tall man arrived alone. As he unrolled a large sticker and placed it over the sign, I wondered had I been sold?

Quietness again returned, my rooms empty, and my windows tightly closed. It was summertime, and I felt as if I could hardly breathe. I longed to throw open my doors and lift my windows. Instead, the hot morning sun blazed on my roof, and as I was about to greet another boring day, my interest sparked at the sound of a car pulling into my driveway.

"Here we are." A man's voice cut through the quietness as my front door once again eased open. I held myself totally still, not wanting any rattles or groans, waiting impatiently to discover who would enter. *Please don't let it be those three young men again.*

The patter of little footsteps sounded across my loungeroom floor as a young couple stepped inside. The young woman opened her arms and embraced my open space, her golden hair bouncing around her shoulders. Memories of a day so long ago came flooding back to me.

"Oh Steve, I'm so happy. I can't believe that we're here at last."

Steve walked toward the young woman, wrapping her in his arms. "Sarah darling, it's ours. It's going to need a lot of work, but it will be worth it. This old house will look new again when we have finished."

Sarah kissed his cheek. "My grandmother owned a house just like this. I love it. I can't believe our luck."

"Mummy, Mummy, come quickly." An excited young voice called from Susan's room.

As Sarah entered, the child looked up in awe. "Look, Mummy, shadows are dancing on the wall. Can this be my room?"

"Of course, it can, darling." Was the reply. "Let's open the window and let some fresh air in before the truck arrives."

As my window opened, a beautiful fragrance of rosemary, sage and roses filled the room. Looking out towards the garden, I knew it would be you. First, your upturned face gazed at me as you smiled your gentle smile. Then you nodded, just once, before you slowly drifted back to John.

Yes, Emily. Once again, I have my family.

# THE BOY NEXT DOOR

## *HANNAH SMITH*

*"Nothing eases suffering like a human touch."*
- Bobby Fisher

Lola thrashed about in her bed, the sheets caught around her flailing arms and legs. She wanted to run, but her feet were rooted to the ground beneath her. The darkness was closing in around her as she cried, "No! Stop! Would you please not come near me? They'll see! They'll take me!"

A bright figure was slowly walking towards her in the darkness, arms outstretched, calling her name. As it reached her and gently laid its hands over her shoulders, she let out a scream. It wasn't the touch out of the shadows that scared her, but the fear of what might follow. She knew she had to leave. She shouldn't be there. She willed herself to move and turned to run, but it was too late. The shrill sound of sirens surrounded her, and the doors to the van opened.

"Shriek! Shriek! Shriek!" Lola sat bolt upright, breathing fast, trying to block out the screech of the alarm clock. She'd had the same dream for weeks now, and although she no longer needed the alarm, it had become a welcome relief from her dreams each morning.

"Woof! Woof", she heard Max barrelling down the hallway, skidding into the bedroom. He bounced up to her bed, licking her face, his tail moving at a million miles an hour. "What are you so happy about?" Lola groaned, rolling over and pulling him in for a cuddle. "Are you not sick of me yet?! So what are we going to do today, Maxie? Holiday in the kitchen, the balcony or the lounge room?" Max cocked his head quizzically. Finally, she crawled out of bed, "I need coffee". And so, another Groundhog Day began.

It had been eight months, one week, three days, 10 hours and 22 minutes since social isolation had begun. Lola started to wonder if she would ever be allowed out to interact again. If someone had told her a year ago, she would go from a successful lawyer working 80 plus hours a week to unemployed, stuck inside the four walls of her shoebox apartment and rarely making it out of her pyjamas. She would have told them they were crazy. But, instead, this global pandemic had shut down the world. Guards patrolled the cobbled streets, waved their batons, and made sure everyone followed the "rules". Groceries had to be delivered, left in bags outside the apartment door and medical appointments by telephone. The only reason Lola could leave the house was to take Max for a 15-minute walk.

She desperately missed her family and her friends, longed for the warmth of another person's embrace. But apparently, isolation was the "only" way to prevent the rising death toll that chillingly flashed across her television screen every night. It was a dystopian nightmare.

Lola had watched from her balcony as guards blew their whistles, barking loudly at people on the street.

"Where are you going? Get over here! Show your pet registration papers! Explain!"

Every day, they loaded people into the back of their white vans. Rumours circulated about detention centres built to house these ordinary people, one person per cell, not allowed to leave under any circumstance. No time outdoors, no sunshine, nothing. She had heard mutterings in the supermarket about cruel and unusual punishments, beatings, lashings and the like but brushed this off as bored fanciful musings of her rumourmongering neighbours.

Lola followed the rules, only leaving her apartment to take Max out for his 15 minutes a day, and each time it was the same. Out of her apartment, down the creaking, cracked staircase, and out through the rusty wrought iron gates.

"Stop! Papers? Where do you think you are going?" the guard would bark.

She would pull Max's registration papers from her bag and say, "I will be back in 15 minutes". The guards would look at her wryly as they waved her past.

The usually vibrant streets were dim and grey. The previously bustling restaurants and cafes dotted along the main road were empty, with thick rotting wood planks nailed across their entrances. Weeds were growing through the cracks in the footpath. She didn't dare venture further than a quick trip around the block, afraid of being out for longer than the allotted time. Instead, Lola found her walks a depressing reminder of the changes the City had endured in just eight months.

Lola pottered around her cramped apartment on that particular day, reading her book with Max curled at her feet. She glanced up from her book, the orange and pink hues across the balcony catching her eye. Her favourite time of the day was approaching. The sun was low in the sky, a flaming ball throwing coloured light across the dull dilapidated streetscape around her. She stepped out onto the balcony stealing a hopeful glimpse across the way. Her heart skipped a beat as she locked eyes with the boy next door, the crimson rising in her cheeks. He looked to be a similar age to her, tanned skin and large dark eyes, his white t-shirt tight around his moulded arms.

She had seen him on his balcony most afternoons in the warm sunshine, strumming his guitar with his furry red companion sitting by his side. The boy next door seemed to like twilight as much as she did. Lola gave him a meek wave and quickly shuffled over to her deck chair, book in hand.

Lola felt something gently graze her leg. Looking down, she saw a white paper plane on the balcony floor by her feet. She picked it up, feeling confused, looking around. The boy next door was smiling at her. Her fingertip lingered on the delicate folds of the plane, tracing the streamlined shape. She turned it in her fingers, the scrawling writing catching her eye. "Hola! Hello. My name is Marco. What's yours?"

The corners of her lips curled upwards, and she felt her heart thud in her chest. She raced inside, picked up the pen and wrote, "Hi Marco, I'm Lola", embellished with a tiny shooting star. Lola stepped across her deck chair, making her way to the edge of the balcony. The boy next door pointed downwards, slapping his palm to his forehead. Lola looked down to the cobbled street below where a small pile of failed flights had laid to rest.

Lola covered her mouth to hide her smile and, with a graceful flick of her wrist, sent her message gliding over the railing into the warm air. She watched in awe at the majestic, graceful movement of the tiny plane, caught in the gentle breeze, floating and flipping like a small bird. Then, finally, it unceremoniously hit the crumbling grey brickwork of the building across the street and joined the pile of failed attempts in the street below.

The boy next door held his stomach in laughter, shrugged his shoulders and smiled at Lola. It took Lola five attempts of furiously folded paper planes with varying adjustments to the wingspan, length, and weight before one successfully sailed to the balcony of the boy next door. He clapped and cheered, his furry companion barking joyfully and bouncing on his hindquarters.

Over the next week, Lola and Marco sent many gliders across the great divide, often with tiny origami animals or shapes folded within their wings, always with a question, an answer and a little shooting star tucked away beneath a delicate fold. Lola quickly realised there was more to the boy next door. He had fled from an impoverished life in Mexico and worked hard to build a new life here. All that seemed to be crashing down amid the pandemic. He was alone and scared, longing for companionship, for some contact, and the paper planes allowed them to exchange their troubling thoughts and hopeful dreams.

One mainly purple dusk, Lola walked hopefully onto her balcony, and she wasn't disappointed. A bright yellow plane had landed perfectly between the arm rail of her deck chair. The boy next door wasn't visible. Lola opened the careful folds to find his scrawl. "Let's meet. Take Max for a walk to Marigold Park tomorrow at 8:30 a.m." Her breath caught in her tightening chest, "But we can't. We shouldn't… should we?" she asked herself.

The following morning, Lola grabbed Max's collar and lead. Lola patted her bag to feel for his papers and made her way down the stairs and the iron gates.

"STOP! PAPERS!" the short, plump guard seemed, particularly on edge.

Lola watched as the guard from across the street strode over to them. He was as tall as he was wide, his face looked red and blotchy, and he smelled strongly of cigarette smoke.

"Early to be out, isn't it girly?" he spat.

Lola fumbled and passed him Max's registration papers, her hands visibly shaking. "I just want to walk my dog".

That is when she saw the boy next door saunter through the gates opposite where she was standing, no longer a guard to question him and hasten around the corner with his furry companion in toe. Instead, the guard followed her gaze, and she quickly looked to the ground in front of her.

"Not today, girly. STAY HOME. You ain't going anywhere," the guard snarled, shoving the papers back at her.

She knew better than to argue. Lola ran up the old stairs and flung open the door to her apartment, searching for paper and pen. She hastily scribbled "Tomorrow? noon?" and meticulously folded the wings, straightened the nose, and sailed her message across the great divide.

It was a new guard today. He was short and stumpy with a lazy eye and thinning grey hair. "Morning, love. Have you got some paper there for me?"

Lola relaxed and smiled back at him, handing over Max's papers. So maybe this wasn't such a bad idea, after all. Perhaps it really would work.

"Good morning, Sir".

"Ah, don't call me Sir, love. The name's Angus. You have a good walk, hey. But do remember, it's 15 minutes". He winked at her and stepped aside to allow her out to the street.

Lola hurried past the eerie empty streets towards Marigold Park, a vibrant flower garden that sat in the middle of the City. Lola hated to think how dead and in despair the once most beautiful part of the City had become. She started to jog, Max scampering to keep up, and came to the diverged roads that surrounded the park. Turning left, she drew a deep breath and, with wide eyes, took in the warm pink and red heart rose floral archway that stood grand as ever.

Behind the archway, the tulip garden was in full bloom. The orange and red cup-shaped flowers open, their tall stems were reaching to the sun. The sweet citrus scent was filling the air. It surprised Lola. She never expected the Marigold Park to be more vibrant than ever while the rest of the city seemed to be slowly dying. She followed the path around the garden, watching the sunbeams dance on the flowers as Max tried to catch butterflies. Then, movement on the footpath that tracked the right side of the park caught Lola's eye.

Max suddenly raced forward, dragging Lola behind him. They came to the end of the garden path where the cool, bubbling fountain sat, and Lola stopped in her tracks, doubled over and breathing hard. At her feet, Max was licking and nudging another puppy with red shaggy fur. Lola looked up, and her eyes met his, the boy next door.

There they stood for what felt like an eternity, soaking in the close physical presence of one another but still 6 feet apart, not daring to break the rules.

"Hola, Lola", he whispered, a tear rolling down his tanned cheek.

"It's you," Lola said. "It's really you!". She reached her hand towards him, longing to feel the warmth of his body, to feel touch. Instead, she felt the tingling electricity pulse through her body, extending to her fingertips reaching for her boy next door. In what felt like slow motion, Lola watched Marco stretch his hand to meet hers. Without thinking, she took a step forward, her fingers interlacing with his. She traced the soft skin on his hands, his calloused fingertips.

Marco took his hand from hers. He traced the shape of her mouth, the crease on her forehead and brushed her hair back behind her ear.

At that moment, the world stopped, and time stood still. Marco and Lola could have been anywhere, surrounded by the gentle sound of the water streaming down the fountain and the fragrant citrus scent of the tulip garden. But, instead, they stood simply holding hands. Silent tears rolled down their faces, the sheer joy at simple human connection.

The piercing of whistles pealed around them, "OI! STOP NOW! MOVE AWAY! YOU ARE UNDER ARREST".

Two guards were running towards them. Marco dropped her hand, flinging her backwards and turning to stand tall between Lola and the guards. Lola started, "I have papers!" She flinched as she recognised the imposing figure of one of the guards, "I don't care about your papers, girly. You are under arrest for breaking section 2 of the Physical Contact Act 2019. There is no getting out of this one.

What about you, boy? Who are you? Where should you be?" he snarled, standing over Marco.

"Me llamo Marco, *my name is Marco*," he stuttered in broken English. Then, finally, another two guards arrived; one was the guard with the lazy eye.

"She's right, lads. I'll deal with this one," Angus interjected, grabbed her by the elbow, firmly escorting her away and taking the dog's lead from Marco's hands. "I'll see to it she and her dogs get what they deserve".

"No! Marco!" Lola cried. "Come on, love, trust me," Angus muttered under his breath, picking up his pace. Lola looked back at Marco, tears streaming down her face. She watched helplessly as the guards beat the back of Marco's legs. He fell to the ground like a rag doll as they continued to beat him.

"No!!!!!!!!!!!" she screamed. As she and Angus rounded the corner, the last thing she saw was the guards scoop up Marco's limp body, dump him into the back of their van and drive away with her boy next door.

Angus rushed her back down the drab grey cobbled street, gently pushing her back behind the rusted wrought iron gates. "Go home. Stay home. Don't speak to anyone", he said, handing her the other dog lead.

Lola headed straight for the balcony back inside the apartment and sat on the deck chair, trying to digest what had just happened. With swollen eyes, she looked across the great divide, and Marco's apartment was in darkness. Max came and sat at her feet, his new mate following close behind. Lola bent down and looked at the dog's collar, 'Bella'. She scooped Bella up in her lap, gently stroking her red fur, tears silently streaming down her face. She never meant for this to happen.

Desperate to be there when Marco returned, Lola did not leave the balcony until darkness had well and truly fallen. It was after midnight when Lola finally dragged herself back inside and climbed wearily into bed. She could not get the image of Marco laying limp on the ground out of her mind. She had dreams that night she would never wish upon anybody, waking in the middle of the night in a cold sweat, gasping for air and her heart racing.

As the light of dawn peeked through the window, Lola shuffled out of bed and back to the deck chair, watching and waiting for the boy next door. She sent a small, winged messenger over the balcony. Lola wanted him to know that she was still there, that he wasn't alone. Feeling numb, Lola sat in the deck chair until nightfall again, hoping, desperately hoping, he was alive and safe.

And so, the coming days, weeks and months followed in much the same way. She was always waiting, always watching, always hoping. Then, finally, a pile of unread planes had collected in a heap on the balcony of the boy next door. The seasons changed, and Winter's rain and wind washed away the pile of planes from Marco's balcony. Lola watched as the wind gracefully lifted them from the balcony floor and danced them through the air, never to be seen again. She wondered where they would end up, who might find them, whether they might wonder where the paper planes had come from and what they meant.

Eventually, the summer sun came around again and Lola, laying on the couch inside her apartment, looked up from her book, the sky a brilliant shade of pink. She stepped out onto the balcony smiling fondly as she recalled that brief moment amongst the flowers and sunshine. She brushed the dead leaves and cobwebs from the deckchair and sat down to bask in the brilliance of the warm summer sunset.

Tomorrow would signal the start of a new beginning. The news reports had flashed across Lola's television all day, and the crisis was finally over. From midnight, the world was finally free to leave their homes and rebuild their broken lives. She longed to be at her parent's home, to hold them in her arms and feel their warm, safe embrace. But she wasn't going to be alone anymore.

Lola took one last glance across the great divide and was met once again with nothing but darkness. She walked to the edge of her balcony, searching his apartment for any sign of light or life. She gripped the handrail tightly and closed her eyes, imagining the strum of his guitar, ready to say her final goodbye to her boy next door.

As she slowly opened her eyes, a light flickered on in his apartment.

"Marco?"

# THE DIARY

## *ROBYN KING*

Sarah woke with the sound of hammering coming from the rear of the house. Steve, her husband of fourteen days, was up early. He tested his handyman skills during the lockdown and was repairing some rotting floorboards under the leaky kitchen sink. But unfortunately, they had just moved in before the lockdown and didn't even get to meet their neighbours.

That morning, on returning from Bunnings, which was finally allowed to open with restrictions, he had noticed Sarah was still asleep, so he proceeded to repair the dripping water pipes.

The Richard Street house, built in the 1930s, was a simple, single fronted, weather-board dwelling, with two bedrooms, kitchen, bathroom, and a toilet off the laundry. Sarah and Steve bought it for a reasonable price and planned to redesign the décor. Down the end of the passageway was a small lounge room with an open fireplace in the middle of the rear wall. The thin carpet had dark marks where embers had scorched a few of the looped threads. The last room before the laundry and toilet was the kitchen. White laced curtains hung proudly across the window, and in the corner was a wood potbelly stove that would warm the whole house when lit. Unfortunately, the cracked linoleum was old, dull, and well worn.

Steve heard Sarah enter the room. He pointed to a wooden box on the kitchen table. "Look at what was under the floorboards."

Still half asleep, Sarah walked over to the table and studied the box. It was a simple black box, its paint dulled with age. "What is this?" asked Sarah.

"Don't know, take a look."

She released the latch and looked inside. "Oh, wow, look at that," whispered Sarah.

"What is it?" asked Steve curiously.

"A handkerchief. The embroidery is so fine," explained Sarah under her breathe as she caressed it lovingly. "It's a bow-shaped brooch wrapped by the handkerchief."

Under the handkerchief was a little book with the word 'Diary' in faded gold lettering on its cover. Steve carefully lifted the diary out and handed it to Sarah. Then, something fell to the ground. It was a picture of a pretty brunette in a nurse's uniform. A tall, dark-headed man in a white jacket had his arm around her waist. Both were smiling. Written on the back of the photo were the initials. A.S. N.C. 1960.

Sarah placed the photo back in the diary and turned the pages. The writings started in May 1960. Sarah made two cups of coffee and told Steve she would be in the bedroom if he needed her. She propped the pillows up on the bed and started reading.

*This is the Diary of Alice Sutcliffe*
***Thursday, May 2nd, 1960***
*I started working with Dr Nicholas Clarke today. I couldn't stop staring as he reminded me of Errol Flynn, with his trimmed moustache and dark hair. He has the gentlest voice. He's very refined, articulate and*

*a class above. All the nurses are talking about him. He doesn't wear a wedding ring, but that isn't unusual, as most doctors won't wear rings while handling patients and performing surgeries. I know he noticed me as he smiled when I handed him a scalpel. Typically, Sister Carr flirted with him, but he ignored her, and I smirked. She glared at me and told me to watch myself as she brushed past.*

*Ernie goes to the pub on Thursdays. So, he will be home late. Every night he wants steak, potatoes and peas. One night I put two Brussels sprouts on his plate to mix it up, and he threw the contents all over my new dress. At first, I was shocked, but I realized he doesn't know what he's doing when he's drunk. While cleaning the mess, I could only find one sprout. The next day I looked up, and there it was, stuck to the ceiling.*

*I've been trying to get pregnant for ages. I just can't conceive. Our family doctor says she will get to the bottom of it. So, Ernie and I have had all the tests possible. My results show I am not the problem. So, now it's Ernie turn to be tested.*

### Saturday, May 4th 6.30 pm

*Today I met with Sister Ann Hutchins. Ann is plump, loud, and funny all at the same time. We sat in the lunchroom discussing Doctor Clarke, and she agrees that he is easy to work with. "He can use his stethoscope on me anytime. He must be queer, as no man is as gentle and sophisticated." Ann bellowed. I was bursting at the seams with laughter.*

*I told Ann that Ernie becomes aggressive when he's drinking. It makes me anxious. But my biggest worry is, I can't get pregnant. "You have to have sex, you know that don't you?" asked Ann. Blushing, "Yes, I know, we have been trying since we were first married".*

**Sunday, May 5th 7.30 pm**

Last night, Ernie, being a tow-truck driver, had to attend a fatality on Beach Road. South Melbourne. I knew he'd be gone most of the night, so I rang Ann to come over to share a bottle of champagne. Ann has plenty of ideas on how to improve the performance of the emergency ward. I'm sure if we put it past management first, we could get some of the ideas through.

Tomorrow I have to go to the clinic in South Melbourne to get the results of Ernie's test. Ann said I shouldn't worry too much as there is a system where the doctors can help you get pregnant by combining Ernie's sperm with my eggs. It's expensive, though.

I went to mass today and prayed to Our Lady to pray for me so I can conceive and become a mother.

**Monday, May 6th 2.30 pm**

I saw Dr Mary Mason; Ernie's sperm count is very low. Quite distressing. I am too afraid to tell him. He won't take it well. I cried all the way home. Dr Mason told me that my chance of falling pregnant to Ernie would take a miracle. I can't believe it. I will never be a mother. I rang Ann. I needed some positive reinforcement, as she always cheers me up. She suggested we talk and drink more champagne.

**Tuesday, May 7th 7.35 pm**

I haven't told Ernie about the results, as I have come up with a plan. It's a long shot, but I think I should be able to get away with it. I am going to get pregnant with someone else's help. Dr Clarke has been paying me a lot of attention, and today I bandaged a wound on his arm where a patient scratched him. While I was applying some antiseptic, he asked me if I was married. I told him I was. His reply was, "That's a shame" We smiled at each other. Ann tells me he's been *asking about me. Tomorrow I am working in ICU with Dr Clarke. I am so excited.*

Sarah wondered where the woman who owned the diary was now? Is she still alive? What was Alice up to? What happened to Ernie? Ann Hutchins? The Doctor? She continued reading.

### Wednesday, May 8th 7.30 pm

*What an interesting day I had today. Dr Clarke is…. is…well, he's just lovely. He followed me into the nurse's quarters, wanting my opinion on something. I turned, took a step closer, looked him in the eyes, and said it. "You are never far from my thoughts. "I want you to make love to me," He looked at me with his big brown eyes and touched my face. I felt like I was floating. His passionate kisses were gentle and constant. I responded with intensity. He took my hand and led me into the broom closet, where it is dark and private. "Alice, I dream of you all the time. I picture us making love on the beach while the waves tickle our feet. I think of you taking your nurse's uniform off, and I am watching you from afar. It drives me crazy thinking that I might not ever have you." We took off our clothes and made love right there, amongst the cleaning products in the broom closet. Dr Clarke told me that all he ever wanted to do was to make passionate love to me. It's been driving him crazy. He kept telling me how beautiful I was and how he loves the feeling of his skin touching mine. I have never felt so wanted and so out of control all at the same time. He didn't ask me if I was enjoying myself. He made sure I was. I have never felt this much delight before. I felt weak at the knees.*

**Friday, May 10th 7 am.**

Just a quick note for the diary this morning. Yesterday, being payday, Ernie went to the pub after work. Dr Clarke and I met and came back to my place and made love in my home. While we were lying together on the bed, he handed me something. When I unfolded it, I found a brooch inside an embroidered handkerchief. It was exquisite. It had belonged to his mother, and he gave it to his wife on her twenty-fifth birthday, but now he wanted me to have it. He told me that he was married, but his wife passed away two years ago, with complications from an enlarged heart. She was only twenty-five. I really like Dr Clarke. I wish I had met him when I was younger. But I'm married to Ernie. I'm his forever. Dr Clarke had just left when Ernie walked in the door. I wasn't expecting him to be home so early. The timing was too close for comfort. Ernie noticed that I had been singing a lot more than he was used to. He was happy that I was in a good mood. He was in good spirits also. I wondered if Ernie has taken on a lover. No, not Ernie. I couldn't see him doing such a thing.


**Monday, May 13th 7.45 pm**

We were busy at the hospital today. A photographer was doing the rounds, taking photos of the patients and staff for a promotion in the Sun newspaper. His camera was snapping all over the wards. The patients smiled as it lifted their spirits. It brought joy to the hospital for a day. He used his polaroid camera to take photos of the staff and handed them out to us as a thank you gift. Dr Clarke and I posed for one. I took it as a reminder of our time together. So, I will keep it under the sink in my box of secrets, away from prying eyes.

Sarah took a break from her reading. She walked out to the kitchen where Steve was cleaning up. "You won't believe this, Alice Sutcliffe, Steve. She is one shrewd lady. I don't know if I like her or not. Her husband's sperm count is desperately low. She can't conceive, so she's taken on a lover to save money and avoid doctors and procedures. But it seems she is enjoying him. I think her lover is falling in love with her. But she is using him to become pregnant. Or is she? That is what I want to find out."

After making a sandwich for them, Sarah went outside in the sunshine to finish reading the diary. She was not sure if Steve had even been listening.

### Tuesday, May 21st 7.30 pm

*I have been too tired to write in my diary this week. Dr Clarke walked past me the other day and didn't acknowledge me. I was hurt. I didn't know what was wrong. But something was. Later in the day, he pulled me aside and told me that he had been allowed to do humanitarian work in Nairobi, Africa. Please, Alice, come with me. I need a nurse to be my assistant. I want you. Not just as a nurse but to be my lover. I won't go without you. I love you, Alice. I can't go alone. I kept shaking my head. In my mind I knew I couldn't leave Ernie. That's not the plan. I love him and will never hurt him. "Please, think about it. I will pay for everything. You just have to pack a bag. We leave on the August 1st. I can take care of all the formalities. You must come, my darling. I will look after you. I can't go without you. I won't", he persisted.*

*"What is he asking me? I am in a whirlwind. All I could think about is if I wasn't pregnant, I might run out of time. I don't want to go to Africa. I'm scared of flying. Africa would be exciting; another time or another life, it could have worked. But I can't dwell on something that is impossible and just won't happen. Dr Clarke could make love to me every day, and the thought made me giggle, as I do like being*

*with him. I'm so confused. My body feels different in some ways. I could be imagining it. My breasts are tender, and I feel squeamish in the morning. But I can't compare it to anything because I don't know what it's like to be carrying a child.*

Sarah read on through the diary to the end of June. In July, Alice found out she was pregnant and was due February 27th, 1961. Her plan had worked, and she was ecstatic. She became a little distant towards Dr Clarke as she thought it was best for them to end their relationship.

*July 31st 7.30 pm*

*Dr Clarke approached me today. He wanted to know if I was pregnant, as everyone talked, and he noticed a bump. I told him that I was. And that Ernie and I are very happy we were going to be parents. He glared at me. I told him I couldn't go to Africa. And the best thing to do is that we don't see each other anymore. I won't leave my husband. I can't divorce. The church won't allow it. I thanked him for being so loving to me. He laughed at me. I detected sarcasm in his tone. Then he walked off. I meant to return the brooch and the handkerchief but never had the opportunity to do so. Before I knew it, he was gone. I achieved what I set out to do, but I feel strangely torn; it's harder than I thought.*

\*

Alice wrote in her diary periodically. Sister Carr went to Africa with Dr Clarke. Alice mentioned in one entry that she often thought of Dr Clarke but was excited to be with Ernie and having a baby. She worked until Christmas until Ernie wanted her to stop and stay home to prepare for the baby.

A healthy, bouncing baby boy was born on February 28th. 1961. 8lb. 13oz. Twenty-one inches long. Alice took one look at him, with a mop of dark brown hair, dark eyes, fair complexion. Perfectly proportioned face, just like Alice's lover.

Ernie was so proud of his son and Alice; drinks all round at the pub that night.

Alice still stood by her decision. They never discussed the sperm count. She felt she did it for Ernie. And herself.

*

Sarah closed the diary, stood up and stretched.

"Hello, neighbour," said a voice from over the fence. A lady wearing a straw hat and holding pruning shears in her hand peered over the fence.

"Hello, I'm Sarah. Nice to meet you."

"Welcome to the neighbourhood. I am Pat. How are you settling in?"

"Really well, thanks." Have you lived here long?" Sarah was glad to get to talk to one of her neighbours finally.

"All my life. Grew up in this house."

Sarah walked towards the fence. "Did you know the Sutcliffe's that lived here?"

"Yes, Ernie and Alice Sutcliffe. Ernie was her first husband. Back in '73, he died coming home from the pub. Three men jumped him, knocked him senseless. Just at the end of this street." Pat pointed. "Alice was so distraught. Thought she'd never get over it."

"Oh, that's terrible."

"Yes, it was," Pat responded. "She finally got over it and remarried. Her second husband, Nick Clarke, was a doctor. He worked in Africa for a while and returned with a bout of malaria. They were married in 1975. Alice was admitted to a nursing home with dementia about five years ago and has now passed away. Beautiful couple. They adored each other. It proves you can fall in love twice."

Sarah felt a pang of sadness. She felt she had come to know Alice personally by reading her diary. "How many children did they have?' queried Sarah.

"Funny you should ask, Ernie and Alice had a boy, Joe, fine-looking lad, but everything Ernie was the boy wasn't."

"What do you mean?"

"Well, Ernie was short, stocky, brown hair, full of freckles. Green eyes. Joe was tall, dark, softly spoken, just like Alice's second husband. We all thought it strange. But the timing is out of whack."

"What happened to Joe?"

He left home many years ago, mixed with the wrong crowd. It wasn't the same after Ernie was killed. Dropped out of school. Became a recluse. He doesn't want to be found. There was talk he moved up to the east coast of N.S.W. Joined a commune.

Sarah listened without comment.

"If you want to know more, Alice's best friend, Ann Hutchins, lives in the green house on the corner of the street."

Sarah's ears pricked up. "Well, thanks Pat, lovely talking to you. We'll talk again soon."

Sarah, with diary in hand, headed inside. She packed the handkerchief, brooch, photo and diary in the box and walked with a spring in her step to Ann Hutchins house. While she was adjusting her mask before knocking, a grey-haired lady opened the door.

"Can I help you?"

"Hello, Ann?"

"Yes?"

"I've just moved into the Clarke house across the way. I found something you might be interested in." Sarah handed her the wooden box.

"Thank you," she said, looking down at the box and turning it in her hands. "What is it?"

"It's a diary which you should read."

# MYSTERIOUS WAYS, INDEED

## *NORMA SAVIGE*

'Thank you for seeing me, Doctor. I have a health issue that is really getting me down, and I'm over it. Another doctor suggested I see you, and I'm here as a last resort. Nobody else has been able to help me.'

'Sit down, Judy. My name is Karen. You certainly appear to be worried, and I'd like to try to help you. But, first, I need to know more about the issue. Can you tell me about it?'

With a deep sigh, Judy dropped her head and fidgeted with her watch.

'I'm trying not to cry, but it is tough as I've gone over this so many times to no avail. It's a long story, and I get depressed when I talk about it. I know there are many people worse off than I am, but it has been more than ten years, and I'm exhausted.'

'Take your time, Judy. We don't need to rush. I'm here to listen.'

Karen settled back in her chair, rested her hands in her lap as she leaned slightly forward in attention. Then, she smiled and nodded her head for Judy to begin.

'For years now, I have had a difficult problem that has controlled my life. I have seen every type of specialist, had every test known and experienced major surgery, but the result of every investigation has always been, has always been....'

Karen reached over, gently squeezing Judy's arm. 'It's OK.' She said, reaching behind her and pulling a tissue box out. 'Here, have a tissue,' she said, 'and take your time. I'm in no hurry.'

With a gulp, Judy continued, '... the result of every investigation has always been the specialist telling me I am a *mystery*. I'm sick of it. Sometimes I get so depressed ...' she stopped and stared out of the window. The tears now fell like a waterfall. 'I'm sorry. It just gets me down.'

'I can see that. Just take a few minutes while I read your file.'

Going through the thick file on her desk, Karen started to shake her head. 'You've been through the mill and have had every perceivable test and treatment. Except one, perhaps?

Karen looked up at Judy. 'I wonder if you would be interested in trying some acupuncture. I would think that's why my colleague suggested you come to see me.'

'I don't know. I guess anything is worth a try. I'm desperate,' Judy lamented. 'I mean ... um ... sorry, I don't mean it as a put-down – it's just something I've never tried before. It always seemed like a bit of magical thinking to me.'

Karen took up an instrument, leaned forward and smiled, 'I use laser most of the time, and often you don't even feel it. Can I try it on your hand, so you know what it's like?'

She pressed the laser into the web between the thumb and next finger of Judy's right hand, a red light flashed, and then there was a beep. 'That's it.'

'Well, what have I got to lose? I've retired from work; I can't do most of my favourite activities in the afternoons unless I go without lunch that day. I need to be near a toilet and, therefore, I have gradually reduced my life to being home-based.'

Judy sighed, whispering, 'It's not just me. My whole family is affected. I can't visit my family because of the long drives. I can't go to the opera or movies or parties or even take others in my car – *just in case*. Sometimes I have to leave, or even avoid, my book-club meetings or writing group classes because I am unwell. It often feels like my life is over.'

'I have to either be a morning person or have most relationships over the phone. I am like an outcast.' Then, again, the tears began to flow.

Karen stood and reached out her hand. 'Why don't you hop up on the couch and get comfortable? We can try a few treatments to see how you go and then decide whether you want to continue with a few further appointments.'

Judy removed her shoes, climbed onto the couch and lay on her back. She could feel an odd tear, now and then, trickle down the side of her face but was unable to stop it from happening.

'Try to relax, and when you're ready, we'll give it a try.'

Gradually, the tears stopped, and Karen explained what she was about to do. Then, she proceeded to apply the laser to various points on Judy's body – her ankles, wrists, ears, and the top of her head.

Judy relaxed, closed her eyes, breathed deeply and began to daydream about how nice it would be to be just like everyone else – that is, if this treatment worked.

'Heavenly Father, thank you for your loving care and kindness ....'

*What? Who? Who's here?*

Her eyes flew open. Karen stood beside her holding her hands and looking at the wall above the couch.

*She's praying for me. What am I supposed to do? Isn't that a bit of a cheek? Maybe not. Look at it as a great and caring thing to offer on my behalf.*

'...Please help Judy and her family resume their normal, joyful lives without ill-health causing such restrictions on them ....'

*What should I do? I'll keep my eyes shut and pretend I haven't noticed. It's kind of her, I suppose. But, oh, she's finished.*

Judy opened her eyes and whispered, 'Thank you.' After that, she didn't know what else to do.

A few moments later, she was led back to the chair beside Karen's desk and agreed to return for another treatment the following week.

After making the appointment, she walked back to her car in the sunshine. She felt like she had woken from a dream. It was all a bit surreal.

When she phoned her daughter-in-law, Susie, Judy started to giggle as she described 'the incident' in detail later.

The phone became silent for a moment before Susie said tentatively, 'Well, that's nice.' It was almost a question. Neither seemed to know what to think about it. Unorthodox, certainly. Kind and harmless, for sure.

But, who knows? As a non-believer, Judy felt like a bit of a fraud. If it had happened when she was a zealous believer as a child, she would have been on her knees beside her bed that night, reinforcing Karen's prayer before adding her nightly prayers for blessings for her whole family.

Back then, she knew for a fact that God answered all prayers. He heard them all and answered them all. However, she had taken heed of the reminders that whilst he answered them all it was in His own mysterious ways. We didn't always get what we prayed for but what we *needed*. We also had to be incredibly careful what we prayed for – *in case we got it!* She didn't quite get what that meant as a child, but she certainly knew it as an adult.

Now, here she was with this *Thing* in her life that she didn't know how to handle. She told her husband over dinner that night and was unsure how to explain or describe what had happened. She was respectful of Karen's motives and, therefore, did not use her typically flippant approach when talking about the religious behaviours of others. It was almost as if she shouldn't upset the applecart, *in case it worked?* She didn't want to jinx it!

She stopped her occasionally blaspheming talk – no more, 'Jesus Christ!' when things went wrong. No more put-downs or patronising remarks when observing others on TV or social media expressing their faith. What a hypocrite! She chastised herself but was desperate enough to fall into line rather than jeopardise any remote chance of it working.

'I'm not hypocritical. I'm just respectful', Judy told herself.

*

For weeks there was no change in her condition – just as she had secretly feared would be the case. The acupuncture made no difference, although she attended the clinic every Monday. She was relieved to find there were no more prayers, and she began to lose any expectations of acupuncture being the answer. She was still house-bound and often unwell. Often the only respite she received from her solitary life was her French online class. This was an international class run by a teacher based in Brisbane. There were class members from America and other Australian states, and during those sessions, she was safely at home but able to join in each week. It was great comfort in her life as she was able to be just like all the other students and share in the online activities making new friends, and enjoying the class for over a year. It is amazing how being just like everyone else helped her relax and be her usual, cheerful self - at least for a part of every week.

Her life was very much one of ups and downs. When she was well, she would often walk, go to a group meeting or a class and feel safe doing it. When she was not well, she was miserable and sometimes even depressed. Those low times reminded her how limited her life was, what a burden she must be to her husband, and how she could not enjoy her retirement by travelling and following her earlier pursuits.

*

Then came COVID-19!

She, and many others, were pronounced by the state Premier to be *highly vulnerable* and, therefore, susceptible to contracting the deadly virus because they are in the over 70s age group. Restrictions came into place. Cafes, restaurants, cinemas and many other businesses were closed. Her son directed all his staff to work from home, and her daughter was permitted to do the same. Her grandson began his university year with online lectures, and her granddaughter was suddenly unemployed. Everyone was instructed to stay home.

All her groups, clubs and classes were cancelled. No more face-to-face sessions as even tougher restrictions came into being. Schools were closed, and her husband, a school principal, supported staff as they prepared for online classes for the new term.

Now she was not allowed even to go shopping. Her husband did that. She spoke to the family on Facetime, and Easter Sunday brought a Zoom meeting to replace the family dinner they had shared for the last 50 plus years. Her son, granddaughter and grandson had all returned from overseas trips a few days before restrictions were applied, and she had not seen any of them since their return. Her life now became even more constricted and constrained.

She was frustrated to see and hear thousands of people on radio, television and various social groups trying to figure out how they would cope with being stuck at home all day and night. She often found herself muttering, 'Welcome to my world, you miserable lot.'

She agreed with one commentator who declared, 'Our grandparents went to war to protect our future. All we are asked to do is stay at home and sit on the couch to protect their future. Just do it!'

'Yes,' she grumbled, 'this is a lot like the way I've been living for years.'

Because of her health issues, she became one of the toilet-paper *hoarders.*

What on earth were those other people going to do with all that paper? They can't all be unwell.

Apart from her daily walk, her only outings now were to visit the doctor's clinic. Once there, she was not allowed to leave her car until a gloved and masked staff member checked her temperature and then, only after a knock on her car window, was she able to enter the clinic.

Last Monday, she related to Karen how annoyed she was that people complained about staying home for a few weeks. They were even trying to find any loophole to allow them to be exceptions to the rule so they could party, swim, fish, play golf or whatever.

'Why can't they just stay home to protect themselves and everyone else? It won't hurt them to do that for a little while. Good heavens, I've been doing it for years.'

As she lay on the couch for her next treatment, Karen asked Judy if she would like her to pray for her.

What could she say?

'Thank you.'

This time, a more extended prayer included more detail about her husband, family, frustrations, and fears. Karen asked that Judy and her family be able to live life in the same way other families do.

As she lay listening to the prayer expressing gratitude for God's love, her husband, his commitment to his students and the excellent health of the wider family, she felt there was, indeed, much in her life to be thankful for. With a lighter step, she left the clinic in a more positive mindset.

*

At 4.30 the following morning, she awoke and was unable to return to sleep. Instead, she lay in bed reflecting on how, as a society, we had accepted the deadly virus and how easily it could spread between people. Most people followed the rules and were now living and working from home – many with their immediate families.

How quickly lives had changed. People were posting relatively mundane images – a sunrise, a pet, a child's cute dance, a joke. Some were saving money by not going anywhere, and others were spending up big online. Whichever way folk were responding and coping with these changes, in general, there was a camaraderie and strong community spirit not always evident until there is a crisis of some kind.

Suddenly it seemed like *everybody* was living within their own homes. They accepted it as a necessary precaution and even discovered that it was, in fact, tolerable.

*Everyone was like her. Or she was like everyone else.*

*Just what she had wanted for so long.*

Her scalp began to prickle.

Her heart began to flutter, and she felt breathless.

'Oh, no!' she said aloud, 'I know it can't be true, but what if …?'

Sweat began to trickle from her forehead.

'No.

'Stop it! That's crazy.'

*Well, my mother, the pastor, teachers, and my Nana always did say, 'Be careful what you pray for,' didn't they?*

Her breathing was difficult and shaky.

*'Your prayers will be answered but not always as you expected.*

She sat up in a panic.

'Oh, My God!'

'What?' groaned her husband as he turned over, dragging himself out of his sleep.

'What's wrong?'

'Oh, nothing, really. It's just that … I was thinking about how much I wanted to be like everyone else. To no longer be different. To live like everyone else. And now I do. And, well...' she blushed and shrugged her shoulders.

'Nah! It's ridiculous. Isn't it? I mean, worldwide, COVID-19 is a bit of overkill. I'm not that important, am I?'

She knew in her heart that any pastor would tell her that she is as important as anyone else in God's eyes. But, suddenly, she didn't want to even think about that. It was too much.

*But what if …?*

# A DAY OUT

## JUDY NEARY

I was entertaining my five granddaughters today. They love to play hide and seek when they visit, so I have decided to play today.

Their uncle Ken is counting, so we all hurry off to find the best hiding place.

I say, "come on, girls. We'll all go together".

"Yes" is the answer I receive from the youngest one.

We all head down the hallway looking for a spot to hide, opening doors as we go. Scurrying along, we open a door that generally would lead to the laundry. As we all rush to get in, we are astonished to see a long passageway. The passageway is quite dark and seems to go forever. There are torch lights lit at intervals along the length of the passage. The soft carpet beneath our feet is a rich, vibrant red.

We creep stealthily along. At the end of the passageway, we could see a green coloured door. As we listen, we hear scuffling sounds on the other side of the door. When the noise fades away, slowly and with some trepidation, we open the door.

As we step through the opening, the children all shriek in unison as we stand spellbound by what we see. It takes our breath away.

We have stepped into a whole new world, a world of wonder and enchantment, with little puppies of all different sizes and colours everywhere. There are dalmatians with their spotted smooth coats, to tiny terriers with cute little faces.

The girls are all talking together in their excitement, wanting to hold the puppies. We look around and see that we are in something like a fairground. There are many rides and things to do. We spot the carousel and run toward it. The three youngest girls hop up onto beautiful wooden horses that go up and down on their poles. One chooses a black horse with a bright red saddle, another chooses a white horse with a blue saddle, while the third hops from one to the other, finding it hard to decide. She finally settles on a brown horse with a rich gold saddle. The rest of us sit in the sleigh, which seems more appropriate for someone of my age.

From the carousel, we head to the big tent, where we hear music and laughter. Three clowns are keeping the crowd amused with their antics. Riding tricycles and honking horns.

Next into the ring come five beautiful white horses with dancing girls on their backs. They are the most beautiful things to see as they twirl atop the horses and put on a fantastic display. The girls and I are all clapping wildly. Their faces lit up with bright smiles.

We move on the pony rides. The two youngest of the girls are eager to test themselves. The youngest is really into ponies at this time. She straddles a pretty little pony with golden hair and a dark tail and mane. Her beaming smile is delightful as she walks the pony around the enclosure. Next, she is in a trot, her little body bobbing up and down in rhythm with the horse. Someone snaps a photo of her atop the pony and hands it to me. I slip the picture into my jacket pocket, thanking them as we leave.

We spot a young girl twirling cotton candy, or as we know it, fairy floss onto sticks, and we head across to her. We all get canes full of the fluffy pink treat. The girls try to eat it straight from the shaft and finish with sticky pink sweet stuck around their lips and faces. I decide to dive in as well and find myself in a very sticky situation.

The girls are all rolling around in gleeful laughter.

"Nanna, you look so funny", one states uncontrollably, giggling. Finally, we all wash faces and hands before resuming our adventure.

We head to the chairlift. Seated in two's, we glide across the fairground. From our vantage point above the fairground, we can see everything. The tent looks huge from up here, and as we sail across the carousel with the swirling patterned roof, we can hear the music playing. Everything seems so colourful from up here.

"We should head home, girls," I say sadly. "Uncle Ken has been looking for us quite a long time".

"Do we have to?" comes the muted response.

As we head toward the green door, we stop once again at the pups. The girls all have one last cuddle of the cute puppies as they lick and yap around them.

We reach the door and slowly pass through, once again into the long passageway. It stretches pretty far. The girls are excited to be back as we have all had a wonderful day.

We finally reach the end of the passageway and open the door. I find myself stretching and yawning as I come out of my sleep. Has this all been a dream? I have been looking forward to this day for such a long time, being out of isolation.

We are now able to see all our granddaughters again. Have all our adventures just been a dream? I shower and begin getting ready for the day. We are finally allowed to meet in groups of ten after being isolated from this COVID-19 virus for months. I'm ready and extremely excited.

I reach for my jacket and slip my arms into the sleeves. I hear something scrunch in the pocket, and reaching in, my hand touches something. I pull it out gently. It appears to be a photograph, it's a bit bent at the corners, but I turn it over and look at it. I see the smiling face of my youngest granddaughter sitting atop a pony. Her beaming face is alight with joy.

Can this be true? Was it a dream or real?

I look forward to catching up with them today and maybe having some more adventures.

# KLAAS, THE LOCAL HERO

## *BERNADETTE WEISS*

Following a sojourn of 13-years in Europe, we had decided to return to Australia, choosing to live in what we thought of as the sleepy country town of Cranbourne. That was thirty years ago. Our children have grown up, married, had children of their own, and reside in nearby suburbs. Two grandchildren attend the school across the road, as both their parents' work.

Our house is a second home to Madeline, now seven and four-year-old Lachlan. Their mother, Trixie, a teacher in Carrum Downs, drops them off at 8 am on school days. She collects the children after they have eaten their tea around 6 pm. Monica, aka Grandee, always walked Madeline to class, leaving me in charge of Lachie.

However, since the little bloke started prep this year, the role was passed to me. We have had a special bond over the last two years since Trixie has returned to work. There was simply no way Lachie would consider going go to school unless 'his' Poppy' walked him across the road and into his classroom. Monica is a meal on wheels volunteer on Mondays and Thursdays. So today, being a Thursday, I was on my own. I was finishing the daily crossword as the phone rang. The boy was unwell, 'could I please collect him?'

I was looking forward to a few hours alone with the lad and eagerly set off for the nurse's quarters. The nurse, Rosemary, a teachers' aide, commented she continued to be amazed how quickly a sick child miraculously recovered once a parent or carer arrived. Indeed, my grandson was no exception to this rule. Although he looked green around the gills, his feverish red eyes lighting up as he heard my deep accented voice. "Poppy, you came!"

Walking home with a spring in his step, he asked, Poppy, can we play Lego's?"

This statement implied it would be a constructive morning, with both of us working on the race cars we'd started to build the afternoon before. However, Lachie could not settle as he sat at the kitchen table.

"I want a drink!" he muttered.

"You can have a drink, Lachie,' I admonished him,' but remember your manners.".

"Please, may I have a drink, Poppy?"

I offered orange or apple juice, but he wanted cold water from the fridge, please.

Touching his brow momentarily while passing the water to him, I noted he was burning up and realised we were in for a spot of bother. The Lego held Lachie's attention for half an hour when his face reddened, and he began to squirm. Looking me in the eye; he bawled,

"I'm going to be sick!" and began puking. I'd managed to hold the Lego container before him, catching most of the vomit.

"Let's have a rest", I said, taking the crying youngster into my arms.

Within minutes his breathing calmed, turning into a steady snore. Placing beach towels over the recliner lounge, I laid the little chap down and popped a throw rug over him. After cleaning up the mess in the kitchen and generously spraying air freshener, I settled down to watch a replay of an old soccer match on the telly, having first switched the sound off. Almost two hours passed before my little mate showed signs of waking, so I turned my attention to him.

After a drink of water and a toilet stop, he came and sat beside me,

"Can we look at pictures in your family aldibum?"

He hasn't yet mastered the word 'album', but this was not the time to correct his pronunciation. Endearing as it is when he repeats the correct pronunciation while mimicking my deep voice and Dutch accent. He could not get over the fact I had ever been a little boy, and so paging through old albums was one way of proving it to him. He has developed quite a knack for picking me out in the dated snaps which record my youth. He used to point to the little blighter in the photos to ask, 'Is that ME Poppy?' It's a reasonable question. If it weren't for the outdated clothes, it could have been Lachie. He looks so much like me around his age.

However, today's album focussed on my teenage years, so I wasn't expecting him to recognise me. I had matured and was already shaving twice a week by my middle teens. I stood 1.86 cm tall and weighed 100 kilos. My physique served me well on the soccer pitch as the goalkeeper. We'd browsed several pages when Lach pointed to a newspaper clipping dated January 22, 1963, exclaiming, 'Poppy, that's YOU!'

It stunned me to look at the figure he was pointing at in the image of two teenagers. The article referred to an incident occurring the day before and made me something of a local hero.

"Who is the other boy?" As he tried to read the words under the caption.

"What do the words say, Poppy? I can't read them! Poppy, can you read them?"

There is something about little boys of four. They ask so many questions, one after the other, without waiting for answers. Fortunately, he is an attentive listener and sensed I would tell the story rather than read the text. So, as I leaned back in the recliner, I stepped back into my youth. The still queasy little chap crawled up onto my lap.

*

The caption under the photo in The Arnhemse Krant, a regional Dutch broadsheet, said 'Klaas and Jaap after their ordeal'. The article outlined how the 15-year-old hero saved Jaap from certain death during an impromptu ice-skating race on the frozen waters of the Rhine River. It happened the week after we had spent hours glued to the television at Jaap's house. His father was the director at Akzo, the paint manufacturing plant in the adjacent township of Velp. Ralph Van den Berg had purchased the tiny black and white television (the first telly in the whole neighbourhood) with his Christmas bonus.

The Van Den Berg family was held in high esteem for several reasons. As the man of the house, Ralph held an administrative position. He was not a tradie like most of our fathers who worked in the building industry. Heleen, his wife, wasn't a stay-at-home mother. She had trained as a typist and employed at one of the big four banks in Holland, the Rabobank. Their son, Jaap, like me, was a teenager who loved his sport. He had blond hair, was a head shorter and weighed about 15 kilos lighter than me. His lightweight frame was ideal for his work on the soccer pitch as a striker. Since his 12th-birthday, he'd received two annual club subscriptions to watch the local premiers' Vitesse Boys play football on Saturdays. We always attended these matches together thanks to his parents' generosity in ordering the double subscription.

Many people in the neighbourhood envied me. I was one of seven children in a poor working-class family. In fact, as Jaap's best friend, my social profile improved. As toddlers, we played together in the street. We started kindergarten together and had been in the same classes throughout our primary school years. As little tackers, we were not class conscious until we were twelve. We went to different senior schools. Jaap followed the

VWO (higher vocational system of 5-years to prepare for a professional or administrative career). I went to the MAVO (lower educational level for the 4-year preparation for vocational training towards apprenticeship selection). After school hours, we were inseparable, spending many hours at one or others' homes.

*

A cold snap late in November announced an early beginning of a severe winter. The temperatures dropped below zero for ten weeks between December 22 through to March 3 of 1963. As a result, the major waterways like the Rhine River had frozen over, stopping the cargo barges that typically transported produce from the food bowl regions to the towns and cities or taking manufactured goods inland to Germany and beyond.

We sat mesmerised throughout the day by the initial broadcast of the running of the Elfstedentocht. Historically, Friesland hosted similar marathon distance skating odysseys on the natural waterways of their province since 1760. The roughly 200-kilometre race in its present form was conceived in 1890 by the entrepreneur Pim Mulier (1865-1954). The inaugural race had taken place during the freezing temperatures of January 1909. The twenty-two competing men were skating from the Friesian capital of Leeuwarden around a circuitous route of eleven townships to have their race cards duly stamped.

*

The newspaper clipping referred to the 13th running of this race, attracting over 10,000 competitors and skating enthusiasts. Five years earlier, the 12th Elfstedentocht of February 1958 had taken place when we had been at primary school and so meant nothing to us. Now it was a historic occasion, and the first time the national event lasting 11-hours was televised.

While many inhabitants of the Netherlands caught snippets of the race on the radio or storefront television sets, Jaap and I lounged on the carpet in front of the telly in his home. As the race unfolded, the weather conditions deteriorated, causing many riders to pull out well before the finish line. The archives show only 72-competitors and 57-enthusiasts completed the race. In the afterglow of watching the courageous skaters on telly, we decided to test our skating skills on the natural ice blocking the Rhine between Wageningen and Zevenaar.

The euphoria of skating on natural ice attracted many skating enthusiasts from all over Arnhem. Thus, we were but two of many thousands. Most skaters did laps around circuits.

We sought a more significant challenge, setting out for Westervoort some 8-kilometres downstream. We skated smoothly, keeping within meters of the Rijnkade levy bank, pretending to be competitors in the Elfstedentocht. After about four kilometres, one of the straps on Jaap's skates snapped, causing him to lose his balance, pitch forward and go into a 10-meter slide bringing him onto the thinner ice towards the middle of the river. Coming to a halt, he noticed the black ice beneath him. As our eyes locked, he screamed, 'thin ice!'

"Stay down! Spread your arms and legs out! I'm coming! Hang on!"

Time stood still. With adrenalin surging through my body, fears for Jaap's safety spurned me on. Thoughts of my mate slipping through the thin ice and Jaap possibly dying from hypothermia clutched at my racing heart. Skating 50-meters upstream, the only audible sound was my skates slicing into the solidified waters of the Rhine. Nearing the bend in the river, I spun around and raced back, gaining speed with every stride bringing me closer to my buddy. I could hear him screaming with rage. Jaap never swore. Now he was venting his spleen, screaming a litany of abuse concerning my heritage! I slid into a gaol-keepers side-on lunge skimming over the ice straight into him five meters from Jaap. Thwack! We desperately clung together as we slithered across the ice, hitting the left levy bank. Safe at last! Clawing our way up the levy, we assessed the damage. I had a split lip where his remaining skate had cut into me while Jaap's eyes were thickening, hinting at the two black eyes that would disfigure him for two weeks.

"God, you should have seen your face when we collided!"

"When you sped off, I thought you'd pissed off leaving me to my fate. As you sped back,

I realised you were going to tackle me head-on. You could have killed me, you big bastard!" Instead, we burst into uncontrollable laughter, slapping each other on the back.

A passing motorist in a blue and cream BMW Isetta 300 noticed our predicament while picking his way along the slippery bitumen track on the embankment. Stopping, he jumped out to help us and offered to drive us home. Jaap's bruised and bulging eyes met mine. A ride in the latest model of a BMW was a fantastic offer, and we gladly accepted! Mind you, three blokes in a two-seater made for a cramped ride.

As we arrived at my place, Ma flew out the front door. She took one look at Jaap's eyes and lashed out, giving me a clip over the earhole.

"Klaas, what have you done? What will Jaap's mother think? Why did you fight?

The man driving the BMW was astounded and looked from Ma to us before the three of us began laughing. Between gasps, Mr Janssen explained,

"The boys were not fighting! Your lad is a hero! He saved his friends' life!'

As the story spread through the neighbourhood, a photographer and newspaper reporter called around to interview us. The story made the front page, hence the clipping in the photo album.

*

As my thoughts returned to the present, I noticed Lachlan had dozed off. It was 2 o'clock, and Monica wasn't due home for another hour. So, I closed my eyes, wondering what had happened to Jaap. He'd started his two-year national service training as; I'd migrated to Australia in 1969. Was he a fulfilled man and a happy grandfather too? As I nodded off, thoughts of my childhood chum and the good old days in Holland came to mind.

# SECRET HELPERS

## *TIFFANY LEONG*

Madeline scrolls through her Inbox, monotonously jabbing the Delete button on her keyboard. The messages are more or less the same these days. The subject line in bolded capitals with FINAL DAYS or SALE or SPECIAL or DISCOUNTED combines into one category: marketing pitches.

There seems to be a more significant influx of such emails since the Australian Government introduced restrictions to control the coronavirus spread. Perhaps that's why Madeline's desensitised to headlines; they're all somehow linked back to COVID-19, and it's almost a given that the email will have a line acknowledging its impact in some way. The words may be written differently but conveying the general message that 'we're all in this together and doing our best. Online purchases supposedly allow customers to purchase their essentials with minimal disruptions while also boosting the economy.

As Madeline sifts through her Inbox blearily with a mug of black coffee in her free hand, another heading with flashing emojis catches her eye:

©IMPORTANT MESSAGE FOR OUR HEALTH ©. It's from her gym. Curious, Madeline clicks to open the first email she'll read for the day.

*Hey Flexers!!*

*Sorry for the cap locks in the subject line. I personally feel that this is an URGENT email. It's tough times while we adjust to the Government's restrictions on training to be one on one outdoors, so I am offering FREE sessions to any client impacted financially by the current pandemic. We know the importance of exercise and healthy eating for our physical and mental wellbeing, which is why I think personal training is ESSENTIAL, but you know, I'm just another guy, not a politician.*

*So if you you want a virtual session at Alexandra Park next to our gym, we at FlexiBElity are here for you.*

*Feel free to hit Scotty or me up and we look forward to seeing you guys soon. Keep in touch and stay SAFE and HEALTHY!*

*Aaron*

*FlexiBElity Club Manager*

Aaron's words warm Madeline more than the mug which her frozen fingers curl around. Aaron instils the importance of health, which can easily be overlooked and not taken seriously until symptoms or consequences appear.

Realising the enormity of Aaron's generosity, guilt chases away Madeline's fleeting appreciation. She suspended her membership two weeks ago during the outbreak of the virus. Aaron's offer is selfless, and FlexiBElity is his own business; surely, like other small businesses, he may experience some financial strain too.

Quickly strumming her fingers out of their numb state, Madeline prepares a reply. Aaron had blind copied to other members' emails, so she knows that they won't see it.

*Hi Aaron,*

*What a lovely message to read!! Your kind gesture is such a communal action, and I'm sure other Flexers, like me, are touched! I wish to contribute and spread the goodwill you've inspired from me. As I continue working from home, I hope to restart my regular membership payments for other members to use if they can't pay. That way, you'll also still get some income too. Win-win situation, I think!*

> *Hope you're safe and healthy too,*
> *Maddy*

Madeline switches to her work emails with a smile, readying herself for more numbers than words in her role as an accountant.

She checks her emails at a mid-morning break, skimming Aaron's reply. Madeline's heart beats thud loudly in her ears. So he's rejected her offer. She had never anticipated that he'd say *no*.

After a couple of deep breaths and bracing for the finality of his answer, she phones Aaron. Her trainer picks up on the fourth ring. "Maddy, how are you?"

"I'm good, thanks, how are you?" she responds automatically as per usual greetings despite the fact that she's actually experiencing the opposite.

"Well. Keeping busy as I'm sure we all are. Is everything okay?" His warm voice is encouraging, a quality that makes her feel at ease during their personal training sessions.

"Yes!" she affirms. "Thank you for sending that email this morning, it really lifted my spirits, and I'm sure it did for the rest of the team too."

"Oh, no problem, Maddy," Aaron chuckles. "It's the least I can do. All of you have supported my dream of opening a gym. Thanks also to you for your kind offer! I just can't accept, sorry...."

Madeline inhales. "Really? You're sure it's not because of the paperwork?"

That elicits another chuckle. "I really want to support you and the other members too. With other organisations, they offer donations or online purchases for use at another date, there's not much I can do at the moment for FlexiBElity but continue payment, and if the payment is going to good use, I would be so touched. Honestly."

A pause. "Alright, Maddy, you raise a fair point. I'll see what I can do. Thank you."

Madeline feels her lips stretch out into a grin. "No worries."

"I'll reach out later once I work out the logistics... you want to keep the usual payment and commence direct debit if I find others who are keen on your offer?"

"Yes."

"Sounds good, okay, I'll contact you later. Take care, Maddy."

"Thanks, Aaron, you too."

Madeline continues her day, her accounting numbers surprisingly all reconciling in the first attempt, and in her work video call, she receives several private messages commenting that she's radiating happiness. Madeline's cheeks flush at the messages, knowing she's on webcam, hoping that no one notices. Thankfully, no one probes her on her apparent joy; Madeline wants to share the news about her chat with Aaron but worries she'll come across as boasting about her deeds as a good Samaritan, going against her selfless principles. Nonetheless, she thanks them for their compliments and finds other truthful ones to send back. Madeline suppresses a smirk when she sees others blush on the receiving end of her remarks.

When she's ready to log off, she sees another email from Aaron.

*Hey Maddy,*

*Thanks again for your generosity – I've managed to find some interested people. This will start again next week, so your direct debit*

*for 3x sessions a week will commence next Wednesday. Will keep you*
*posted on how we go!*
    Aaron

As she lives alone, Madeline lets out a loud whoop, and even fist bumps the air. It's only now, when she feels the tension leave her shoulders, that Madeline realises how much she'd hoped her offer would be accepted. Because like Aaron, she wants to give back to the community that has supported her – strangers she crosses paths within the change room who compliment her physique or her training efforts; FlexiBElity's social media posts that feature her and how they attract motivation quips amongst the 'like/love' reactions. If money helps in continuing such bonds in her gym community, why not? Besides it's better than spending money on food and bills and Madeline isn't spending her income on anything else.

The irony doesn't escape her as she settles in front of her Smart TV for exercise workouts. She's saved money from not using a personal trainer and driving to work, which gains time for fitness in her usual commute time. Madeline browses the suggested workout videos on YouTube, reading each title and taking note of the video length. It's about ten minutes later that Madeline chooses an exercise she knows will make Aaron and FlexiBElity proud.

*

Weeks' pass, and the days blur into one another, yet the date in the calendar indicates that time continues on. Madeline is constantly busy with numbers on workdays, and she finds herself on phone calls more frequently with family and friends. Sure, she misses interactions in person, the simple gestures such as hugs that she took for granted, but she knows she's giving it up for something much more important – the health of her nation.

Madeline sees an email from Aaron; she hasn't heard from him since the phone call, but her bank statement shows that he has recommenced her direct debits. She trusts him, so it would have felt intrusive to ask: *how's my money being used?*

Smiling, she opens his email.

*Hey Flexers!*

*What a whirlwind couple of weeks, hey?! Trust you're all well and great to hear from so many of you. Thank you for all the different types of kindnesses you've shown. For a bit of team building and checking how we're all holding up, how are you all placed this Friday at 7pm for a Zoom social event? Drinks optional!!*

*Stay safe and healthy!*

*Aaron*

*FlexiBElity Club Manager*

Since Madeline is essentially free every non-working hour of the day, she responds with an immediate, "I'm free!"

*

Friday evening arrives quickly, and Madeline flutters around her kitchen. Should she have a drink ready for the call? Cocktail or wine? Perhaps something non-alcoholic? After all, she's meeting with people who recommend alcohol in small doses. Should she bring a snack instead? If the meeting is long, Madeline knows she'll get peckish, and won't it be rude if she excuses herself to grab a bite?

Madeline decides on soda water with a dash of raspberry syrup. The cool drink will pass off as either alcoholic or non-alcoholic, and it's easier to sip through a straw so her lipstick won't smudge. With a final last check in her mirror, Madeline settles in front of her computer with her soda.

After signing into Zoom, she's greeted with a message that the host will let her in shortly. Madeline wonders who, and how many will be present. Although it's a local gym, she hasn't met everyone due to their different scheduled times, especially as most of them only have one on one training with the personal trainers.

At exactly 7.01pm, the screen signals her admission. After the tiny square pixels sharpen, all attendees simultaneously scream: "Thanks, Madeline!!"

Shocked and confused, Madeline is vaguely aware that she's probably gaping back.

"Hey, Maddy," Aaron says from the square in the middle. "These are the people you've helped in your generosity of donating your payments."

"With your help too, Aaron!" chimes a person from another square, and the group laugh.

Realising she's been silent too long, Madeline manages an "Oh wow…!"

"So," Aaron continues, always a leader and taking charge. "You can see there are seven members here. I don't think any of you have met one another, but you can see each other's names. With your usual schedule, Maddy, we've managed to rotate all these people to fit in a regular workout routine."

"We are so grateful," a lady named Sherry pipes. "With my kids studying from home, expenses skyrocketed and having a PT session forces me to exercise… running after the kids don't count *or* help!"

"You're welcome," Madeline murmurs dazedly.

"It was Sherry's idea to come up with this Zoom meeting," Aaron adds. "We had to make sure you're free as we ALL wanted to say thank you."

The members echo in agreement. Madeline takes a long sip of her soda, casting her eyes downwards. She's always had trouble being the centre of attention and seeing the care shine back in these strangers' eyes will set off the tears quickly welling behind her eyelids.

"Once everything goes back to normal, we'll organise another way to say thank you," declares a teenager named Ian. "This is just an interlude!"

"Yes!" the others nod.

Madeline laughs shakily, blinking back the tears threatening to spill. In the last couple of months, she's only just recognised the many different ways to show appreciation. "Once these restrictions are over, I look forward to meeting you all at the gym."

There's a chorus of agreements.

"Now that we've thanked Maddy," Aaron prattles on. "Why don't we all do a meet and greet kind of thing, because even though we're all connected by Maddy, we're all essentially strangers. Though I know every single one of you here, you just don't know anything about each other!"

There's another round of nods and yesses.

"Well, we'll start with the person responsible for why we're all here – Maddy!!"

Although they are all in their respective homes, there's applause as if Madeline is called on stage. For a second, all Madeline can do is stare in awe as Aaron's words sink in – she has unknowingly united this newfound group.

Another second later, Madeline realises they are waiting for her once again.

She sips her fizzy drink and clears her throat. She's ready to immerse herself in the ripple effects of one goodwill to another.

# I BELIEVE

## *HANNAH SMITH*

Charlotte thought she was a young girl like any other, except that she wasn't really like you and me at all. All this happened once before, and it will no doubt happen once again. All you have to do is close your eyes tightly, make a wish and believe dreams really do come true.

It was a warm summer's night, and Charlotte and her mother were singing and dancing around the kitchen while her mother cooked dinner. Then, Charlotte heard a loud clap of thunder and let out a scream.

Her mother, laughing kindly, pulled her in for a warm hug. "This is where the magic happens, Charlotte! Come on! Come and see!" she said in a sing-song voice, pulling her outside.

Charlotte felt the refreshing sprinkling of summer rainfall across her face as her mother took her by the hand, twirling her around and singing, "*The fairy sings, a bell rings, a new baby is born. The feast begins, and the celebration brings on the new dawn*".

A bright rainbow appeared in the sky above them, and her mother laughed. She bent down, holding Charlotte's hands, and looked at her with such love. "The fairies are here, Charlie! Whenever it rains, go outside, and see if you can find a rainbow. If you can see a rainbow, it means the fairies are celebrating that a new fairy is born! If you find the rainbow, you can find the fairies! Search high, search low, close your eyes and find the glow".

Charlotte giggled, "But Mummy, I have never seen a fairy! Never, ever, ever! I wish I had seen a fairy. I want to see a fairy! But, Mummy, have you seen one?"

"Oh, my sweet girl, one day, you will see. You have to believe, and they will come. So make a wish, close your eyes and believe my baby!" Her mother continued singing as they danced in the rain and jumped in puddles together.

Charlotte's father was standing on the front porch shaking his head at them, "You girls are going to catch a cold!"

Charlotte and her mother didn't care; they were having too much fun to worry about silly things like getting sick.

But Charlotte's mother did get sick, and it was much worse than a cold. Her father reassured her it had nothing to do with them dancing in the rain, that those were the times her mother had been the happiest. Her father also told her that her mother was extremely sick and that one day when she went to sleep, she might not wake up, but she would go and stay with the fairies.

Charlotte remembered coming home from school one afternoon, and her mother was in bed asleep again. She looked so little in the big bed, and her father looked like he had been crying. He came out to Charlotte and told her, "It's almost time, Charlotte. Mum is going to go to sleep and be with the fairies soon." None of it made any sense to Charlotte at the time, but she knew she would not be able to see her mother again, and that made her incredibly sad.

A year after her mother had gone, her father decided they needed to move to a new home.

"Come on, Charlotte. Grab your bag. We have to get on the road," her father called from the front door.

Charlotte didn't want to leave her friends, her school or the house she loved, but her father insisted, "It will do you good Charlotte. And me. It is a new start, and I am sure you will make new friends. There are too many memories in this house". She cried as she packed her most special toys in her backpack, making sure none were left behind. Then, as she climbed into the car with her father, Charlotte looked sadly back at the house where she grew up, the place where she lived with her mother.

It felt like they had been driving for hours before the car turned down a long dirt track. Charlotte looked around and saw nothing but long-dead grass, overgrown trees, dirt, and dust.

As they reached the end of the dirt track, her father said, "Here we are, Charlotte, our new home".

Charlotte thought "new" was a stretch. The house looked big, that was for sure, but the paint was peeling from the front, the window shutters were falling off, and the vast garden was overgrown, covered in tall, long grass and thick bushy trees. Charlotte shuddered at the thought of what creatures might be living in there. She pulled her backpack from the car and followed her father to the front door. He took the big ornate key out of his pocket, unlocked the wooden door, and swung it open. If she could get past the dirt, dust and cobwebs, Charlotte could imagine what the old house must have looked like once upon a time. She looked around the giant entryway and climbed the grand old staircase in search of her new room.

Her father called out to her from the end of the hallway, "Here you go, sweetheart. This is the room I thought you would like". He stepped aside to let Charlotte walk into the room.

Charlotte gasped, "Whoa!" as she turned and looked around. A beautiful light purple covered the walls. Painted pictures of fairies and colourful mushrooms decorated the space next to the big bright window.

"Your mother would have loved this room," her father said quietly. "I hope you can love it too". Charlotte felt tears well up in her eyes as she reached over and hugged her father tightly around his waist. "It will be okay Charlotte, we still have each other, and I love you very much," he said, trying his best to force a smile.

Over the next few days, Charlotte and her father unpacked their belongings and set up their new house. As much as her father tried, it just didn't feel like home to Charlotte. She spent much of her time in her bedroom reading the books her mother had given her. Closing her eyes, she let memories of her mum flood her mind. She missed her so much. She missed dancing around the kitchen, looking for rainbows, jumping in puddles and looking for fairies.

Her father spent most of his time locked in the study writing his book in their new house. Charlotte knew writing made him happy, but she felt so lonely. They sat at the big wooden dining table in silence at night as they pushed their food around their plates. Her father wasn't much of a cook, but he was trying hard.

One night he said to her, "Charlotte, you should go outside and explore the garden before you start school. See what you can find! Your mother wouldn't want you to stop believing, Charlotte, she would want you to find some magic. I could come with you. We could look together". But every time, it rained, and Charlotte just wanted to stay inside.

Sitting in her room one morning, Charlotte thought how much her mother really would have loved this room, and as she looked up from her book, she noticed light raindrops falling on the window. She climbed down from her bed and walked towards the window.

A gold flash flew past her. "I must be imagining things," thought Charlotte. And then she saw it again, but it was gone again in a flash. "I wonder…" she thought.

Charlotte pulled open her wardrobe and found her favourite purple raincoat, with fairies on it, of course, and pulled on her gumboots. Then, running downstairs, she found her father sitting on the kitchen bench.

"Daddy, is it okay if I go outside? I just want to go for a walk in the garden. I promise not to go too far".

Her father sat up, placing his cup of tea on the bench. "Of course, darling," he answered. "Would you like me to come with you?"

"Thanks, daddy, but I will be okay. I think I will just go for a walk on my own".

"Okay, sweetheart, I hope you find something special," her father replied.

"Magical," Charlotte muttered under her breath as she stepped out the back door.

Charlotte walked unhurriedly down the garden path as the light sprinkling of summer rain continued, and as she looked around, she noticed a vibrant rainbow in the sky. It seemed to end right at the end of their very own garden. Charlotte felt something move close to her face and heard the quiet, gentle ringing of a bell. Her eyes followed the sound, but as she looked around, all she could see was the thick bushy trees and tall overgrown grass across the garden.

"That is strange," she thought. But then an old wishing well at the back of the garden caught her eye, and as she walked towards the wishing well, she again heard the quiet tinkling of a bell. Placing her hands on the edge of the well, she closed her eyes and made a wish. "I do believe in fairies; I do believe in fairies. Wish I might wish I may, please let me see a fairy today".

The bell chimed again but louder this time. Charlotte lifted her hands and noticed a light gold sprinkling of what looked like sparkling gold dust on the palms of her hands. It tingled and quickly disappeared. The ringing of the bell became louder and louder. It seemed to be coming from behind the thick trees, just where the rainbow seemed to end. Charlotte needed to know where the sound came from so, she walked to the dense clump of trees, desperately searching for a way through. She eventually found a small space between the trees, just big enough for her to get down on her hands and knees and crawl all the way through. Pushing the branches and leaves out of her way and pulling the cobwebs from her face, Charlotte finally stood up on the other side of the trees. As she brushed the dirt from her hands, she looked up and let out an excited cry.

Charlotte had entered a beautiful wonderland and could hardly believe her eyes. The grass was a perfect green, and a stream ran beneath a beautiful waterfall. Giant red and white toadstools scattered along the water's edge, with colourful flowers growing in between them. Frogs were hopping across the lily pads in the stream, croaking loudly. Charlotte rubbed her eyes,

"Wake up, Charlotte," she said. "This must be a dream."

As she opened her eyes, she heard the bell again, and a light on the toadstool caught her eye. Walking towards the toadstool, Charlotte saw a trail of gold glitter dust appear in the air as the bell sounded again and sitting on top of the toadstool, she saw it. It was a real-life fairy!! It was the size of a large butterfly and had long silver hair and large bright purple wings that were gently fluttering. The little fairy was wearing a sparkling purple dress with little silver shoes on its tiny feet.

"Well, hello there. I am Charlotte. What's your name?" she stuttered. The little fairy rose in the air, leaving a trail of gold sparkle dust behind her, the bell sounding louder than ever. "Are you really a fairy?"

The little fairy nodded her head smiling. "Am I dreaming?" The fairy seemed to laugh at her, bending over and holding her stomach.

"Please, may I call you Violet?" Charlotte asked the little fairy. "It was my mother's name, and it matches your dress". The little fairy nodded. "Are there others, or are you the only one?" Violet shook her head again before she sped off.

"Wait! Not so fast!" Charlotte called, sprinting to follow the gold sparkle trail in the air that Violet left behind. She ran along the side of the stream, ducking between the big bright purple and orange flowers. The fairy led her to the waterfall at the top of the stream. The water from the stream sent a fine mist into the air.

"The summer rain!" Charlotte exclaimed, stopping in her tracks. She could hardly believe her eyes or her ears! There were hundreds of fairies, all with their colourful dresses and beautiful vibrant wings, flying around the waterfall. The ringing of bells was quite loud now, and Charlotte could hear it. The little boy fairies in their pom-pom hats were flying in leaf carriages pulled by small birds amid the waterfall. Other fairies were dancing on the side of the stream. Finally, a parade of fairies was sailing on lily pad boats, floating down the cool, clear water.

Violet was fluttering just above Charlotte's shoulder, clapping her hands and pointing to the most miniature lily pad at the front of the parade. Charlotte bent down and rested on her knees by the waterfall, her hands in her lap. The little fairy landed on her shoulder, gently tickling her neck with her beautiful wings. Charlotte looked closely at the lily pad and saw a tiny fairy with long silver hair, dressed in a white dress, lying in a flower bud. This little fairy was about half the size of Violet.

"Is that… is that a baby?" Charlotte asked.

Violet fluttered her wings, floating in the air in front of Charlotte's face. She placed her hand softly on Charlotte's cheek and nodded.

"Mother was right. The fairies are celebrating that a baby has been born! I do believe, I do believe in fairies!" Charlotte cried. She had not felt this happy for the longest time.

Charlotte spent the day in the fairy wonderland, dancing and twirling between the flowers, climbing on the toadstools, and sitting quietly with Violet watching the fairy parade. Violet showed her the tiny fairy houses scattered along the edge of the stream and sitting on the trunks of the big old trees. The fairy houses had little mini toadstool tops and carved wooden doors, and Charlotte thought they were just perfect.

Violet led Charlotte to a vast old tree that sat in the middle of the beautiful green grass. From its branches flowed the gold sparkle dust that followed the fairies wherever they flew. The sparkle collected onto the leaves resting on the ground glittering brightly. Violet placed her hand in the stream and sprinkled the gold dust over her head.

"Does this help you fly?" Charlotte asked.

Violet nodded, flying high up in the sky and twirling around. "Will it make me fly?" Violet shrugged her tiny shoulders.

"Can we try?" asked Charlotte. Violet nodded, gathering some gold glitter dust in her hand and sprinkling it over Charlotte's head. Charlotte laughed in delight as she felt a warmth spread over her body.

Closing her eyes, Charlotte whispered, "Please, please, please let me fly!" but as she slowly opened her eyes, she saw that she was still standing on the ground. "Hmmm…I guess children can't fly!" she said, laughing.

Violet sprinkled some more gold glitter on Charlotte's head. Suddenly, Charlotte's feet lifted from the ground, and she felt herself floating up into the air. Violent was clapping wildly.

"I am flying, Violet. I am really flying!" she cried. Charlotte and Violet spent the next hour flying through the air and around the old tree together. Oh, how her mother would have loved to be here, to see the fairy wonderland and to fly with Violet.

When the magic glitter dust wore off, Charlotte and Violet floated downwards to rest on the ground. Charlotte sat, yawning, when they returned to the stream, while Violet rested on her lap. She thought what an adventure it had been as she lay back on the grass, taking in another big yawn. Charlotte felt Violet's hand on her cheek again as her eyes slowly closed.

"Charlotte? Charlotte, where are you? Charlotte!" she could faintly hear her father's voice in the background.

"Oh, my goodness, Charlotte! There you are!" Charlotte slowly opened her eyes and saw her father rushing towards her. She looked around, feeling confused. Charlotte was lying on a patch of grass in front of the old wishing well. As she looked around, she could no longer see the stream, the giant toadstools, or the colourful flowers.

"Violet?" she called. "Violet, where are you?"

"Who are you talking to, sweetheart? I have been worried about you. You have been out for hours!" her father said, hugging her tightly.

"Oh, daddy, I have had the most wonderful day! I love our new home. I love living here. Please promise me we will never ever leave!"

Her father laughed at her. "I am glad to hear that, Charlie. Tell me all about it," he said as they started walking back to the old house.

"I saw them, daddy. Mummy was right! I saw real fairies," she said excitedly.

"Oh, Charlie, it sounds like you had a wonderful dream".

"It wasn't a dream, daddy. Violet gave me some magic dust, and I flew! All the way up into the air!" she said, twirling around with her hands in the air.

Her father laughed, opening the backdoor. "Well, I am glad to have you back inside, I was worried that you had run away," her father said, giving her a gentle kiss on the top of her head. "You better go and get changed, Charlotte. You are filthy, and it is time for dinner".

Charlotte ran up the creaky old stairs into her bedroom, still barely able to contain her excitement. As she opened her bedroom door, she looked at the beautifully painted wall and could hardly believe it. Right next to her bed, there was a perfect painting of Violet with her long silver hair and her purple dress, smiling back at her. A trail of gold glitter dust was trailing behind her, forming a love heart shape. Charlotte smiled to herself and knew her mother was watching over her constantly. It had been the best day ever.

# DREAMS GALORE

## *GRACE DE VISSER*

Dreams, dreams, dreams galore,
We all have them by the score.
To help make them come true,
Is something we all must try to do.

Some are big, some are small,
Make them come true one and all.
Sometimes it's very hard to do,
Mine might seem so strange to you.

We all have different dreams to dream,
Some are also the same it seems.
To achieve them we can but strive,
Really try to make them come alive.

When our dreams finally arrive,
It is then we really feel alive.
We shine with our heart aglow,
Forever forward we must go.

Dreams are what help us thrive,
As we go about our waking lives.
Then on to the next dream so it seems,
There is always time for one more dream.

# DRAGONFLIES

## *GRACE DE VISSER*

Dragonflies make my heart sing,
Their darting bodies and silver wings.
Darting here, there and everywhere,
Sometimes they just stop and stare.

They spread their wings so unaware,
That danger could be in the air.
Not stopping for long, off they go.
Off to where I do not know.

On glass like wings, they do glide,
Throughout the lands so wide.
Many colours I have seen,
Blue, red, yellow, and green.

Swarming in their thousands,
Breathtaking flying over the lands.
Freely flying grand and elegant,
Surrounding huge herds of elephant.

At first, I could not believe my eyes,
Were they really dragonflies?
They came so close to my touch,
The sight of them was almost too much.

Dragonflies make my heart sing,
Their long bodies and glittery wings.
Darting here, darting there,
Sometimes I love to stop and stare.

# BUTTERFLIES

## *GRACE DE VISSER*

Butterflies are very symbolic,
They can represent so much.
A beautiful wondrous sight to see,
Their bodies not meant to be touched.

Their wings are fragile, yet so strong,
With gentle movement, they traverse so far.
Together in a group we like to belong,
As Individuals we too can shine like a star.

They have no song or sound,
Not like us we have a choice.
So many opportunities abound,
For goodness sake to use our voice.

Some tell them dreams they cannot share,
I like to watch them in flight.
Some just chase them everywhere,
I like to see them landing so light.
A glorious dance in flight,
Many brightly hues to see.
It always fills me with delight,
Always makes a smile on me.

The sight of them lifts my soul,
They make my heart fill with delight.
A feeling that never grows old,
Lifting and soaring like a kite.

Butterflies have a very short life,
They live it to their best.
We have one life to live,
So, we should give no less.

We should be like butterflies,
Carefree, young, and free.
Young at heart with love in our lives,
I love butterflies and being me.

# STORIES

# WRITTEN

# DURING

# LOCKDOWN

# WORTHLESS

## *DIANE BROWN*

The scorching January sun beat down on my head, and the soles of my feet burnt on the hot pavement. I just wished I had my sneakers, but someone stole them, and there was nothing I could do about it.

I was homeless once again, and I didn't know where to go. One of the other times he threw me out, I spent two nights in the schoolyard. It was easy to hide in the playground during the night, there was a spot I could crawl into just behind the bins, and sometimes there were flattened cardboard boxes that I could cover myself with to keep me warm. The drink bubblers were outside so I could get plenty of water and even have a wash, and if I were lucky, I might find scraps of food from the left-over lunches before the bins get emptied. But no, it was now school holidays, so it was pointless looking for food in an empty playground.

He's done it again, that drunken lout my mother married after my dad died. He pretended to be a nice man before she married him, but he didn't fool me. I never trusted him from the first time I met him. Mum used to be such a happy person, but now she never smiles, and she walks around like a zombie. Some days she doesn't even brush her hair or put any lipstick on, and she always looks so sad.

I hated him. He always picks on me when he's drunk, which is every night and most of the weekend. He'd come in after the pub closed, yelling at Mum to get his dinner. She had kept it warming on a saucepan all night, and when she put it on the table, he took one sniff, picked it up and threw it at the wall.

"Why can't you cook something decent, you lazy bitch?" he bellowed at Mum as he staggered off his chair, his fist clenched in a tight ball.

Mum cowered in the corner, knowing what was coming. I spotted my little sister half asleep, standing in the doorway, her face as white as a sheet, her eyes wide open with fear. That's when I snapped. Diving on his back, I yelled, "Leave Mum alone." I punched into his back and head as hard as I could. "Don't you dare touch her!"

He bent forward, throwing me over his shoulders. As I hit the floor, I felt his boot connect with my ribcage. I can still see his yellow teeth, his sneer and hear his mean voice. Dragging me from the floor, he twisted my arm way up my back as he threw me out the front door, yelling after me that I'm nothing but a worthless piece of shit.

*I know you were frightened, Mum, but why didn't you stop him. I'm only 14, where do you expect me to go?*

The last time he threw me out, I stayed away for three days, but then I had to go home, to cry and beg him to let me come back. I knew I'd cop a beating, and I did, but I had no choice. There was nowhere else for me to go. That was the time he gave me a black eye. My teacher was a bit suspicious, calling me into the Headmistress' office, asking what had happened. Still, luckily, they believed my story about being hit in the eye with a ball while playing cricket in our backyard. What a laugh. Who would want to play in our backyard, uncut grass up to your waist and old car parts and junk all over the place? I don't know if the teacher rang Mum, but he stopped hitting me in the face and head after the black eye. But gee, he certainly made up for it around my back and stomach. He could knock the air out of my lungs with one hard punch, and then he'd laugh when I lay panting on the floor. He never used my name. The only way he referred to me was "Worthless." "Hey, Worthless, do this. Hey Worthless, do that."

*Mum, am I really worthless?*

The hot sun burns into my skin, and my feet still hurt, so I head down to the beach. It's only a short walk, and there's always a crowd at this time of the year. I spot some left-over pizza in a box that's poking out of a bin. God, I'm so hungry. I wander along the grass as it's cooler under my feet, bending down to pick up a stray ice cream wrapper. It's sticky, and there are a couple of black ants crawling over it. Searching the many faces to see if someone is watching, I pop the wrapper into the bin, then quickly grab the pizza slices from the open box. Great, there are two slices—food at last. Cramming one into my mouth, I greedily take huge mouthfuls. It has gone a bit hard and dry, but I don't care.

At last, something to eat. If only I could find something to wash it down, I would be fine. But, looking around, I cannot see a tap anywhere, so I'll have to stay thirsty for a while.

As I hobble across the hot sand, my feet feel so painful. I'm not used to walking around barefoot, and as I reach the water's edge, I stand there. Motionless, not moving at all, just enjoying the white foam from the waves dancing over my hot, sore feet and circling my tired legs.

*I guess I'll be safe on the beach tonight. My sneakers are gone, so there's nothing else to steal.*

*I am so thirsty—God, what I wouldn't give for a cold drink.* Shaking the wet sand from my feet, I head away from the beach. I must find something to drink. As I shield my eyes from the glare, I spot an outdoor shower at the top of the sandy, concrete steps.

Great, hopefully, I can get a drink of water there. Standing behind a row of kids while I wait my turn, I listen to their chatter. Wow, they all seem so happy and carefree. Finally, at last, it's my turn. No one seems to notice as I stand under the shower wearing all my clothes, turning my head upwards as I take huge gulps of water. That feels so much better, and my wet clothes cool my skin.

Returning to the grass, I plop down on the cushion of green softness. Tiredness surrounds me as I look up at the sky, watching the brilliant blue turn pink as white seagulls float on the breeze. The fear of last night comes back to haunt me. It feels as if a hand is clutching my belly. After he kicked me out of the house, I felt so alone, and I didn't know where to go, so I'd curled up in the corner of a bus shelter, hoping to get some sleep. And then they arrived, four of them, all laughing and smelling of grog. Once they spotted me, I was fair game. They circled me, wanting to know my name. When I told them my name was "Worthless", they laughed.

"Well, Worthless. Boys like you don't need sneakers," and two of them held me down while another one grabbed my sneakers. Then, after punching me in the gut, they all ran off. I cried when they left. I just couldn't help it.

I didn't feel safe in the bus shelter after that, so I walked back to the empty schoolyard, taking up my well-known spot behind the emptied bins. Wrapping my arms around my knees, trying to keep warm, I heard a scratching sound. I froze, fearful that it was a rat, but then a soft meow and a fluffy coat brushed my skin again. Someone's cat was out exploring the night. It felt so soft and smooth, and it made me feel safer. As I curled up on my side, trying to sleep, it nestled beside me, its warmth easing the pain in my aching ribs and sore stomach. It had disappeared when I woke up this morning. I don't know where it went.

The sky is darkening back at the beach, so I jump down on the sand and huddle up against the rock wall. The sea wind has picked up, burrowing through my still damp clothes, making me shiver. I feel so lost, so alone. I just cannot face going home again, begging him to let me in, taking yet another beating. Finally, I can't take it anymore.

*Mum, Mum, where are you? Have you been looking for me? Please help me. I don't know where to go.*

Darkness arrives, but I cannot sleep. So many strange noises fill my ears, and fear keeps me alert. I sit upright, my eyes straining into the moonlight. Dozens of little creatures are popping out of holes in the wet sand. Tiny crabs, scuttling across the beach. Moving back as far as I can against the rock wall, I hope they won't crawl around me. The sand has turned cold where I sit, but at least it's still dry.

I must have eventually nodded off as the call of seagulls wakes me as brightness creeps through my closed eyelids. As I stand to stretch my stiff body, I double over in pain. My ribs feel so painful, and when I pull up my T-shirt, I notice a large purple bruise covering my left side and wrapping itself around my back.

"Bastard," I whisper to myself. Another day, so what do I do. I need a toilet. That's first on my list. There should be unlocked public restrooms somewhere at the beach at this time of the day. After that, I'll have to find something to eat. I'm hungry again. Walking towards the toilet block, I notice that all the rubbish bins were empty.

*Damm! Those council workers must have started early.*

Great, the toilet block is open, the concrete floor is still wet. The sink looks pretty clean as well, so I manage to splash water over my face and dry it on the bottom of my shirt. My mouth feels furry, but I can't do much about it without a toothbrush. I wet my fingers and rub them over my teeth. That's better than nothing, I guess.

What will I do today? I don't want to sit in the hot sun again as the back of my neck feels quite sore, and my arms have turned red. I'm not sure where I can go, but I stroll up the street past the shops as I'm pretty bored. My feet are still sore, but the footpath is not too hot as it's still only early. The street's incredibly quiet at this time of the day, not many people around, just the odd one or two going into the newsagents and a few shopkeepers setting up their shops. As I walk towards the fruit shop, I spot a big fat guy unpacking a carton of oranges, placing them neatly in rows in a barrow at the front of his shop. Just as I reach him, a couple of oranges drop from his grip. He struggles to pick them up, so I bend down to help, grabbing the fallen oranges before they roll into the dirty gutter. When I hand them back to him, a beaming smile covers his face, and his white teeth gleam in the morning sun. In his heavily accented voice, he tells me I'm a good boy. Turning to pick a small bunch of grapes and an orange from his display, he places them in a brown paper bag, holding it towards me in his big hairy hand, his dark eyes crinkling as he smiles.

"You take these, good boy." He smiled. "Gunna be a hot day, and footpath get very hot. Maybe you need to wear some shoes."

I can't believe my luck, food again. As soon as I'm out of the fat man's sight, I bite into the orange, the sticky juice running down my chin as the sweetness fills my mouth. I carefully place the grapes in my shorts pocket. I'll eat those later. I know that food will be hard to come by, so I need to ration it out.

I think today is Tuesday. Already I'm losing track of the days. Walking past the newsagency, I notice the date on the paper ad outside the shop. Yes, it's Tuesday. Today was the day I should have been going back to school, and I was so looking forward to starting Year 9, but now it looks like the school is a thing of the past for me. I remember my little sister is starting Middle School today, and the urge to see her fills my thoughts. I wonder how Mum is. Has she been trying to find me? My sister will be walking to school, so if I'm careful, maybe I could catch up with her.

Crouching behind a clump of bushes in the parkland near our school, I peer down the street. I can see Sally in the distance. Good, she's by herself. As she approaches the bushes, I call out. "Sally, Sally, over here."

She looks towards my voice, startled at first, but then she spots me, hurrying over with an enormous smile on her pretty face. She drops her school bag and gives me a big hug. It feels so good, and my tears well up.

"I've been so worried about you," she whispers, even though there is no one else near us. "Where have you been? I haven't got long, as I can't be late on my first day."

"I've been around," I mumble, pulling away from her soft hug. "How's Mum? Has she been looking for me?"

Sally's expression changes. It's as if a cloud has dulled her eyes. "Mum's OK. But she can't look for you as he's checking her every move. He gave her a walloping the other night and accused her of driving around the streets looking for you, so now he checks the kilometre reading on the car every night. He's started leaving work to come home at different times during the day to make sure she's there. He's made her give him a list of where she's been, the time it took and all that. Mum's too frightened to look for you. He's even started to check your clothes and things to make sure nothing's missing."

"Gee, I'm sorry, Sis. I never meant it to get to this."

"It's OK, we'll manage, but I can't meet you here again. He might be checking up on me as well. So I'll have to go, but here, look." Sally's eyes darted around as she held out her hand. "He was so drunk the other night; he must have dropped this outside when he was fumbling for his keys. I found it the next morning. I was going to give it to Mum, but I hid it instead. So I've been saving it for you."

I glanced at Sally's hand. She was holding out a $10 note. Grabbing her in a bear hug, I held her close. As I breathed in the smell of her shampooed hair, I knew I wouldn't see her again for a long time. I couldn't risk if anyone sees her talking to me. My eyes blurred with tears as I watched her walk towards the school.

Tucking the $10 note into my shorts, I was careful not to squash the grapes. Today had been a lucky day, first some free fruit and now $10.

The footpath was heating up as I headed for the beach. The walk is now becoming familiar. It's down the street and around the corner, passing a row of shops, before crossing the main road to the beach. I have nothing better to do, so I stroll past the shops, checking each window to see what they sell. Wow, I hadn't noticed it before, but there's an Op-Shop, next door to the newsagents.

The tingle of a bell sounds as I open the door and cautiously walk inside. A lady sitting behind a glass counter looks up as I enter.

"Hello, young man," she smiles at me. "Why aren't you in school today?"

I take in her grey, curly hair and light blue eyes that match the colour of her blouse as I cautiously reply, "I left school last year and am looking for work."

"Oh, my mistake." She smiles at me again. "You don't look old enough."

Feeling braver now, I smile back. "Yep, I'm 17." Then, after a few seconds of silence, which seem to go on forever, I add, "I'm looking for some sneakers. But, unfortunately, I managed to lose mine."

I follow her behind the racks of clothing to an extended display of second-hand shoes. "Here, try these," the lady holds out a pair of old sneakers. "They're a bit worn, but they're a good brand, and I can let you have them for $2." As I bend to try them on, I feel my T-shirt slide up my back. Too late. I realise she has seen the dark purple bruise that has spread around my ribs and back. I quickly stand upright, pulling my shirt down, but not before noticing the concerned frown wrinkling her forehead.

"Why don't we look at jackets while you are here," she says. "The nights will be getting cold soon, and a warm jacket never goes astray." She grabs a couple of jackets, holding one out for me to try on. "We just have too much stock at present," she adds. "So, some of these are just giveaways."

As we walk toward the register, I'm surprised to see loaves of bread piled on a side table. "What's all the bread for?" I ask, turning towards the delicious smell wafting from the table.

"Oh, the local baker gives us the day-old bread to hand out to the needy," came the reply.

"Here, I'll grab you a loaf, as it will be too stale if it stays here much longer. I'll pop it into this old backpack here, along with your jacket. It will be easier for you to carry."

As I'm about to leave the shop, another grey-haired lady appears from the back room. "Gladys," I hear as I open the tingling front door. "Gladys, you are not giving things away for free, are you?"

"No," comes the reply. "The young man paid for the sneakers, and the other stuff was just throw-away. It's always the same with these kids, Mary. First, loneliness and despair, then come the drugs, the alcohol and sometimes prison. I hope an old backpack and a free jacket gives him some comfort."

My stomach stops rumbling after eating some bread and a few grapes, but I feel so lonely, so unwanted. Wrapping my arms around my knees, I stare at the surf as the waves roll in and out on the wet sand. I angrily brush away tears that run down my cheeks.

*What did I do to deserve this? What will become of me, and how will I survive without anywhere to live and no one to care about me? Who am I? Am I really Worthless?*

Gladys' words keep rolling around in my head. Drugs, alcohol and sometimes prison. No, I positively don't want to go down that path. Maybe I could go to school and tell them I have nowhere to live, but they might force me to go back home or, even worse, put me in a Boys' Home. I've heard about those places, and there's no way I'm going there. I'll just have to take it one day at a time and see what happens.

Another moonless night closes in, and once again, I huddle against the rock wall. At least I feel more comfortable than I did last night. The OP shop jacket feels quite warm, and the backpack softens my body as I lean against the cold rocks. I finished the grapes and ate a few more slices of bread before dark, and I even managed to get a drink of water in the toilet block before the council locked it for the night. Again, I'm finding it hard to sleep, as so many strange noises surround me. One noise seems to stand out from the others. Straining my ears above the pounding of the waves, I could hear the sound of laughter, which seems to be growing closer. I try and huddle closer into the wall, hoping to make myself invisible.

*God, please don't let anyone hurt me.*

A soft voice fills the darkness. "Hey matey, what are you doing here?"

"Trying to sleep." I nervously answer.

"You need to keep awake at night if you sleep alone because that's the difficult time. Best to leave sleep for daytime."

As my eyes adjust to the moonlight, three young faces peer down at me.

"Hi, I'm Steve. So, what's your name?" The closest face asks.

"Ah, the old man calls me Worthless."

"Yep, that sounds familiar. Mine called me Shit-Face, Bella's called her Hopeless, and Lonnie's called him Useless. If you're planning on a bit of street living, you'd best hang out with us. There's safety in numbers, and we can clue you in on how to cope. C'mon, I bet you're hungry, come, and we'll grab something to eat."

I follow them along the sandy pathway until we reach a fish and chip shop, where we look through the window watching the owner finish his last clean-up. Then, finally, he calls Steve over to his door, handing him a large parcel. It smells great, and when Steve opens it, we discover many warm chips wrapped inside. We quickly sit on the damp grass, placing the chips in the middle of our circle, and when I take the rest of my bread from my backpack, we all greedily eat as I listen to their chatter. They tell me the names of the shopkeepers who are kind enough to give them left-over food and also where it is safe to sleep.

"The only people you have to watch out for is the coppers," Lonnie mumbles through a mouthful of chips. "If you don't cause any problems, they'll leave you alone. Sometimes they move you on if you're sleeping in shop doorways and stuff, but they know there's not enough places for kids like us, so they're pretty cool. So, what about it, do you want to hang out with us?"

"Sounds good to me." I shyly reply.

Days turn into nights, and nights turn into weeks. The four of us stay close together. Steve is the leader, calling the shots, deciding where to sleep and how to find food. He and Bella are close. He's always looking out for her, giving her his share when we have very little to eat. Bella often screams during her sleep, and Steve holds her close until she's properly awake. We all look after Lonnie. He seems pretty unwell sometimes. He talks to himself a lot, and some days sits perfectly still for hours, holding his arms outright and staring at his hands. Other times he says he is a genius and is going to save the world. Steve says Lonnie suffers from delusions.

Summer has disappeared, and the nights are turning very cold. We need to move into the city away from the beach, heading off to the local railway station. Unfortunately, none of us has a train ticket, but no one checks, and after a couple of hours, we end up in Fitzroy just as the night shadows cover the street.

I'm feeling anxious in these new surroundings. Living at the beach had turned out well. The fat man at the fruit shop often gave us bags of overripe fruit, and the fish shop man gave us chips. I was able to shower at the concrete steps at least once a week, wearing my clothes, so they got washed as well, and now I'm in a strange place where I don't know anyone. I'm feeling uneasy, frightened.

"So, where to now?" I nervously ask.

"Don't worry, Matey," Steve replies, patting my shoulder. "I've been here before."

Walking together down the narrow footpath, I notice the rubbish littering the ground and the bareness of this place. Old terrace houses line the street, some with front doors opening right onto the footpath. There are no trees or flowers and no grass.

Lonnie walks beside me. "Is your real name Matey?" His voice breaks the silence.

"It will do," I reply, the streetlight highlighting his frowning face.

"Well, I am Jesus." He adds with conviction. "And I am going to save the world."

"Course you are, Jesus." I smile at him. "Course you are."

I don't know why I never told the group my real name. I guess it's because it's the only thing that I have left that's mine, and I want to keep it to myself.

As we turn the corner, Steve's face breaks into a huge grin. "Get a load of this, Matey. Hot food."

My eyes cannot believe what I am seeing. There must be at least thirty or forty people standing around a van. The smell of food makes my stomach rumble. I cautiously walk towards the truck. A young man's face smiles at me as he holds out a paper cup and a sandwich. I stare, not knowing what to do, but he smiles again, not speaking, just nodding. I reach for the cup with one hand, tucking the sandwich into my jacket pocket with the other. He nods again, another smile.

*Can this be real? Are these people actually giving us free food?*

Finding a spot away from the others, I sit on the dirty concrete sipping my soup. It's so delicious. I savour every mouthful before taking a bite of my sandwich. Ham and cheese, it's been months since I've eaten ham and cheese. I'm so busy devouring the food that I don't notice the man with the smiling face moving towards me. He's joined me on the concrete.

"Hi there," his voice is strong, "what's your name?"

"Matey, will do," I grumbled a reply as I eyed him suspiciously.

I don't want to talk to this guy. He could be a copper in disguise. He seems OK, but I'm wary, just the same. He chats about his studies. He says he's an economics student at Uni and works on the food vans two nights a week. He asks how old I am. I tell him seventeen. Steve has warned me not to let anyone know I'm only fourteen, or I could be sent back home or made a Ward of the State. As I finish my soup, I stand up, planning to return my cup to the van. Instead, the smiling face man follows me and asks me to wait. Expecting another cup of soup, I take a deep breath, surprised when he returns carrying a large bundle.

"Here, Matey," he holds the bundle towards me. "This will come in handy now the nights are turning cold."

Returning to the concrete, I study the bundle. It's a sleeping bag, neatly rolled with carrying handles and tucked under the straps is a plastic package. Excitement floods over me when I open it. I can't believe my eyes. Inside there's a cake of soap, a toothbrush, toothpaste, and some warm socks—tears of gratitude stream down my face. I've wanted to brush my teeth for weeks, and now I can.

As the van leaves, Steve rounds us up. We need to find somewhere to sleep. He says there are some old sheds down near the railway line, so we head down there. Lonnie seems even worse tonight, talking rubbish. Nothing he says makes sense. We've all been given a sleeping bag, and it feels just like Christmas. As we enter the shed, the smell of dampness is overpowering, and there's a pile of rubbish in one corner, but it will have to do until we can find something better. Trains constantly rattle past, the noise vibrating through the thin walls. Lonnie tosses and turns, muttering to himself, something about stopping the trains so he can sleep.

A burst of cold air hits my face with a blast, awakening me from a deep sleep. I sit upright. *Something's wrong.*

As my eyes adjust to the darkness, I can see the shed door is wide open. Glancing towards the others, I notice that Lonnie's not in his sleeping bag. Perhaps he's gone for a pee, but I'd better check, as he's been acting very strange tonight. I slip out of my bag, trying not to wake Steve and Bella. It's a clear night outside. Straining my eyes in the darkness, I can't see Lonnie anywhere. Then, at last, I see him, standing motionless on the railway lines, arms raised to the sky. As I stumble down the hill,

I fall, twisting my ankle on the uneven ground. God, it hurts. I can hear the rumbling; a train is getting closer, and Lonnie is still standing on the railway line.

"Lonnie, Lonnie," I cry into the wind.

He doesn't move. Pain seers through my foot as I race towards him. I'm so close, but the train is closer. I hear the screech of brakes. The smell of metal against metal fills my nostrils. I scream as I take in the scene. Lonnie, upright with arms raised to the sky, the train, smoking wheels, flashing lights, Lonnie has disappeared.

I don't know how long I've sat beside the line, unable to stop sobbing. Lonnie was my friend, and I couldn't save him. My body aches, my head hurts, and my foot is throbbing. But worst of all, my heart is broken.

*Mum, Mum, I want to come home.*

I feel the arms around my shoulders before I realise someone is there. It's Steve.

"C'mon Matey," his voice is gentle. "Time to go back to bed."

As I hobble up the hill, the flashing lights from the police and ambulance vehicles disappear into the distance. I can't stop shaking. My sleeping bag beckoned.

"Here, take this." Steve leans over me, a small white tablet in his hand.

Bright lights start to dance behind my closed eyelids. I feel as if I am floating. Colours flash brightly, and music fills my ears. I feel weightless.

*What was in that pill?*

Gladys appears, floating into my vision. She is holding out a jacket, her blue eyes looking troubled. "Loneliness, despair, drugs, alcohol, prison." She repeats the words over and over. They bounce around my brain, trying to escape through my tears.

The smiling face rests on a flower. "Study, study," its gentle voice drifted around the petals. My little sister reaches towards me. A $10 note clutched in hand.

*Mum, are you looking for me?*

Sitting upright, I call into the night.

"Lonnie. Lonnie. I am not Worthless, and I am not Matey. My real name is Benjamin."

# THE OLD STONE BRIDGE

## *NORMA SAVIGE*

She hadn't realised where she was going when she left his parents' home. She just knew she had to get out of there. Her poor parents were probably still there, stunned, out of their depth and not knowing what to do next. So now here she is on her own on the old stone bridge. This bridge is usually her *happy place* in her hometown, but today she is as miserable as she can ever imagine being. Her heart feels like it is made of lead, weighing her down.

As she reaches the top of the bridge, with its platform and a seat, the sun comes out. Despite her misery, her eyes are, as usual, drawn to the view. The river runs deep here, flowing slowly and smoothly, like silk with barely a ripple. Both banks of the river are covered with willows which wave down to the water, and ahead is a large pond enjoyed by birds, aquatic animals, ramblers and fisher-folk alike. Paths follow the banks, and because the bridge carries only foot traffic, bikes and the occasional horse, this is a safe walking loop for families, couples and solo pedestrians – young and old alike. A happy place for them all.

This seat has been her sought-out space when she is happy, sad, stressed, or even bored. As a seven-year-old, she came here when her best friend didn't invite her to a party. New romances and those broken have all been celebrated, regretted or commiserated on that seat. When she needed to decide about beginning her nursing career, she spent quite a few hours here going over the pros and cons of training in the local hospital or moving to the city. She sometimes wondered if missing the bridge, its seat, and the view influenced her decision to stay local.

This visit, however, is filled with a terrible, panic-stricken dread. Her life seems unbearable, and, unusually for her, she struggles to calm down and look at her plight objectively. Instead, her feelings flit from joy, panic, fear, excitement, stress and shame, then back again.

Pointlessly, she asks herself how she could be pregnant. Of course, she knows how but that doesn't help – this is her, not just anybody. Why? Why? Why? It can't be undone. She knows that but still, somehow, hopes that some magic will happen. It will all be a bad dream and disappear. *If I just sit here in the sun, take a deep breath, cross my fingers, and wait patiently, it will all go away.*

Of all people. A nurse! Dumb! Dumb! Dumb! Her *Mat Med* lecturer has covered the new contraceptive pill. A good Catholic, he condemned it, criticising all its possible side-effects to a horror level. He also insisted it was only available to married women, and she would need a script from him, anyway. Too embarrassing. Now, this. Her dreams of completing her training, moving on to Darwin for her Staff Nursing year then going to London, where hospitals are begging for Australian nurses, are all disappearing before her eyes.

Finally, she calms enough to begin considering her options. The view before her helps to slow down her breath which, in turn, helps her organise her thoughts. Of course, she can get married, as attested to by her boyfriend and her parents. Although his parents have violently disagreed, she knows, in the end, there is an unspoken social rule of the time – marriage should happen.

Does she want to get married? Who is this man, really? Has she known him long enough to decide? Could they afford it? Is there any choice, though? The social disapproval, gossip and judgement passed by one-and-all for an unmarried mother is to be dreaded. There is also the issue of the label her child will carry if born out of wedlock. Bastard is the official title. What child should carry that burden? If she doesn't marry, she will have to leave the town and lie for the rest of her life – invent a father for the child and a partner for herself.

Another option coiuld be to go away to a place for *girls like her* to have the baby, give it away, then return home as if it never happened. But the horror stories about places where girls are beaten and treated like slaves - like wanton sinners getting exactly what they deserved, came to mind. Babies removed with or without their mother's consent, with the girls returning home and gossip following them anyway. Could she possibly give away her baby? Probably not.

She could choose to keep the baby. Go away, find a place to stay, maybe with a city aunt and uncle. She knows that could be possible. She could keep the baby, but then what? Money, work, somewhere to live with the child, food, clothes. How would they survive? Would that be fair on any child? A life of poverty and, probably, shame.

The last choice open to her seems to be to have an abortion. Oh, God! Kill the baby? It's not their fault. As a nurse, she has seen the results of botched butchering carried out in back-street kitchens. Sometimes even resulting in the death of the mother and the child or lasting infertility or other medical issues. Or even worse, failed abortions with a severely damaged child. She also remembers a girl from her year-eight class in school who had died. Now her own boyfriend's parents want this for her. What would they care if she died? They would be happy to get rid of the baby and, probably, getting rid of her would be a bonus.

Her heart breaks for her parents. The shame of being pregnant out of wedlock is enormous: it's as if it were the eighteen-sixties, not the nineteen-sixties, for goodness' sake. It's not just the shame of being pregnant but the shame of having had unmarried sex. Those who *get away with it* go on in life with no impact. Those who *get caught* suffer intolerably – the woman, her family, the child, her friends and her career. It's certainly not the same for the man involved. How is that fair? Is there ever going to be a time in this world when society will treat women more gently?

What is the immediate plan? Don't panic. Just stand up, turn left and return to the boyfriend's house to plan a speedy wedding, or turn right and return to her room at the hospital to prepare a solitary life with or without the child. Don't panic. Make a well-considered choice. Sit a while longer and ponder all the options and their pros and cons. Then, finally, turn left or right. Simple.

She leans back on her favourite seat, gazes out over the river and the pond beyond, wraps her arms around her abdomen and finds herself talking to the child.

'What do you reckon, Sweetie? Could we go it alone? If you were me, what would you do? Left or right? What should I do?'

She closes her eyes, takes a few long, slow breaths and enjoys the warmth of the sun-baked stones of the bridge. How familiar this all is. The sounds of the river, the bird calls and the people haven't changed over all the years of her life. In her mind's eye, she can see what will be happening around her. She has always used this spot to make decisions, and today is no different. She lets her thoughts wander here and there as she considers all her options again, discarding some as time goes by.

After a few hours, the sun is setting, and the shadows are growing long on the river banks. The stone seat is cooling as the sun leaves it. She shifts on the bench, stands up and stretches as if waking from a dream. She has made up her mind. She is keeping this child with her forever. Deep down, she probably knew from the start that she would. She slowly smiles and turns neither to the left nor to the right. She steps ahead, leans out wide over the rampart of the bridge, and lets herself go. With a floating sensation, she and her baby slip together into the warm water's soft, silky embrace. Together forever.

# THE POSTMASTER'S COTTAGE

## *BRONWYN VAUGHAN*

Days turned into months, months into years, and Jane found herself immersed in the calling of the land she loved and knew so well. *Time had never stood still*, Jane thought to herself. Now approaching her mid 40's and having lived in this home longer than the one she grew up in as a child, Jane began to recollect her life twenty years into marriage. 'These have been the best of days!' she breathed quietly at the footstool of the sitting-room hearth.

Jane was a small statue of a woman born from an English family who immigrated from England in the late 1850s. She was the only child of Thomas and Ellen, who came to Australia as a newlywed couple, resettling in the inner suburbs of Melbourne.

Thomas, her father was a banker in London and Ellen, and her mother was a seamstress. Having received the call from the local congregation to sail abroad and help establish a new church, her parents set about building the place they now called home. Thomas grew up in a manor house located in an estate of grand squares and cream-stuccoed terraces in London, which made him eagerly sought after, not only for his banking experience but also for his town planning and design love.

Ellen began her seamstress business, sewing gowns and accessories to the Melbourne based clientele, and on Sunday, they would travel to the local church in a horse and buggy with little Jane seated between them.

Sundays were the grandest day of the week for Jane as a child. She rose early to help her mother collect the eggs from the barn house and milk the jersey housed in the paddock adjacent while her father chopped the kindling for the kitchen woodstove and sitting room fireplace. Then, in the heart of the house, her mother would bake eagerly on Saturday, before Sunday chapel.

Jane particularly loved the winter months of Melbourne, and she often found herself running between the fence lines of neighbouring properties to exchange a morning greeting to her closest friends. Sunday was no exception. Instructed by her mother, she would hand-deliver half a dozen eggs and a pint of fresh milk to her neighbours before going to church. She did this until the age of 17 years. Grace lived to her right and Jessie to her left, both born within months of Jane's birthday in 1866, and they became the best of friends. Neighbours would often hear the girls calling each other and singing made-up melodies as they crossed between each other's properties.

'Grace and Jessie', called Jane. 'Come out and see, I've your fresh eggs and milk for the week. Mother says I must hurry, as father's getting the horse and buggy ready to leave for chapel.' And within minutes, each appeared on the porch of their homes, running out to meet Jane with thrupence to spare.

It was a delight to see Jane at school but especially on the weekends. Jane's parents were well respected in the Melbourne socialite community and often hosted frequent parties for their business acquaintances and church friends.

In those days, money wasn't scarce, and her parents delighted in sharing what they had with others.

'I must go now,' called Jane as she ran home after delivering produce to her neighbours. 'I'll see you again Monday. We'll talk then.'

By the time she got back home, she knew it was time to leave for chapel.

'Jane', called father. Father had led our horse to the front gate with the buggy attached in preparation for Mother and me to mount. The chapel was a short ride into town, taking approximately half an hour, and it was already a quarter past nine. Her mother appeared dressed in a warm lilac dress. She had hand sewn it herself with matching hat and gloves, Father had his best suit on, and Jane dressed in a stitched coat mother had made especially for that winter.

We arrived at the inner-city chapel laden with homemade pastries and loaves of bread, wild jam and butter. After each service, the church community would share in fellowship together, chatting with each other over a pot of tea, while the children would play 4-square and made plans for the next week.

Monday arrived, and Jane would walk the 1-mile distance to school with Grace and Jessie with their lunch swinging by their side. It was a two-classroom building in those days, with a hall, a kitchen and fireplace, all under one roof. There was also an outside play area.

Mrs Bridge was both the school's headmistress and the senior class teacher. Ms Paige taught the junior classroom. School hours commenced at 9 o'clock each morning and finished at 3 p.m. Jane, Grace and Jessie often remained behind for extra tuition each day. Jane had already decided at the age of six that she wanted to be a teacher. However, she would have to wait until her 18th birthday for this to happen.

The years passed, and as each season led into the next, Father's banking career developed. Mother became highly sought after for her seamstress business, and studies became increasingly more attractive.

It was nearing the end of Jane's school years where she would graduate, and with a further 3-months of teacher instruction, she would soon be able to take a class herself. However, she'd already turned seventeen, and it was coming into summer. It was then that the unthinkable happened. Jane had been out all day with Grace and Jessie when her mother met her on the front step. She looked white, almost ill-looking when she grabbed Jane by the hand.

'Come inside. I have news to tell you!'. Jane didn't like the sound of it and couldn't possibly imagine what her mother was about to tell her.

Her mother led her into the 2-bedroom portico home with a sitting room, dining room and woodfire kitchen. She spent most of her days growing up here, and it was now only days until her 18th birthday. The chaplain was seated in an upright chair by the far window, and mother motioned that I should sit close. Mr Francis, as we called him, appeared calm, but Jane could tell he was concerned. Finally, mother began to weep, and she pulled out a lace handkerchief that she had sewn with her initials.

'We're sorry to have to tell you, Jane, darling, but your father was found at the rear of the property early this afternoon. He, unfortunately, passed away with heart failure. The police have visited and established there's no foul play.

'No, it can't be. It's my 18th birthday in a few days, and father was so happy." Jane's eyes began to fill with tears, and she leapt to her feet. "This can't be true. It's not real. Tell me where he is!'

Without even thinking, Jane found herself running to the back door through the kitchen, and the door swung loudly behind her. She found herself racing towards the back of the family's property where she spent countless hours during childhood, close to the creek and the dappled floor of her father's orchard, often painted in purple and gold.

Her mother was right. Father wasn't there. But Jane could tell he had been since the rake remained leaning against one of the lime-green elm trees with father's hat still placed securely atop. Jane sat down on a paling seat, just as she and father often did after a tiring day either from school or tending the property. It was here Jane reflected that held her fondest memories. From within the lining of her apron pocket, she often wore to protect her best dress, she pulled a small diary and began to write. Tears streamed down her flushed cheeks, smudging the etchings of the paper-thin parchment. Her father had encouraged her to write with a presentation each birthday of a simple little diary with daily quotes, readings and poems that she often read to inspire her writings.

'Jane, Jane', her mother called with a piercing voice from the back verandah. 'Come inside, it's near dark, and I've prepared dinner.'

Noting the chill of dusk in the air and the sun's setting over the west ridge, Jane reluctantly walked the two hundred yards back home. "Tonight", she melancholy thought to herself.' It was to be the beginning of a new era'. Wherever the path now took her, she knew she would be taking her father along with her. He was her strength for years and would still be.

Summer arrived with a burst of fragrant heat in the first days of December. Jane particularly loved the first month of summer with birthday preparations and Christmas festivities. However, this year the planning was for it to be a little more reverend and subdued. It was Jane's 18th birthday in the first week of the month of summer, with a small gathering planned for just Jane, mother and her closest friends Grace, Jessie and Wilhelm. Mother had prepared a quiet affair with the most delicate English pastries and cakes, placed upon an ornately decorated table with a cloth hand-sewn years earlier. There was nothing more satisfactory than an afternoon tea celebration, and Jane accepted the opportunity to gather particularly with Wilhelm, whom she'd met only recently at the local chapel.

After father's death, Jane and her mother continued to attend each Sunday travelling the distance by walking the two miles, until Wilhelm one morning stopped by and suggested that he prepare the buggy for the trip into town. Wilhelm was a few years older than Jane and lived in the country over 30 miles away, born of Lutheran descent. He had decided earlier to try his luck in gold prospecting and was often seen by Jane's side on a Sunday helping around the property on his way back home. The journey would often see him travel from the foothills of the ranges to the goldfields, stopping to rest and grab a meal with the chapel congregational members. This gathering was part of their service to the community and inspired primarily by the chaplain, who encouraged families to open their homes.

The few months for Jane were some of the best days she'd had since her father's passing. She obtained her teacher's certificate, and Wilhelm continued to court her, even having a little success in his gold prospects. Wilhelm became very fond of Jane and loved listening to the stories told of their immigration from England, reminding him of his heritage from Germany. Wilhelm had saved enough money to purchase land and build within the township he grew up in as a child. Wilhelm now owned the property only a few minutes from High Street, close to the shopping precinct and in a prime position. It was then that he decided to ask for Jane's hand in marriage.

It was a beautiful autumn day that Wilhelm took Jane down to the paling seat by the creek and asked her to marry him. Wilhelm knelt on the ground on one knee, he pulled from his pocket a small velvet pouch tied with a ribbon, and Jane knew this was going to be a critical moment of her life. She had noticed petals from the rose garden had been scattered on the ground, and ribboned lace hung from the elm tree's vivid green foliage. 'I think mother was in on this idea', Jane thought to herself, and a smile gently appeared across her face.

'Will you marry me, Jane?' asked Wilhelm with a strong and assuring voice.

'Oh, yes, Wilhelm!' Jane replied eagerly. He reached for her hand and placed a small signatory gold band with one solitary diamond on her left hand.

It began an engagement of four months to prepare for the wedding to start and build the last house. Mother, of course, gracefully committed to assisting with the wedding preparations from the silken gown and dainty lacework, veil and matching buttoned slippers to preparing the wedding banquet for the guests on the day. Jane engaged herself with the invitation guest list, making suggestions to her mother for gowns for Grace and Jessie, while Wilhelm constructed a small pavilion at the rear of the property close to the creek. It was Jane's way of being close to her father.

The garden was immaculate on the day, with the orchard dappled in purple and gold and a path for guests and wedding attendees to walk covered in rose petals. Ribboned laced was again placed strategically on the surrounding elm trees. Mr Francis, the pastor, was in attendance, as were the many guests from the Melbourne social lite community, congregation and business clients. Wilhelm had invited family and friends from the region, and all were encouraged to share a glorious banquet afternoon tea into the late afternoon hours. Even a small-rounded parquetry platform for dancing allowed both Jane and Wilhelm to dance a quick waltz around the garden to the enthusiastic applause of those in attendance. Guests began to throw rose petals, and the couple farewelled with a motherly hug from Jane's mother.

As she did, she whispered in Jane's ear, 'Your father would've loved to have been here to celebrate this day with you both, Jane!'

'Yes', Jane replied softly, returning the warm embrace. 'He was here with us!'

Jane awoke for the first time in a newly built cottage in the heart of a rural landscape with a suite of new friends and family she was yet to get to know. She'd taken leave from teaching for a week and set herself the task of establishing a new daily practice of rising with her husband in the early dawn, completing the morning chores and working on the finishing touches of the newly acquired house. In contrast, Wilhelm worked with his brothers in the local building and carpentry establishment, which had just recently commenced. The house itself was a two-bedroom finely built cottage with lemon-coloured timbers, an external verandah that wrapped itself around the building, olive green trims on the posts, window frames and door and a solid tin roof to withstand the rains renowned in the area. It would sometimes snow delicate white snowflakes, and Jane would love to watch the miracle and gift of creation from her window.

On entry, a sitting room to the right held a large, open fireplace leading to the generously sized dining room, the left, the bedrooms and the central kitchen at the rear of the house. The outside porch area contained a wash, utility room. The gardens were expansive with room not only for a proposed orchard like Jane's fathers, but the property had recently acquired a vegetable patch, chicken barn and dainty cottage garden towards the front of the tree-lined property.

'Wilhelm', Jane called from the back porch. 'Supper is ready!' Jane had prepared the meal for herself, Wilhelm and his parents, who were the first immigrants to migrate into the area. They embarked, having landed by ship in South Australia on a walking trek to find a farmland district resembling their homeland. Listening to the descriptions, Jane had gathered that the main street was very much in appearance to the Lutheran town they had left behind.

They spent the next year working about the village, attending the local chapel service with other settlers, teaching, building and hosting Sunday afternoon gatherings for family and friends. 'Yes', Jane thought to herself, 'These were the best of days!' Not long after, Wilhelm and Janes' first child was born, a beautiful baby boy with fair hair, a European complexion, striking oceanic eyes and the most peaceful of natures for a child. Ernest was a contented child, the second born into Australia, from a long lineage of first-borns who schooled at the local primary excelling in all academia, training at the local post office and eventually gaining the title of postmaster. They were incredibly proud of all their children.

Nonetheless, Ernest became renowned for his wit and intelligence and gainful employment during World War I as a morse code transcriber within the nation. Still today, the Postmaster's Cottage remains intact with its ornate, decorative verandah fixtures and gardens with stories of olde to tell for those with an ear to listen.

# THE JOURNEY
# CONTINUES

## *(A SEQUEL TO THE STORY IN VOL I)*

*JUDY NEARY*

## *TOGETHER*

Faith kicked hard to remain afloat in the stream. Then, as she began to sink below the water, she gave one extra little kick to bring her back to the surface once again. As she turned her face upward, she felt the warmth of the sun upon her wet cheeks. Water cascaded down from her hair and tickled her face. She felt so alive.

Her face lit up in a smile as she looked towards the bank where Isaac sat watching. Then, with smooth, swift strokes, she headed for the bank, hearing splashing, and coughing behind her. She looked back to see

Heather struggling, her gangly limbs flying in all directions.

Three months ago, neither could swim, but every time they stopped near a river, or stream Isaac would get them in the water to teach them. Faith had taken to it like a pro, whereas Heather had struggled.

Reaching the bank, Faith exited the water. She turned, hearing cursing behind her.

"Damn, bloody water". Heather cursed, "I will never get the hang of this thing called swimming".

When we last left this trio, they were travelling, trying to find a facility somewhere that may be able to discover what was wrong in Heather's brain. Heather had escaped from RHYTHM, a giant pharmaceutical company, where she had been held and used in many experiments for several years. Both Heather and Faith's mothers had been on an experimental program carried out at RHYTHM when pregnant with the girls. And as a result, they both seemed to possess unique qualities. Faith had not been under RHYTHM's control and had adapted natural attributes, while Weaponry was Heather's skill.

The three of them had some time ago come to believe that it had been no accidental escape for Heather. RHYTHM had deliberately let her go to lead them to Faith. Whatever they had implanted in Heather's brain was being used for tracking, among other things.

Heather always remembered the slight tug on her, drawing her in a particular direction towards Faith. Faith had already met Isaac after he saved her from drowning. Isaac had shared his story with Faith which made Faith question her existence. Faith knew she was different, she would see some things, mainly flying things, and she could become that thing, like a butterfly, a bird, even rainclouds.

Heather's arrival took Faith entirely by surprise, landing on her back and knocking her down. Faith could see that she was in terrible pain. Knowing Isaac and Heather's story and looking into Heather's eyes, Faith immediately realised she was Isaac's lost sister. The eyes gave it away instantly.

The fireballs raining down on the village where Faith and her surrogate parents had resided for some time were destructive, and rained havoc on the village. Her parents did not survive. Luckily, Faith, Heather, and Isaac had escaped.

The three of them had travelled for several months, aware they were being followed and constantly wary of strangers. RHYTHM wanted Heather back and now also wanted Faith.

Isaac, Heathers older brother, had searched for her for many years, and now they were reunited. He was determined to protect both she and Faith. However, he was still in awe of Faith's powers and her ability to share her capabilities with Heather.

Faith tried to get Heather to see her powers naturally and always encouraged her. She was always cheerful and encouraging where Heather was concerned. As they travelled, they had learnt so much about each other.

Often when they camped at night, Isaac would sit strumming on his guitar. The three would sing. Faith couldn't hold a tune, whereas Heather possessed a lovely voice, very unusual for someone with no training. Her favourite song was 'Somewhere Over the Rainbow'. She would often sing as they went about their daily routine.

Heather had developed one quality she had not yet shared with Faith or Isaac. She knew it would be handy one day, but she had not had the opportunity to test it. Faith and Isaac were always nearby, worried about her and the headaches she constantly suffered.

Sometimes the headaches were so debilitating. All Heather could do was lay and rest. Faith would make up a potion from plants and some roots that seemed to soothe the pain.

Heather was a tall girl, at about 5ft 7inches, very slender with long limbs. Her mouth was almost as wide as her face, and her brown hair was shoulder length. Her eyes were her standout feature, brown with gold flashes. Her pale complexion made her look quite frail, but she was anything but frail, being through so much in her short life.

Her brother had those same eyes. Isaac was tall and athletic. His body was strong and quite handsome, with brown wavy hair, grown a bit longer now as he grew older. When he smiled, he displayed dimples, although it seemed a little crooked and never seemed to quite reach his eyes. His eyes always had a little sadness in those amber depths.

Faith, the third member of this trio, was only about 5ft 3inches with green eyes that sparkled with mischief. Her body was curvy, and she had a tan complexion. Her hair had grown much longer now, with red tinges throughout the long tresses.

Today, as they travelled, they came across a small village where they could trade for supplies. Faith always used the healing skills she had learned from her surrogate mother and was able to help with minor health issues in many villages. For example, she knew many plants and barks used in potions to heal different disorders.

Faith stopped them and pointed towards a small bridge across a creek bed leading to a large town or village. Maybe here, they would find what they sought. They skirted the houses checking for anything suspicious. Faith had taught them this as a precaution against RHYTHM.

"Seems okay," Isaac stated. "I think it's safe."

*

# CAPTURED

As they entered the village, Faith and Isaac decided to meet at a particular place before sundown.

"If something goes wrong." Isaac said with a furrowed brow, "we meet there regardless."

With a nod of their heads, they parted ways, Isaac to see if he could gather more supplies, while Faith and Heather looked for any medical facility that might exist in the village. Faith spotted a large building in the centre of the town and guided Heather towards it. The building seems to be still reasonably intact, not like many other structures, some even reduced to rubble.

This village would have been quite a large town before the event that brought the world to destruction. Some structural parts of buildings had remained intact, with what appeared to be pathways surrounded by garden beds, which could have displayed colourful flowers and bushes. Now, these garden beds looked like they had vegetables and practical food supplies growing in their midst.

The girls noticed a big red cross painted across a wall, indicating a medical facility.

"Come on." Faith said excitedly, dragging Heather behind her.

Upon entering the building, there was no one at the reception desk. Looking around for signs, Faith spotted a sign which said 'Pathology', with an arrow to the right and another sign 'Radiology', pointing up to level one. Heather hesitated, but Faith found the stairwell, and they headed up. Opening the stairwell door that reads level one, they found themselves in a long passageway.

Suddenly a man wearing a white coat and carrying a clipboard stepped out through one of the doors and into the passageway. Heather immediately went into panic mode. She remembered all the white-coated people who experimented on her and caused her so much pain. Faith placed her arm around Heather's shoulders to calm her.

The man is surprised when he noticed the girls. "I believe we have finished for the day." He said, looking around and up and down the passageway.

"I just need my friend seen to, she has terrible pain in her head, and we need help urgently." Faith gave him her most radiant smile, hoping to influence him.

"Oh, okay, come in, and I will set up a scan. After all, I have nothing much else to occupy me." He stated with a guarded look on his face.

A few minutes later, he ushered them in. Heather had to lay with her head inside a sizeable drum-like machine. Faith and the white-coated man left the room and stood where they could view the scan. Faith saw a round object implanted in Heather's brain on the screen, which appeared to be turning slowly with a blue light at the core.

The technician was quite shocked at what he saw.

"What is it?" Faith asks, her face going quite pale. "Is there any way you can remove it?"

"I'm no surgeon," the man replied, waving his arms around. "But maybe I can find someone to have a look." He moved across to a drawer and removed a syringe and small bottle with a colourless liquid, filling the syringe.

Moving in Heather's direction, hesitating, he said. "It's just a little sedation. It will keep you calm. My name is Peter, by the way." Heather was shrinking back on the bed, trying to appear as small as possible.

"No," Faith shrieked, "no sedation."

Peter laid the syringe in a petri dish, and with a shrug of his shoulders, he leaves the room.

Faith sat next to Heather, trying to calm her. "We may have found what we have been seeking." Faith felt very optimistic and could hardly contain herself. Heather, on the other hand, had always been a pessimist and still looked worried.

They had been waiting for some time, so Faith decided to go and see if she could find out any information. Stepping into the passageway once again, Faith moved slowly towards the stairwell. She heard voices and walked in that direction, coming to a standstill, listening. What she heard sent chills down her spine.

"Yes, two young women. One has something implanted in her brain. Something I have never seen before." It was Peter who was talking. He was intrigued. Somebody spoke on the other end of the line, and Faith heard Peters reply. "I will try to keep them here as long as possible. I will expect a substantial reward for my services."

Faith doesn't wait to hear anymore. Instead, she sprinted back to the room where she left Heather. She burst through the door, exclaiming in a shrill voice. "Heather, we have been betrayed and must get out of here." Grabbing Heather by the arm, they begin to move towards the door.

Peter stepped through the door blocking their exit. "Wait, I have someone coming to look at the scans." He reached out, trying to stop their departure, stepping away from the door and waving his arms around.

Faith took the opportunity and plunged the syringe filled with the sedative into his arm and released the fluid. She pushed down hard to hurt as much as possible. Peter screamed in pain, falling to his knees as Faith pulled Heather behind her while escaping through the door.

Running along the passageway and opening the stairwell door only took a minute. Just as Faith and Heather enter the stairwell, they hear the siren shrieking. It was pitch black, so they cautiously made their way down.

As they reached the ground floor, Faith screamed in a shaky voice, "we must get outside." Faith pushed Heather along until they somehow found themselves outside, and as they looked skywards, they could see giant fireballs raining down on the village.

They run towards the bridge on the outskirts of town, sprinting along the tree line, hoping no one saw them. Unfortunately, there were soldiers everywhere firing at random.

Faith and Heather threw themselves into the creek bed. They couldn't see Isaac anywhere. Peering out, they stared at the utter chaos in the village.

Then they saw him. Isaac was trying to stay in the tree line for cover, but several of the soldiers had seen him and were in pursuit, shooting at him. He went down, rolling as he hit the ground.

Faith roses from her hiding spot and flew into the air, becoming a giant eagle. She grabs Isaac with her talons, lifting him into the air.

Two soldiers were already upon him. Finally, she lost her grip, letting him go.

Still hiding in the creek bed, Heather seized the opportunity to use the new power she acquired. Sprinting, she became a blur, as she is running so fast. Then, finally, grabbing Isaac, she threw him over her shoulders and began to sprint away. Faith rose into the air to follow. Heather kept running, stopping only when she reached their campsite from the night before. Isaac seemed to be okay, just a bit stunned.

Heather turned as she looks for Faith. She can't see her.

"Oh no, oh no," she wailed, "where is Faith?

Heather ran back the way they came, once again becoming a blur. As she neared the creek, she changed into a small sparrow and lands high in a tree. Then she saw Faith. The soldiers had her. She was unconscious. One of the white coats appeared and injected something into Faith's arm, *probably a sedative* Heather thought. Faith was already shackled and was placed into a cage with chains to hold her down.

Heather looked towards the hospital, where she noticed Peter waving his arms around in all directions, conversing with one of the white-coated people who looked familiar.

Heather gasped. She knew this person. It was her main torturer and tormentor when she was in captivity.

Peter was pleading for the promised reward for betraying Faith and Heather. With a dismissive wave of her hand, the scientist turned her back on him, walking away. Heather was shocked when one of the soldiers pulled out a gun and shot him. She realised that her friend Faith had just been taken prisoner by the same people who held and tortured her for years.

Sprinting back to where she had left Isaac, Heather's head was beginning to pound with pain. She came across Isaac. He had started back looking for them.

Heather lets out a sob, falling into Isaac's arms. "They have Faith," she cried out. "They have our friend."

Isaac carried her back to the campsite, laying her under the shelter of an overhanging tree. Heather is clutching her head in pain.

Isaac found the bark and made a poultice as Faith had shown him, wrapping it around Heather's head and holding it in place with a scarf. He didn't dare try to make up the potion Faith used. One wrong ingredient could have made things worse.

He thought about going back to see if he could help Faith but daren't leave Heather in her vulnerable state.

Lying next to his sister and unable to sleep, he watched the stars twinkle above as he tried to decide what they needed to do the next day.

After eventually falling asleep, Isaac woke to the tweeting of birds and the sun shining down. He turned to see Heather already awake. She looked recovered from her ordeal and ready for what they needed to do next.

"We know where they will take her," Isaac stated with conviction. "You know where the facility is, the one you escaped from. We need to go there and hope an opportunity arises for us to help Faith."

Heather was afraid but also determined. "It will be dangerous," she replied with a shake in her voice and a gulp of air, then jumping to her feet, "I am ready, let's go."

*

# SACRIFICE

Gathering all their supplies, they moved out of the camp, knowing that it would take them some time to reach their destination. Heather was still in pain, but soldiers on, not allowing the pain to dull her resolve.

As they travel, Heather showed Isaac what she had learnt about her special powers. She can run so fast as to become a blur, and like Faith, she has mastered the art of changing her form.

Heather's headache got worse as they approached the scientific facility. It is all she can do not to collapse with the pain. This place still had a hold on her. Isaac and Heather stay on the rise overlooking the facility. It seemed quiet, not much activity, which could be a good thing. But unfortunately, the soldiers haven't arrived with Faith as yet.

Heather felt that little tug on her brain. "They're not far away," she said bravely.

The two of them waited. "They're here," Heather finally stammered as a parade of soldiers, scientists, and the cage come into view.

On their arrival there's a lot of activity. Faith still seemed to be sedated and unconscious in the cage. It was carried towards the centre of the facility which appeared to be four long buildings, a bit like aeroplane hangars.

Heather remembered this place well. Remembered the pain, the torture, and the intimidation, practices that were used to their fullest when she was here. Heather was so afraid of what would happen to Faith. But, looking down over the facility now, Heather willed herself to stay focused.

There seemed to be a difference of opinion about how the soldiers should transfer the cage into the hanger. The soldiers had already unchained Faith and were in the process of lifting her out, when Heather decided to act. She moved out of her hiding place, a streak, a blur, picking Faith up, sending everyone into chaos.

Heather had been waiting for her chance and extracted Faith right from under the soldier's noses. Then, returning to the hilltop and carefully handing Faith to Isaac, she stammered shakily. "You must take care of Faith now. I must destroy this facility forever."

Heather leapt into the sky as Isaac ran to her.

"Stop", he called," dismay in his voice. It was too late.

Heather turned her attention to the buildings below with one last look and a kiss thrown in his direction.

Isaac looked up to see Heather become a missile.

He screamed. "Heather, please no, don't do this." It was all to no avail.

The missile targeted the building in the centre of the facility. Straight down it went, slamming into the structure and burying itself deep down.

Isaac had begun to run down the slope he saw what was going to happen. He ran back at full speed, throwing himself on top of Faith's inert body.

The explosion was intense and destructive, the shockwave rolling over the two of them. Standing and looking down over the site, Isaac was shocked at what he saw. Nothing was left intact. The whole facility was a black mess, with spot fires burning everywhere.

Isaac laid close to Faith throughout the long night, afraid to close his eyes for fear he might miss something, eventually falling asleep towards dawn.

When Isaac awoke, Faith was stirring beside him. He moved to the edge of the slope to look over the devastation. There were still small puffs of smoke rising into the morning sky from the ruins of the building.

Isaac sat with his head in his hands in a defeated pose.

Faith sat up, dazed, and confused, next to him. The sedative had left her feeling quite fuzzy. She saw Isaac turning towards her with utter dismay and sadness on his face.

Faith looked for Heather. "Heather, where's Heather?"

Seeing the helplessness in Isaac's eyes, she sobbed, running to him and placing her arms around him like a blanket. Then, she sees the puffs of smoke still rising from the ruins. Faith turned to hold Isaac, still crying.

They remained like this for some time. Then, when Isaac felt ready, he related what took place with a tremor in his voice. They slowly walked arm in arm amongst the ruins. The ground was still blackened with the burnt embers now cooled. They wandered into the centre of the ruins, where the main building once stood. It was where Heather plunged deep when she became a missile. They stood for quite some time in reflection, both remembering Heather in their way. Faith felt a slight tug on her senses and smiled.

Searching Isaac's face, she said. "Watch."

Rising a few feet from the ground, she begins to twirl, around and around.

Suddenly she turned into a beautiful green butterfly, the exact colour of her eyes. Then another butterfly appeared, then another, until there are several butterflies, all different colours fluttering around this particular place.

Isaac's face lit up. Faith dropped back down, stepping away from the circling butterflies. They sat in silence for a while, both feeling relatively calm. They would spread the word about this facility so that no company will ever be allowed to grow and have so much power again.

As they strolled away, Faith looked back. The beautiful kaleidoscope of butterflies had followed them. Faith felt that little tug on her senses once again. She hears singing in that little sing-song voice they have grown to know so well over the past months.

"Isaac, can you hear the song? Her song."

Isaac shook his head.

Faith began to sing in that beautiful sing-song voice.

Isaac is amazed as he looked down at Faith and smiled. He's not sure what was happening, but he feels happy.

As Faith and Isaac travel, Faith would sing in that lovely voice, and they would always feel that connection. Heather was still with them.

# A SURPRISE PURCHASE

## *NORMA SAVIGE*

Emily was smiling to herself as she stepped out into the sunshine. It was quite a while since she had met with her old friend, and they had caught up on all the news from both families over a delicious lunch in their regular bistro. They had known each other for most of their lives and now enjoyed their individual retirements – albeit in different ways and different places. Of course, they did not have wine with their lunch, but she still felt relaxed and at ease, that warm and fuzzy feeling she always had after being with Helen.

As she turned towards her car, she felt a tap on her shoulder and turned around to find a stranger staring intently at her. He was a tall young man with red hair and a sprinkling of freckles across his nose. He also had the greenest eyes she had ever seen.

She smiled at him as he leaned forward and whispered in her ear, 'We know who you are and what you did. It took us a long time to track you down. But here we are. You will get what you deserve very soon.' He shook his head and grinned. 'You can't get away with anything forever, you know.

Somebody always knows somebody who knows somebody else who knows something. You are sprung, and the day of reckoning will come, and it will be a big surprise when it happens!' Before she could register what he said, he glanced up and said, 'Oops! Gotta go. See you soon, though.' He smiled and disappeared into the crowd of office workers returning to their desks for the afternoon.

This was always a busy time in the square. It housed many offices and crowds of workers spilt out onto the pavements for fresh air, a cigarette, or to find some lunch. However, the rush was always over quickly, and the street soon emptied. Emily could see no sign of the redhead and wanted to sit down but couldn't move. Her heart was pounding, and she felt nauseous. She was perspiring and could feel sweat prickling her face and the back of her neck.

'Are you alright, love?'

Emily looked up to see a waiter from the cafe frowning into her eyes. 'I… Yes… No… I don't know.' Emily knew she couldn't stay where she was, blocking the doorway but thought she'd fall if she tried to walk unaided.

'Would you mind just helping me to my car over there? I suddenly feel a bit woozy and have to sit down. I just need to catch my breath.'

Her head was spinning, and she tried to make herself concentrate as she felt gently supported across the square to her car. She couldn't think straight. *We know what you did. You'll get what you deserve.* What? What did she do? What did she deserve?

'Thank you. I feel a lot better now. Must have stood up too quickly.' She tried to laugh and shrug off the concerned look of the waiter. 'Really, I'm fine now. Thanks again.' And she nodded him away.

'Well, if you're sure, then I'll be off – meeting my girlfriend for a quick bite to eat. Better not be too late,' he smiled and blushed, 'I'll leave you to it.'

She waved and watched as he jogged through the square to the park then slumped into her seat. Her head was still spinning. What should she do? Go home? Would she be safe there? He seemed to indicate he knew all about her, and that probably included where she lived. Go to the police? And tell them what? That someone she had never met had threatened her with a vague *day of reckoning*, whatever that meant, for something she has no idea about doing?

Emily realised her hands were sweating. She was clinging onto the steering wheel as if she'd fall if she let it go. Her thoughts were reeling from one thing to another, flitting around like the proverbial bee in a bottle. She knew she was heading for a panic attack but didn't seem to have the strength to ward it off.

'Stop this now! You've got to get a grip,' she scolded herself under her breath. 'You've got to be able to think straight and calm down. Take some slow, deep breaths, drop your shoulders, and relax. Breathe in. Relax. Breathe out. Calm.' Her breathing was jagged, and her voice shook. She knew she must think clearly and make a plan of action – what to do, where to go next? Make sense of what had happened.

Slowly Emily felt herself settle down. She was exhausted and just wanted to go home, crawl into bed and sleep. 'Surely I'll be safe if I drive home. I'll zap the garage open, drive in, zap it shut while I'm still in the car, then race in through the inner door and lock myself in the house. I've got the alarm system and my phone. Anyway, I'm probably safer at home than parked out here like a sitting duck in full view of anybody who wants to pay me back for something I've done to them.'

'You know,' she tried to reassure herself, 'This is probably all a big mistake, and it wasn't me, or they misunderstood whatever had happened. Yes, that's probably it.'

Emily put the car in Drive and gently pulled out of the square. Still shaky, she almost drove through a stop sign without stopping. 'Perhaps I've inadvertently caused an accident and killed someone. That's possible. I think we're all lucky at some time when we are aware that a car or pedestrian has suddenly appeared, and we have wondered where in the hell they came from?' Maybe I did that without realising.' She struggled to bring her thoughts to driving and to concentrate on the task at hand. 'Don't want to cause an accident now, while I'm thinking about possible accidents in the past.'

*

'You need a baseball bat,' her friend Helen said.

'A baseball bat. What on earth for?' She stared at her phone as if the answer might appear on the screen.

'You say, you won't, or can't, go to the police, so you need to find some protection. I've read about people keeping a baseball bat beside their bed when they've managed to fight off a home invader.'

'I don't know if I could fight off anyone – baseball bat or not,' she sighed. 'I feel sick. I don't know what to do. All I can think of is to try to disappear. But how could I do that? They managed to track me down before, so I guess they'll find me wherever I am. I just don't know what I can do.'

'Well, can you try to work out what their complaint is? Do you honestly not remember anything you have done to harm someone?'

'Look, I've wracked my brains. When you reach a ripe old age, there have been many opportunities to harm – even unintentionally. The thing is, I have no idea. Honestly, I can't think of a time when I deliberately or neglectfully caused harm to someone else. I have tried to live a good and decent life, have not taken advantage of anyone and have certainly not cheated someone out of their rightful possessions or position.'

'Did I expel someone's beloved child when I taught, or did someone die on my shift when we were nursing? Could I have overlooked the suicidality of a young person I counselled? These are all possible over the years, but most people would accept them as part of my job and because I always did my best to be ethical I never expected this.

'Did I not give a job to the worthiest candidate by mistake? I swear I am going insane here. I feel sick and can't stop panicking.'

*

Shortly afterwards, when Emily glanced through her front window, she noticed a red car parked opposite her house. She peered closely and was sure the driver, just sitting there, had red hair. 'Now I'm getting paranoid. Why would he just sit there and not come in and attack me? Probably a delivery man searching for an address. God, I am so scared, and I need to do something about it.'

With that, she turned on her computer and started to Google *Personal Protection*. What an Aladdin's cave! There were advertisements for anything you could want, including the ubiquitous baseball bats – wood, including maple, hickory or mahogany and metal, including cold steel or aluminium. There were personal alarms guaranteed to painfully and permanently deafen any attacker. There were ferocious dogs, already trained to attack and even more brutish-looking men to act as bodyguards. Some of them looked as if they could murder her in her sleep, anyway. There were bullet-proof vests, nunchakus and knuckle dusters along with knives of every possible description. Lastly, there were Mace, Pepper Spray and Tear Gas on offer – there were even videos demonstrating the effectiveness of each. 'What has happened to this world?' she asked herself out loud.

'This is ridiculous. If I get any weapon to wield, I'm sure I won't be able to protect myself before it's taken from me and used against me. I can't get one of those horrible dogs, and a bodyguard is way out of my league. I should get a gun and be done with it. To hell with the consequences.'

*

'Oh my God! How easy was that?'

Emily couldn't believe that she could arrange for a gun so easily. And with some lessons about safety and hints about how to use it for self-protection. 'This is Australia and shouldn't happen here, but I quite like the look and feel of it. I never thought I would want or own a gun. But here it is in my bag when I go out, on the side table in the lounge room whenever I'm relaxing and in my bedside drawer when I'm in bed. A Smith and Wesson with a built-in laser, no less.' She wasn't sure how a laser would help, but it came for the same price, so why not?

The man who delivered the gun and the free lesson seemed genuinely nice when she met him in the bush park close to home. He said he was genuinely interested in helping her keep safe. 'If we all had guns, love, there'd be a lot less gun crime, I can tell you. Bullies like your bloke would have less chance of throwing their weight around so freely.'

Emily had heard the quote, *God made men, Sam Colt made them equal, and John Browning made them civilised,* somewhere. Maybe there was something in that? She did feel safer. In fact, she felt like a different woman. More confident, more relaxed and, finally, less anxious.

*

For a week, Emily settled into a different lifestyle. First, she did not go out unless it was absolutely necessary and ordered her shopping and medications online. When she did go out, she placed her trusty gun in her bag and felt reassured. It did not have an exposed hammer that could catch on her purse or clothing, and the long trigger pull prevented it from accidentally firing, so she was confident it was safe.

*It was safe.... she was safe. She was a woman with a gun!*

Occasionally, she thought she saw a glimpse of red hair but did not immediately go into a panic. Let him come to me and discuss his issue. I'll be able to sort it out because, with my gun, I can get him to slow down and listen.

Sleep did not always come easily, though, and she sometimes slept with the gun under her pillow. 'Small steps,' she reminded herself. 'You are certainly coping a lot better than a few days ago. It will all work out OK.'

When Helen rang for her daily check-in, Emily told her she was coping a lot better. She still couldn't determine her alleged crime, but the redhead would probably help her sort that out.

*

One evening just before dinner, as darkness fell, she was closing the drapes when she noticed, to her alarm, the same red car pulling up to her front path. She raced to the side table and took out the gun. It felt reassuring, and she quickly memorised the instructions she had received in the park.

Her heart was racing as she peered out at the car. The driver was, again, just sitting there. 'Is he just trying to creep me out? Make me panic?'

'I'll sit here where I can see through the glass panels in the door. If he tries to get in, I'll see him.'

The door had three glass panels that always gave a view of an adult's head, waist, and legs standing on the other side. 'I'll be right. I'm glad the waiting is over at last. It'll all be finally sorted out, one way or another.' She sat down with her gun pointed at the door and waited.

'Come and do your worst,' she thought, 'I'm sick of the pressure. Just get it over with. I think I'd rather die than continue to live like this.'

Suddenly, an outline of a tall man appeared through the door panels.

Emily took a deep breath, breathed out slowly and, speaking calmly to herself, said, 'You've got this.' She waited with all her senses awake and alert. One way or another, she was going to settle it today.

Her hand was shaking as she aimed the gun at his head. She felt nauseous and lowered the gun to aim at his body. If she had to shoot, she wanted to incapacitate but not necessarily kill. 'How ridiculous is this? I'm even considering where to hit him. So calm and calculating.'

'Boy, having a gun really does change you.'

*

Her doorbell rang, and almost immediately, there were impatient, loud raps on the door frame. She jerked up in her chair, panicking, heart pounding. 'So much for being a new, calmer, self-controlled woman.'

'What do you want?'

'Come out and see,' he laughed.

He was so confident he could overpower her. The arrogance! 'God, I've got no hope.'

Sweating and shaking, she suddenly lowered her gun and fired at his legs. She just could not make herself aim higher – despite what her trainer had said.

The glass smashed, and she heard a scream, then a terrifying roar. Then, through the glass, she saw the man crumble down in a heap, his red hair leaning against the broken panel.

Emily stood frozen to the spot. She could hear a lot of noise outside and could see several legs surrounding the man. 'Call an ambulance.'

'What the Hell happened?'

'He's been shot.'

A woman screamed and that shook Emily back to her senses. She gingerly opened the door just a crack and peeped out at bright lights, a camera, a woman collapsed on the lawn, sobbing, while two people attended to the shot man.

The man was clutching a massive bunch of flowers even as he writhed around on the front porch.

As she opened the door wider and stepped out to stand beside the injured man, she was vaguely aware of the camera pointed at her and a small crowd had gathered.

*

'What's going on?' she stammered, glancing down at the man, his red hair damp with sweat.

'What's going on?' the woman on the lawn screamed. 'You've shot my grandson. That's what's going on!'

A TV reporter she recognised from a news channel approached and held out her microphone to Emily. 'Do you have anything to say, Ms Jackson?'

The cameraman shouted to the reporter, 'Get back. It's not safe.'

Puzzled, Emily stammered, 'I don't know what's going on here. Who is this man? Who is his grandmother? I don't know them.'

The ambulance arrived. The paramedics leapt into action, clearing people off the porch before cutting open the leg of the injured man's jeans. Suddenly one of the paramedics noticed the gun in Emily's hand. They both stood up and moved away. 'We need to call the police. We can't attend to him while she has the gun.'

Emily glanced down and realised she was still holding the gun. As she raised it, everyone tried to take cover. Her fingers had frozen around the handle, and Emily used her other hand to free it, one finger at a time. She carefully placed it on the floor inside the house and closed the door behind it.

'Please come back and help him. The gun's inside. Please. He's bleeding a lot.'

A paramedic took the flowers from the injured man handing them to the reporter, who looked towards Emily. 'These were for you. He and his Gran wanted to give them to you. What do you have to say, now?'

'Why?' she snapped at him, 'Did they finally realise they'd made a mistake? That it wasn't me after all? Why not tell me that instead of letting me live in terror all this time?'

'It *was* you!' the grandmother shouted as she rose from the lawn to hold her grandson's hand as the paramedics wheeled him to the ambulance. She turned back to face Emily. 'We tracked you down over all these months. We were so looking forward to finally catching up with you today.'

\*

Two police officers emerged from their car, putting on their hats as they approached. 'Is there a weapon here?'

Emily pointed to her door, explaining it was on the floor inside. The male officer slowly approached the house, asking, 'Is there anyone else in there?

'No. I live here on my own.' Emily replied as the female officer moved to stand beside her.

'What's your name, Ma'am?'

'I'm Emily. Emily Jackson.'

'What's happened here?'

'I don't know, honestly. That man warned me they were going to pay me back, and I don't know why. I don't know what I've done. I've been living with a gun for a couple of weeks now. I have no idea what's been going on. I just feel sick. Can I sit down?' Emily struggled over to the chair on her porch and sat down with a groan, and put her head in her hands.

'Why is the TV camera here?'

'I don't know. I know nothing. I opened the door, and they were just there with lights and the camera focussed on me. I think the reporter must know what's going on.'

The officers called the reporter over. 'Do you know what's going on here?'

'I know a bit, but not about the shooting. Jamie and his Gran have been trying to find Ms Jackson for months. Gran was in a Lotto shop and had ordered some lottery tickets when she discovered she had left her purse at home. Emily, here, stepped in and insisted on paying for the tickets. She wouldn't leave her name and just left.

'One of the tickets won a *huge* amount of money. Gran had raised Jamie on her own, and they never had a spare cent. They lived close to poverty and suddenly found themselves wealthy enough to buy a house and still have hundreds of thousands of dollars left over.

'They set about tracking down Emily to reward her as a thank you. Unfortunately, it took them a long time, even with a private detective, to finally track her down.

'Jamie started to tell Emily what they had done but then he saw Gran fall on the roadway near a square in town, and he had to race off to help her.

'They contacted me,' the reporter continued, 'because they wanted Emily recognised for her good deed and today was the day. Jamie was going to give her the flowers, and Gran would give her a cheque for a hundred thousand dollars.

'A good news story for a change. But,' the reporter looked around, shaking her head, 'she shot him.

'And there they are. And here we are.'

# THE GLADE

## *MELISSA SAYERS*

The trees were a vivid green – so green they almost seemed to luminesce; the leaves shaped perfectly as a child had drawn them. Tiny white blossoms dotted the foliage, and a honey-sweet scent filled the air. Although the morning sun was only peeking gently over the hills, the grass was still icy and crisp from the chill of the night before.

Hills rolled and began to awaken to the east, though still shrouded by the early morning mist and to the west, flatlands, tall grass, and sporadic clusters of bushes. A small herd of deer meandered around the perimeter of the grove, grazing on the green grass they found there. Bird noises began to echo from each direction, and flocks took to flight, propelled by a soft breeze that swished and swirled.

And I was here at the entrance to the magical glade, where I came to meet her. She would be here soon.

Ahead of the trees was an old wrought iron gate, highly decorative and black. I slowly strolled towards it. There was no rush, though my hand reached out in expectation. She would not be here until the sun had fully risen. As I walked to the gate and placed my hand on it, an antique creak rang out as it opened.

And there it was – the crystal pond. And the glistening waterfall. The place where she and I could be together. I strolled to the edge of the pond and gingerly sat on a cold boulder right at the water's edge and waited. I daren't dip my toes – the frost had barely broken on the surface of the water.

I was suddenly lost in her beauty as I pictured her in anticipation. No more than 11 or 12, a young girl, wearing a white cotton dress sporting brown curly hair hanging loose but seemingly perfectly formed. Her eyes were bright blue, and her face betrayed a memory of my own. Yes, she was mine, my angel child. So, it was how she always came to me, periodically in my dreams, to remind me, comfort me, and love me. And for me to love her.

I felt the sun begin to warm the back of my neck, and I revelled in its heat. The crystals on the surface of the pond started to melt, revealing the pristine water beneath. I deeply inhaled the morning air, and my whole body felt energised.

I heard her before I saw her. Lost in my daydream, her dulcet humming, the sing-song of some childish tune, invaded my pondering.

Each time I saw her, it felt like the first. I thought that I had never seen anything so beautiful, so perfect. She skipped lyrically towards me and hugged me. I held her desperately, so tightly, and I kissed her tenderly on the forehead. She squirmed from my grasp.

"Mama," her words were like music.

"Hello, my darling," I said, taking her hand and standing enthusiastically, longing to know where she may lead me.

We ran eagerly towards the other side of the pond, where a field of white and golden daisies seemed to spread for miles. We tumbled, lost in euphoria, and rolled in their delightful softness, laughing and grabbing handfuls of the perfectly formed blossoms. Then we sat and bound the daisies into rings, just long enough to encircle the circumference of our heads. It was a painstaking task, and she curled in the lap of my crossed legs, concentrating intently on her work. Finally, when we had completed our work, we proceeded to crown each other with mock pageantry, bowing with sombre faces while stifling sniggers.

The sun was on its way to its peak now, and she left her toil of daisy rings and ran giggling towards the pond, leaping into the water, her white dress clinging to her skin.

I walked over to watch her swim. It filled me with pure joy to watch her play. My eyes transfixed as she danced with the water. I scrambled over the rocks towards the back of the waterfall and reached out, touching the streaming flow and watching my angel through the gap the water formed, a white light aura surrounding her. She frolicked, she was free, and for that moment in time, that freedom was all I needed to know. Knowing she was at peace and I could be with her, here, in my dreams, made me feel whole. When I lost her, I lost a piece of me – here I was, complete again.

She moved toward the waterfall, tipped her head back, face glowing brightly in the sun, and swam through the waterfall. Her hair clung to her face, and for a moment, every feature was perfect.

"I have to go now, Mama," she whispered and kissed me on the cheek.

At that moment, I felt pure joy and pure sadness at the same time.

"OK, baby. I love you."

She began fading into evanescence.

"I love you too." Her voice became a whisper which echoed of the walls of the glade. Then, turning, she disappeared into the water, leaving me alone and on the edge of wakefulness.

My eyes slowly opened. I looked at my window, and through the plantation blinds, the sun danced with the dust forming streaks on the walls of my room. I closed my eyes, desperate to recapture the moment. But she was gone, and the gate closed.

But as I opened my eyes fully to face the day, I heard her voice whisper in the wind, "I love you too", and I smiled. She was always there.

# THE ELIGIBLE MARKUS SUKRUM

## *ANNA ROBERTS*

People often saw Markus at the café Buza drinking his morning coffee in his white suit, his white hat hanging off the chair next to him. Even on the hottest days, he never seemed to sweat. Stroking his imaginary beard and then looking up from his expresso, Markus would pick out tourists to hook that day, offering to take them sightseeing.

Markus enjoyed taking tourists to the home of Marin Drzic and telling them to sit on Marin's bronze statue and rub his nose for luck. Unfortunately, Marin's figure has a Jimmy Durante style nose discoloured from all the rubbing, as well as sporting a bullet hole in the statue's neck, a sovereign of the war. He was considered Dubrovnik's equivalent to Shakespeare, writing dramas and comedies portraying Renaissance Dubrovnik in a no holds barred way, mostly from his own experiences.

Markus Sukrum is twenty-five years old with a slim athletic build, honey-blond hair and a distinctive moustache that he twirled till the ends, pointed upwards. His blue eyes were like the Adriatic Sea, and as his mother would say. "they could tempt mermaids out of the water."

Growing up in Dubrovnik, Croatia, with its slow pace, was like being on holiday all the time. But, being such a handsome man, you could believe that Markus could whistle the birds out of the trees. Women loved him, and men admired him even though they didn't entirely trust him with their wives or daughters.

All his sisters were married, and some of his family had even migrated to the United States and Canada. But unfortunately, the family had, over time, lost touch with many of those living overseas.

Markus was a man's man, physically fit and always had a story or joke to tell, and some were only suitable for men's ears. An eligible bachelor, he was the life of the party, and if Markus saw a wallflower in the corner of the room, he would flatter her, asking her to dance. In turn, this would arouse the curiosity of other men, and they, too, would ask the wallflower to dance.

By showing a lot of interest in a rather dull creature, Markus would ensure that other bachelors would try and woo her, not wanting to miss out.

Later that year, the wallflower's parents would give Markus a large tip placed in a plain envelope at her wedding, slapping him on the back and thanking God that they unloaded yet another daughter. His grandfather called this practice taking the bull to the cow.

Women were fascinated by Markus and a little intimidated as well. They felt like they had no willpower to resist his charms. He was the local tour guide in their coastal town, where he grew up in a stone house with his parents and six sisters.

The home was lovely and cool in summer. But, when the sun was in full force, beating down on the rocky shores, the family wondered, from their comfortable abode, why foolhardy tourists would risk their skins in the blistering heat.

Markus and Josip had been friends since school, and although Josip had settled down and was raising a family with Elena, he loved to hear the stories of Markus's exploits and conquests.

Josip was short in stature with dark curly hair and a beard to match. Markus would tease him, saying that he looked like an orthodox priest, while Josip would respond by saying that he'd never seen a priest with a moustache like the one Markus had.

Josip often thought of how Markus, being a Roman Catholic, entered the church of St Ignatius, Loyola, showing tourists around and wondered how the building had not collapsed on such a sinner. Josip contemplated that even God had a soft spot for a bad boy like Markus.

He attended church every Sunday, and he could hear his grandmother's words ringing in his ears, "only sinners need to go to church so often." So, leaving the church after mass, Markus would put on his hat and sunglasses, sit at the cafe nearby, watching the ladies stroll by.

Markus was a dapper dresser and was very particular about how he looked. However, he was incredibly proud of his fine physic in swim trunks. You could almost hear the ladies sigh at the sight of him.

As a young lad, Markus's father had threatened to send Markus to Italy as his schoolwork was not up to the standard expected. He wasn't dim, but rather just lazy. He was the sort of chap that just cruised through life.

The thought of having to go to Uncle Zoran's home to live was enough to make him pull up his socks and receive better marks at school. His Uncle Zoran was a mean-spirited character, with a leathered face that had a permanent frown. The family would jest saying he looked like a wild boar about to charge. So, when Aunt Teresa ran away with Branko, the kind-hearted and passionate gardener, no one could blame her. He was the total opposite of Uncle Zoran.

As a choir boy, Markus ran home one day to announce that he was going to be a priest. His mother walked quickly to the church that day to ask God to make his hormones kick in early as she wanted grandchildren and not a Pope in the family.

Markus's grandfather had shocked him by saying, 'Priests should not be married and should be castrated.' 'Who are they to lecture us about matrimonial problems when they don't have wives.'

Two of his sisters had also announced when they were younger that they wanted to be nuns, and their mother had prayed that they would soon show some interest in boys. So she sighed in relief when one day her prayers were answered. Eventually, she knew she didn't have to share her home with a load of nuns and a priest.

Markus's first love was Clara. She had the body of an angel with her firm breasts and slender hips that swayed like the sea lapping the shore. Her dark wavy hair reached her waist and was often tied back with bright coloured ribbons. When she walked past the baker's shop, the baker would stop kneading the dough and gently caress the mixture until his wife slapped the back of his head, bringing him back to the present, and he would continue to knead the bread in earnest.

All the men tipped their hats upon seeing Clara, and schoolboys would whistle and wonder why older men would shove them out the way so they could watch poetry in motion.

Markus fell in love with Clara in his teens, but her father felt that Markus wasn't good enough for his daughter, so Clara and Markus met secretly at Orlando's column holding hands and sharing an ice cream. Standing by the statue of the knight who helped keep Dubrovnik a free trade city, Markus would tease Clara by holding the ice- cream so high that she could not reach it. Clara tried to grab the ice cream standing on tippy-toes, which gave Markus a chance to steal a kiss.

Word filtered back to her parents, who told Clara to stay away from

Markus. She pleaded with them as she loved Markus. Her father yelled and threw his glass to the floor with shards flying, telling her she was too young to know what love is.

Clara was sent away to boarding school, and upon her return, she was married off to the Svek family, who were wealthy landowners. Her father thought she would live a privileged life, never wanting for anything. Ivan's parents hoped she would give them beautiful grandchildren.

Ivan showed no love towards Clara, and no matter what she tried to do for Ivan, it was never good enough. Clara began to fear him as his moods were so unpredictable. His parents treated her like a peasant, but Ivan's lack of affection was like a dagger driven into her heart. Doubts lingered for Clara after overhearing the servants talk about the fact that Ivan preferred the company of men.

Ivan was not a popular man in the old city. Many working at the market would divert their eyes upon seeing him, unlike Markus, whom the locals loved exchanging friendly banter with, often throwing him an orange.

Ivan had straight black hair and a curved back caused by a childhood accident; his eyes gave off a vibe of pure evil. His persona was sour enough to rot the fruit, and when he did smile, it made people even more uncomfortable. The stallholders would joke that if Ivan held his nose any higher, his nostrils would sprout grass with the help of the sun.

Markus hated violence against children, women, or the elderly. He would come to the aid of anyone in need and use rough justice to correct the situation. If he heard someone was brutalising their spouse, Markus would wait in the shadows late at night for these drunken slobs and give them a few jabs, sending them staggering home, their ears ringing with the threat that he would finish the job if they ever hurt their wives again.

Talk among the town was that Clara's husband Ivan was very jealous and quite sadistic, yet she stayed even though it was a loveless marriage. Ivan controlled her daily life, not allowing her to leave the house without an escort, so when Ivan mysteriously fell off the cliffs to his death, many thought Markus had done him in.

Josip knew that Markus did not kill him and had heard talk that the men Ivan owed money to through gambling debts; had followed him one night after losing a substantial amount. Yes, Markus had beaten him up earlier that evening, but he had also helped Ivan to his feet, sending him home, not knowing he would never set eyes on him again.

An inquiry held into Ivan's death stated the verdict was death by misadventure. However, gossip around the old city kept Markus from going to see Clara. Markus didn't want people to think that they had conspired to kill Ivan.

Ivan's father, Zlatko, put out word amongst his men to find the culprits responsible for Ivan's death. Luka and Rajko were sent to retrieve the money Ivan owed their boss, Tomislav. But Ivan was fed up that night after the punches he received from Markus, and so he fought back hard against the two goons, striking his assailants multiple times before losing his footing and plunging down the cliff to his death.

Tomislav had Luka and Rajko beaten up and sent to work for his brother Filip in Serbia. But Tomislav resigned himself to the fact that you can't get your money back from a dead man. Ivan's father, Zlatko, wanted the men killed, but Tomislav believed it was an accident, so instead, he banished them from their hometown.

Although heartbroken at losing the love of his life when Clara was married off, Marcus pursued many women, but they were just his playthings. There could never be another woman to replace Clara.

Saturdays, for Markus, were for sleeping in, having long lunches with his cousins then going out for drinks. Sometimes skinny dipping late at night with the naughty girls, as he called them. Then, half asleep and blind drunk, he would rub his hands along the buildings from the foreshore to home, all the while hoping to find his bed. Finally, he would shut his eyes with the gentle sea breeze from his window and dream of Clara sauntering towards him with her arms outstretched. But the following day, Markus would awaken to see that the other pillow was untouched by Clara; he'd clasp his hands to his face to calm himself and accept the reality of the situation.

Sundays were for church and dinner with his family; he was often late and would kiss his mother, so all would be forgiven. However, his father would chastise him, saying, 'Why are you always late? It's like waiting for royalty to make an entrance every time you come to dinner.'

Markus loved to play Briscola with Josip and his two cousins, an old Italian card game. When time permitted, they would take a trip to Split or Korcula, using the main road from the city that runs through the forest on the island of Blato.

He would perform magic tricks for the children there while catching the eye of some bored housewife who would go home with a smile on her face after spending the afternoon with Markus. Even the ladies selling fish would smile when Markus walked by, tipping his hat and winking at them. He was hard to resist, rather like a Madjanca layer cake that could entice even those with the strongest willpower.

All the men wanted to see Markus settle down while all the women loved how he would surprise them with a visit just for a coffee and some home-baked almond slice, all the while complimenting the ladies and maybe giving a kiss or two on the cheek.

Even women in their eighties, aprons on, preparing food for lunch, would perk up when talking with Markus while waiting for their husbands to return from their early morning walk. After lunch, the old dears would cuddle their husbands, hoping for a bit of afternoon delight. Surely this would bring a smile to both of them. A bit of romance meant that all was well, and that life was good in Dubrovnik.

*

In old movies, we often see calendar pages ripped off by the wind with autumn leaves floating past, followed by the sound of a blizzard, then by the chirping of birds, signifying the passing seasons. Just like the movies, six years indeed had passed quickly since Ivan's death, and a lot had happened during that time. So many births, deaths, and marriages filled those years, and there were many lonely nights for both Clara and Markus.

Markus's cousin, Jelena, married and gave birth to twin girls naming them Isabella and Marissa. Jelena's daughters had long wavy hair, which reminded Markus of Clara. He often visited, doing magic tricks to delight the little ones. They loved to see money appearing from behind their ears which made them giggle with delight. During those visits, Markus wished for a family of his own.

Markus now worked for a tour company, booking tourists on day trips. Sometimes he took ladies on sightseeing tours of the old city. He showed them around the ancient city, taking in sights such as Sponza Palace.

Sponza Palace was a favourite tourist destination, rich in history and craftsmanship. The handrails are huge carved white hands holding the railings. Fine artworks throughout the building. An inner courtyard that at times has been used for weddings. The Palace was at different times a customs office, a mint, a bank, and an armoury.

Markus had some favourite spots like the little Onofrio fountain, constructed in 1442, with its phenomenal gothic decorations, still supplying free drinkable mineral water which flows from under dolphin heads.

He often walked past an inscription above a historic gate, making him stop and nod while contemplating the words, "Non-Bene Pro Toto Libertas Venditur Auro" (Freedom is not to be sold for all the treasures in the world).

Recently, Markus was also working several shifts at Cognito cafe, home to a clowder of cats. Otto, the owner, often joked that Markus must be moisturising his hands with anchovy oil as the cats would appear from every direction, running to greet him when he arrived to start his shift. They rubbed up against his legs almost in a frenzy, making him feed them quickly so they would settle down.

Coffee was the most ordered drink in this establishment, with iced coffee popular during heat waves and artisan ice creams to satisfy even the fussiest of patrons. The cafe had red-checked tablecloths and benches outside so people could relax and take in the sea view.

Otto discovered that Markus was a great asset to his business. His looks and engaging approach with the customers kept them coming back while many also booked a tour.

Otto loved him like a son, and he felt Markus's pain. He, too, had lost the love of his life many years ago and never found anyone that could honestly fill the gap.

At night after work, the two men would enjoy a few shots of liquor while closing the cafe. Then, finally, Markus would wave goodnight and head home, lying in bed and some night crying, for he wanted Clara's body next to him, his sleep so tormented that he would kiss his St. Joseph medallion and hold it in his hand over his heart.

Waiting at the jetty some mornings, Markus would scan the sea, searching for the elusive mermaids' that his mother mentioned. On the ferry, Markus would claim that he swam the 600 metres every morning to Lokrum, winking, smiling in his cheeky way, making people on the ferry laugh and relax, knowing they would have a good time. This tour would not be presented by a stodgy history teacher but rather by a fellow who engagingly talked about history.

Markus explained that Austrian archduke and short-lived Emperor of Mexico Maximilian once had a holiday home on the island. A Benedictine monastery and a botanical garden with 800 exotic plants still survive from that era at Lokrum.

Markus liked to take tours of Fort Lovrijanac, still called Dubrovnik's Gibraltar, with walls facing the sea twelve metres thick in some spots; it deserved its given title. An imposing structure, offering impressive views of the city and the sea from the impenetrable walls built on rugged rock formations. You can view the red roofs of Dubrovnik from the fort walls, which overshadow two entrances to the city, one from the sea and the other from land. Black swifts flew overhead, making their nests in crevices. Markus had read about these birds and marvelled at how they spent most of their time catching food, collecting nest materials, even occasionally sleeping while in flight.

Clara stayed on to look after her mother-in-law, Petra, after Ivan's passing. But, unfortunately, Petra's depression seemed to worsen each day, finally refusing to eat or drink. Gone was the attractive looking woman Petra once was, now with wiry thin hair and a skeletal frame; that would shock even the servants. The doctor had given her iron injections to keep up her strength, but nothing brought her comfort. She eventually was placed in an institution by her husband, Zlatko.

Zlatko was a man not to be trifled with. He was tall with broad shoulders that tapered down to a trim waist. His hands were rough and calloused from many years of hard work. Zlatko had a cigarette permanently in the side of his mouth and never a kind word for anyone, including Petra.

Clara could not bear to stay in the house with Zlatko after Petra left, as he did nothing but drown himself with alcohol, swearing at her every time he saw her. His anger was so raw, blaming her for all the bad luck that had engulfed his family. She had cared for Petra for two years, but Clara fled back to her mother when her mother-in-law was institutionalised.

The locals rarely saw Clara on her return; she was happy not to have people looking at her as though she was a jinx. Instead, her mother, Ana, would often find Clara staring into space, rubbing her eyes repeatedly as if a great sadness had followed her home.

Clara dreamt of Markus every night, wondering what her life might have been—trying to stay optimistic by hoping and telling herself they would be reunited someday.

Markus kept busy working and saving his money. He planned to buy a small house close to his mother and never gave up hope of having a family of his own one day.

Greta, Markus's mother, had noticed an enormous change in him. He was planning for the future, something he'd never worried about before. This change seemed to come about after his father, David, died suddenly from a heart attack. He even stopped staying out late drinking; Greta was happy that Markus was starting to make better choices.

An invitation to his cousin Ruza's wedding arrived, and Greta wanted Markus to accompany her. Markus sat heavily in his chair, trying to decide on his answer. He would want to look his best and hoped he might see Clara at the ceremony. Finally, he agreed, going out the following week to shop for a new suit.

Ana, Clara's mother, had told Clara of the wedding she was attending and fought hard to convince her to attend. 'You can't lock yourself away forever. People will think you have something to hide, but you have nothing to be sorry for! I'm the one who is guilty of allowing your father to give you over to the Svek family, and if I had known what was going on, I would have brought you home sooner and told you to divorce him.'

Ana waved her hands in the air as if she trying to slap someone then bringing them to her face to cry. Her chubby body was shaking with each tear that fell. Seeing her mother sad was too much for Clara to bear, so she placed her hands on her mother's soft grey hair, kissing her forehead and agreeing to accompany her to the wedding.

'Before your father died, Clara, he told me it was his biggest regret, forcing you into that marriage.'

The big day had arrived. Clara admired the dress her mother made her. It was dark blue lace with short sleeves, well fitted and extremely elegant. She combed her hair up high, adding silver butterflies clipped randomly throughout her curls. Her mother had arranged for the local cobbler, Stjepan, to attach the same blue material to her shoes. It was indeed a striking outfit.

'Clara, you might outdo the bride', her mother said.

'I hope not, as it's supposed to be Ruza's special day, mama.' She hugged her mother warmly and kissed both her cheeks.

Greta took her son's arm, trying to calm him down. Markus looked like a nervous teenager about to go to his first dance, realising he'd forgotten to put his trousers on just before leaving the house.

Markus wore a deep blue suit with a pale blue embossed vest underneath. A gold chain linked across to his vest pocket, a gift his grandfather Antonio had given him that afternoon before the wedding. 'Wear this, my son, and may you have as much happiness as I have had wearing it over many years.'

Arriving at the church Clara and her mother were surprised to see some men outside tip their hats. They acknowledged the men with a slight bow as they reached the church door. Ana wore an emerald green suit with a gold brooch her husband David had given her on her wedding day.

In church, you could feel the gush of anticipation by the congregation as Clara entered. A nervous smile crossed Markus's face when he saw his beautiful friend enter. He turned his head to focus on the alter and catch his breath.

Ana tried to control her trembling hands as she sat down on the pew. Clara tried to hide her nerves, her lips felt dry, and she started to fidget like a naughty child whose been told to sit still. Once seated, Clara felt her hands becoming clammy, reached into her bag for a handkerchief. Clara glanced at Markus and smiled, thinking he looked even more handsome than she remembered.

The bride, Ruza, wore a beautiful white gown that had belonged to her grandmother. It had beading down both sleeves, beading also on the bodice depicting two doves. Her mother had altered the dress to fit Ruza's slender body. As she entered her groom, Christofor was mesmerised by her loveliness; he had to be steaded by the best man as he looked as though he would faint.

Christofor had known Ruza since they were small and had even declared that she would be his bride at the ripe old age of five. Naturally, his family had laughed at him, but he never waived in his resolve to marry Ruza. Christofor had short dark hair with a well-crafted beard rather like a musketeer with soft, hazel eyes; he could easily have been on the cover of a fashion magazine.

Later at the reception, Ruza thanked her cousin for his very generous gift, Markus had paid for their honeymoon in Spain. Christofor was so excited that he gripped his arms around Markus and swung him around, lifting him off his feet. 'Careful of my suit Christofor, it's brand new,' Markus said, laughing as he spoke, putting the groom at ease.

The reception was full of energy, lots of chatter, fun, food with wine flowing freely. Antonio asked Clara to dance; they walked hand in hand to the centre of the dancefloor, smiling at each other. Guests at the reception clapped as they knew Antonio was a fine dancer, and as he stepped past Markus, he winked, tilting his head as if to say, *come on, lad, here is your chance, don't blow it. Otherwise, someone else will steal her away.*

Taking a deep breath, unbuttoning his jacket Markus tapped his grandfather on the shoulder and took Clara in his arms. Markus placed his left hand gently on her waist and lifted his right hand just out of reach, so Clara had to rise to tippy toe to reach it. They danced without speaking, looking into each other's eyes. Finally, Clara spoke, saying how nice it was to see him again. Markus told her how much he had wanted to hold her in his arms once more. It had indeed been a long time since they touched.

Antonio was very agile for his age, and he asked as many ladies as possible, both young and old to dance. Just one dance, then he would accompany them to their seat and kiss the back of their hand. He was a real smoothie, much like his grandson Markus. Antonio saved the last dance for his wife, Ema.

Ema shook her head, 'Old man, we need to go home and sleep.'

'You're right, my dear, but I saved the last dance for you, and it's only three in the morning', replied Antonio.

Antonio had soft white hair, a full beard with a chubby face, always smiling; he'd lived a contented life. Parents told local children that Antonio was St Nicholas. Children seemed to be on their best behaviour around him. A Croatian custom is for children to leave their boots on the windowsill, hoping that St. Nicholas will bring them gifts, usually sweets. Unfortunately, St. Nicholas is accompanied by Krampus, a hairy demon. While Nicholas rewards the good children, Krampus leaves sticks for those who have misbehaved. Needless to say, no child wants sticks for Christmas.

People began to tap their glasses when they saw Ruza and Christofor dancing. Tapping glasses is a way of making the bridal couple kiss. Only a kiss will stop the tapping, so Ruza and Christofor kissed for the longest time. The crowd cheered when the married couple left the reception at about four in the morning. The men returned to their drinking while the women continued to chatter and eat the wedding cake.

Clara and Markus seemed inseparable that evening. No bachelors dared ask Clara to dance, as she looked so content in Markus's arms. Then the tapping began again, so Markus asked, 'may I kiss you, Clara?

Clara declared, with a broad smile, 'I've been waiting for this moment for such a long time, Markus.'

Ana and Greta hugged each other when they saw Clara and Markus finally kiss. Both had hoped to see their children find happiness.

Markus was not going to lose his chance to win Clara's heart. Leaning towards Clara's ear, Markus whispered, 'would you like to meet me at Orlando's column tomorrow. We'll hold hands like the old days, and I'll even buy you an ice cream.'

'I wouldn't say no to that. Markus.' Then, laughing, Clara added, 'as long as you don't hold my ice cream up too high.'

Ana and Greta began tapping their glasses again.

Markus asked, 'Kiss me again, Clara', and without replying, she did.

# THE RICKSHAW MAN

## *MARYANN GRIGSON*

The scorching sun beat down on my bare body. The short sarong tucked around my waist was drenched in sweat as I slid my blistered feet into a pair of worn, brown sandals. Finally, I was ready to work, determined to earn two hundred rupees every day.

I was born in India, but I never had the good fortune to be loved by a mother or a father, for I didn't know where they lived or if they still existed.

Brought up in an orphanage with about forty other boys of different ages, sometimes we ate bread and lentils and sometimes we had red rice with a mixture of vegetables cooked into a thick soup. We slept on tattered straw mats spread out on the floor.

The supervisor in charge of the orphanage was tall and middle-aged. He had grey hair, big black eyes, and a beard. He always dressed in long dark trousers, white short-sleeved shirts, and black sandals. We didn't know the man's name, but we called him Sir.

The man took his job very seriously. He taught the boys to talk in Tamil, although they came from different parts of India. He also taught us to speak in English, saying it would help us find work when we were older. However, 'Sir', as we called him, was extremely strict with the boys, and we were all scared of him. A long rattan cane sat on his table in the room, which he used to flog the naughty ones.

Life in the orphanage was miserable. I was constantly hungry with only two meals a day. As I grew older, I thought of leaving the orphanage. I finally ran away when I was fourteen years old and joined a group of urchins living on the streets of Chennai. Some of them were older boys who had lived on street corners all of their lives. They were very cunning, and they taught us younger ones to beg and also how to steal.

We bathed in the rain, wore grimy shorts and torn t-shirts, and walked barefoot on the hot pavements. We shared whatever food we could lay our hands-on, often rummaging through dustbins to find anything that would satisfy our pangs of hunger. People who passed by sometimes gave us food parcels, especially on holy days. We thanked them and bolted around the corner, crouching on our haunches and devouring the food like a flock of hungry crows.

Being the quietest of the gang, I often wondered what it felt like to be loved by somebody. I envied every boy who passed me dressed in crispy new shorts, shirts, and shiny black shoes. *What had become of me,* I thought? *Where was I from? What would my future be?* These were questions I often asked myself, but I had no answers.

At night we slept in an abandoned old building on the other side of the main Chennai Road. The cracked walls had holes in them, but the roof was strong and sheltered us from the sun and the rain. However, the overpowering smell of garbage and rotten food hung around everywhere. We had no choice but to sleep on the dirty cement floor. We woke up every morning and ran to the water tap in the neighbourhood, sloshed water on our faces, rinsed our mouths and onto the streets again. We lived from one day to the next, hoping to beg or even steal to fill our hungry bellies with at least a morsel of food.

Although I was just a street urchin, I was interested in everything around me. I envied the man who drove a bus or a motor car, a van or even a truck. I stood on the pavement and watched the tuk-tuk drivers creep in and out of traffic. I was jealous of the cyclists who rode past me. Any type of vehicle that travelled on the road interested me. I thought to myself that someday I would like to find a job as a driver.

The older boys taught the younger ones to become pickpockets. They had always stolen wallets to buy any food, and they were able to teach us how and when to pick somebody's pocket. So I stood on the street corners of Chennai and watched the people walk by. I was a tall fifteen-year-old boy, dark-skinned and skinny. My curly black hair had grown quite long and curled around my ears. I worked with Kumar, a younger boy who looked up to me and thought I was a hero.

Kumar was also an orphan, following me like a shadow. The little chap had dark brown hair and dimples, and his face lit up when he smiled. He carried a piece of velvet cloth that he used to shine shoes. We usually stopped gentlemen on the street on their way to the office and asked if they would like to have a shoeshine. While my helper was busy polishing the man's shoes with the velvet cloth, I stood behind the guy and slipped the wallet out of his pocket.

Sometimes I was lucky to collect two or three wallets in a day, but the older boys were extremely mean and they watched and waited. They grabbed the wallets from me and took all the money. I was given a few meagre rupees in exchange for my hard work. I always gave Kumar 10 rupees and put the rest of the money in a tin can I hid in the abandoned building where we lived. In this way, I was able to collect a few rupees each day.

One day the police caught me in the act. I was terrified when a policeman dressed in khaki shorts and shirt pounced on me from behind. He handcuffed me and threw me into a prison cell with four other boys. Although I was given a prison sentence by a magistrate who wore a white wig, he told me that he would double my sentence the next time he saw me if I did not reform myself.

I was terrified and shivered with fear. I was worried about my little helper Kumar. The boys in the cell were older than me. They were wicked, and they bullied me and abused me in that prison cell. I became a blubbering mess in their midst.

Meals were meagre and had no flavour. The other four in my cell ate first and threw the leftover scraps to me. I was constantly hungry. My stomach made funny noises to which the others laughed. I was miserable, and I became fragile and bony.

Days followed nights, and I lost count of what day it was. The older boys always ganged up and hurled insults at me. They frightened me, so I kept my distance and stayed in the darkest corner of the cell, lost in my thoughts.

*What would be my fate? Where would I end? When would I be released from this hellhole,* I wondered? These thoughts went round and round in my head until finally, they became so loud that I hardly slept at all.

I promised myself that I would never steal again or do anything wrong to anybody when I was released. I remembered the magistrate's words and was determined to be a good person, find a job and build a life for myself. These thoughts comforted me, and I continued to dream about the man that I wanted to be.

I finally walked out of prison after six months, glad to feel the sunshine on my thin body and to see blue skies again. It was good to see ordinary people walk by and hear the street vendors trading goods. I gave the old haunts a wide berth, and I was determined not to venture anywhere near them. The day I got out of prison, I crept into the abandoned building when my old gang was out and collected the money that I had hidden. Thankfully, no one had found it.

I left Chennai that very day and caught a bus to the seaside town of Velankani in the south of India. It was the first bus leaving that night, and I didn't care where it was going as long as it took me out of the city. I was hoping to get a job of some sort, and any place would do. It was the first time I had ever been on an inter-city bus.

The trip took most of the night. There was a television on board the bus with an old Tamil movie on repeat. As the bus reached the highway, it began to move at great speed. I was sitting by a window where the heavy wind started to make me feel cold. Some people on the bus were sleeping while others watched the movie. I just gazed out of the window. At some time during the night, the conductor turned off the TV. In a short time, most of the people on the bus were sleeping, some snoring loudly. I couldn't sleep thinking about what I was going to do when I arrived at my destination. It was pitch black outside, and there were hardly any streetlights, so all that was visible to me were silhouettes of places we passed.

The bus finally reached the seaside town as the sun was beginning to rise. The bus station was quite busy, but it was half the size of the one in Chennai. Small shops, food kiosks, and restaurants selling various goods lined the station perimeter. I could see the gleaming white towers of a Christian church peeping over the buildings in the distance.

Across from the bus terminal was a boutique (small food shop) that looked busy. Wandering over, I paid for a mug of tea with some of the money I had saved from picking pockets.

The owner who sat behind the counter was short and stocky, his bald head covered with drops of sweat, and a thick moustache covered his upper lip. He wore a grimy *banion* (singlet) and a checked sarong and looked harassed. I noticed him scrutinising me when I counted the change to pay for my tea.

The boutique was located in a central spot and served food and beverages to weary bus passengers, its shelves stacked with all kinds of snacks. I could see that it was a busy place with many customers coming to eat and refresh from their journey's.

After I finished drinking my tea, I decided to be bold and ask the man for a job.

'I am looking for work,' I said, bowing my head to him in deference. I had learned on the street that ordinary people would react more positively if you showed them some respect. 'I will do anything to earn some money.'

'Where are you from?' he asked, looking at me strangely. 'I have not seen you around here before.'

I was hot and tired after the long bus trip and weak from hunger. But, if I wanted sympathy from the man, I had to be as truthful as I could.

'I am from Chennai, sir,' I said, looking straight at him. 'I am an orphan. I left the city to get away from a street gang. I don't know anyone here, and I will do any work that you can give me.'

'You don't look like you've had enough to eat,' he said while pouring tea from a battered tin kettle that he picked up from the burner.

'I eat when I can afford to.' I shook my head at him sadly. 'I don't always have money to buy food.' I couldn't remember the last time I wasn't hungry.

The man whose name was Thambi must have seen something in me, so he offered me a job to clean tables, sweep the floors and wash mugs and plates. I felt so relieved, and I smiled. Here was my chance to start anew.

The boutique opened at seven in the morning and closed at eight at night. I was allowed to sleep on the veranda outside the boutique. I was fed and paid a small wage, and I worked hard every day. I built up my stamina by eating big healthy meals. I saved every cent that Thambi paid me because I was determined to leave India.

Over time Thambi and I became friends. He knew that I was an orphan, but I didn't let on about my past habit as a pickpocket. The man trusted me and sent me on all sorts of errands with money to pay various people. I had turned my back on that old habit of stealing, and I never let him down.

As the days went by, I heard many stories from my friend. Thambi was a Tamil man who had grown up in Ceylon with his parents and two older brothers. His family had lived in Galle, a famous town in the south of the island. His father was a *mudalali* (proprietor) who owned a boutique that sold groceries. He told me that Ceylon is a tiny island known as the *Pearl in the Indian Ocean*. He said it is a beautiful place with lovely beaches and friendly people and the best mug of tea a man could ever drink. I pricked up my ears and listened carefully to everything my friend said.

That night I sat on the outer veranda, but I couldn't sleep because I was excited about all the things that Thambi had told me about Ceylon. *Wouldn't it be an excellent place for me,* I thought?

I worked hard in the boutique for five years. I saved all the tips the customers gave me and most of my monthly wages too. Finally, I decided now was the time to quit and start a new life. Regretfully I had to tell Thambi that I wanted to leave the boutique.

After the boutique had closed the following evening, I decided to speak to him about my plan. So we sat down together to have dinner that night.

'Thambi, my friend,' I said, 'I think it is the right time for me to leave.'

He was shocked and nearly choked on his food. He sipped from his glass of water and looked at me curiously. 'Why do you want to leave? Are you not happy working with me?'

'I am glad that I met you, Thambi and thank you for your kindness in giving me a job when I was so desperate, but when I heard your stories about Ceylon, I decided to go there. I want to start a life of my own and be a part of a family. I think I can do it there.'

Thambi studied me for a moment and then nodded his head in agreement. It made me feel better. I owed this man so much.

'I have never regretted taking you in, and I am sorry that you are leaving,' he said as he hugged me. 'Good luck, my boy,' he said, 'just be careful.'

I had become strong and hardy, a man with an adventurous spirit, ready to discover the world. Unfortunately, I could hardly read or write, but thankfully, I learned to speak the English language in the orphanage. Now I was determined to find my way to Ceylon.

I left the boutique the next day with my clothes packed into a brown cloth bag I slung over my shoulder. I tucked my wallet with the money that I had collected safely into my trouser pocket and walked out into the sunshine. As I walked along, I heard the sweet sound of the birds chirping. I knew that I was doing the right thing, and my heart felt lighter with every step that I took.

While I had been working at the tea boutique, I often overheard people talking about the fishing boats, that for a price, would smuggle anything or anybody across the Bay of Bengal into Ceylon. So I had often sneaked down to the fishing harbour and talked with the owners of the fishing boats, and I knew which of them would take me across the water.

I walked the short distance to the jetty and approached a man who stood beside a wooden fishing boat I knew was from Ceylon. I had seen him around the harbour many times and heard that he was a people smuggler.

'How much do you charge for a boat ride to Ceylon?' I asked the man.

He was a big guy with long hair that reached down to his shoulders dressed in khaki shorts and a blue t-shirt. He looked around carefully before answering.

'We are almost full, but if you give me 1,000 rupees right now,' he growled, 'I'll take you across, but it has to be tonight.'

I nodded so he motioned that I should get into the boat. I paid him the fare which was a lot of money, but if I wanted to cross into Ceylon, I had no choice but to pay him.

It was my first trip on a boat that looked too small to cross the sea. Conditions below deck were cramped, crowded with men and women, sitting with their legs crossed almost on each other. There was barely any room to move. There were two containers of water for us to share. The rest of the containers contained fuel.

The sea was rough, and the journey was uncomfortable. The salt air and the sound of the waves dashing against the boat made me sick, and I vomited. But the thought of starting a new life in a new land hardened me. I knew that once I reached Ceylon, things would be different.

After two long days, the boat finally reached the northern Jaffna peninsula. The rain was coming down in torrents, and we were soaked to the bone as we stepped out from the little boat. Nevertheless, I felt happy for the first time, and I ran with my bag to a bus shelter and stayed undercover until the rain ceased.

The rain clouds disappeared, and the sun began to shine. I was curious, and I wanted to know more about Ceylon. I looked around me. Almost everything looked similar to my birth land. Two crows perched on a tree branch made a racket as they feasted on a dead squirrel. A cockerel crowed and ran across to the other side of the road. Cars and motorbikes honked and tooted and sped by at great speed. Men and women traded goods by the wayside in this land called Ceylon.

The locals spoke in Tamil using words I couldn't recognise. Then, looking around, I saw a middle-aged man near the bus stop smoking a cigarette.

'I am sorry to disturb you, sir,' I began hesitantly. 'I am new here. Could you please tell me where the busiest city in this land is?'

He looked at me curiously. 'Why do you want to know?'

'I am looking for work, and I think it will be the best place for me to find something.'

'It is down south in Colombo, the capital of Ceylon, where interesting things happen.' The man replied.

'How do I get there?' I asked him.

'You have to catch a bus to the Jaffna railway station and buy a train ticket to Colombo.' He told me.

After catching two busses, I just managed to catch the night train to Colombo. It was exciting to be inside a train for the first time. I looked around at the many people in the compartment. Small children slept on their mother's laps. A lady sitting next to the window looking out. A man wearing a sarong and shirt walked through the compartment, selling hot tea and biscuits, calling out his wares. Tired after the long trip on the boat, I paid the man for a mug of tea, drank the hot mixture, stretched my legs, clutched my bag, and dozed off. The rhythmic rattle of the train as it picked up speed finally lulled me to sleep.

I awoke to the shrieking sound of a whistle. It was morning. The train had stopped at the Dehiwela Railway Station, located in a southern suburb of Colombo. I had slept through the whole night. I got off quickly as people shoved and pushed to get to the exit. I held onto my bag and walked outside to bright morning sunshine.

The road sign next to the station read Station Road. So I walked up the road until I came upon a milk bar. I bought a bottle of chocolate milk and drank it with a plastic straw. I had to find a place to live, so I asked the milk bar owner in English how to rent a room.

'Where are you from?' he asked, looking at me curiously.

'I have just arrived on the night train from Jaffna.' I had decided that I wouldn't tell anyone that I had initially come from India.

'I have a room that you could rent for 100 rupees a month', he said.

I smiled at the man and told him, 'That would suit me fine.'

I paid him the rent for a month and went into the room behind the milk bar. It was small but sufficient for my needs. I left my bag on the narrow bed, had a shower in a simple bathroom, changed my clothes, then walked to a bakery nearby. I paid for my breakfast, a bun and banana and a hot cup of tea.

I was eager to start my business and get some information on how to begin the trade. The money I had saved when I worked in Thambi's boutique would help me to begin work. But the dream of working in the transport business was fixed in my head. I had been lonely all of my life, and I wanted to be with people, talk with them and enjoy their company.

I walked the streets of this busy suburb for some time, and at last, I found a place that hired rickshaws. A rickshaw is a chariot with two steps to climb into with two big wheels and seats facing each other and brown wooden poles on either side for a man to pull the rickshaw.

The older man who owned the place looked grumpy. His big round eyes stared at me from behind his spectacles.

'What do you want?' he growled.

'I want to hire a rickshaw. What do you charge per day?' I asked the man.

He gave me a fee which I thought was too high. I decided to bargain with the older man. I told him very firmly.

'Your rickshaws aren't new, and your charges are too high. I shall look for another place to hire a rickshaw'.

The look on his face told me that he hadn't had any trade at all today. Finally, he turned towards me and said, 'If you pay me 50 rupees a week, you can hire a rickshaw'.

I paid the grumpy old man the money he wanted and inspected the five rickshaws in the shop. I chose a black one with shiny silver wheels, which looked less beat up than the others. I pulled the rickshaw along the black tarred road and returned to my living quarters. I parked it on the side road, locked the rickshaw and walked into my room.

I was so excited and couldn't sleep that night. I was in Ceylon, where the people were friendly, kind and helpful. The transport business was my dream, and I was about to start. *What more could I ask for?*

I parked my black chariot the following day at the top of station road, and

I waited, hoping someone would hire me. Finally, a man and two young girls dressed in white school uniforms, long white socks and shoes approached me.

He approached me and asked, 'How much will you charge to take my daughters to the convent close by?'

What an exciting moment. It was Monday morning, and my work has just begun and here was my first ride. I smiled with the man and replied, 'Pay me fifteen rupees sir, and I will take your children to the school'.

The man gave me the money and went on his way. I pulled the rickshaw along the dusty road right up to the convent. The two young sisters giggled all the way. They stepped out, saying, 'thank you for the ride'.

My business was off to a good start. The job kept me extremely busy, and I was certainly one happy man. People liked to ride in my black rickshaw with its shiny wheels.

My customers became friendly, and we chattered with each other. On school days, I took boys and girls dressed in white school uniforms to different schools. I also transported beautiful ladies, young and old, dressed in pretty gowns, hats and shoes for Sunday mass. Gentlemen dressed in dark suits, shirts and ties rode to the office in my rickshaw. Women who worked as nurses, dark and fair ones dressed in white frocks and caps, used my rickshaw as I dropped them off at the hospitals. Every one of my customers was cheerful and friendly. I was a satisfied man.

Time passed swiftly, I worked harder and longer hours each day and saved enough money to buy a second-hand rickshaw which I got fixed to look almost like new. Having my rickshaw increased my self-esteem, so I changed my attire from sarongs to shorts and t-shirts and my usual customers, who were now my friends, looked at me differently.

One day, I noticed that a small vegetable kiosk had sprung up across the road from where I parked my rickshaw. A middle-aged woman and a young girl sat inside the booth selling vegetables and fruit. I was curious and wondered who they were?

The following day after my school drop off, I decided to buy some bananas, so I crossed the road and went up to the kiosk.

As I entered, the young girl said, 'Can I help you?'

'How much is a kilo of bananas?' I asked. She was about my age, tall, and slim with long wavy hair and gleaming white teeth. She wore a floral skirt, a green blouse, and a pair of sandals. She looked beautiful.

'We charge five rupees for a kilo. Do you want them?' she said demurely.

I smiled and told her that I wanted a kilo. I stood and watched as she weighed the bananas and put them into a bag. I paid her five rupees, and she glanced at me when she took the money and handed me the bag. I could sense the older woman watching us.

After my work finished, I went to my little room and had a shower. After that, I ate a packet of rice and curry, which I had bought from the bakery. Then I lay in bed and thought about the girl in the vegetable kiosk.

*Wouldn't it be nice if I could chat with her and be a friend*? So I thought while drifting off to sleep.

A new day dawned, and I woke up excited. I showered and dressed in a pair of khaki shorts and a blue striped t-shirt, brushed my hair, and put on my sandals. Then I pulled the rickshaw along the road to begin work. I took six children on different school routes in the morning and transported a nurse to the hospital nearby. Next, three foreign ladies wanted to ride to the Mt. Lavinia Hotel in my rickshaw. They climbed out when we reached the hotel, patted my shoulders, and paid me an extra fifty rupees for transporting them.

Life was good, and I was happy. I whistled a tune as I ran along with my rickshaw to pick two girls after school and drop them off at home.

I looked across the street and found the kiosk open. The mother and her daughter were standing outside. A lorry drove up and dropped a large gunny bag filled with vegetables just near the booth. I thought they might want some help, so I crossed over and offered to carry the gunny bag inside. Both women smiled and thanked me. I told them that I am the rickshaw man from across the street and offered to help anytime.

The young girl said her name was Savithri and her mother's name was Kamala. I had a short break before the evening shift, so we chatted for a while, and my heartbeat quickened each time she flashed her friendly smile.

*What was happening?* Thoughts rushed through my mind. I never had any feelings for anyone and didn't understand why I felt this way. *Was I falling in love with this girl? How would I know if she felt the same way?*

I decided I wouldn't rush and bide my time, not frighten her. So I paid her the money for two guavas and went back to work.

Within a year, I saved enough money to rent a small house a few streets away and furnished it with some necessities. I dropped in at the kiosk every day after work and chatted with both women. We discussed business and things of interest and eventually became good friends. Now my greatest desire was to win this young girl's heart and ask her to be my wife.

A week before Christmas, I bought a pink sari and jacket from a shop in Dehiwela and presented them to Savithri. She was so excited and opened it in front of her mother.

'Thank you, my friend, but how did you know pink was my favourite colour?' She jumped up and down like a child.

I glanced at Kamala, who had a satisfied smile on her face. 'I looked at many other colours and finally decided that pink would suit you best,' I replied.

Her mother seemed happy and content with our friendship, being older and wiser. Maybe her mind was already made up about her daughter's future as a rickshaw man's wife.

Savithri and I hope to be married soon with her mother's permission. I will finally acquire the family I've always longed for, and I will never be alone again.

My life as an orphan, a street urchin and a pickpocket now seem like a bad dream. My name is Velu, and I am the happiest and the most satisfied rickshaw man in Ceylon.

# THE GIFT

## *MELISSA SAYERS*

It was a chilly Tuesday morning, much like many others, but this morning was different. Tilly Hart opened her eyes, stretched her arms and legs and smiled. Light filtered through the opaque roman blinds casting a delicate glow over the room. She climbed out of bed and flung open the blinds. Soon she would need to close the block-outs for her husband, who would be on his way home from the night shift, but for the moment, she wanted to soak in the sun and the bright blue sky. Yes, something was different this morning.

Tilly glanced over at the test strip on her nightstand, smiled and caressed her belly. They had been trying for so long. Tilly slipped out of her winter pyjamas and into a knee-length black satin slip because there was something to celebrate this morning. She wrung her hands in anticipation.

"Hurry up, Gordon. I can't wait to tell you." She giggled and did a little dance where she stood.

She and Gordon had met at nursing school, and from the moment they met, they had been virtually inseparable, moving in together after only a couple of months and marrying a year to the day they met. They finished each other's sentences, always held hands and embraced at every opportunity. They seemed to glow in each other's company.

Generally, on a weekday, Gordon would creep into bed around 7, grab a quick cuddle, then kiss Tilly on the forehead, signalling the need for her to get up and start the day. But, these last few months, they had passed like ships in the night, Gordon on night shift and Tilly on day shift.

Tilly stroked her belly again. There was so much to look forward to. Her mind was awash with all the things the future held.

Out of the silence, Tilly's phone rang. "Don't tell me you're running late, Gordon Hart. I can't keep this to myself much longer." She answered with a smile on her face. "How late are you going to be?" She asked, whispering a silent prayer that he would not be too much longer.

"Tilly, it's Amanda." Amanda was the night charge nurse at the Royal Melbourne Hospital. "I need you to sit down and try and stay calm for me."

Tilly collapsed to the floor. *No, it can't be. No, he wouldn't do that to me. Not now. Not this morning.*

"Tilly, there's been an accident." Tilly gasped, and for a moment, felt she couldn't breathe. "A drunk driver ran through a stop sign and ran straight through Gordon. I'm so sorry Till, his head injuries were too severe. We tried, we tried so hard, but he lost so much blood. There was just nothing we could do. Again, I'm so sorry Till." Tilly dropped the phone into her lap and began sobbing uncontrollably, her chest heaving and tears flooding from her eyes. It felt like half of her was gone. Like she had lost a limb.

*Why now? Why today? Why this morning? This can't be right. Surely, he wouldn't do this to me.*

"Till..." came the echo from the phone in her lap. She took a deep breath, consciously exhaled and picked up the phone.

"Yeah, Manda," she whispered, trying to compose herself.

"I hate to do this to you, but can you come down and identify him? You're his next of kin, honey."

"Yep, I'll be there shortly." Her voice cracked down the line. "Thanks, Manda."

Changing from her slip, Tilly ran her hand over her belly again, and the tears began to flow as she looked at the side of the bed where Gordon would normally lay. Where Gordon would never lay again, and she grabbed his pillow. It smelled like his aftershave. Sweet and musky. She loved that smell on him, loved nuzzling into his neck and breathing it in.

She changed quickly into jeans and a flannel shirt and grabbed her purse, phone and keys. Normally one to drive with the music blaring, she made the trip this morning in silence. Tears fell soundlessly down her cheeks, her breathing laboured and shallow.

She found a park in the visitors parking, grabbed a ticket and slowly, methodically, walked towards the emergency department. She stopped at the door; her feet frozen to the floor.

*I can't do it,* she thought. *Not today!*

But she bolstered herself, took command of her body, wiped her tears and stepped into the ED. She was buffeted with that old familiar smell of sanitiser and wiped her hands before she entered.

It was a strange sensation entering the department on the other side of the glass wall as a family member, not a staff member.

Amanda's face dropped as she saw Tilly walk through the sliding glass doors. She immediately came to embrace her, and the tears began to flow again.

"Did he suffer?" Tilly asked.

"No, honey. He had a massive brain haemorrhage. He was out when he got here and never regained consciousness." Amanda quietly explained. "It would have been quick."

"I need to see him." Tilly's voice was coarse and ragged.

"Of course." Amanda wrapped her arm around Tilly and guided her to the familiar room where family members were brought to say their last goodbyes. Tilly stood at the door, hand on the handle, and took a deep breath.

There he lay. The love of her life. So serene. Like he was just asleep. Slowly, deliberately, she stepped towards him. Unable to control her emotions any longer, Tilly collapsed into the chair beside Gordon's bed.

Then out of nowhere, peace came over her. She gently placed his hand on her belly and rested her head on his shoulder.

"I have something to tell you." She whispered, almost mischievously. "I have your baby in my belly. A piece of you, so I will never be without you."

She leaned up and kissed him tenderly on the cheek, lingering a moment, breathing him in. She placed her hand over his, where their child silently grew. She felt a sense of infinite connection and strength.

And with that, she stood, glanced one more time at the man who had forever captured her heart and walked purposefully out of the room, all the while knowing that she would carry him in her heart forever.

# EGYPT, JORDAN, AND THE HOLY LANDS

## A CONDENSED TRAVEL JOURNAL FROM BEFORE THE PANDEMIC.

### CORINNE KING

It was the final realisation of a childhood dream. We were getting organised to embark on a series of holidays to explore countries of incredible history, scenic beauty, intense spirituality, and inspiration. Ian and I were on our way to Egypt, Jordan, and Israel. We planned to spend four weeks exploring and walking the soil with historical and spiritual connections. We also planned to visit Sri Lanka, the land of my birth, afterwards. However, there were many hurdles to accomplish before we could embark on this epic journey scheduled for early November 2019.

Our travel day finally dawned with a feeling of freedom and blessings from above. I had experienced a few nail-biting days of anxiety over a medical condition that needed treatment in the days prior. Finally, cleared to travel,

I could leave on my trip, a most satisfying and long-awaited outcome. What we did not know at the time was that a new coronavirus had started to do its deadly work in far distant China and that this would be the last overseas trip we would be doing for a while.

The Emirates flight from Melbourne to Dubai was a tedious fourteen-hour flight, whereas the flight from Dubai to Cairo was a short three hours and twenty minutes. After arriving in Cairo, our tour guide greeted us, and we checked in to the Marriott Hotel in the city centre. Extremely tired, we crashed after a light dinner as we had an early start.

We were travelling with an APT/Travel Marvel Group who had come from all over Australia. Meeting our fellow travellers at breakfast was an exhilarating feeling, as was the realisation that we would finally be exploring many beautiful places of interest.

On Day Two, we had chosen an optional tour, a 3-hour journey to Alexandria to visit its ancient Egyptian Catacombs, the old Egyptian Museum and have lunch at the Fish Market Restaurant on the foreshore.

Alexandria is a beautiful city looking out at the stunning azure blue Mediterranean Sea. After a delicious lunch, we drove to the world-famous Bibliotheca Alexandrina Library. Half a day isn't sufficient to take in the entire building with the main library exhibitions, the planetarium and science centre and its numerous internal galleries and permanent displays. I would say one would need six months to enjoy the countless artefacts therein. What fascinated me in the short time we had was the Nobel Prize Winners section, where every winner of the prize had a head monument and individual plaque sitting on a single stand.

Our coach driver and guide were both university-qualified graduates holding degrees in Egyptology. Listening to these two knowledgeable men give us a detailed history of the city combined with what we were observing was a great experience. We were fortunate to be allocated coach seats right behind the driver and next to the guide. We gradually got used to their

Egyptian accents on the long drive back to Cairo for our official 'meet and greet' over canapes and drinks at the Marriot.

On Day Three, we all met for early breakfast before leaving for a full day of touring to the Pyramids of Giza. The breakfast buffet at the Marriott Hotel was as impressive, a diabetic's dream. After a hearty meal, we excitedly boarded our coach for the drive. I had eagerly awaited the moment I would finally set eyes on the Pyramids.

To see the monuments even from a distance gave me the fulfilment I had yearned for all these years. Finally, at 11 am, we had a clear view of the Pyramids. Tears streamed down my cheeks as I gazed in awe at the magnificent sight ahead of us. It was the same emotion I had experienced when I first set eyes on the Grand Canyon and LA's Disneyland in the USA, the Niagara Falls in Canada, the Taj Mahal in India, the Terracotta Warriors, and the Great Wall in China. This day was to be yet another repeat of emotional joy and disbelief to fulfil another childhood dream.

The Pyramids of Giza were spectacular. When we reached our destination at the historic and ancient site of Egyptian culture, we walked right up to the first and largest pyramid, the Great Pyramid of Khufu, which is the oldest of the Seven Wonders of the Ancient World, the only one to remain largely intact. We sat on the bottom row of the massive slabs placed so precisely by ancient builders between 2580 to 2560 BC in the 4th Dynasty.

We paid an extra 200 Egyptian Pounds to go inside the Great Pyramid. Tourists are allowed to enter via the Robbers' Tunnel, which was cut straight through the masonry of the pyramid in ancient times. We passed through the solid stone blocks that make up the pyramid's core to explore its cramped, hidden passages and chambers. The use of cameras and videos was strictly prohibited.

Our second stop was around the corner to see both the second and third pyramids from a vantage lookout point. Then it was back into the coach to drive a bit further down the road to view the Great Sphinx of Giza, known as the Great Monument of Egypt. The Great Sphinx is a limestone statue of a reclining sphinx, a mythical creature with a lion's body and a human head.

It was sad to get back on the Coach and leave the Pyramids behind as we headed off to the Papyrus Museum. Here we witnessed how Papyrus paper, a mindboggling ancient artwork of the Egyptians and the forerunner to the writing material we use today, was made. The papyrus plant, which once flourished in the River Nile area, has gradually disappeared, although the plant grows in other parts of Africa and the Mediterranean. It was fascinating to feel the real papyrus which is extremely strong against a sample of 'fake' papyrus paper made from banana skins.

The lunch break on this warm day in Cairo was welcome as we were all starting to feel 'pangs' of hunger. We drove through a picturesque landscape, enjoying the ambience of a botanical gardens-style park surrounding for lunch. Lunch was a bowl of chicken soup and local pita bread straight out of the oven. The main course followed. A sticky rice ball served with chicken and beef kebabs and salad. Dessert was an Egyptian-style rich milk rice pudding with sultanas and nuts sprinkled on the top and served in dainty porcelain bowls. That evening after a short afternoon rest, we attended a spectacular 'sound and light show' against the backdrop of the Pyramids.

On Day Four, we proceeded to the central Egyptian Museum to visit Nefertiti's artefacts and Tutankhamun's treasures excavated from the excavation in 1922 by British Archaeologist Howard Carter. This fascinating Museum housed the mummified remains of King Tutankhamen's great grandparents, Yuya and Thuya. We stood in awe as we viewed their mummified remains in an elaborately constructed sarcophagus, stone coffins carved by exceptional craftsmen.

On our way back to the hotel, we had brief tours of the Mosque of ibn Tulun, the largest in Cairo. We also visited the Synagogue of the Levantines in Old Coptic Cairo, reputed to be where the Pharoah's daughter found baby Moses on the banks of the Nile. These experiences will be etched in our minds forever. Having experienced a fulfilling day, we looked forward to dinner and a rest in the luxurious Marriott Hotel, our Cairo home.

On Day Five, our last day in Cairo was a 'free day' to pack, relax and enjoy the grandeur and splendour of the city. We spent the time strolling along the picturesque River Nile and resting.

The following day, we were up at 2.30 am, had breakfast by 3.15 am left as early as 4:00 am to catch an early morning flight to Luxor. There, we were to embark on our four-night River Nile cruise.

Our 7:00 am flight was one hour and fifteen minutes long. It was fast baggage-retrieval in Luxor and out into the coach to drive to the famous Karnak Temple. We toured the 'Temple of Karnak' and 'The Luxor Temple', which were breathtaking. Sadly, most of these buildings are in ruins as they date back over 3,400 to 2,300 years BC.

We left the temple complex to board our vessel, the Movenpick Ship R.V Royal Lily, which was to be our 'home' for the next four nights. Our first meal on board was a buffet of enticing and delicious dishes.

On Day Six, we stopped at Edfu and visited the Valley of the Queens and the Valley of the Kings. The coach trip to the Valley of the Queens and Kings was long, resulting in many of us having cat naps. The morning was strenuous, walking in 'searing' heat with bottles of water to rehydrate. But, amazingly, one doesn't feel so exhausted because every fifteen minutes, we saw an ancient tomb or the fascinating hieroglyphics, which made us wonder at the incredible history of this ancient culture. A phenomenal experience indeed.

We were invigorated when our guide announced that we were returning to the ship for yet another tasty buffet lunch, followed by a 'free' afternoon where we could relax and savour the ambience of Edfu. Unfortunately, the nightlife on the vessel was limited, and we were not encouraged to keep late hours because of early morning rises and tight schedules.

On Day Seven, we went into Edfu in a horse-drawn carriage, indeed a great experience. The Temple of Edfu was a sandstone temple dedicated to the Falcon God Horus. The temple's gables depict artwork of historic festivals. After lunch on the boat, we visited the Temple of Kom Ombo, a very unusual temple. A long uphill walk was necessary for this visit, but it was worth the struggle and helped reduce some kilos that were gradually piling up with the delectable meals served on board.

That evening, we toured the ship's galley, a must to anyone travelling like this. We learned what goes on behind the scenes on board regarding the culinary aspect of food preparation. Another fascinating tour was the Captain's Bridge which gave us an insight into the navigational skills of a Ship's captain and the intricacies of steering a river cruise ship. Most cruise ships sail throughout the night when all their passengers are asleep.

That afternoon's itinerary was a leisurely cruise down the River Nile to Aswan. We were all in a great mood that evening as excitement filled the air. We all dressed up for the 'Egyptian Night of Nights'! We did well with the head attires purchased from the ship's clothing shop on board. Ian and I played the part of 'The King & Queen of Sheba'! It was an impressive sight as everyone had gone to the trouble of dressing up, Egyptian style, for a most enjoyable night of fun and frolic on the luxurious ship.

Day Eight in Egypt - yet another full itinerary lined up. We boarded a Felucca, a small traditional wooden sailing boat propelled by oars or lateen sail and sailed around El Nabatat or Kitchener's Island, named after the British Consul-General for Egypt in 1914 who owned it. Drifting alongside this island now turned into a picturesque Botanical Gardens, we saw many luscious plants native to Aswan.

We were getting used to travelling by coach and other modes of travel in 'searing' heat as we had a short sightseeing tour to the unfinished Obelisk Temple. Afterwards, we rushed off to the Aswan Airport for a short domestic flight to Abu Simbel to visit the magnificent temples once buried under centuries of sand and restored in 1813 for all civilisation to appreciate.

Visiting the Abu Simbel Temple was a realisation of its history and magnificence, which is beyond imagination. It was beautiful to see the Key of Life or the 'Ankh' in the door. The Key to the Nile or 'Crux Ansata' in Latin means 'Cross with a Handle', the ancient Egyptian Hieroglyphic character that read 'Eternal Life'. Egyptian Gods are often portrayed carrying it by its loop or bearing one in each hand and arms crossed over their chest.

We marvelled at the two awe-inspiring temples considered masterpieces of ancient Egypt. We enjoyed the breathtaking ambience around us and strolled around this phenomenon of ancient history in 38°C of intense heat at noon. We were prepared for this heat as we travelled adequately attired and hydrated for searing temperatures.

Our guide informed us that we were heading to the Abu Simbel airport for our short 'EgyptAir' flight back to Aswan, where the ship anchored. An exhilarating experience for our second last day in Egypt. We were exhausted, and two-thirds of our fellow travellers decided to return to the vessel at 4.30 pm to get some rest. It was only a minority that braved the heat and went on a visit to the Essential Egyptian Oils and Aromatherapy Factory.

Not with tons of energy, but coping well, we showered and dressed up for our second last evening for a Nubian Folkloric Show organised onboard the vessel. These types of shows are popular in Egypt. Nubian music is performed in Arabic and relies on drumbeats, clapping, fiddles, flutes, and various other percussion instruments. Nubia is an ancient region in North-eastern Africa, which extends approximately from the Nile River Valley (near the first cataract in Upper Egypt) eastward to the shores of the Red Sea.

Day Nine of our Egypt exploration dawned in a melancholy way. All good things do come to an end as we prepared to leave our 'home' for the past five days. It was indeed a treat to have been a passenger on this great ship that sailed the River Nile.

We were up early to complete our last two sightseeing excursions in Egypt and, after an exquisite buffet breakfast, we were on our way at 7 am for a day excursion to the Aswan Dam.

We flew 'Nile Air' from Aswan Airport, an internal flight to Cairo Airport, to go our separate ways. Saying our 'Goodbyes' to the group we had mingled with for many days and shared spectacular and awe-inspiring moments was sad.

It was soul-wrenching to leave Egypt, a country that we could never forget for its ancient culture and history. Our guide and coach driver who had enraptured our imagination with their immense knowledge of the history of their native land they were so proud of, enabling them to talk to us with such a learned sense and sensibility of place and date.

On a balmy night in Cairo, we drove to the airport to fly to Amman to begin our next tour of Jordan, Israel, and join the Holy Land Pilgrimage.

At 12.45 am on 16th November, we landed in Jordan and looked forward to the next chapter of our tour. First, we went through Customs, meeting with our Visa Officer, Issi, who handed us our Visa Certificate. Then, after collecting our baggage, we walked out of the airport terminal to meet with Rabah, who took us to the apartment block we had booked into for the night.

The morning dawned with us having only four hours of sleep, but we had to be 'bright and chirpy' to meet our new group of fellow travellers. We met our new coach driver and guide, locals who told us that we were in a territory with constant unrest, considering that the 'Gaza Strip' was only eighty kilometres away from Jordan. Electrifying news for the start of a new trip!

At 10:00 am, we travelled to the Amman airport to pick up Gillian, who joined the tour and proceeded to Petra in Jordan, driving four hours and twenty minutes. About two hours into the drive, we stopped at a complex for lunch and a restroom stop. The three-course meal was a delightful blend of Middle Eastern Cuisine and cost us Dina 12, a mere song in dollars. Then, we boarded the coach and continued to our overnight abode at the Amra

Palace Hotel, a picturesque and breathtaking place with palm trees and window boxes to each room with a view across to the City of Petra. At night it looked like a fairyland across the valley.

When checking in, we learned that it would cost us $25 per person to attend a Jordanian Cultural Folklore Show in the Old Village Resort in Petra. For us and another couple, this was a 'pièce de résistance' that was too good to refuse. So we arranged for a taxi to take us to the designated venue, be given a meal, and safely brought back to the Amra Palace Hotel by midnight.

Amazingly our stamina pulled us through after a quick shower and a change of attire! It was gratifying to witness Jordanian Folklore Culture at the concert and feast on tasty food from recipes from Old Jordanian culture that came to us in various small bowls. These intriguing desserts were merely a 'taste test' as I would have termed it, as I could have had a salad bowl of each.

The historically accurate and colourfully choreographed Cultural Show of Fine Art in Ancient Dance techniques deserved great admiration. After the show, the 'Director of Choreography' and the 'Financial Director' of the Cultural Arts Centre approached us to discuss what we had witnessed and canvas our personal views. We learned from them that only in August 2019 were the ancient Jordanian traditions of dance and lifestyle resurrected at the Art Centre. The final 'icing on the cake' for us that night was when our taxi driver from the Amra Palace Hotel took us for a lovely night drive through Petra to witness the city at night.

After four hours of sleep for a second night, we were up early, breakfasted and dressed, with our bags outside our doors for a quick getaway in the coach. We were off at 7:00 am on a long drive to ancient Petra, a tedious journey passing through barren land for kilometres on end. When we reached our destination, our guide advised us of a long walk ahead and comfortable in whatever mode of transport we undertook to take. We requested a horse and cart as we thought the long walk ahead of us in searing temperatures would be oppressive. We paid a handsome sum of US$60 for the horse and carriage with a driver to make the eight-kilometre return journey. I would never have been able to walk that distance in the oppressive heat, and by being elevated in a horse-drawn carriage, the views of the rock formations along the way were spectacular.

Petra is sometimes called the Lost City. It was rediscovered in 1812 by the Swiss traveller, Johann Ludwig Burckhardt, who tricked his way into the fiercely guarded site by pretending to be an Arab from India wishing to sacrifice at the tomb of the Prophet Aaron. Amazingly, he got away with his story and discovered Petra's Treasury Buildings' magnificent historical and archaeological site and ancient tombs.

Also known as the 'Rose City', the prehistoric city is an incredible spectacle. The history of Petra established by the Nabataeans was fascinating. It was the capital of their Kingdom, strategically located along major ancient trade routes. Two main elements were the driving force behind the Nabataeans existence, their prosperity and their power. The first was their advanced and ingenious water systems, which enabled them to move around the desert areas of Arabia where others would perish, thus linking coastal parts of the Arabian Peninsula. The second was their aptitude for trade. Together, these elements enabled the Nabataeans to grow wealthy by gaining control of the incense trade. As a result, they built the beautiful 'City of Petra' and consequently left behind a legacy that continues to astonish historians and visitors alike more than two millennia later.

The long passageway of tombs along the cobblestoned roads was fascinating. The Treasury Building was iconic when seen through the steep, red-stoned rocks. Our horse stopped in the gap for us to take photos of the building with the two Roman soldiers on sentry duty. The Treasury is one of the most elaborate temples in Petra, a city of the Nabatean Kingdom inhabited by the Arabs in ancient times. As with most other buildings in this old town, including a monastery, these spectacular ancient structures are carved out of the red sandstone rock face.

Petra has been a UNESCO World Heritage site since 1985, and in 2007 it was voted one of the new Seven Wonders of the World. The Nabataeans, who were a nomadic people of Arab descent, are speculated to have come from Wadi Sirhan in the Northern Arabian Peninsula. They were masters in their trade and became wealthy as a race in the east after Alexander the Great.

Our lunch was at a quaint restaurant called My Mom's Recipes, an enchanting place for dining where meals were delicious, reasonable, and well presented in the buffet of exotic Jordanian-style dishes.

Another early start on Day Three, 18th November 2019. After a wholesome breakfast at the IBIS Hotel in Amman, we boarded the coach. We drove to the Allenby Bridge on the Jordanian border to begin stringent border control formalities with Israel. We were pleasantly surprised to go through painstakingly detailed customs procedures without any hiccups. Female officers examined all the ladies and male officers the men. The experience was questionable, but then again, it was their Border Control system, and we had to adhere to their regulations.

Fortunately, we experienced no hiccups. Next, we awaited a new tour guide and driver who arrived with a coach. All formalities accomplished, our names ticked off on the list and bags loaded on to the coach, our guide introduced himself as Hannah, and our driver as Ed, again two knowledgeable men with well-educated historical and cultural backgrounds. We were once again strategically seated next to Hannah as he informed us that our afternoon tour would be to the Inn of the Good Samaritan. We would then view the Sycamore Tree, which Zacchaeus the Tax Collector had climbed to see Jesus passing.

It aroused everyone's enthusiasm when witnessing the many historical sites mentioned in the Bible. A feeling of great excitement and satisfaction came over me to see road signs with Jerusalem, Bethlehem, and Nazareth on them. We stopped at a local restaurant on our way to Jerusalem for lunch and souvenir buying. It was our first souvenir shopping expedition, something that every woman loves to do!

Ed was a very jovial character and drove at very reasonable speeds to allow us to film and take photos. Hannah gave us detailed facts and figures of what we were viewing. He pointed out the Dead Sea in the distance and told us that it was the lowest place globally and the saltiest sea with its water so dense that one does not sink but floats instead on the surface. Hannah promised us that we would visit the Dead Sea the very next day.

We drove into Jericho, the 'Oldest Ancient City of the World', where we stopped for a quick lunch and restroom break. From there, we could view 'Mount Temptation', a place where Satan tempted Jesus.

It was here where I got 'teary and sooky' as I stood and looked across at Mount Temptation after just having stood by the Sycamore Tree. All this was very overwhelming for me, as again I was re-living childhood dreams and visions of sometime in my lifetime the possibility of visiting these places.

Our next destination was the Manoly Plaza Hotel, our abode for the next five days. We checked in at 3.30 pm, and Hannah informed us that we had a free afternoon. Ian needed this time of rest as he had a fall down two steps and felt shaken. He had no broken bones, but it could have been a disastrous outcome.

It had been a relatively short day of adventure and exploration in the land of the Bible. The views across from our hotel window were breathtaking as we had a clear vision of the Valley of Bethlehem. We could see sandstone peaks of many hues of yellow with rays of sunlight reflecting on them. As evening approached, the night views were even more spectacular.

Our evening meal in the main dining room was an endless buffet where the Maître de allocated us a private table. The hotel was full of fellow travellers from all over Europe and Scandinavian countries exploring the Holy Land. It was interesting to see so many other cultures and people all talking in various languages. They all excitedly tried multiple dishes and shared their daily experiences in a constant babble of voices.

Day Four of the Holy Land tour was the day to visit the Dead Sea. On the way, we drove to Masada to experience and view the ancient excavations of Herod's Palaces, the bathhouses, the storerooms, and the ramp. We visited the oldest synagogue in the world. We also visited the home of Mary and Martha and Lazarus' Tomb. Mary and Martha's home is now a Church and referred to as the Number One Church, where we followed a short service.

The Qumran was our next place to visit. An archaeological site in the West Bank managed by Israel's Qumran National Park is where the Dead Sea Scrolls were hidden in caves in the desert cliffs and found in excavations done in the early 1950s. Finally, we visited the 'Dead Sea Restaurant' for a delicious lunch to complete our time at the Qumran.

We finally experienced floating in the Dead Sea with 'dead sea mud' spread on my legs by Nimi and Denise as a healing source. We took great care not to swallow the heavy saltwater or even get it into our eyes as it would burn our eyes.

Afterwards, we continued to Jericho, passing by the 'Inn of the Good Samaritan'. We also went to Ein Gedi - where David fled from Saul as he wanted to kill David. We also witnessed the Mustard Tree behind the fence, the sign reading 'You will find the Mustard Tree only in Bethany'.

A highlight of this afternoon was the visit to two popular tourist information and jewellery shops, where some of us purchased souvenirs of our visit to the Dead Sea. Then, after our short spell of excitement, we got back into the Coach and were taken back to our Manoly Plaza Hotel. Along the way, we visited the Tomb of Lazarus and 'The Tower of the Jewish Church of Ascension', both sites located across the Valley of Jerusalem. We also witnessed many projects underway to restore buildings with historical and biblical backgrounds.

We did enjoy the fact that we could sit in the various loungeroom areas of the hotel to discuss our day's activities. As we exchanged views and highlights relaxing with our bottles of cold water, we could not help mentioning how we had seen date palms in Masada, a sight only related to the area of Masada, also known where Herod had his fortress. Furthermore, it was an unusual sight to have also witnessed Mountain Deer, which came close to us without fear of human beings.

Another day dawned, our fifth day in the Holy Land, and we were to visit the 'Wailing Wall' built in 19BC, which is the most religious site in the world for the Jewish people. The 'Wailing Wall' was an inspirational and holy place of reverence where we all placed prayer requests in the many crevices. The faithful believe that God would eventually answer these prayer requests. The Wailing Wall originally got its name from European travellers who witnessed the mournful vigils of pious Jews.

On our way to the wall, we visited the Al Aqsa Mosque and the 'Dome of the Rock' - a very spectacular place to witness. The Dome built of solid gold is visible from outer space. Next, we viewed the Mount of Olives through the Five Arches in the Square of 'The Dome of The Rock'. Next, we visited the 'Jaffa Gate' for lunch and walked around Market Square. After lunch, we visited the 'Pool of Siloam' where Jesus sent the blind man to wash his eyes, thus restoring his sight.

We were getting weary but still eager to soldier on as our next stop was on to Hezekiah's Tunnel built under the 'City of David' in Jerusalem. It was a tunnel built by King Hezekiah for an impending siege by the Assyrians. We next visited Israel's Museum to view the 'Second Temple' model, a fascinating piece of architecture. The Shrine's story began in 1955 when the Israeli government decided to construct a suitably distinguished 'Treasury' to preserve and exhibit the Dead Sea Scrolls.

Our final visit, and a fascinating one, was to the Holocaust Museum. It was also known as the 'Yad Vashem' built by the Holocaust Martyrs and Heroes Remembrance Authority in 1953.

Our day six, we took a brisk walk to the 'Shepherd's Field' Church in the back street behind the Manoly Plaza Hotel. Then, having covered this early morning sightseeing trip on foot, we walked back to our hotel, a downhill walk to board our coach for the journey to the Old City of Jerusalem to visit The Church of the Nativity - the Church built over the birthplace of Jesus Christ.

We waited for at least two hours till we could have our chance to walk down into the basement to view the massive 'Gold Star' monument, which has a view over the exact place where the Manger was where 'Baby Jesus' was born. We were all mesmerised by this and didn't want to leave the basement crypt area—the Church of the Nativity constructed over the original area of the Manger of Christ's birth. So, in the 'Church of the Nativity', we lit candles as we descended into the 'Holiest of Holies' in the basement crypt. Then it was back in the Coach for another drive up to The Mount of Olives, where we visited the Church of the Ascension of Jesus. The Church erected where Jesus ascended into Heaven. In fact, to this day, the 'footprints' of Jesus on the rock are still visible 2000 plus years later.

We then took in a brisk walk to the 'Pater Noster Church' also referred to as The Church of The Lord's Prayer on the Mount of Olives in Jerusalem. It is part of a Carmelite monastery, also known as the Sanctuary of the Eleona. The Church of the Pater Noster stands right next to the ruins of the 4th Century Byzantine Church of Eleona. We explored Churches all day, going to 'The Chapel of Dominus Flevit', where Jesus wept over the Old City of Jerusalem. The 'Dominus Flevit' is a Roman Catholic Church on the Mount of Olives, opposite the walls of the Old City of Jerusalem. Again, archaeologists uncovered artefacts dating back to the Canaanite period and tombs from the Second Temple and Byzantine eras during the sanctuary's construction.

Our last visit for day six was a visit to the 'Church of Agony', the 'Garden of Gethsemane' and 'The Church of All Nations - 'The Church of Gethsemane'. We spent over an hour in the Church of All Nations in the

'Garden of Gethsemane'. The Dome and altar were beautifully painted, with murals extending around. The stone floor near the altar is from the original block of stone where Jesus sat. The stone block was behind a steel rope, but it still enabled us to bend forward and touch the stone.

On our way to the hotel for the night as weary travellers, we made one last stop at 'The Church of St. Peter of Galli Cantu' in Jerusalem. The Church had a distinctive double entrance door in solid brass. The painting at the main altar was significant, depicting Christ ascending into Heaven on the day of His Transfiguration. This Church was notable for its many illustrations and altars all around.

Day Seven was going to be testing for us, so we prepared for the feat ahead of us with thought and prayer. We were mentally preparing to undertake the six-hour walk known as the Stations of the Cross, the walk that Jesus walked on his last day on earth. Nevertheless, I resolved with faith and determination to achieve this prodigious journey where Jesus carried His cross and walked the journey to His Crucifixion.

It was a fascinating walk with many stops along the way. We walked through laneways, churches, marketplaces, and wayside cafés and although under warm atmospheric conditions. One of our fellow travellers had an 'app' on their smartphone, measuring the distance we were walking and counting our steps.

Our day started at 8.30 am, and at 2.30 pm, we were still walking. Having started at the Gate of the 'Old City of Jerusalem through the 'St. Stephen's Gate', the 'Gate' where the stoning of Saint Stephen happened. We then walked the 'Pool of Bethesda', this was where Jesus healed the disabled man after thirty-eight years. Next, we visited the 'Church of St. Anne', where the Virgin Mary was born, now managed by white-robed French priests. As we entered the Church, a lovely statue of 'The Virgin Mary' was a young child with her mother. This visit was a highlight and very uplifting. Finally, we continued along the Via Dolorosa (Way of the Cross) with stops at every 'Station of the Cross'.

We were fulfilling an unparalleled coverage of places, either heard about or read of in the Bible. Our next and vibrantly stimulating stop was 'The Church of the Holy Sepulchre' of Mount Calvary and Golgotha. The 'Dome' of this Church was of spectacular architecture, with the walkway to the courtyard rugged with cobblestones. We were all weary and needed a stop for lunch and a restroom break.

After we walked on to Mount Zion to the Upper Room and the Dormition Abbey, 'The Last Supper' location. The Dormition Abbey is located on the crest of Mount Zion outside the walls of Jerusalem's Old City and is near the place where the Last Supper took place. The 'Dome' of the room of The Last Supper was very ornate. This incredible building is also known as the Cenacle. It is a fortress-like building with a conical roof and four corner towers and stands south of the Old City's Zion Gate. We next walked to the 'Dungeon' where history says Jesus was held before being taken to trial. The route to the Church built on Caiaphas's house is very scenic, and you can get beautiful pictures. Inside, we walked the Holy Stairs down to the Dungeon, where the Roman soldiers held Jesus during His trial the night before His Crucifixion.

Our final stop was to the Garden Tomb or Gordon's Calvary. It was advantageous to receive 'Holy Communion' at the Tomb of Jesus Christ. An emotional and uplifting time for us all as every step taken on this pilgrimage was the same that Jesus had walked himself on His last day on earth.

I saw some conspicuous signage for the 'Garden Tomb', which indicated that the site was owned and maintained by the Jerusalem Association based in the UK. The Garden Tomb site was recognised as a 'Christian Holy Place' by Israel's Ministry of Tourism and designated as an antiquity site by the Israel Antiquities Authority.

A sign of note at 'The Garden Tomb' read – Jesus Christ - Declared with Power - To be 'The Son of God' - by the - Resurrection from the Dead - Romans 1:4

We were now at the end of our pilgrimage, which had covered 6.65 kilometres, measuring 9,669 steps—an exhilarating journey, to say the least, and biblically a trek of no comparison. The 'Way of the Cross' is a religious path following the sites of 'Jesus' Passion'. It begins at the Praetorium where Jesus was condemned and whipped and reaches Calvary (Church of the Holy Sepulchre), where Jesus was crucified and buried.

The present route was crystalised during the 16th Century and slightly modified later. The actual way includes fourteen stations where every Friday, the Franciscan Priests lead a procession along this route, beginning from the yard of the building across the way. All pilgrims are welcome to take an active part in the spectacle on Fridays.

Our eighth day - 23rd November, was different as we were all packed and ready to leave the Manoly Plaza Hotel after five nights. The food was delectable, the rooms comfortable, and for weary travellers returning from our daily explorations, it was home.

We left our hotel on schedule at 8:00 am and drove along well-maintained highways to Tel-Aviv, the commercial capital of Israel. Next, we proceeded to Jaffa, the home of the best oranges and mandarins and biblically, where Peter raised Tabitha from the dead as written in the Acts of the Apostles. Next, we visited St. Peter's Church - a Catholic Church now and fleetingly visited the 'House of Simon, the Tanner'.

We encountered breathtaking scenery travelling north to Caesarea to view the Roman Theatre built by Herod the Great and the Roman Aqueduct, which provided water to the City of Caesarea. It was a remarkable engineering feat of early times to view the water supply system that served the city. Continuing to Haifa, the third-largest city of Israel, the home of the Israeli Navy along the stunning coast as the city rises on an outcrop from the sea. Our next visit was to St. Peter's Monastery, where the symbol on the front of the Church depicts the hands of Jesus and St. Francis. Again, the Altar and Dome of this magnificent Church were superb works of architectural splendour. Finally, a brief stop was at Mount Carmel's Stella Maris, the Cave of Elijah the Prophet. We completed the walk around the premises and then took in a shortstop arriving at the Bahai Hanging Gardens of Haifa.

All these stops were brief as we had to arrive at the Stella Maris Monastery for a 2.30 pm lunch and unloading our cases for our night's stopover. It certainly proved to be different as married couples were all given twin-share rooms! Sister Esther, who managed the monastery, provided us with relatively simple but wholesome meals. The Sister turned out to be a passionate and caring person with loads of humour and personality. After dinner at the designated time of 6.30 pm, she took us up to the rooftop of the monastery to view 'The City of Nazareth' by night, a simply breathtaking view that was indescribable. It was undoubtedly unforgettable and picturesque.

One small story that will be imprinted in the minds of our group when the elevator was coming down to ground level got stuck mid floors. The wiser ones chose to come down the two stories on foot, and a few weary ones decided to take the elevator. Unfortunately, a disaster happened when our elevator got stuck between the floors. The incident turned out to be a source of great excitement and giggles for the group, but I went into a panic and 'thumped' the back of Ken standing in front of me through sheer fright. I screamed that someone should press the alarm button on the panel, and I accidentally jabbed my phone into Rukmal's face causing her to have a facial bruise.

Sister Esther came to the rescue by getting the elevator to continue its journey to ground floor level, much to my relief. When we reached the ground floor, I fell out of the elevator to breathe a sigh of relief and apologise to Ken, who was most gracious about my repeated thumping on his back. This incident was a source of fun and chuckles until we all said our 'goodnights' and dispersed to our rooms.

On Day Nine, after a basic breakfast, we left the Stella Maris for our next drive, which ended up in a calamity just ten minutes on the road, when we heard a loud 'bang'. The thought crossed my mind that someone had shot at the coach. Instead, however, it was the suspension on the coach breaking. We all dismounted as Ed rang around for a replacement vehicle.

Once our replacement vehicle arrived with Hannah and our cases transferred into the new coach, we drove to Caesarea Philippi, an ancient Roman city located at the southwestern base of Mount Hermon. It was the place where Jesus gave Peter the keys to the Kingdom of Heaven. After briefly stopping at this sacred place, we drove on to Capernaum, the second home of Jesus, to see the ancient synagogue and St. Peter's House site. Then it was a quick visit to the Church of Multiplication, the place where Jesus blessed the fishes and the loaves. Again, these were brief stops that covered biblical areas of interest that we were all familiar with throughout the Scriptures and in our days of Sunday School.

Our next quick stop was to the Mount of Beatitudes, the Venue of Jesus's Sermon on the Mount. Then, again, a brief visit and back on the Coach to head to Tiberius to partake of a complete fish lunch on the shores of the 'Sea of Galilee' - a fascinating meal so authentically served to us at St. Peter's Restaurant.

After a delicious meal, we boarded our coach to head to the pier to take a boat trip across the Sea of Galilee, as taken by Jesus and His Disciples. A thrill for us all to experience as we were over an hour on a large wooden boat built similarly to what existed in the era of Jesus. The vessel styled in the same manner looked like 'Noah's Ark'. The boat driver and his colleague, locals, made us feel happy when they played Australiana songs!

We came ashore from the Pier area to walk into the Sea of Galilee. I was the only one that ventured knee-deep into the water as I prayed for a 'healing' of my legs. My unfettered faith and personal prayer in this sacred expanse of water have indeed been an answer to prayer. The crowds were mixed at the water's edge of the Sea of Galilee, and yet it was a place that I marvelled to realise that I was standing in this 'Sacred Sea'.

We were all weary and glad that we had one last stop to the Yardenit Baptism Site at the River Jordan, where many people renew their baptismal vows by being immersed in the river. It was where John baptised Jesus in the River Jordan. According to the Holy Scriptures, it is here where John baptised Jesus, and as He came up out of the water, He saw the Heavens Open, and the Spirit descended upon Him like a dove, and a Voice from Heaven said, 'Thou art My Beloved Son, with Thee, I am well pleased' - Mark 1: 9 – 11.

On day Ten - 25th November, we headed to visit Nazareth Village, an authentic way of life in the time of Jesus over 2000 years ago. It was a fascinating place to visit as the friendly group of locals were dressed in the folklore clothing of that era, the heavy clothing and the sandals made of animal hide. They tendered their animals and had mud made living quarters. It certainly was an eye-opener for us used to comfortable living conditions.

We moved on to Mount Tabor, the Mount of the Transfiguration, where Jesus ascended the Mount and went to Heaven. A significant place to visit as we are aware of the Transfiguration of our Lord. Our next stop was to the Church of the Annunciation, where the Angel Gabriel appeared to the Virgin Mary and announced that she would be carrying a child born of the Holy Spirit. These short stops were significantly familiar to us all.

Our last stop for the day was to Cana, where Jesus performed His first miracle of turning the big jug of water into red wine. The massive 'jug' is visible in a glassed-in room. We met a couple renewing their vows here. The last evening and night's stay was finalising our packing and get organised for the trip back to the Border of Israel and Jordan as we took our separate flights to our following destinations.

Day Eleven - 26th November, our final day, was acknowledged with sadness that it had come to an end, with bags packed and Passports ready for entry into Jordan. However, our drive to the Sheikh Hussein Bridge in Jordan was stimulating as we only saw the desert and mountainous terrain.

We said our goodbyes to Ed and Hannah at the border and met a new driver and tour guide. They passed through Customs and drove us to Mount Nebo, believed to be the tomb of Moses, situated on a lonely windswept hill with an astonishing view of the Jordan Valley, the Dead Sea and the 'Spires' of Jerusalem. On the Mount was sculptured the face of Moses, a giant sculpture that overlooked the valley towards 'The Promised Land' - a significant landmark.

Our last stop was Madaba - a drive of thirty kilometres south of Amman, where we saw some of the finest Byzantine mosaics in the world. The most famous is the 6th Century Mosaic Map of Palestine, supposedly the oldest 'Map of Palestine' and possibly the oldest map of the Holy Land in existence.

It was time to say our goodbyes to Theresa, Peter, Chitra and Iromi at the hotel on completing the tour. Then, a final trip to Amman Airport to board our designated flights, with Ken and Nimi flying to Singapore, Rukmal and Nirantha on to Dubai, and Fred, Denise, Gillian, Ian and I to leave for Colombo in Sri Lanka.

Ian and I had planned an additional twenty days in the land of my birth with an eleven-day rest at the Mount Lavinia Hotel, a popular and well-known colonial-style seaside resort just south of Colombo. We had also planned tours of the Wilpattu Wildlife Sanctuary and Central Highlands of Sri Lanka.

But that's another story.

# THE RISE OF ADRIAN NICHOLLS

## A PREQUEL TO THE NOVEL 'CRY IN YOUR SLEEP'

### BRUCE HEWETT

*I fixed those bastards*! Adrian Nicholls said proudly to himself as he swung to and fro in his high-backed, office leather chair. *Whoever thought a boy from Mt Willsmore would be seated in the Vice-President Asia Pacific of Anux Pharmaceuticals chair.*

Adrian looked out the window of his forty-second-floor office window in Sydney's Central Business District, taking in the natural beauty of Sydney Harbour. The Harbour Bridge and the Opera House, with the sun reflecting off the rippling waters as the harbour snaked its way past Middle Head to the entrance and emptied into the Pacific Ocean. He stood up from his desk, walked to his office door.

"Please see I am not disturbed for the next 30-minutes, Greta. Give me a call when everyone is ready to start the afternoon management meeting." After receiving an acknowledgement from his PA, he closed his door and returned to his desk, where he took a sip from his mug of steaming hot black coffee. Adrian wanted to indulge himself for just a moment and think back on the journey that saw him today, sitting for the first time in the boss's chair.

His Mum brought up Adrian in one of Sydney's lower socio-economic, outer western suburbs, Mt Willsmore. His alcoholic father had disappeared from their state housing commission home not long after his birth, and to this day, he had never met his Dad. Life had always been a struggle for the family. However, his Mum worked long hours in the local grocery store and always managed to provide the essentials of life for the family. She had a fantastic ability to stretch the value of every dollar she earned and was a great role model for her son.

With his drive to succeed and make his Mum proud, Adrian excelled at high school academically and in sports, especially rugby. Being tall and athletic brought him to the attention of the many attractive young women in his class. They appeared to be intent on causing him to lose his virginity before he finished high school, but he ignored their advances and instead focused on his studies. He wanted to make his Mum proud. Adrian successfully won a scholarship to the prestigious Macquarie School of Business in Sydney, where he graduated with Honours with a Commerce and Marketing Degree. The qualification provided him with immediate entry into a marketing position within a high-profile department store chain in Sydney. He made excellent progress and soon had a very bright future within the organisation.

An email pinged onto his screen, which he opened. The message confirmed his two-year working visa for under thirty-year-olds for the UK. A jubilant Adrian fist-pumped the air. "Lookout, world, here I come!" he yelled. It was his ambition to head overseas from Australia to seek his fame and fortune. He vowed he wanted to earn enough money to buy his Mum a place of her own on the waterfront. She deserved someplace lovely for the many sacrifices she made in raising him.

Adrian knew it would be a great shock to the management when he handed in his resignation at the end of the day. He was sure they would offer him inducements to stay, but he saw his future as one day heading up an extensive global organisation. Courtesy of a former fellow graduate, Dougie Richards, there was a bed, well at least a couch on offer in London, to get him started on the next stage in his life's journey.

*

The screech of tyres on the tarmac and the pressure on his seatbelt digging into his stomach roused Adrian Nicholls from his semi-conscious state. It heralded the safe arrival of his flight into London's Heathrow Airport. He peered out from his window seat in the last row of economy on the QANTAS aircraft. Adrian was craving the opportunity to get his legs moving again after cramming his large athletic frame into his seat for the wearisome 14-hour journey from Singapore.

It was early morning, and the sun had not risen on this wintery day. Thick fog blanketed any view of other aircraft or the terminal buildings. After seeing the fog, Adrian was amazed the aircraft was able to land in such conditions. There was no way they could land back home in Sydney in such extreme conditions.

The aircraft seemed to taxi forever in search of the arrival gate. Then, like a swarm of bees, the passengers started to prepare for the mad scramble into the terminal building to complete arrival formalities. Passports removed from bags, last-minute searches for a pen to fill in the UK arrival card, and the buzz of excited conversation energised the cabin.

The seatbelt sign finally extinguished, signalling they had arrived at the gate, which set off a surge in humanity. Passengers extracted coats and bags from overhead lockers and a mass of impatient bodies flexed in the congested aisleways to get their blood flowing again and keen to escape the cramped confines of the aircraft.

Adrian was one of the last to exit, looking enviously at the spacious environment in the business class cabin on his way to the door. "This is where I want to be seated," he whispered to himself. "No more row 59 ever again. I want to travel up front from now on!"

On reaching the exit door, he immediately felt the bite of a London winter's morning and regretted his Mum's advice in not buying that thick coat before departure. He was hoping to get something cheaper on arrival in London to preserve his limited cash reserves after giving his Mum some money during a teary farewell at Sydney Airport. He promised to call her regularly and assured her he would be home soon as the visa was only for two years.

The long-distance walk from the arrival gate to the Immigration counters provided his body with the opportunity to warm up. He was becoming excited about what lay ahead for him in this great adventure. However, his happy mood quickly evaporated at the teeming mass of humanity that greeted his arrival to clear Immigration. He looked longingly at passengers sauntering past with passes for the shorter first and business class lines and those with EU passports accessing their automated entry facilities. Finally, all he could do was join the vast sea of humanity in the arrival's hall. He shuffled his way forward, nudging his carry-on bag along the ground with his feet, wondering what lay ahead for him. Then, with his passport stamped and suitcase collected from the baggage carousel, it was down into the bowels of the airport and onto the London Heathrow Express for the 20-minute non-stop journey into Paddington station.

With his limited knowledge of the London public transport system, Adrian spent some of his precious British Pounds on a taxi to take him to Dougie's flat in Camden, adjacent to the tourist mecca, the Camden markets. It was just like in the movies stepping into one of the famous London hackney carriages, complete with his luggage stacked around his legs in the spacious rear compartment.

"*A London taxi, first thing on the to-do list ticked off!*" Adrian thought to himself. "*Wow, the Abbey Road studios and the famous crosswalk, with people everywhere and cameras flashing.*"

Arriving at Dougie's address, Adrian noted the fare on the meter as 19-Pounds 50-Pence. As he realised from his exposure to television and the movies that he was now in the world of tipping, his heart beat faster. He boldly thrust a 20-Pound note in the cabbie's hand, "Keep the change," he announced and quickly extracted his luggage out of the cab.

"Typical bloody Aussie," the cabby snorted. "Just me luck to get one of you cheap bastards to start me day. Have a good one."

A red-faced Adrian did not look back as he headed towards the entrance to Dougie's flat. The flat was located above a shop close to the Camden Town Tube Station and accessed via a street-front door adjacent to the entrance to the convenience store. A white entrance button located about chest height to the right of the door had seen better days. The flaking paint revealed multiple layers of various colours underneath the current, mainly dark green. Adrian pressed the button and, not hearing any sound, hoped that Dougie would answer.

After a brief wait, Adrian heard a weary sounding "hullo?" from the speaker next to the button.

"It's me, Dougie. I've come straight from the airport."

With a buzz, the lock on the security door released, and Adrian faced the prospect of humping his suitcase up a steep climb of dark, dusty timbered stairs. Looking up, he saw the entrance to the flat open at the top of the stairs and Dougie standing there in a white t-shirt, boxer shorts and bare feet.

There was the obligatory questioning from Dougie. "How was the trip? Do you want a cuppa?"

After handing Dougie a bottle of duty-free Bourbon, a tired Adrian dropped heavily onto the couch, which would be his bed, he hoped for only the next couple of weeks. But, from the feel of the sofa under his bottom, he knew he had to find work quickly and find a place of his own, as it would not be easy to sleep on this old piece of spring laden furniture. Sipping their hot cuppas, they reminisced over days past and quizzed each other on what they knew of the exploits of their fellow graduates spread around the world.

"Pretty cosy place you have here, Dougie," Adrian said, taking in the tiny apartment. Little light penetrated the darkened, painted windows facing the street, which looked permanently shut. Adrian noted a small windowless room looking through the open bedroom door. It held a single bed and a wooden chest of drawers with a mirror mounted above it. Shirts and other clothing apparel were hanging from a portable Ikea-like stand on wheels. In between the bedroom and the basic exposed kitchen, an open door revealed a bathroom, miniature by Australian standards, which consisted of a tiny shower cubicle, squashed up next to a toilet and a small wall-mounted cupboard with sliding mirrored doors.

*I will have to be a contortionist given my size to move around that bathroom*, he thought.

Dougie observed Adrian surveying the flat, "It is about all I can afford on what I make working in the local pub," replied Dougie. "But it does the job until I head back to Sydney in a few weeks."

"How come you are heading back home so soon?" quizzed Adrian. "I thought you would be looking for something a bit more exciting and challenging than pouring beer in a pub?"

"I started applying for a few jobs, but my Mum hasn't been well and has been diagnosed with breast cancer, so I have decided to head back home. replied Dougie, "She's not been doing so well with the radiation treatment and the chemotherapy."

"So sorry to hear the news Dougie," replied Adrian. "I like your Mum. I hope she will be ok."

"Maybe have something for you that may be of interest," Dougie continued, his eyes searching for a document, which he found lying on the dark, wooden coffee table, stained with circular markings from decades of coffee mugs and beer glasses. "It was something I was going to apply for before I got Mum's news. It's a job with a pharmaceutical company, Anux Pharmaceuticals, a big American company rapidly expanding here in the UK and worldwide. They are looking for sales reps to launch a major new product. The advertisement states no previous pharmaceutical sales experience necessary, with full training provided for successful candidates. A competitive salary with an attractive bonus scheme is on offer."

"I certainly don't know anything about selling pharmaceuticals, but I like the sound of a competitive salary and the attractive bonus scheme," said Adrian taking the advertisement from Dougie. "No experience necessary, you say. Reckon I will give it a go. Nothing to lose."

"Here, I have some info on the company," Dougie handed some printouts to Adrian. "I started to do some research in case I was successful in getting a job interview."

"Wow, that's great, Dougie. Thanks a lot, that will be a great help. Could be a good start."

"Also, I have spoken to the landlord, and he is happy for you to take over the remainder of my lease, which will help you get underway," added Dougie.

"Thanks, Dougie, much appreciated."

After Dougie left for his shift later that morning at the local pub, Adrian settled into the apartment. After a shower, he started to study the information provided on Anux Pharmaceuticals. They were listed on the stock market in New York, with a market capitalisation well into the billions. The potential of their new pain-relieving product AnuxuDone was driving the share price. The medication was about to be launched in the UK and then rolled out through Continental Europe. However, in the information provided by Dougie, there were reports that several international regulatory bodies had cautioned the company about the inappropriate promotion of AnuxuDone, a potentially addictive analgesic product.

Adrian gained the impression that Anux Pharmaceuticals would bend the rules to drive its success and eventually recoup its substantial investment. Maybe they were the perfect company for him and his drive to succeed. His mind started spinning with visions of being awarded company shares and options. Even perhaps stepping into a senior position in the New York head office. However, first on the ladder to success was securing the sales representatives job here in London.

*

Adrian sat nervously outside the office of Gareth Jones, the Assistant Sales Manager for Southern England for Anux Pharmaceuticals, waiting for his job interview. His leg was twitching, and he picked up a copy of the Financial Times and was aimlessly leafing through the distinctive orangey coloured pages but not reading any of the articles. His mind raced with possible questions he could be asked. Being in England, Adrian thought it best to take a conservative approach and dressed in his dark grey suit, with a white shirt and plain navy-blue tie. His freshly polished black shoes glistened under the fluorescent lighting. In his mid-twenties, Adrian was in the prime of his life.

The office door opened, "Adrian Nicholls?" asked Gareth Jones as he smiled and extended his welcoming right hand. "Please come in and take a seat. Tea or coffee?"

"No thanks, I'm fine," replied Adrian starting to relax after the warm welcome. "I just had a coffee before coming to the office."

"That Aussie accent is a bit of a giveaway," smiled Gareth. "Even without looking at your CV, which is very impressive, by the way."

Adrian immediately felt comfortable with Gareth, who he thought to be in his late thirties. His sandy, blonde hair was slightly balding on his crown and his protruding waistline, indicating he regularly liked to consume a few pints of lager.

Gareth continued to describe the job and expectations regarding time commitments, depth of product knowledge acquired, and call rates with the doctors in the designated territory. Adrian thought the salary to be low by comparison with a similar job in Australia. However, it was a start, and the bonus scheme sounded attractive. At least he would be able to manage to take on the lease of Dougie's flat easily. Anyway, it was the first rung on the ladder of success, and who knew where the job could lead.

"We need to make a quick decision on appointments as we have to get the four-week training course underway as soon as possible, ready for the new product launch," said Gareth. "You have presented yourself very professionally, and with your background, I would think Ms Marlow in Human Resources will be in contact with you shortly."

*

Having been notified of the success of his application for the sales representative position, Ms Virginia Marlow, the Assistant HR Manager, summoned Adrian for a meeting. He would be required to complete the necessary paperwork and receive instructions regarding the training course commencement.

The door to the inner sanctum opened, and there stood a lovely Virginia Marlow. She was around 5-foot-ten in her flat black open-toed shoes and dressed formally in black, tight-fitting trousers, with a matching jacket and white blouse. With her long blonde hair tied back in a ponytail, Adrian guessed she would be in her late twenties, a little older than him and looked after herself.

"Mr Nicholls," she stated, extending her right hand, ushering him towards her office. "I see that you have recently arrived in London from Sydney. Please take a seat."

Adrian thought he perceived a slight tremor in her voice as she directed him into her office. Adrian knew the impact he made on members of the opposite sex and immediately sensed the mental appraisal Ms Marlow was making of him.

*

Virginia Marlow was impressed with what she saw. Adrian Nichols was a classic Aussie. A little over six feet tall, tanned, dark hair, intense blue eyes and broad, muscular shoulders tapering down to a narrow waist. He looked fit. She mentally scolded herself for allowing her mind to wander and concentrated on the task at hand and his job interview.

"Mr Nicholls, please take a seat," said Virginia as she pointed to a plain timbered chair on the opposite side of her spartan desktop, adorned only with her open laptop and a nearly empty intray.

"Please call me Adrian," he invited. "Hopefully, that is not being too forward for the company culture?" Adrian added, maintaining eye contact with her.

Virginia felt herself blush, looking down at the notepad on her desk, scribbling something unintelligible to avoid meeting his intense gaze. Then, composing herself, she looked up. "Here is the paperwork you need to complete, including applications for your National Insurance and Tax File numbers. You can drop them back to me when you return tomorrow morning to start your training course. Oh, here is your security pass. We better not forget that."

"I look forward to seeing you again," said Adrian as he stood and clasped Virginia's hand.

*What came over me?* Virginia thought to herself as she watched Adrian leave her office. *I was acting like a schoolgirl!*

*

The four weeks of the training course passed quickly. A few of the applicants dropped out, finding the intensity and expectations for sales of the new product to be too demanding. However, Adrian excelled and, after feedback from Gareth, expected to receive one of the territories with a high sales potential, such as the rich London territory of Chelsea. Therefore, he was somewhat surprised to learn he was assigned an area in South London, with some lower socio-economic areas like Brixton. Sales for existing company products were historically much lower in this territory and consequently likely to have a lower bonus earning potential.

Despite difficulties with the English language, Gabriela Sanchez was given the much sort after Chelsea territory. Gabriela was a stunning, Latin black-haired beauty, with her slim body somehow squeezed into hip-hugging skirts. She had recently arrived in England from Spain. Stories circulated she had become very friendly with the Product Manager, Tim Hewson, who delivered the new product knowledge training. Tim Hewson coincidently was a good friend of Gareth's boss, the Sales Manager Alan Hadley.

Virginia saw Adrian walking down the corridor towards her, with his head down, deeply lost in thought. He was just about to crash into her when he instinctively looked up, " Oh, I am so sorry, Ms Marlow," apologised Adrian. "I had something on my mind."

"You are now officially a member of the Anux Pharmaceuticals team. Please call me Virginia," she said with a smile. "What seems to be the problem?"

"How about I share it with you over a drink?" Adrian asked. "My treat."

"Sure, I'd like that. I'll get my coat," Virginia replied. "I know just the place. The Robber's Dog pub, just around the corner. It will be quiet this time of day."

There were only a few patrons in the pub sitting on stools perched over the bar top leaning over their frosty pints of beer. The dark timbered décor seemed to soak up the light from the few light fittings affixed to the walls and the glow emanating from behind the bar servery area. Virginia and Adrian settled into a high-backed booth at the rear of the pub, which would hide them from any office staff entering. Virginia was eager to learn what Adrian had to say and did not want to be interrupted.

Virginia nursed her glass of Chardonnay, as Adrian, between sips from his pint of Guinness, relayed his tale of woe. "Gareth Jones indicated to me that I was one of the best of the new sales reps and should command a top territory to launch AnuxuDone. However, I ended up with South London, one of the toughest territories, with it being one of the lowest bonus earning territories in the company. Gabriela, who can hardly speak English, gets the prime territory of Chelsea. The whisper is she's very close to Tim Hewson, who's best mates with the Sales Manager, Alan Hadley."

Virginia studied Adrain before replying. "I have heard the rumours floating around the HR Department about Tim and Gabriela. You have learnt a tough lesson in corporate politics, and you can treat it in two ways. You can either make a big issue of it and complain, thereby making enemies within the company hierarchy, or show people in management what you can do. Bring yourself to the attention of those people who I would describe as kingmakers in the organisation. They will help decide your future."

Adrian thought for a moment before taking a sip of his drink. He then looked deeply into Virginia's eyes before replying, "Thanks, Virginia, that's good advice. I'll show the bastards. They'll be working for me one day."

That first drink broke the ice between the two of them. After that, it turned into regular drinks at the Robber's Dog, then eventually an invitation for dinner, which inevitably turned into regular romantic rendezvous in Virginia's flat. Adrian was becoming very fond of Virginia. He, however, was not a fan of the very feminine décor of her flat with lots of shades of pinks, fluffy cushions and stuffed animals adorning her bedspread. Nevertheless, it was a lot more comfortable than his place on the positive side, so it wasn't tough to regularly stay overnight.

*

With the support of Gareth's coaching and his teaching of some of the trade tricks, especially with some promotional activities, it was not long before Adrian started to produce excellent results in his South London territory. With Adrian achieving prescription numbers well above expectations, Gareth put pressure on Alan Hadley to transfer Adrian to the Chelsea territory. Gabriela had performed below expectations and repeatedly called in on Monday mornings, advising she was not feeling well. Tim coincidently was also unwell on the same Mondays.

Despite Tim's protestations, Alan, with pressure mounting, finally moved Gabriela on from the company before the end of her probationary period. However, with Adrian taking over her territory, it brought him under the scrutiny of Tim Hewson and Alan Hadley. That Aussie had made them both look bad with senior management, and they were out to get him.

Alan Hadley dropped into Tim's office. "Tim, that Aussie has done amazingly well in South London. Too well for a novice, I think. So what's his secret?"

"I overhead Gareth talking him up to Virginia Marlow in HR about his performance. That is another good reason to get rid of him, in case she starts mentioning him to senior management," said Tim. "I snuck into Gareth's office and looked at Adrian's promotional planner on the wall. It appears he does a lot of educational evenings involving a series of presentations by Professor Barnard from the London School of Medicine. The Professor performed a lot of the early research on AnuxuDone and would be a drawcard to the doctors in the territory. In addition, I found receipts for food and wine and an email to the Professor about travel to the USA."

"I know Professor Barnard is very friendly with Gareth, so no doubt Gareth has helped arrange for the Professor to speak," said Alan. "But those receipts and email sound very fishy. I bet he is in breach of the industry promotional codes. That would bring the company into disrepute, and I would see that as grounds for his instant dismissal."

"Mm, I like the way you're thinking," grinned Tim. "I say we pay a surprise visit to tonight's educational evening, with cameras ready. We must defend the company against any episodes of impropriety."

*

It was early evening with Alan and Tim sitting expectantly in Alan's car outside the Brixton Community Hall, watching Gareth and Adrian greeting the delegates at the entrance. It was a chilly London night – the motor still running to keep the heat pumping through the vehicle.

"Let's wait until we hear the applause coming to signify the end of the Professor's presentation, and then we can burst in to capture the largesse," said Alan with a smirk on his face. "We can capture that Aussie flouting the industry regulations by serving them expensive booze and fancy eats. That will see the end of him!"

"How dare he bring the company into disrepute!" Tim mocked.

They waited patiently in the car until they heard a burst of clapping. Then, they nodded to each other and headed straight to the meeting room's double doors. They stepped into the meeting room with cameras flashing. A stunned audience of around fifty people swivelled in their white plastic, stackable seats.

"What is the meaning of this?" Professor Barnard roared at two men from his podium.

A quick scan of the room showed not a drink or morsel of food in sight. Adrian stood smiling, pointing at a sign at the rear of the room which stated in bold red letters, 'No food or drink in the meeting room'. Alan and Tim turned quickly on their heels and fled from the room, not even stopping to close the door.

"Friends of yours?" queried the Professor with a raised eyebrow as he continued to hand out scientific papers to the doctors who attended the meeting.

"Thanks for the heads-up, Gareth," acknowledged Adrian with a thumbs up.

"Yes, I saw Alan snooping around my office when I came back from lunch," said Gareth. "I knew they were after you, ever since Gabriela's termination."

Adrian stepped up to the podium. "Apologies, everyone, for that inexplicable intrusion. I don't know what it was all about. It looked like some people were in the wrong place at the wrong time. By the way, there will be a gift basket sent to your surgeries tomorrow in appreciation for your attendance this evening."

Gareth reached inside his coat pocket with the last of the guests departing and passed an envelope to Professor Barnard. "Thanks, Prof, for your support. You have been such a drawcard for the doctors in this area."

*

"I think you gentlemen know why you are here," said Virginia. "A leading Professor from the London School of Medicine has reported some very inappropriate behaviour on your part in front of him and a large number of doctors from the South London area. You have embarrassed the company, and I expect your resignations on my desk by the end of the day. Otherwise, I am afraid the company will not hesitate to take action."

"But…," started Alan.

"No buts about it," interjected Virginia. "We have already received several complaints about your actions, let alone some of your recent employment decisions and indiscretions. So go and empty your desks, and I want your laptops and security passes now."

Alan stood and glared at Virginia, "The pharmaceutical industry is a tight industry, and everybody knows everybody, so someday, some time, I am going to get that Aussie bastard!"

*

Virginia and Adrian sat up in bed and clinked their glasses of champagne. After a couple of sips, Adrian stretched across Virginia's naked body and, finding the switch, turned off the very bright pink coloured lamp shade. Adrian wrapped his arms around her and pulled her towards him.

"Oh, Mr Nicholls," she giggled. "I hear there is a vacant Product Manager position now available. Any interest?"

"I certainly could be tempted, Ms Marlow," smiled Adrian as his hands started to explore Virginia's smooth body.

*

Over the next couple of years, with his visa extended to permanent residency status, Adrian's star continued to rise in the Anux organisation's London Office. From Product Manager, he was steadily promoted to Marketing Manager for the UK and ultimately Marketing Manager for all of Europe, with the rollout for AnuxuDone continuing into the major markets of France, Germany, Spain, and Italy.

Over time he had continued to spend more and more time at Virginia's flat, and finally, one day, she presented him with a key to the door. With their substantial combined incomes and Virginia now Head of the HR Department, she dropped hints about getting a more permanent place together.

One Friday afternoon Virginia slipped away from the office earlier than usual and called Adrian on his mobile, asking him not to be late as she was preparing dinner. On entering the flat, he smelled the familiar aroma of freshly roasted meat. He was surprised to see the dining table set for two at one end of the glass-topped table. Freshly pressed white linen placemats with Virginia's finest silverware and wine glasses and pair of flickering red candles adorned the table. Virginia looked up from a pot of vegetables she was straining through a colander into the kitchen sink, while a roast of beef just removed from the oven lay resting on a cutting board. A gleaming razor-sharp carving knife and fork were ready for action.

"What's this all about?" Adrian asked with a puzzled look on his face as he placed his briefcase and laptop on the pink two-seater couch. "Is there a special occasion?"

"Well, Mr Romantic, this is the third anniversary of the day we had that first drink at the Robber's Dog," Virginia replied. "I thought we could make a special night of it. Why don't you open some wine rather than just standing there? There is a chilled Chardonnay ready to go in the ice bucket on the dining table."

The beef was perfect with a hint of pink, served with a red wine jus and some hot English mustard on the side. Again, Virginia had pulled out all stops. The meal was complete with a dessert of hot apple pie, topped with clotted cream.

"That was some meal, me darlin'," said Adrian as he reached for and squeezed Virginia's hand. "I'll need to go to the gym in the morning after that."

"Glad you liked it," Virginia smiled. "There is something I have to say…. about us."

"What about us?" asked Adrian with a furrowed brow. "We have a pretty good thing going."

"Pretty good thing going! I am not getting any younger and am now into my thirties, and I think it is about time we talked about the future," she replied. "I want to know where we stand. I want a permanent relationship. I want a home, and I want children."

"Well…umm. I don't know what to say." Adrian was tongue-tied, his mind racing, trying to figure out how to reply. "I am very fond of you, and we have had great times together."

"Fond of me, and we have great times together," she mimicked. "Is that all you have to say?"

"I am not the marrying kind, Virginia. I don't want our relationship to change," Adrian shrugged. "I am happy the way it is right now."

Virginia glared at him. "After three years, it seems like you don't share the same feelings. I think it is time you left."

Adrian made his way back to his flat. He tossed and turned all night and decided he would try and makes amends with Virginia first thing in the morning. On the way to the office, he bought a bouquet of assorted spring flowers at the Camden Tube Station and, on arrival, went straight to her office, but her door was closed.

"Is Ms Marlow in?" Adrian asked her PA.

"I'm sorry to say we received notice this morning that she has resigned and will not be returning to the office," the PA replied, looking at Adrian quizically.

Adrian nodded, placing the flowers on the PA's desk and headed down the corridor to the elevator and the solitude of his office. He made numerous attempts to call Virginia's mobile without success.

*

Despite numerous attempts over several weeks to speak to Virginia, Adrian was unsuccessful in contacting her. He knew this could be a major regret in his life, and his focus on his career and the drive to the top may have potentially cost him the love of his life and the type of family he had not been able to experience growing up. Was his life growing up without a Dad, the reason why he had not seen what Virginia wanted in a relationship?

With Virginia now gradually becoming a distant memory and following successful product launches in Europe, Adrian's mind firmly focused on ascending the corporate ladder, and much to his surprise, the opportunity came up sooner than he expected. He was invited to the head office in New York to present a proposal on managing product launches in the Asia Pacific region, including Australia, China, Japan and Korea. The presentation would form part of the selection process for the position of Vice-President Asia Pacific to be based in Sydney.

*

Newton Sinclair, Head of Marketing for AnuxuDone in the USA, sat in his office looking at the agenda for the forthcoming presentation, which was on the company's rising star product's rollout in the Asia Pacific region. He anticipated having the job as the new Vice-President Asia Pacific for the company. He even told his wife to start packing and telling her friends that they were bound for Sydney, Australia.

Newton thumped his desk when he saw that he would be competing for the job against some Aussie called Adrian Nicholls. But, unfortunately, he did not know who the person was. "Let me see if I can take him out of play before he even gets started. Firstly, a visit to Helen Rogers in HR."

Newton took the elevator down to the HR department and boldly walked straight into Helen's office without considering it necessary to knock before entering. An annoyed Helen looked up from her laptop and, seeing it was Newton, asked in a curt voice, "what can I do for you today?"

"I had the impression that I am the only candidate for the Asia Pacific VP position," he stated, getting straight to the point. "Now I find I have some unknown coming over from London to pitch against me. So what's going on, and who is this, Adrian Nicholls?"

Helen was used to Newton's brusque manner. "He has performed exceedingly well as Marketing Manager for the launch of AnuxuDone in the UK and throughout Europe, and senior management believed they should see what he has to offer," Helen replied. "There have been glowing reports on his capabilities from the hierarchy in Europe, so he has earned the opportunity."

"We'll see about that," said Newton as he turned on his heels and made a hasty exit from Helen's office. Returning to his office, he locked the door and extracted his keys from his trouser pocket. Unlocking the bottom drawer on his desk, Newton retrieved a small metal box containing a clear plastic re-sealable bag labelled *Columbian Heaven*. He set two white lines on his desktop blotter and snorted deeply into nostrils. Then, with a shake of his head, he picked up a burner phone housed in the lockable drawer.

"Pueblo, I need your help with a problem I think you can help me get rid of," said Newton. "Is Candy available tomorrow night? I need her to make a special delivery."

After Newton finished speaking with Pueblo, he dialled Helen. "How about I take Adrian for dinner tomorrow night. It will be nice to get to know him socially before presenting to the big bosses the next day. May the best man win."

"I'll be meeting him tomorrow morning when he arrives at the office and will let him know," she replied with some hesitancy in her voice.

*

"Welcome to Anux Pharmaceuticals Head Office, Mr Nicholls," welcomed Helen. "Come in and take a seat. I have your itinerary for the next couple of days."

"Please call me Adrian. We Aussies don't stand on too much formality," he replied with a smile and looked deeply into Helen's eyes. Adrian reckoned she was in her mid-thirties, dressed in classic American conservative business attire, knee-length, dark grey skirt with matching jacket, atop a white button-up blouse. She was not wearing a wedding ring. She looked down when he made eye contact.

"I have an itinerary worked out for you, Mister...I mean Adrian," she blushed. "I will take you on a tour of the office this morning and introduce you to a number of the senior management group. We will then go to Tony's Seafood Restaurant for lunch. After lunch, I will find you a quiet spot to catch up on your emails and prepare for tomorrow's Asia Pacific presentation. For tonight Newton Sinclair has asked to take you out for dinner."

"Isn't he competing with me for the Asia Pacific job?" Adrian asked.

"He told me he wants to get to know you, whichever way the decision goes with the appointment," said Helen. She leaned forward, lowering her voice. "I would be very cautious with him. He has the reputation of being a bit of a snake, prepared to do anything to get his way to the top. He said he would meet you here at the end of the day and take you back to your hotel after dinner."

*

"Adrian, Newton Sinclair. How you doin'?" asked Newton as he walked into the office allocated to Adrian. "Ready to head off for some dinner?"

Adrian mentally appraised Newton. In his late thirties and just under six feet with the development of a bit of pot belly. Indeed, not at as good a level of fitness as he was. His hairline was slightly receding from his forehead, with flecks of grey sprouting amongst his black hair in the temple area. His black suit highlighted tiny spots of dandruff nestling on his shoulders. There was something about his flickering beady eyes that reinforced Helen's words of caution.

"My hotel is just down the road, so I'll drop off my laptop and briefcase, and we can head out," proposed Adrian. "I am starting to feel a little hungry but will need an early night with London five hours ahead."

"Great," replied Newton. "There is a nice Italian place, Giovanni's, just around the corner from your hotel. I didn't think you would want a late night with the big presentation tomorrow morning. Of course, we'll both want to be at our best."

They entered Giovanni's, where Newton was warmly greeted at the door by the Maitre'd. It was a long narrow restaurant with booths comfortably seating four people against a left-hand mirrored wall. A row of two and four-seater tables down the centre with a walkway leading to the kitchen and restrooms completed the restaurant.

"Your usual table, Mr Sinclair?" asked the host, immediately leading his guests, following an affirmative nod from Newton. They were seated and handed menus, with Newton also receiving a drinks list.

"How about an Australian Shiraz?" Newton asked as his eyes scanned the list.

"Sounds good to me," Adrian affirmed.

The waiter returned, unscrewing the cap on the bottle of a Barossa Valley 2017. The waiter poured the wine after an obligatory swirl, sniff and taste.

"Cheers and welcome to New York," toasted Newton with a clink of Adrian's glass.

"Well, I do declare. If it isn't Newton Sinclair," boomed a loud voice.

"Hey, Candy. What a nice surprise," said Newton. "Like a drink?"

"Sure, and I think I will take a seat next to your good-looking friend," she said, snuggling up next to Adrian.

Adrian started to wonder what that was all about and recalled Helen's warning about Newton from earlier in the day. *It can't be good. I will need to keep a close eye on the pair of them.*

Candy was a little over the top, blonde wig, bright red lipstick, heavy black eyeliner and dark eyebrows. She wore a short, hip-hugging red dress, exposing a lot of her breasts, which protruded out the front of her navy-blue jacket."

After taking a sip of her wine, Candy let out a loud sneeze. "You don't have a handkerchief, Newton? It must have been the red wine."

Newton unfurled his plain white handkerchief and passed it to Candy, who wiped her nose, placing it into the pocket of her jacket.

"Oh, it's yours," she said, retrieving it from her pocket and passing it back to Newton, who quickly placed it into his suit pocket

To Adrian's eye, it seemed as though there was something concealed within the handkerchief.

"Better be going," Candy said as she stood. "Thanks for the drink."

"What was that all about?" Adrian asked. "She seemed in a bit of a hurry."

"She used to work for me in another company," Newton replied. "Must have seen me coming into the restaurant and wanted to say hi."

Adrian thought the response about Candy was implausible, and he was on high alert, keeping a close eye on Newton's flickering eyes. He seemed nervous and was taking a lot of interest in Adrian's wine glass. On commencing a refill, he clumsily knocked over Adrian's glass, resulting in a minor spillage of wine onto the white, starched tablecloth.

A waiter appeared from nowhere to attend to matters. *It looked as though he deliberately knocked over my glass,* thought Adrian suspiciously.

Newton's hand slipped into his suit pocket and, with the waiter gone, picked up Adrian's glass. Then, using the other hand, he picked up the wine bottle and proceeded to refill Adrian's glass.

Something was not quite right, and with Newton on the verge of proposing another toast, Adrian stood and headed for the bathroom. "Back in a moment. I'll just have a comfort stop before we get something to eat."

On Adrian's return, Newton indicated he would also have a bathroom break before their meal arrived. With Newton away, Adrian quickly switched their wine glasses. *Just to be safe. Something is not kosher!*

After finishing his main course, Adrian apologised for needing to head off to bed. "I have had it. I'm sorry. We both need to be fresh for the presentation in the morning. Thanks for a great evening and all the best for tomorrow. May the best presentation win!"

*

Adrian was in the meeting room, being introduced to the senior management team members and getting ready for his presentation when Helen Rogers entered the room.

"I just had a call from Newton Sinclair," she said, looking at Adrian closely. "Unfortunately, he has been vomiting all night and will not be in today."

"Must have been something he ate," said Adrian, smiling as he turned and nodded to Helen.

*

A gentle knock on his office door brought him back to reality, "they are ready for you in the meeting room Mr Nicholls," said Greta as she entered his office.

"Thanks, I am on my way," Adrian stood and strode confidently out of his office.

# DINOSAUR HUNT

## *GRACE DE VISSER*

I didn't want to get up or climb out of my bed today. My bed was so warm and snugly, and I love my soft fluffy doona. It's as light as a fluffy cloud. So Steggy and I hid underneath it, surrounded by pictures of our brightly coloured dinosaur friends. Of course, there are blue ones, red ones, green and yellow ones too.

"Pretend colours," Steggy tells me. At least, I think that's what Steggy means, and we roll around laughing. What if they were to come to life! Wouldn't that be funny! They're not real, only pictures. What if the real Tyrannosaurus Rex, or the Triceratops and the fat body long-headed Diplodocus, had been the colours of the rainbow. What a sight that would have been. Poor things they would not be able to hide anywhere.

We love to hide, Steggy and I, we often play tricks on each other, hiding. Laying ever so still, hearts thumping waiting to be found and then jumping out and making each other giggle in delight. Unfortunately, Steggy sometimes falls asleep, and I have to go and look for the lazy lump. One day

Steggy could not be found, and when I found Steggy's chunky little body stuck, wedged tight underneath my bed, I had to come to the rescue. I got stuck between the timber slats and the wooden frame and had to yell loudly for Mum to rescue both of us! What an adventure that was.

I like talking, and Steggy's an excellent listener. He doesn't interrupt me all the time, particularly when Mum or Dad growls or are just a bit grumpy. We hold each other tight. We even have a secret handshake. We both love eating chocolate and bickies. I don't like eating broccoli, peas or sprouts, but Steggy loves eating greens! We also love dancing and stomping around to music only we can hear.

Sometimes when Daddy comes in to see what all the noise is about, he shakes his head and gets a little red in the face, especially when he sees the cushions and bedding and toys all over the floor.

"What's going on in here?" he says in his grumpy voice. "What a mess you have made." He has prominent deep wrinkles on his forehead when he tells me to pick up all my toys. Mummy knows our games and shakes her head and smiles, but not in front of Daddy.

It's Saturday today, so I get to stay in bed as long as I want. I like school days when I get to see all of my friends. Steggy doesn't go to school but stays at home to play and sleep. I like my teachers and my school and learning new things. But I do enjoy the weekend too.

I can stay in my room and have my adventures. But I like it best when I tuck myself in the cave with Steggy. We are more than just best friends. Our cosy den is a little dark, but we are unafraid. It is safe here. We make each other smile most of the time and we have so much fun playing tickling games together.

When we leave our cave and go on adventures, we climb over rugged mountains and trudge through rocky valleys and dark, dark tunnels. We often pass tall timbers and struggle through the woolly bushes under a sky of a beautiful blue with white fluffy clouds that seem painted. Today, the quietness surrounded us as we crept along past the enormous Tyrannosaurus Rex with its long tail, little, short front legs, sharp claws, a big mouth and sharp pointy teeth.

"Shh, Steggy, don't let him catch us," I said, crawling ever so slowly past the Triceratops with its large, frilled shield around its neck and three spiky horns. One is almost on the tip of its nose. I would not like one of those sticking into me!

Quietly sliding past the monstrous Stegosaurus, looking rather scary with its two rows of rigid pointy plates running down its back and tail, it could smash us with his four heavy spikes on the bottom, but I don't think it will. Nevertheless, it makes us a little nervous; our shaking ripples through our bodies as we squeeze together for comfort until we get past. On our way, we notice one of the usual dinosaurs we meet is missing. Where is Dino, the Diplodocus who hangs around in the mysterious forest? I wonder if its big body with stumpy legs, long neck and long tail will be nearby. Maybe he had too much to eat and fell asleep near the pool of the glittering blue waterfall or underneath the shade of the purple mountains.

Steggy and I crouch down low, trying to spot Dino, but we can't. So we try to see who can stay still the longest without moving. Steggy usually wins! A creaking sound reaches our ears as we lay on the green grass. Is that the sound of a dinosaur's creaking knees? We quickly realize the sound is coming from much further away. Immediately we head back towards the cave. Suddenly the sound becomes louder, and it's coming from the hallway. It's the floorboards creaking. Then a loud snuffle, followed by a grunt, made my ears twitch, then slightly getting louder.

Bump, thump, bump, thump as it tries to tread lightly down the hall and fails. Was it a big dinosaur-like Dino sneaking down the hallway? I listened as hard as I could, I'm sure it must be, as it doesn't sound like Daddy's thump, thump as he stomps down the hall. I cupped my ears and felt more like an elephant than a small child with auburn hair. I wonder does the intruder have freckles like me. Does he look like his mum? I do.

Will he be as tall as Daddy, and that is very tall. Mummy is a lot shorter than Daddy. I'm tall for a six-year-old. Steggy is not very tall, maybe short is a better word, but Steggy doesn't like that word.

"Where has the dinosaur been? I wonder where he had been hiding?" I asked Steggy in a quiet voice, and a shake of the head tells me Steggy doesn't know either. Mummy would not like it if he's been hiding in the hall cupboard. If he messed up the linen, she would be very cross. When Mummy gets cross, the wrinkles on her forehead make her look like Daddy. That would be funny. I suddenly sat up and listened. That sounded like a burp. The poor Dinosaur must have overeaten and had indigestion. I quickly crawl out of my cave and stand up tall. Steggy is close by my side.

I could hear more burping and coughing noises from the hallway. I needed to see what kind of Dinosaur was lurking in our house, lurking in my very own hallway. Was it Dino? In my mind, I could picture him already, big and green with stumpy legs, long tail and neck swaying slowly from side to side as he walked down the hallway. I tiptoed across the carpet of green grass, squishing it under my dinosaur feet. I slowly turned the handle of the door, as not to frighten him. The door creaked as I opened the door just a little way. As I pulled the door open, it squeaked, and just for a second, I saw the long shadow moving along the wall. My heart went thump. My knees were shaking as I started down the hallway dragging Steggy close behind me as we followed that big green lumpy thing.

I could still hear him as he headed towards the kitchen. My nose twitched, has the dinosaur been using Daddy's aftershave? I hope not. Daddy doesn't like anyone touching his things! Oh no! The dinosaur was heading straight for the kitchen. I'm too late to stop him!

Mmm, the yummy smell of freshly cooked bacon and toast. I wonder if dinosaurs like bacon and toast. I love bacon and toast, and now my tummy is rumbling loudly underneath my blue and green pyjamas. Steggy is hungry too. I try to tiptoe, but my feet make a pitter, patter, pitter, patter sound as my feet hit the hard pale floorboards. What will Mum and Dad say seeing a dinosaur in the kitchen? I quietly poked my head around the kitchen doorway. I managed to take a big deep breath in and took a small step into the kitchen. I searched around the room with my big brown eyes. They almost popped out of my head. I could not believe what I was seeing. I could see the white wall to wall cupboards, the sunshine sparkling on the sink bench. I could see Mum standing at the stove, the bacon sizzling in the red frying pan.

Dad was standing in front of the fridge, reaching inside and bringing out the milk. But where was the dinosaur? Was that top of a great big head poking out above the fridge and the green tip of a tail beside the refrigerator that I could see? No couldn't be. There was not enough space for him to hide there. He is way too big. He couldn't be hiding near the fridge, and Dad would have seen him! Dad was wearing his jeans and black t-shirt and continued to make the coffee for his and mum's breakfast. I was sure the Dinosaur came in here, but where did he go?

Daddy turned and smiled at Mummy as Steggy, and I crept into the room. "Look who's out and about." Then turning towards us and ruffling our hair with his long, lean fingers. "Morning, sleepyheads, I thought the smell of food would bring you out."

Mummy looked up at Daddy, her face glowing. "Here comes double trouble." Then, although Mummy was wearing her faded slim blue jeans and white t-shirt, she turned and smiled at Steggy and me gracefully.

"Good morning, my little dinosaur girls. I see you are still wearing your dinosaur pyjamas and slippers." Then, smiling at Steggy and me, Mummy looked at us with that knowing twinkle in her green eyes, "How was your adventure this morning?

My shoulders felt droopy, and my bottom lip trembled and dropped. Steggy's shoulders drooped too! I could see nothing of the dinosaur. He was much too big to disappear.

"We couldn't find Dino anywhere in the forest, and we thought we heard a real dinosaur in the hallway."

Shaking her head, her shoulder-length auburn hair catching the sunlight as it shone through the window and glistened like gold. "Don't look sad! Instead, have a look beside the fridge. You may find what you are looking for," said Mummy with a knowing smile and a twinkle in her eyes.

I looked beside the fridge and could not believe my eyes. There was Dino, our favourite Dinosaur. My heart jumped for joy as we ran over to him, shrieking and bubbles of giggles floating through the air and gave him and each other a great big cuddle. Now how did he get there? He is, after all, only a stuffed toy!

# A PENNY WHISTLE
# FOR CARA GREY

### *ROBYN KING*

The execution of witches was a significant event in townships across the British Isles in the sixteenth century. Scotland was one of the first to execute, burn alive and torture them. Most people supported the idea of getting rid of the scourge of sorcery and believed these witches worshipped Satan and had the powers to sink ships and bring on storms, famine and diseases. Any loud-mouthed, undignified, lazy, unfaithful women were considered witches.

Arran Douglas, a cloth merchant in Dalkeith, Scotland, believed women were sacred beings and should be loved and nurtured. In turn, women saw him as a wealthy eligible prospect with integrity and kindness. He dressed well, and his shoe buckles were always shiny. But what he earned, he put back into buying the very best fabrics for his business. He loved making people happy and wanted to provide them with quality. Young women would chatter amongst themselves, gossiping and giggling at the prospect of him taking notice of them.

Arran's parents were from good fishermen stock, but the sea made him sick. He found the cloth business quite by accident. When Arran met Anice Macmillan, she introduced him to her father, Stuart Macmillan, who sold pottery and wares at the markets around Scotland. He needed someone to help with his new venture, working with all kinds of cotton, silks and threads. Arran, with his natural charisma, was just the man for the job.

Stuart wanted Arran to sell his wares to wealthy English customers, the upper crust from the big towns, as the Scottish were very miserly with payments, always wanting to argue the price. Though they were Scottish born, they found English buyers knew quality products and didn't mind paying the price.

Word got around that he had quality materials, and in turn, he built a reputation with ordinary folk, and progressed to wealthier people. He would give his clients extra services by measuring them, cutting the fabric to size, and delivering to their homes. Arran's most respected customer was Lady Sarah McWilliams's daughter of the late Baron Jeffery McWilliams. She passed on her recommendations to King James's staff saying that Arran Douglas sold the finest cotton in Scotland.

Arran received word inviting him to a meeting with Mrs Cosgrove, the Royal Lady-in-waiting in Edinburgh. She was selecting clothes for the adornment of the marital bedroom and for the arrival of the soon to be Queen Anne of Denmark. They needed new cotton for curtains, linens for sheets, and nightwear for the upcoming nuptials. The marriage to King James was in three months, and there was a heightened sense of urgency.

Giles, Arran's trusted footman and a longtime friend, loaded up the cart with fabrics, threads, and lace for sale. He suggested taking more samples just in case Mrs Cosgrove took a liking to them. Next, he organised provisions for the horses and food, ale, and water for themselves.

Pulling into Edinburgh, they noticed a crowd surrounding six shackled women.

"Devil worshipers, whores, witches!" The people in the streets screamed, waving their arms.

The shackled women were dishevelled and crying, pleading their innocence.

"Giles. What's going on?" cried Arran.

"I don't want you fainting, sir, but I see it's the witches burning today."

"What?" cried Arran. Born to a loving family, he hated cruelty of any sort.

The two men from Dalkeith had never seen anything like it. The crowd were revelling in the commotion. People were cheering, yelling language that should never have come out of people's mouths. Arran saw vendors selling ale, whiskey, bread, pies, clothes, musical instruments, and memorabilia of the burnings in the market behind.

It was a carnival atmosphere; magicians, jugglers and a man swallowing a fire stick lined the streets. A stall of cloth and linens caught Arran's eye. But, unfortunately, on closer examination, the quality was of a lower grade.

"This cloth would fall apart too quickly," he muttered to himself. "I have no concern about these sellers, Giles. My bolts of cloth are more superior."

"Aye, sir, they are," Giles replied.

The crowd was growing at an alarming rate. Arran noticed a young lady sitting on a rock, busking in the spring sun. With a pennywhistle in hand, she sang with an angelic voice as she entertained the children surrounding her. There was a black case by her thigh, which she periodically opened and placed the coins in that she was collecting. Her voice was of an angel and intermittently she played the pennywhistle. She made it sound unusual. It was the way she moved her tongue. He also noticed the whistle had a split in it because when she hit a high note, the split made the pennywhistle screech.

"That wasn't supposed to happen, to be sure," Arran said to Giles.

When she was resting, Arran walked up to her and asked. "Where did you learn to play so beautifully?"

"My mother taught me, Sir."

"You sound so lovely," he declared.

"Thank you," she said, turning a rose red.

Two passing people placed a halfpenny on the cloth that lay on the ground. Arran pulled out a pound, handing it to the girl.

"Thank you, sir. You are truly kind," the girl gasped. "Are you rich?"

Arran laughed. "Oh goodness no. What is your name?" he asked.

"Cara Grey, sir", she replied.

"Pleased to make your acquaintance, Cara Grey. I am Arran Douglas, and this is my friend Giles Mack. We're from Dalkeith." Arran extended his hand but realised it was too formal as Cara just put her head down. "Sorry, Cara, I didn't mean to…."

"That is alright, sir. I didn't want to…."

"I understand, Miss Cara Grey. It's been a pleasure." Arran nodded. "We must be off now, be safe, Miss Cara. It seems pretty unsafe around these parts.

"Thank you, sir. I will."

Cara looked up. Her smile was absent. "Here they go, Mr Douglas. They blame women for all that goes wrong and call them witches. The crowds are the vicious ones. Cara explained with a tear running down her cheek.

They turned to look at the women tied to pine stakes as three men pulled them up by rope. They placed wood shavings, twigs, dried grasses, and logs around their feet. They then poured alcohol on the woodpile and lit it. Once the fire was well lit, the men lowered the women over the fire. They urged each other, with no empathy for the agony they were causing. The women were looking for their loved ones in the crowd, and after one last goodbye, their screams echoed through the hills.

Flames flew into the sky, spitting embers, the women dying a cruel death—

the stench of burning flesh clogging to the nostrils of all who stood around. The crowd wooed in unison as the bodies perished in gouts of flames.

"Whores, Satan's children, let them die," shouted the crowd.

"Don't waste alcohol on these witches," a voice called out, followed by a roar of laughter.

"These people are monsters, Mr Douglas. They burned my mother last year. She mixed spices for Mrs Mackellar while in child, but alas, her boy was born with broken bones. My mother helped everybody. It was only lavender oil with aniseed, and it would have done no harm. But Sara May Bligh came and took her away, said she was a witch." explained Cara.

Arran was in disbelief, watching another tear stream down her cheek. He felt a pang of sadness and wanted to stop her pain.

"Cara, do you come here often?" Arran asked, trying to change her focus.

"Yes, with my father. He sells pies. You see, he cannot talk proper. He fought Sara May when she was taking my mother away. He pleaded her innocence, but she accused him of being a liar. So the Magistrate ordered they put the brank on his head for seven days, and when he moved, it cut his tongue. That's what they do to liars."

*

Arran's fiancé Anice was in Edinburg shopping to add to her bottom drawer. While walking through the market, she noticed Arran talking to a young girl sitting on the green singing to the children. A pang of insecurity rattled Anice.

A lady in a blue dress got Anice's attention by saying, "A penny for your thoughts."

Anice turned. "Pardon!" she replied.

"You look deep in thought. So, a penny for your thoughts." The lady replied.

Anice looked back to Arran, Giles, and the girl and pointing in their direction.

"See that girl with those two men. Well, one of those men is to be my husband, and she is flirting with him. I am wondering if this is the first time they've met?"

"In my experience with men, my dear, they are flirting. She is giggly and turning red. I'd be worried," The lady in blue laughed with a touch of haughtiness and walked away, as she did not care for Anice's response.

Anice thought she saw something that was not there. She felt Arran was a faithful man as he was always claiming his love for her. So, she went on to shop for her upcoming wedding.

*

After talking to Cara, Arran and Giles continued on their way. "It's not safe for her here. Giles." Arran said, concerned.

Giles nodded but didn't reply.

When they arrived at The Royal Mile, the horse picked up the pace to the castle's gates and around to Holyrood house, the King's residence. Statues lined the entrance to the court. Flower adorned the windows, and white pebbles were in amongst the flowerbeds.

Giles attended to the horse while Arran stepped onto the residence with materials in hand. A footman came forward to greet them. Arran handed him the invitation. After a glance, the guard looked up and motioned Arran to follow him.

"Mrs Cosgrove is expecting you," he murmured.

The King's dwelling was in disarray. The main room's paintings were on the floor. Materials on a large table sprawled out, ready for cutting. Pins and threads lined the shelves. He had never seen such a great set-up for the making of garments, curtains, and tablecloths.

Mrs Cosgrove entered the room. Around Arran's age, the lady held herself tall and straight. Her attractive face looked unfriendly.

*She looked too young to have such an important job. She must have married when she was a wee child,* thought Arran.

But when she spoke, she bellowed out her words. "I hope you brought what I wanted. If you can't deliver what I'm asking for, we are wasting your time Mr Douglas."

"Of course, I did, Mrs Cosgrove," Arran responded.

Mrs Cosgrove held herself in high regard. Arran realised she knew colours and textures as she carefully unravelled the fabrics, pushing her fingers through to test the quality. Arran thought she looked impressed but said nothing.

There was a knock on the door. "Enter!" Mrs Cosgrove shouted.

The uniformed man that Arran met at the gates entered. "My apologies, Ma'am, but Mr Mackenzie is here with some goods he wants you to look at."

"Send him in." Mrs Cosgrove responded, turning away. "I'm finished here."

"But you haven't ordered anything, Mrs Cosgrove," Arran exclaimed with a worried frown.

"I'll take the lot," she said, her stern face breaking out into a smile. "Your quality is the best I have seen for a while."

Arran smiled back. The lady was not as ferocious as she appeared to be. "Aye, of course. Thank you, Mrs Cosgrove," as he helped to clear the fabrics off the table.

"Leave your bill with Von Smoy," she said, indicating the uniformed man standing by the door. "He will pay you in full before you leave."

"Thank you, Mrs Cosgrove," nodded Arran.

"Will you be able to return in two weeks with more? You see, the Queen cannot wear the same dress twice." Mrs Cosgrove explained.

"Aye, I can. It would be a pleasure. Mrs Cosgrove." Arran nodded again. He was astounded. The price was Four hundred and eighty pounds, including food and wine and provisions for the journey. Mrs Cosgrove hadn't even questioned him about the price.

After dealing with Von Smoy, he handed Arran a bag of money.

Mr Mackenzie was also leaving as they were exiting Holyrood House.

They nodded hello to each other. Mr Mackenzie asked Arran if he would like to look at some musical instruments, he had brought to show Mrs Cosgrove. "They are of the finest quality."

Arran nodded, wanting to look at what the man was offering.

Mr Mackenzie opened the case he was carrying. It contained a flute, a harmonica, and something wrapped in velvet cloth with gold trim, which had twine wrapped around its body. "What's in the wrapping?"

"It's a pennywhistle," Mr Mckenzie replied, taking it out of the bag and unwrapping it. "It's a fine instrument."

Picking up the pennywhistle, Arran whispered, "This is a beautiful instrument. I know just the person who would love this. She sings and plays for the children on the Green."

"Do you mean Cara Grey?"

"Ahh, so you know her?" Arran asked with interest.

"Aye, her mother, Mary Grey, is my cousin."

"It's a small world," replied Arran.

"Aye. Mary argued with Sara May Bligh. The next thing she was careered off, and that was the end of her. That woman is someone you keep a fair distance from, I tell you. Plenty of people want Sara May's head. But no one will stand up to her."

"It's the second time today someone has mentioned this lady," Arran responded.

"Sara May also wanted to take Cara off on that day but didn't, maybe because on account she was only fourteen." Mr Mackenzie shrugged his shoulders. "She is dedicated to looking after her father now. She's a good girl."

"Aye, Cara told us about her mother and her father," Arran said. "We heard her play and sing, but her pennywhistle has a split in it."

Mr Mackenzie nodded. "Oliver, her father, bought that whistle for her.

Then, when the women forced their way in to take Mary away, Cara hit Sara May over the head with it."

"Did you say women?" probed Arran.

"Aye, Sara May's helpers are all women. They get a fee, you know to dob people," Mr Mckenzie said, shaking his head. "They are liars, and the Magistrate doesn't seem to care. She finds evidence, through witnesses, all liars they are. So, the job gets done."

"This group shouldn't get away with it," Arran said while holding his hand out to shake Mr Mackenzie's. "Arran Douglas is my name. I will buy the pennywhistle."

"Aye, I am James Mackenzie. You will find me at the market on burning days."

Mr Mackenzie and Arran concluded their business quickly.

"Pleasure. I will look out for you when I'm passing through." Then, waving at each other, they parted ways.

Arran showed Giles the whistle. "I bought this for that lassie in the market. What do you think?"

Giles just shrugged. "Arran Douglas, you are a sucker for a pretty face."

"I'm just doing a young girl a courtesy, my friend."

The day was getting darker, so instead of shivering from the cold, Arran and Giles booked themselves into the Bull's Head Inn for the night.

\*

Packing up her money box, pennywhistle, rug, and hat, Cara walked over to help her father pack the pies. Two savoury, one apple and pear were left. Just enough for dinner tonight as the Kemp girls were coming over.

"A man gave me a pound today, father," Cara said with a smile.

"What!" With dribble running down the side of his mouth, he wiped with the cloth that he always carried.

"His name is Arran Douglas, and he liked my singing. He said he'd look out for me when he comes through here again."

Oliver Grey smiled. He noticed that his daughter was growing to be a fine-looking woman. Once home, Oliver put the pies on the wood burner and set the table for six. Cara cooked some turnips and beans she'd brought from the market.

There was a knock on the door, and Kath Kemp entered with her sisters, Maddy, Grace and Marilee. The four spinster sisters supported them after Cara's mother, Mary Grey, had died.

These nights together were a happy and gay time for everyone. Dinner was delicious. They drank ale and sang songs. Cara played a tune while Oliver took out his Lyre, rested it on his lap and played his version of "The Plough song". The women sang along in harmony while Maddy and Marilee played backgammon. Cara boiled a pot of tea and handed out the cups. While the ladies sipped their tea, Kath swirled the leaves around one by one, tipped the cups upside down, and closed her eyes. She explained that she glances at the contents and says what comes to her mind.

Kath did her ritual and turned her cup upside down. "There's a storm brewing.

"Show me your cup, Maddy."

"Look, the storm is in yours also."

"Can you read mine?" asked Cara.

Kath looked in Cara's cup, and the storm was in hers as well. Kath swirled the leaves around. "There's a bunch of blooming flowers. Kath says they represent new people with love and new experiences," explained Kath Kemp.

"Oooh, with love", replied the girls in unison. Then laughter.

Then her little sister, Marilee's cup. "Look, there is a storm in yours also. And I see wealth, lots of little stones too. I think they are children. But these storms are a worry. We are in for something very soon, and we have to prepare." Kath said seriously.

"All these storms are making me tired," yawned Marilee.

*

Meanwhile, Anice arrived in her room in the Bull's Head. The first thing she did was to head to the community bathroom and take a long hot bath. While drying herself off, she heard a conversation between two ladies at the vanity bowl. Anice peeked through the bath curtain, listening. The lady in the blue dress she met earlier at the market talked to another lady who Anice did not know.

"Sara May, I know it's a long shot, but we need to look at this."

"Elizabeth, what are you talking about?" replied Sara May.

"A girl named Cara sings at the Green."

"Do you mean Cara Grey?"

"Aye, that's her," replied Elizabeth.

"I was talking to a lady at the burnings today. Cara is laying with the man who is to be married to the lady," Elizabeth explained.

"How do you know that?" asked Sara May.

"Cause she told me! And I saw the lovers today, on the Green at the market, and they were talking about their time together and arranging another meeting place," lied Elizabeth.

" I have heard that Cara is meeting with the Kemp sisters tonight at her house. So we can arrest them all at the same time. Kath Kemp screamed at me one day and told me she would put a spell on my family. My father has been sick ever since," cried Elizabeth.

"Right, we'll do it tonight. Meet me at Corbiehill road. It will be worth it just to get the Kemps," devised Sara May.

Anice was shocked at how a small conversation could get so exaggerated.

*

The Kemps and Cara were clearing up when a group of people barged in through the front door. Sara May Bligh led them.

"Here's the storms, girls!" yelled Kath.

Sara May Bligh yelled for everyone to stay still.

"Cara Grey?" pointing at Cara. You are under arrest for using your home for this gathering. These women are witches."

Sara May looked at the cups on the table. "Here'sere's more proof. Who does the reading? You are all under arrest. Come with me."

Maddy fell to the ground, crying, screaming, knowing what it meant.

Sara May grabbed Cara by the hair and yanked her towards her. "Cara Grey. I thought you would have learnt a lesson, with your mother, being a witch an' all. I have a witness who says you have been with a man promised to someone else. Who is it you have been lying with? What's his name?" she pulled Cara's hair harder.

"Harr! I lay with no one," hollered Cara in pain.

"Who is he?" Sara May pulled her hair harder.

"There's no one."

"Liar! Where is your father?" shouted Sara May, looking around.

"I don't know," Cara screamed.

"Liar!"

Sara May and her army led the women to the gaol and went to speak with the Magistrate. There would be a hearing in the morning.

Other prisoners woke when they came in. Some screamed in protest, one prisoner recognising Cara. "Cara, what are you doing here?" Cara glanced at her but said nothing.

The jailers shoved the women into a stone-cold freezing room, its walls dripping with water and smell of mould.

The night was long, cold and damp. The smell of sickness was rife. Many prisoners coughed a dry hollow cough. Cara heard crying. Cara learned that some prisoners had been there for months with no court hearing. The ladies were at a loss as to how this could have happened. Discussions through the night gave no answers.

Cara put her head on Kath's shoulder. In turn, Kath put her arm around all her sisters to keep warm, and they fell asleep.

*

Arran and Giles travelled into town. They tied the horses and entered the popular Edinburgh Inn to eat. Jolly, intoxicated men sang songs of their kin and drank. Finally, they ordered a drink and found somewhere to sit when a busty woman with a flowing yellow dress approached them.

"What would you fancy, my friends?" she asked.

"Pottage for two. Haggis, onions and turnip, Fish and cabbage, two tankards of ale, and a large chunk of bread for dipping." They ordered.

They watched the rowdy crowd fondle the waitresses. The women would slap anyone who would go too far, then collected their tips and move to the next unsavoury man that was sloppy with his money.

The delicious food filled their bellies. Arran rubbed his belly and talked about the sale to Mrs Cosgrove and the pennywhistle in his sack. He was looking forward to giving it to Cara. Arran asked a local man whether he knew where the Grey's lived. He gave Arran directions with his fingers drawing on the table.

"There's talk that witch's meet at the Grey's," the man replied.

Arran shrugged his shoulders in disbelief.

"People have seen it. If you go down around midnight by the loch, you will see them dancing, singing, chanting to the devil. There are lots of them. And now we have more disease and famine than ever. Look at all the problems we have had since they have tried to take over. They want to destroy humankind as we know it. My brother saw it. He said they caused the flood last season up north. Wiped out the crops and towns there, they did. People and children have washed away. Get rid of all witches, I say."

Arran shook his head angrily. "All gossip."

Just as Arran and Giles were leaving the inn, Arran saw Anice walk in. He waved to get her attention. Anice noticed him, ran towards him and hugged him. She told him about the conversation the two ladies had in the community bathroom.

"Arran, we have to stop these women! They have their sights on the girl from the Green. I think they are going to arrest her. It's all my fault. I saw you talking to her, and this lady called Elizabeth asked me questions. I told her that I thought you were flirting with her. And now they are saying she has been laying with you. I'm so sorry, Arran. Please forgive me," pleaded Anice starting to cry.

Arran was shocked but he put his arm around Anice, consoling her. "You're not to blame. I've heard about the witch hunters. They are cruel, brutal people, and we must stop them."

*

The morning sun was beaming down on a frosty layer of condensation that blanketed the ground. Arran and Anice took a walk to Corbiehill Road. A slight breeze tickled Arran's face as he smelt the fragrance of a Daphne tree nearby. Reaching the small single fronted stone house, he noticed the shingled roof needed some repair. Some shingles had moved, and he hoped that rain wasn't getting through. He knocked on the door, but it was already ajar.

"Aye. Mr Grey," he called out. "Anyone? Miss Grey!"

On entering Grey's humble home, they saw that it was in disarray. Broken cups lay on the table with a backgammon board turned over, its pieces scattered.

Following sounds coming from further inside the house, they saw Oliver Grey sitting on his bed, head in hands, sobbing uncontrollably.

Arran put his hand on Oliver's shoulder. "What has happened here, Mr Grey?"

Oliver Grey looked up with a jump. His thin, drawn eyes were red with sobbing.

"Hooo r oooooo?" Oliver mumbled.

"Mr Grey, I'm Arran Douglas. Where's Cara?

"oooo r eason shhh as aken awa"

"Slower, sir, I can't understand you," begged Arran.

"Oooo a eason shhh as takke away." Oliver desperately tried to make Arran understand.

"How can I be the reason? Taken where? Arran said, puzzled.

"Sawa May By. Takke er away. Call Cawa witch."

"A witch?"

"Aye, takke evewe one away. Misses Emp, Gace, Matty, a Ara. takke away."

"Others were taken as well," questioned Arran. "Who were they?"

"Aye, aye," replied Oliver, nodding. "The Kemp sisters."

Arran picked Oliver up off the bed and led him to the kitchen to boil water for a pot of tea. "I'll talk, and you nod for yes, and shake for no," said Arran, looking at Mr Grey, who looked tired and sad.

"Was it Sara May Bligh and her army?" asked Arran.

Oliver looked up. He let out an almighty wail. "Aye, call Cawa whore and a witch."

"I see. Where have the women been taken?" Arran asked, scared of what this frail older man was telling him.

"ourt ous," Oliver said, grappling with words and slobbering. Finally, Oliver stumbled to the breakfront and picked up some coal from the burner. He wrote "Courthouse" and shook the paper in front of Arran's face.

Arran stood. "Mr Grey, I will try to get her back."

Anice looking on felt compelled to help Cara and Mr Grey.

"We will help as much as we can, Mr Grey." Explained Anice.

"ank u ank u." Oliver pleaded something unintelligible while wiping the dribble from his chin.

Arran felt this man had been through enough. And now, he might lose his daughter.

"I will do my best to get Cara back, Mr Grey."

Head in hands, the older man just nodded.

Arran and Anice walked to the courthouse, where a commotion was ensuing. They heard from the guard that the hearing was underway.

Arran, Anice and Giles watched as the women were led out one by one from the damp cells to the courtroom. People lined the courtroom walls as they witnessed the proceedings, tutting and snorting at anything they disagreed with. The Magistrate had to call 'order thrice. Arran and Anice watched as the accused sat in front of the Magistrate stating their cases.

Then Cara was escorted into the courtroom.

Father Fergus, a priest from Dublin, was prosecuting Cara. Father Fergus was reading from his notes. He explained to the Magistrate that Cara was bedding a married man. The man's wife saw them together at the Edinburgh Inn.

"Lies! None of this is true!" cried Cara, sobbing.

The crowd hollered and hissed.

"Order! Order. Miss Grey. Sit down! Do not disrupt the court!"

"Identify this accuser, Father Fergus," asked the Magistrate.

"Sir, she doesn't want to be identified because she's a pillar of the community, and it might affect her standing. Father Fergus made it all up as he didn't know who made these accusations."

"No witness, No evidence! Dismissed!" He banged his gavel on the wooden block. "Is that all, Father Fergus?"

"No, Sir, there is the question of witchery. When arrested, Miss Grey was in the company of other known witches. Fortune telling was evident at the dwelling of Cara Grey. Eerie music was playing. Sara May Bligh will provide proof of this."

With a wave of his hand, the Magistrate asked Sara May to come forward.

"What do you have, Mrs Bligh."

"I have it all down, your honour. Can I please read from my notes?" asked Sara May.

With a flick of his fingers, the Magistrate responded. "Carry on. But be quick as we have a full day."

"We entered the premises of Cara Grey; strange music was playing.

There were teacups turned up for tealeaf reading, evidence of fortune-telling. There were vials of concoctions on the shelves, like this one. Sara May held up one of the concoctions she took from Cara's house. These are for spells, of course, as I have experienced this in the past in other witches' houses.

The Magistrate turned to Cara. "Miss Grey, do you have anything to say in your defence?"

"Sir, I am not a witch. I had my friends over for a meal. We played music and backgammon and drank tea. I look after my frail father, who needs me. Please believe me, sir," Cara pleaded with a pitiful squeal.

"I can't dismiss that you organise meetings and practice witchcraft. Your family has been known to practice it in the past. You are lucky you are so young, Miss Grey. It could have been a lot worse. I hereby sentence you to one year in prison. Take her away!"

Cara screamed a death-defying scream. "I am innocent. I want to go back to my father. Please! He has no one else. Please!" she begged."

Ignoring her cries, two men grabbed her and threw her back into the dungeon. The pungent odour that reeked through the cells made Cara feel ill.

"What have you done in here?' queried Cara holding her mouth.

"Cleaned. We will cleanse you for lice to wash your piety to Satan." replied the guard.

"But I don't follow Satan. I don't. Please believe me," cried Cara uncontrollably.

"That's what they all say." He grunted.

Cara slowed to a whimper when the door opened. The two guards threw Kath Kemp in. "Four years, for something that is a tradition in my family for generations," she cried.

"We are not witches, Kath. So why do they think we are?"

"I am so sorry, Cara," replied Kath.

Maddy and Grace came in soon after. Marilee was hysterical. Kath grabbed her and tried to calm her down.

*

Arran was dumbfounded by what he just witnessed. *What is going on in this town? Sara May Bligh was a law unto herself,* he thought. He walked up to a guard standing at the front gate.

"Can I visit Cara Grey? He asked.

"You would have to get permission from the magistrate." The guard replied. "Here he comes now. Talk to him."

Arran waved him down.

"Excuse me, sir. I want to visit Cara Grey. Can I get permission?"

"Are you the man she is laying with?"

"No!" replied Arran in a firm voice.

"No visitors, a physician will see her today. She is vomiting, I've been told, and her nose is bleeding. Be a smart man and let this go. There is nothing you can do. Proof is all the King asks for. Sara May Bligh has presented it in court today. It is out of our hands now. That is all I am going to say," demanded the Magistrate, waving his hand and brushing Arran off.

Arran met with Giles and Anice, but he felt defeated. Giles, the man of reason, suggested they try and get her out.

"That is too risky, Giles." Arran had grown his business by being smart about where he placed his bets. "The King is our only hope to end this debauchery," said Arran firmly. "Come, Giles, we are paying the King a visit."

Arran looked at Anice who was looking quite pale. "This is not your fault, my love. Sara May Bligh would have done this with or without you. Someone must stop her. You go home, and I'll see you when I return. I love you," explained Arran with a kiss.

Anice felt safe with Arran. She admired Arran's concern and wanted him to fix what seems to be unfixable.

"I love you, Arran. Would you please help her go home to her father? She has been through enough."

"I will. As soon as I can, I'll be back in Dalkeith."

Anice nodded went on her way back to her home.

\*

Arran and Giles arrived at the palace and asked the guard if they could see the King.

"I can't just let you in without talking to His Majesty first," was the reply.

"Certainly, I understand. However, tell the King it is a matter of urgency. Tell him there is an injustice in the court system. Innocent people are being arrested and subject to the most horrific punishments. The Magistrate presiding this morning put five women to years of gaol on hearsay alone. Not proper evidence. Who knows how many more have suffered the same fate?" pleaded Arran.

The guard listened. Arran could tell he was concerned.

"Wait here. I'll go and see if His Majesty will see you."

Mrs Cosgrove happened to be walking past and overheard the commotion. She noticed it was Arran Douglas asking to see the King. So she accompanied the King to see what was going on. She explained along the way that Arran was the man that sold her the materials for his Queen who had been extremely pleased with the purchase.

King James who was a strong handsome man, held some papers in his hand. He listened to Arran's plight, nodding as he spoke. This information must have stirred something in the King to get things moving quickly. Flicking the papers, the King responded, "You are not the first who has brought this to my attention. Complaints by trusted folk have made me aware of this woman, Sara May Bligh's underhanded actions." The King turned to the guard. "Get the horses and tell John Williams he needs to gather some men in front of my quarters as we are going to arrest this lady. I want her tried for her actions. Immediately." Then turning back to Arran and Giles, "Thank you for your concern, Mr Douglas. Now that it is obvious that innocent people are not being listened to, I will deal with this matter. I can give the prisoners a new trial with this paperwork, signed by the town's people. But keep this in mind, Mr Douglas, if they are witches, they will be re-arrested." he said.

Looking at Mrs Cosgrove standing next to the King. "Mrs Cosgrove here is extremely impressed with the fabrics you sold her. I am looking forward to dealing with you again in the future." They shook hands.

"Thank you, your Majesty. Thank you." Arran replied, bowing with a glimmer of hope.

*

Lord Justice General John Williams's men forced themselves into the house of Sara May Bligh soon after. Then, holding the document, he stated, "King James has presented an arrest document to collect Sara May Bligh under the suspicion of false imprisonment, inciting violence and giving false accounts to pursue an arrest.

Sara May Bligh looked up in concern at the sudden intrusion and declaration. She remained calm and demanded to see the paperwork. John Williams held it out to her. The Lord Justice insisted she came with him quietly or he would order her to be taken by force. She went quietly. The men took her to the holding cells.

The Lord Justice looked through a small mysterious black book taken from Sara May's home. Sara May Bligh's name was on the heading. It stated names of accusers and witnesses and addresses. There were descriptions of people's frantic looks when arrested. He got the impression that when the evidence was weak, she had to strengthen it by exaggerating. She wrote about husbands wanting to be rid of their wives by falsely accusing them of being witches. A housemaid was arrested for stealing a vase given to her as a reward for loyalty and services. There was more. In the book, Sara May Bligh admitted to lying to further her cases. She wrote of fees paid by the Court Clerk.

*Executions; twenty pounds.*

*Adultery; fifteen pounds.*

*Thieves and swindlers; ten pounds.*

*Gossips and liars: ten pounds.*

Payments to her helpers were marginal—a pound each for each arrest. However, towards the end of her writings, Sara May had written that she was responsible for the economy's upturn, noting that she should be thanked as people were employed because of her.

John Williams was astounded by the money she was making. He doubted the King was aware of these payments.

*

Sara May Bligh was held in prison for sixty days before a hearing. People from all over Scotland gathered to witness this monster facing justice.

She entered the court, her hands and feet tied, her greying face looking gaunt. The local people that were once supporters now turned. Hating her, yelling, "Liar! Monster!" The people were angry at the deception, and she was paid all that money. They wanted her head.

A new Magistrate from England read her writings in the black book. He, too, was convinced that Sara May needed to be dealt with harshly, as she embarrassed the monarchy.

Sara May Bligh's head was down, and she looked defeated. Her tough exterior was gone. When asked if she wanted an opportunity to state her case, she declined.

John Williams looked on as the Magistrate gave her the death penalty. He gave her the option of hanging or burning. She took hanging. She was to be escorted to Gallows Hill in Lancashire in thirty days and hanged until she was dead.

The Magistrate spared her army of workers from the death penalty. But they were marched through the town in shackles, then strung up by their feet for seven days.

Others eligible for a new trial and were still alive were given it, including Cara Grey.

Kath Kemp told the court that her three sisters were innocent as she reads tea leaves, not her sisters. The Magistrate dismissed the charge against Maddy, Grace and Marilee Kemp after questioning Kath. However, he gave Kath four years in prison.

Cara was then put back on the stand. Witnesses for her defence came forward and said Cara was an exceptional girl as she had a beautiful voice, and she sang and played her whistle for the children.

The Magistrate was happy to give Cara her freedom and warned that she should choose wisely, with whom she dined. She was allowed to return to her father.

*

Arran and Giles had returned to Edinburgh to witness Cara's court case. They were ecstatic when the Magistrate set her free. They escorted Cara back to her home. She asked the men if they wanted to stay for their famous delicious savoury meat pies. It was the least she could do for all the support they had shown her. Arran explained he had to get back to Dalkeith as Anice was waiting for him.

"Cara, before we go. There's a reason I returned, to see you. I bought this for you," Arran said, pulling out the velvet package and handing it to Cara.

Cara untied the twine, and the cloth fell open. There it was, a brand-new Pennywhistle. With her mouth a gasp, she said in a quivering voice. "Oh, thank you, Arran." She put it to her mouth immediately and played a couple of high notes, and the whistle didn't screech. They both laughed. They hugged.

"We do have to be going now. Please, Cara, be safe."

Cara was thankful for his kindness. However, she felt sad they were going. She watched as the two men disappeared over the horizon. She waved until she could see them no more.

*

Arran and Giles were exhausted with the journey back to Dalkeith. Giles dropped Arran off and headed home to his family. Anice was at the door when she heard the horse pull up. She ran towards Arran greeted him with open arms.

Arran walked into the bedroom. He discarded his boots and fell onto the bed. Anice said she would cook him a beef pottage and dine when he has a rest.

When Arran awoke from his deep sleep, he wondered where he was. Then getting his bearings, he remembered he was home, and Anice was here somewhere. He sat up, got off the bed, looked around the room, still half asleep; he opened his sack on the floor to empty the contents for washing. He realised the bag belonged to Anice as ladies' undergarments fell out. Amongst the clothes was a pennywhistle with a split in it.

He saw Anice at the corner of his eye, standing in the doorway.

"What is this?" he asked.

"I found it at the Green at Edinburgh. It was on the grass." She explained.

"Why do you ask, Arran?" asked Anice with a soft, unassuming voice.

"This belongs to Cara. I suppose she won't be needing it now 'cause I bought her another one."

Arran looked at Anice. She had an unhappy look on her face.

"Aye, that's right. I saw it was a split whistle and bought Cara one off a man at the palace."

After dinner, Anice and Arran sat on a seat in the garden and talked about their future. They accepted that they were good together and there were to be no secrets. To speak to each other when there was a problem, except that each had flaws and be faithful. Arran was pleased to have this conversation with the woman he loved.

*

The Douglas's future was filled with promise. They were happy for many years to come. After they married, they moved to Edinburgh to be near the palace as they both worked for the King and Queen. Arran continued to provide fabrics to the court, and Anice learnt dressmaking and made clothes for the prince and princesses Henry, Elizabeth, and Charles.

Mrs Cosgrove became a trusted friend and godmother to the two of them and their four children. They made a substantial income and volunteered at the courthouse for people who were summons to court for witchery. But it was futile. The future of witches got worse. Forty-five years later, the hysteria spread to Salem, Massachusetts, in America. There, men and women were placed on trial and found guilty, just like what Arran witnessed in Scotland all those years ago.

Through the hysteria, some people even believed they were witches and admitted to it. No one knew why this happened. Legend says the people got caught up in the hysteria, and if they felt different or saw unexplainable things, they blamed witchcraft and the devil.

*

Oliver Grey died of natural causes one year after the trials. He was content with his life. But the stress of all the difficulties took its toll.

Thomas from London, who travelled with The Jongleurs, a travelling group who performed tricks, sang, and danced, noticed Cara Grey singing for the children on the Green. He asked her to join him and his wife Lorraine on tour through Europe. With her beautiful singing and knowledge of the pennywhistle, she would make a perfect addition to the cast. Cara being on her own, accepted the offer.

Kath Kemp did her time in gaol. She never reread a tea leaf again. Kath was fifty when she died in 1620 of dehydration caused by dysentery. Some said it was retribution for leading a sinful life. Others said she was finally at peace, as she had never regained her life to any form of normalcy after her stint in prison.

Her sisters Maddy and Grace lived together and never married; they were traumatised by their experiences and lead tranquil lives. The youngest,

Marilee, looked after her sisters financially and emotionally. She married a courtier to Queen Anne and had six children.

They all wanted peace and to live a normal life. But it was always in the back of their mind, that they could be a product of people's gossip and were well aware of the hardship of living in a time of witches.

# ADAMS SECRET TREASURE

*ZOE SKJELLERUP*

Good afternoon. My name is Adam Jones, and I am 14 years old. For most of my life, I lived on an old, decrepit ranch in Houston, Texas. But, of course, that was before my parents sent me to the orphanage three years ago. So how did I end up an orphan?

Well...

Ever since I can remember, my parents told me that I was a unique child and stayed with them at all times. I'd never been to a real school before, as my parents needed help around the property. I just wanted an education at school like the other kids, but my parents said it just wasn't possible. We were running too low on money, so I didn't have a choice but to stay and work on the farm. I wished life were different.

It was hectic! Every day, my job was to feed the animals - cattle, horses and chickens. But, I didn't mind doing the chores outside. I loved the freedom-the smell of the fresh country air and the cool breeze hitting my cheeks. I didn't mind helping my mother prepare a meal for supper either.

How I miss these memories, now they're gone.

My family's house was two storeys, made out of weatherboard with a gable roof. Inside, it was warm and cosy, but to me, the place felt confined. It was all I ever knew, and it had become boring. Day after day, I was doing the same old chores. But, looking back, it was much better than the orphanage.

The ranch gradually became too much work for my parents to maintain. We had to let some of the animals run wild, and my many duties decreased.

*Perhaps now I will have time to go to school?* I wondered.

I didn't want to leave my parents behind. But I wanted a bright new future at school.

*I have to try.*

That night I was helping my mother Yolanda prepare a meal for dinner. My family were having a delicious homemade chicken and vegetable soup.

"Mother, do you think I could start going to school soon?" I asked as I grabbed the kitchen knife and started chopping the vegetables.

"Certainly not!" Mom declared, keeping her focus on the simmering soup. "We're losing control of our property right now! You know we need your assistance on the ranch."

I felt the anger bubble violently inside my stomach, "Please let me go! I've done everything you wanted, and I'm bored with the same chores every single day! All I want to do is learn, and you won't allow it! What makes me so different from everyone else, anyway?"

Mom hesitated for a moment, scratching her head and raising her eyebrows. I could see the nervousness in her eyes.

"Adam, If you entered the community by yourself, something bad might happen. So my decision is made, and you will stay here!"

"What on earth are you talking about?" I puffed deep breaths through gritted teeth. "I don't understand! I feel scared, mother! What is wrong with me?!"

Then, suddenly, I felt an intense pain strike inside my hands.

"Argh!" I jumped backwards in fright, dropping the knife onto the bench. I glanced down at my hands covered by blue sparks. My heart pounded in my chest. I felt the heat flushing through my cheeks.

"Mom! What on earth is happening to me?"

"I will explain, but you need to control yourself first!" she spoke calmly, looking into my eyes. "Listen to me. You need to breathe."

Seeing the distress in Mom's face, I took a few deep breaths and tried to remain calm. As I watched, the blue sparks on my hands began to fade away.

Finally, I glanced back toward my mother.

"Listen, you're a special child compared to the others. You have a gift! You were born with a unique power, just like I was, and my father before me. This ability has passed down through the family for generations."

I was stunned. *No way! Power in our family? Like magic?*

"Wait, does that mean you have the same power I do?" I asked.

"No, you see... every generation's power is different. I had telekinesis, and my father said that he had the power of fire. So it looks like you have electricity. But I don't have my power anymore. When a child is born, their parents no longer keep their gift."

"What is telekinesis?" I asked.

"Telekinesis means having the ability to control things with your mind. So, for example, I could clean my bedroom without having to lift anything physically."

"Wow, that's pretty cool! I wish I had that power. It would make my life so much easier."

A slight smile broke across Mom's face as she walked over to the kitchen sink. "Yeah, it was pretty handy! First, however, I'm guessing that you'll need to learn to control your anger, just like my father and I needed to."

"Wow, that's awesome! So, once I've figured out how this power works correctly, I can finally go to school?

Mom paused and looked out the kitchen window, "No! You must keep the power hidden. We already said that we need you here!"

"But Mom, I'd be careful!"

"Enough, Adam! I hate to break this to you, but you could become a threat to society. We just can't worry about you like that."

I grimaced as I felt my chest tighten.

"What? I'm not a threat to anyone, mother! Take that back." I looked down at my hands. They were glowing again.

"Calm down now!" Mom said, trembling with anxiety. "Your palms are glowing! The power is activating itself. My father said that his hands would glow red every time he became angry. You have to relax."

Suddenly, the electricity in my palms combined into a circle of blue sparks.

"Oh no!" Mom shouted, "Adam, STOP!"

A blinding light blasted from my hands through the air towards my mother. She dived behind the kitchen bench, narrowly escaping the ball of energy. It smashed into the window behind the sink, sending shattered glass and blue sparks flying in every direction.

My eyes widened, my heart thumped against my chest. I breathed heavily. *Oh no! What have I done?*

I looked down at my hands. Wisps of grey smoke floated from my fingers into the air.

Suddenly, I hear the door open behind me. I turned around to face my father, Zachary.

"Oh my god! What on earth happened?" He asked as he burst into a sprint towards me.

Mom emerged from behind the bench, panting heavily. She peeked around the room, making sure that everyone was safe.

"Zachary, it's time..."

"It was an accident," I sobbed, "a blast of energy... I'm sorry! It was uncontrollable. Am I punished?"

Dad pulled me into an embrace, "Shh!" He soothed. I noticed a tear roll down his cheek, "Yes you're punished. You need to learn to control your anger next time."

That was the last night I spent with my parents. I awoke the following day in an orphanage, far away from my home. The matrons told me that my parents could no longer take care of me. But I knew that it was punishment for my anger.

To begin with, I thought life in the orphanage was excruciating. I was terrified that matrons and orphans might discover my secret power, so I chose to remain quiet in my bedroom. There was absolutely nothing for me to do.

All day long, I could hear rambunctious little kids outside my door. Their running and squealing left me with a headache every night.

When I did spend time outside of my room, the older orphans would throw me into an old storage room and lock the door behind them, laughing. I would slide down the wall and bury my head in my arms. All I could smell was the stench of dead mice filling the room and the dust from the old blackbutt floorboards. Insects and beetles scurried across the floor. Once, they crawled up inside my top. I felt goosebumps on my skin.

"Ewww!" I yelled, jumping to my feet and shaking my shirt.

The orphans would bully me because I look different. I have silver eyes! Both the matrons and orphans constantly ask about their rare eye colour. But there's no way I'm going to tell them the truth.

The orphanage was much older than the ranch and far more isolating too. This place - it wasn't an ordinary orphanage. The matrons told me that it used to be a mansion many years ago, but the owner had disappeared.

The mansion was once luxurious but had fallen into disrepair with its vast stained-glass windows developing cracks, and their colours faded over the decades. Tattered leather furniture occupied the rooms, and the swimming pool next door was filled with insects and cobwebs instead of water.

Most importantly, I discovered that the mansion had a library, where I spent many hours reading. Unfortunately, some of the chipped wooden shelves had collapsed. The books were disintegrating and covered in dust, but that did not deter me. These books taught me everything I could imagine - more than I ever could have learned at school. They became my only friends.

*

Three years have passed since being abandoned at the orphanage. The year is 1952, and here I am - still trapped in this place, hiding away in the library with my books. Clutching a book against my chest, I feel a tear slide down my cheek.

*Mom and dad don't give a damn about me anymore! I don't have any friends here. I feel like I don't belong here. I feel so alone!*

I am startled by the sound of rustling papers. Then, I become aware of a low humming noise coming from inside the library.

"Hello, is anyone there?" There's no response.

I quickly brush the tear away and stand up, heading past the broken shelves. Tucked away in the corner of the library, I spot a small office with a chipped and decaying oakwood door displaying rusted hinges. Beside it, a small window with pieces of shattered glass spread across the carpet in front of me.

*I've never explored this part of the library before! I am not even sure if I'm supposed to be here, but I don't care. Instead, I'm intrigued to figure out what's behind this door. I have begun such an exciting adventure; I can't possibly stop now!*

Wooden blinds have been left closed inside the window, and I peek through them cautiously. A fluorescent lamp is on inside the office, and I can see paperwork scattered across the floor. An old tanker desk sits against the right wall, and behind it, a ripped fabric study chair.

*Strange! Someone must've been in the middle of work! But there's nobody here...*

I head inside the office. Suddenly, the lights all around the library flicker off, throwing the room into complete darkness.

I feel my heart pound in my chest. I'm stuck, frozen with fear. I can't see anything anymore, but I can still hear the loud humming sound nearby.

"Who's there?" I call out again. My voice is unsteady, but there's still no response. *If I only had light in this room.* Suddenly, I feel a tickle between my fingertips. I glance downwards. I notice ten circles blinking as if they're dancing.

*I haven't seen this one before. What could the power be doing now?*

The electricity forms a long string and floats into the air towards the light bulbs. Then, finally, it makes a loud popping sound and disappears. I frown.

*Well, that was disappointing. It didn't seem to do anything.*

The lights suddenly flicker on again.

*Wow! It actually did something worthwhile. I can see quite clearly now.*

Taking in my surroundings, I glance around the office. The wooden desktop is untidy, with paperwork left scattered across the surface. In addition, a metal fan has been left on the desk, blowing paperwork around the room. Heaving a sigh of relief, I realise that the source of the humming sound was just the running fan.

As I scan the office, I notice a destroyed frame left on the carpet.

*It must've collapsed from the wall above me. Surely, someone would've dealt with this mess by now!* But, instead, the frame was smashed, and the print inside missing.

*What could the picture have shown?*

Beside the frame, I find a sizeable foolscap print that has been left on the floor, covered in dust.

*It must've been the missing print from the frame!* I wonder as I step over the shattered glass and pick it up. I dust it off so that I can see more clearly. It's a black and white photograph.

The picture shows a young gentleman standing in front of the mansion. The massive building behind him was white and clean, with a manicured garden and a prominent water feature in the middle of a cobbled path.

*This must've been what the orphanage used to look like before!*

I look more closely at the man. He's dressed in a dark overcoat and holds a straw hat. He looks like he might be in his late thirties, with dark greasy hair perfectly combed to the side. The man appears to have silver eyes, and they almost glimmer back at me from the photograph. I gasp.

*No way! Silver eyes. Just like mine. And I've always thought that I'm the only one!*

Flipping the photo over, I was surprised to find the words 'Tommy Smith' written in cursive writing.

*I've heard of this guy before! He was the old owner of this mansion.*

I tuck the photograph into my jeans pocket.

As I examined the paperwork, I notice a letter. It's unfinished and addressed to a doctor. It read:

*June 21st 1934*
*Dear Dr Ross.*
*The medication you've given me seems to be helping a lot. My headaches are reducing, and I'm not as fatigued as I was before. However, my senses are growing way sharper. Thank you so much for-*

I could feel my head spinning.

*That must have been why Tommy had to leave because he was sick. But this was written almost twenty years ago. So why would it still be lying around? Shouldn't the owner have done something about it by now?*

As I turn to exit the office, I notice something in the corner of my eye.

Tucked away behind the desk, I see enormous slashes on the carpet. My eyes widened. *What on earth happened here?*

As I make a closer inspection, I realise that the slashes gave way to a gaping hole in the floorboards underneath.

*A person wouldn't have done this! It looks more like a creature but of what kind? And where could this hole lead to? Maybe a basement? I need to find out.*

I scan the office for a light, but there's nothing.

*Oh please, there's gotta be something!*

As I glance towards the desk, I notice an old rectangular lantern on it.

*Perfect. I just need something to light it with.*

Suddenly, It happened again—another tickle in between my fingertips. I glance downwards. Ten circles were blinking.

*I've noticed this before! It's really weird.*

Suddenly, the electricity zaps and ignites the lantern, sending blue light in front of me. I gasp.

*Wow! The electricity must be connected with my thoughts somehow. This is totally wicked.*

I take a deep breath and head towards the gaping hole.

*Should I do this? I only discovered this room a minute ago. Oh, stuff it. I'm going in.*

I peeled back the tattered carpet and cautiously hopped inside, gripping the handle of the lantern.

As I shine my lantern around the basement, I notice the thick wooden beams stabilise the building above. Insects and cobwebs dangling from the beams. Empty shelves line the walls - some chipped, and some even collapsed like dominoes. I find old, empty bottles scattered across the floor.

*That's strange! Who would leave empty bottles down here?*

Amongst the rubbish, I track a trail of blood. It leads further into the darkness. I follow it cautiously.

*What could have done this? But, I'm determined to know where this path leads!*

The blood stops at the corner of a shelf, and I immediately peek around. The lantern shines upon what looks like a moving shadow in the far-right corner. It is gigantic and horrifying.

I stumble backwards with fright, and I hear a loud crunching noise underneath my shoes. I glance downwards and notice that it's broken glass from one of the bottles.

My heart pounds in my chest. I press my back against the shelf and close my eyes for a moment. Silence spreads throughout the underground area.

*Could it be gone? Did the sound of the glass draw its attention?*

My eyes spring open, and I peer around the shelf again. I notice that the shadow has disappeared, and nauseous rises in my stomach. I glance around the basement, just to make sure. I can't see the shadow anymore, but that doesn't mean the creature isn't here. I step away from the shelf.

*What was that thing, anyway?*

I notice what looks like a pair of creepy eyes shining out of the darkness. I'm struck frozen, just staring at those eyes. I can't make out what it is as darkness surrounds the creature's body.

Before I know it, the creepy eyes disappear. I tremble with fear in the dark.

"Where are you?" I call out as I quickly shine my lantern in every direction, searching for the eyes. I can't see anything, and the basement is quiet once again.

Suddenly, the creature rises out to attack me, and I jump back with fright. My eyes are glued onto the beast as it slowly moves towards me. Its ears are pointed forward, and its tail is straight and unmoving. The lantern shines upon its face, revealing a pair of sharp, gnashing fangs. It looks like a werewolf.

I retreat slowly, moving backwards as the wolf approaches. I was trapped in the basement with a ferocious wolf. My cheeks are burning, and I feel myself trembling with fear.

I am startled as I feel my back collide against the wall.

*There's absolutely no escape now. I'm doomed!*

I feel the lantern slipping from my hand. It extinguishes as glass shatters on the ground.

I hear a whimper, and in a split second, the werewolf leaps up and strikes, leaving a deep gash across my cheek with its sharp claws.

"Argh!" I yell, placing my hand on the wound. I can feel blood streaming down. I can see daylight towards my left, but I can't sneak out. My only option is to fight back!

Adrenaline courses violently through my body. I feel the power activating.

Sparks appears in my palms and combines into a circle. Then a blinding light blasts through the air towards the wolf. The intense force of the power pushes the animal backwards. There's a loud screeching noise on the concrete as the wolf skids away, creating long claw marks that lead into the darkness. There's an enormous thud in the distance.

*The wolf crashed into a shelf!*

I hear a scrambling sound nearby. Then, after a brief second, it disappears, leaving the basement quiet once again.

*The werewolf! Where on earth is it?*

I spin wildly, looking in every direction for the wolf. I can't see it. My heart is pounding.

Suddenly, I notice claws flying towards my chest. It has jumped out of the darkness to attack me again. The werewolf pushes me down, its claws almost piercing my skin as they pin me to the ground. The creature snarls above me, its massive jaws ready to strike.

*This is it—my final moments.*

Suddenly, I feel an intense pain strike inside my shoulder. The werewolf is sent flying away from me.

"Argh!" I yell.

The creature whimpers as it lands with a heavy thud.

*It must have received a shock of my electricity!*

I pull myself to my feet and see the creature lying on the ground, staring back at me.

Looking deeply into the werewolf's eyes, I see that they're not as creepy as I thought. They're actually quite a beautiful silver colour - almost familiar, like the gentleman I saw in the photograph. My eyes widen.

"Tommy," I whisper.

The wolf tilts his head slightly as if the name seems to ring a bell.

"Adam..." He growls before limping away into the darkness.

*How... how did he know my name?*

As the shock wears off, I begin to feel the pain of my wounds. I wince as I carefully touch my cheek.

*I have to get out of here... before Tommy comes back.*

I climb out of the gaping hole, back through the library and towards my room. It's always a challenge to remember the way, as there are many long narrow corridors leading in every direction- It feels like a maze. It's bewildering, especially now that I know the truth about the mansion and its past.

*

One month later, I hear a knock at my bedroom door. A smile breaks across my face.

*What could this be about? Nobody ever knocks on my door!*

I reach for the handle to answer it. Behind it, I find a young gentleman smiling at me. He looks familiar, with his dark hair combed perfectly and bright silver eyes - like the man who gave me the scar. My smile fades.

"What on earth are you doing here? You scarred my bloody cheek!"

"Adam! I think that I owe you an apology...." He pauses to look behind him as if whatever he needs to say is a secret. Then, he turns toward me and whispers into my ear.

"I have a condition that turns me into a werewolf, and I need to learn to control my hunger.

*Like me, with my anger.* I think.

"May I please come in? I would like a word with you." I pause and look away, glancing at the wall.

*Should I? I don't believe him after what he did, though, but I need to know what he's got to say.*

"Where were you all this time? Everyone told me that you were missing, presumed dead."

"If you would just let me in, I'd explain everything!"

I widen my door, gesturing towards my bed and heaving a deep sigh. "Fine!"

I make myself comfortable on my bed, and Tommy stands in front of me.

"I was on the telephone to my sister, Yolanda, just a minute ago-"

My eyes widen. *Wait, my mother is Tommy's sister? This doesn't sound right!*

I glance downwards onto the floor. "First you gash my cheek, then you're telling me you're my uncle. You can't be serious right now!"

"Hey! I was a wolf at the time, Adam. I wouldn't have known who you were. I'm sorry, I wasn't there in your childhood." He continues. "I was dealing with the sickness of becoming a wolf. I have been living in the basement beneath the mansion ever since, and I couldn't let anyone else know about it. Not even your mother knows."

Tommy reaches into his jean's pocket for something. He takes out a little piece of paper and flips it over. I see a picture that shows my mother huddled up with a young gentleman. He's Tommy!

I'm left speechless.

"I feel so bad for hurting you! I'm sorry! Can you please forgive me?"

I glance towards the wall and take a deep sigh. "That depends. Can you please fix my cheek?"

"I'll do whatever I can. How did you end up here? We have to get you back to your parents."

I shake my head. "No, thank you! Mom and dad don't care about me anymore. All because I smashed the kitchen window with a blast of my electricity. I was so angry that I couldn't go to school. But it was uncontrollable at the time. That's why I'm trapped in this orphanage."

"Excuse me? Doesn't she want you? That's ridiculous!" Tommy exclaims, shaking his head. "Right! If they don't want to look after you, I'd be more than happy to take you home."

A smile breaks across my face as I stretch my arms out for an embrace. "Really? Do you mean it? Thank you!"

"But first, we'd need to do something about that scar. The matrons would never let me adopt you if they knew I put that scar on you!"

# BLACK DOG/WHITE DOG

## *MELISSA SAYERS*

She couldn't tell you where or when it began. On a calm and sunny day, or under the curtain of thundering rain, whether she was alone or in company, whether she was drunk or sober, she just knew somehow, she snapped. One moment she was sane. The next, she had lost all her faculties. Though there had been signs, in retrospect, it had crept up on her. And given her history, the death and destruction in her teenage years and early 20's, it was no great surprise.

Karyn's father had been shot and killed as an innocent bystander in a bungled bank robbery when she was 13, a cruel twist of fate that cut her profoundly. Her mother was never the same and plummeted into a deep depression, resulting in electroshock therapy to cure the great malaise. As a result, she lost the essence of who she was and was nothing but a shell of her former self when she died tragically at her hand in her late 40's.

An abusive relationship in her early 20's only worked to compound Karyn's emotional issues. It took three years to extricate herself from that hell, and from that point on, Karyn always viewed herself as damaged goods. Unworthy.

However, things began to turn around when Karyn struck out on her own and started attending University to study Psychology. Her mood improved, and her preoccupation with the darkness inside her faded. By her early 30's, she was feeling like things were finally coming together for her. But by 32, though, she was drifting. It started with the odd miserable day, but days turned to weeks, and misery became sheer desperation, blackness, and a failure to function on the most fundamental levels. Days on end were spent under the covers, motionless, praying for the reprise of sleep. All was dark. The sun and moon both seemed to hide and slide into each other as the curtains stayed closed. Days were spent at the bottom of a bottle as she stumbled in the darkness, cold, alone and lost. The empty bottles on the top shelf of her kitchen betrayed her story. When her head is awash with whiskey, or vodka, or wine, nothing else mattered. The pain stopped, and numbness set in. Then the morning would come, where her head would pound, and it seemed like she was drowning under ice, scratching for the surface till her fingers bled—not knowing what to do or how to get out.

But through all this, there were sporadic periods of euphoric and dangerous mania. During these times, everything seemed so magically amplified and appeared to have an ethereal glow about it, like an aural photograph or like the Southern lights. Sunsets shone bright fluorescent pink. She felt like she could rise towards the sun, soaring through the heavens and above the clouds. She was not afraid, or sad, or confused. Instead, she felt weightless, untouchable, shrouded in warmth and infinitely wise. Spinning naked with all her imperfections and insecurities laid bare, yet no compulsion to conceal them. At that moment, she felt strength through weakness and power beyond measure.

So she bought a new car she definitely couldn't afford, on a whim, and walked from one side of Melbourne to the other in red stilettos at 3 am, because she had spent all her money on drink and her friends had run out of steam long before her. And she really didn't care.

During one episode, she ran 10km in the pounding rain.

Or, in this invisible high, she could sit cross-legged on her bed surrounded by books and consuming words of grief, of love, of sanity, of psychology. Her brain was on fire. She would sit for days at a time without sleep, absorbing information like a lion devouring a fresh kill.

Or there would be the rage. Anger so deep it felt like a fire engulfing her, like black spirits consuming her, a wave of vengeful, hurtful anger that did not care for its consequences, nor for the pain it could cause to herself or others. She did not care about the holes in the wall or the smashed glasses or the stitches required to her right hand when she smashed a wine bottle on her kitchen bench after a particularly combative phone call with a lover who tried to call her out on her fluctuating moods. It was an infinitely energetic emotion, a poison she knew too well and loathed yet could not dismiss. And it, too, was fuelled by alcohol. It was like standing outside herself and watching herself destruct, with no capacity to intervene. It was a parasitic dis-ease, spreading with every heartbeat and out of Karyn's control. And it manifested in ways that deeply scarred the people she loved. Very few are left now.

Then there would be the crash. Darker and deeper than the last, every time. Just when she felt she had reached the bottom, she would fall lower into the rabbit hole, and the entrance seemed further and further away, a pin-prick of light that she could barely see. The sorrow seemed overwhelming. She didn't eat. She didn't sleep. She didn't communicate. She didn't shower. She didn't function. Period. But the darkness was worth it for the sweet, bright light, even though the periods of brightness were far shorter and more transient than the darkness.

However, there were tiny moments of space in between. So still. So sweet. So fleeting. The calm was palpable. White light filtered tenderly through the silence. Karyn felt soothed and reassured but simultaneously fearful. There was an ephemeral moment of not knowing which way the pendulum was going to swing, a solitary light from a blackened tunnel. This is the half-light, the place where logic and emotion, fear and hope both exist. There is nothing but silence, rare and beautiful. Her most private mind at rest. Her heart still for a moment. Boundless freedom. And then, here it comes, the light, a freight train. As it bears down on her, she braces for impact and takes cover in a bottle of whiskey.

# FRED

## *DALE WALKLEY*

My life had revolved around my father, but we had help in the house with Nanny. MrsLingstrum was our housekeeper, and Raoul, the gardener.

I would have happily lived this way, not knowing any different, but that was not to be. I was 12 when I found out I had a grandfather living in Johannesburg. Since the first meeting with him, we both have made up for lost time with many visits and holidays.

My father, however, remained aloof, and to me, he always was the non-caring person. I had my friends Geordie and Liam, with whom I spent most of my time and considered my brothers. We went to school together and were now at university, where Geordie studied to become a Sports Doctor and Liam, a Lawyer. I was studying Accounting as my father expected me to join the family business. Still, unbeknown to him, I was also studying Photography and was well on the way to earning my living.

My twenty-first birthday was coming up in March and Geordie, Liam and I were looking forward to a camping weekend. About two weeks prior, I received a letter from a Mr Abrahams from Abrahams, Lithgow and Palmer, Solicitors in Johannesburg. *Who or what did a solicitor want with me?*

So here I sat, in Liam's living room, beyond nervous and terrified, waiting on a gentleman by the name of Abrahams.

There was a knock on the door. I opened it tentatively to find a man about my father's age dressed in a dark charcoal suit, grey shirt and red tie. He carried a briefcase and a coat over his arm. He was pleasant to look at, clean-shaven with iron-grey hair cut in the military style.

"Frederick Johannsson?"

"Mr Abrahams! Yes, sir, please come in. This room is my friend's. He thought we might be more comfortable here. Can I get you a drink?"

"A black coffee would be nice. Thank you."

My anxiety abated as I prepared his coffee. He looks like a nice man. Maybe I was worrying too much.

"Shall we sit while I explain the reason for my contact?"

"Yes, please do so," I replied, watching him settle onto the sofa. "I must admit, sir, that I am intrigued. I cannot think of anything I have done to warrant a visit from a legal firm."

Mr Abrahams smiled, nodding his head in understanding. "What do you know about your mother?"

"I have a photograph and know that she died when I was about three years old."

"Is that all you know? If so, this is going to be quite harder for you to hear." He paused, shuffling some papers he pulled out of his briefcase. "Yes, your mother died when you were three, but she left a sizable estate that comes to you when you turn twenty-one. Has your father never mentioned anything of this?

"No, sir. He never talks about her. Her bedroom has remained locked and unchanged since her death. It is something he refuses to discuss with me. I was twelve when I found I had a grandfather living in Johannesburg".

"Oh dear, it is worse than I thought. What about your grandmother?"

"Grandmother, what Grandmother?" I was puzzled by his question.

"Your mother's mother. She has looked after you all these years. Surely you realised who she is?" Mr Abrahams looked at me in surprise.

"My Nanny is my grandmother?"

"Yes, that's what you always called her, my Nanny, so I assumed you knew."

"No, sir, I did not!" Different thoughts were churning through my mind. I was confused. *What was he trying to tell me?*

Mr Abrahams must have seen the confusion on my face. "Would you prefer to postpone this meeting, and I can come another day to discuss your mothers will?"

I struggled to pull myself together. I had to know what this lawyer had come to tell me.

"I always knew there was something special between Nanny and I, but I never thought it had to do with my mother. After I found out I had a grandfather, I saw my first photograph of my mother." I took a deep breath. "Mr Abrahams, please go ahead with what you have to say because I don't think anything else could shock me today."

"If you are sure?" Mr Abrahams asked, looking at me cautiously.

"Yes, I am," I nodded firmly.

"I have a letter from her for you, to be given on or near your twenty-first."

"A letter", I interrupted. "My mother left me a letter?"

Mr Abrahams nodded, pulling out an envelope. "Would you like to read it now or later?"

"Now, please." I was beside myself with everything he told me so far but holding something she wrote was beyond my wildest dreams. Mr Abrahams handed me a long buff- coloured envelope, the words *For Freddie on his 21st* written on it.

*She called me Freddie* I was touched.

Opening the envelope carefully, I shook out the letter and gazed upon the hand of someone I have never seen,

*April 4th, 1989, My darling Fred,*

*If you are reading this, then I am no longer around. I do hope I didn't leave you too soon, but this hideous illness will determine when I go, not me.*

*Your father is a loving and kind man and will not cope very well with my passing.*

*No, he just shut you away and pretended you weren't ever here, I thought.*

*I hope that by leaving Nanny, my mother, things will be easier for you. She always loved me and will undoubtedly love and care for you. But, please, son, don't be angry with her if she doesn't reveal who she is, there will have been very good reasons for it.*

*Aah, a lightbulb moment for me. That is why Nanny calls me her Fred.*

*Mr Abrahams will have delivered this letter to you. Whatever you decide to do with the information, please think long and hard because above all it must be your decision because your father will either be devastated or delighted.*

*Remember to look after him if you can, he is a good man, and I loved him very much. I will love you always and will watch over you.*

*Mummy.*

I felt tears were streaming down my face. I looked up at the man sitting opposite me. "My mother loved me and didn't want to leave?"

"Yes, Frederick, she loved you much."

"I can't cope with any more today. May I come and see you tomorrow if you are still in Cape Town to discuss the rest?"

"Of course, I am staying at the Hilton and will be here for at least a week. So, if tomorrow doesn't suit, ring me and arrange another day. Here is my card."

Mr Abrahams stood up to leave and shook my hand. "She would have been very proud of you and all that you have achieved so far."

I reeled with the shock that my mother had left me a letter. Geordie and Liam burst into the room, interrupting my deep thoughts.

"Are you okay?" they chorused.

"Yes, I must see that gentleman again, but I couldn't cope with what he was telling me. I have a letter from my mother. I found Nanny is my grandmother. And he says he has other important things to tell me. It's something to do with her will, apparently."

"But are you alright?" Geordie asked, his concern obvious.

"Do you know what? I am angry, and before I confront my grandmother, I need to calm down. So how about we go get a drink?"

"This is beautiful. I wish I had something like this from my mother," whispered Liam reading the letter Fred had left lying on the bed.

"Oh, Liam, I am sorry I didn't think when I left that there."

"What does it say, buddy?" asked Geordie.

"That she loves him and didn't want to leave and that his father was a good man." Replied Liam.

"Just no soul," I replied.

I worked my way through the rest of the week, but I arranged to visit Nanny the following weekend before I went home. She was one Lion, or should I say Lioness, I would deal with first. I was still angry but more confused about why she couldn't or wouldn't reveal who she was all these years.

*

Nanny was in the kitchen and heard Frederick enter the house.

"Grandmother, where are you?" he called out.

When he referred to her as 'grandmother' her heart skipped a beat. *Oh God, he knows. Now what?* Taking a deep breath, she left the kitchen and walked towards Frederick.

"Hello, my Fred."

"Hello Grandmother, care to explain?" he asked with a smile on his face.

She knew right away that everything was going to be alright.

"Tea is in the kitchen as usual," she said. "Sit, and I will explain why I did what I did."

She poured a cup of tea to steady her nerves and sat down next to him at the kitchen table. "When your mother was dying, she asked me to look after you, so that is what I did. You always called me 'Nanny', so we didn't see the need to get you to change."

After taking a sip of tea, she continued. "As time went on, it got harder to unravel the deception. Finally, I had this conversation with your father before you finished high school, suggesting that we should tell you, but things got in the way, and it came down to Mr Abrahams." She sighed and reached for his hand. "I am sorry, really I am, but I still love you whether I am Nanny or Grandmother."

"I can understand that the story got bigger than the lie," Fred asked. "Why not talk about my mother so I could have known her while I was growing up. Instead, all I have is one photograph that father gave me when I turned twelve."

"Oh, Freddie, no! You have so many of her things. Whose cameras do you think I gave you when you showed an interest, whose coverlet covered your bed all your childhood years. Yes, she loved Lemurs too. The bookcases and some of the books were all hers. I surrounded you with her, but I couldn't tell you. It upset your father too much. Did you ever wonder why he never came to tuck you in at night? It was because he could not bear to see her things? The China that Mrs Lingstrum made sure you ate off for every meal was all hers. It was our way of keeping her alive for you. All your life, she has surrounded you. Even the orchids Raoul grows were her favourite flower. Although they were never in the house, her bedroom had a fresh vase every week."

"But, why? Father never mentions her, and it was only by chance that I saw the photo on the desk that he told me was of my mother and gave me a copy."

"He was devastated when she died as we all were, and the only way he could deal with it was to lock it all away, including his heart. So, their bedroom is as it was the day she died, nothing has changed, all her clothes, cosmetics, trinkets are all there. She could walk in there tomorrow and find everything as it was. Ingrid keeps it clean but is not allowed to move anything."

"Who is Ingrid? Fred asked.

"Mrs Lingstrum! Ah, so Abrahams didn't tell you that story then." Nanny looked down, adjusting a napkin on the table, gathering her thoughts.

"Ingrid Lingstrum is your aunt. She is your mother's sister or, should I say, half-sister."

Fred looked perplexed.

"I have been married twice. Ingrid is from my first marriage, and when my first husband died, I was left alone until I met and married your grandfather, and we had your mother."

"Everyone refers to her as my mother. Did she have a name?" Fred asked.

'Of course, she did. Her name was Elspeth."

"Elspeth?"

"There is a chest in the attic with her things in it. Ingrid will get it for you."

"Chest in the attic?" Fred was parroting everything she said. "Why does father not want her memories around him and to remember?"

"He has a living memory, you, you are the living image of your m…….. Elspeth, so he can't help but remember. He's essentially a good man, but he has forgotten how to live, love and enjoy himself. There are some video films of him and your mother somewhere. Watch them, then perhaps you might be able to understand him a little better. Are you still angry with me?'

"No, I was never really angry, just disappointed, I suppose," responded Fred. "What was that saying you used to tell me? I told fibs. Oh, what a tangled web we weave, when we practise deceiving. You all certainly did an excellent job. But no more? I love you, but now I have bearded one Lioness. I must go beard another lion. It is going to be a busy weekend."

"Take care, my Fred. I won't ring Ingrid or your father to tell them you are on your way. Drive safely now."

"Bye, Nanny, I guess that is what you have always been, so that is what you will stay," kissing her, Fred climbed into his car and proceeded down the street.

*

I left Nanny's and drove home, parking my car in the garage as I would be home for the next couple of days. Father's car was not there, so I would have time with my Aunt before he appeared. As I walked from the garage to the back door, I looked over at the greenhouse full of orchids and smiled. I shared my passion for these along with Raoul and my mother. Stepping into the kitchen, she had her back to me stirring something, so I opened with

"Hello, Aunt Ingrid, I am home, and we need to have a chat."

"Oh, shit," the spoon fell on the floor as she turned to look at me.

"Finish what you are doing. A few more minutes won't hurt."

She turned, picked up the bowl of peas and a saucepan, then sat at the table. I looked at her for the first time. I could see Nanny in her, but her face was more angular, and her hair was thick and dark, worn in a bun at the base of her neck. Her eyes were blue, not unlike mine, I suppose.

"You know?" she asked, studying him.

"Yes, I have just left my grandmother. It's alright, and she is alright. I was angry but not that angry. Now it's your turn to explain. How long have you loved my father? Where the hell did that come from?"

His Aunt spluttered and coughed and started podding the peas. "I had been recently widowed and was coming home to my mother when your mother...."

"Elspeth," I interrupted.

"Yes, Elspeth. When your mother became ill, and as I was a nurse, I stayed to look after her. When she died, your father was devastated, and you were only a little boy, so I decided to stay and look after you both. It was decided for appearance's sake that I would be called Mrs Lingstrum, which is my married name, and everything would be proper to the outside world. Never has there been a moment of impropriety".

"Aunt Ingrid, that might have been the original reasoning behind it all, but I am almost twenty-one. Did none of you think that I might have liked to know my mother?"

"No, it was easier to keep the story going and not rock the boat. Mother and I talked about it, and she said that she told your father to tell you the truth at least once. It wasn't our place or story to tell."

"Bullshit!"

"Frederick, language!"

"You aided him in keeping my mother from me. Do people really grieve for eighteen years, or was it the easier option?"

His Aunt shrugged her shoulders. "That is something you will have to ask him."

"I intend to. Do you have the key my mother left behind? There is a chest in the attic that is full of my mother's things. Do you know what it looks like?"

"Frederick, I am sorry, but I only did it because I promised Elspeth that we would look after you. But, unfortunately, I don't have any key, and the chest is a large leather thing. I can go get it for you."

"Aunt, I know you did what you all thought was right, and I can forgive you for that because a deathbed promise is significant. But, like I told Grandmother, I was angry but more disappointed that I was so isolated about mother. I know that you surrounded me with many of the things she left behind, but it would have been nice to know that is what they were. Do you still have my cover from my other bed as I want it on my new one?"

"Hmmm. Do you think you are too old to hug your aunt? I will go get the cover and put it on your bed."

We mended some open wounds over a hug, a giggle, and a few tears. "It's been a long time, but your father still mourns Elspeth," she whispered.

I shook my head. "I don't think, so it has just become routine with him because he doesn't know what else to do. So you need to be more assertive."

*I predict as soon as I leave the room, the two lionesses will be on the phone with each other*, I thought. But for now, I need to see what is in the attic. I do remember coming up here once before. Why I don't know because until now, I had no reason to come up here. So dumping my keys and jacket on my bed, I head up the stairs. The key is still in the lock, although I assume no one ever went inside. The door squeaked loudly on opening; I wonder if the lights still work, so flipping the switch answered that question.

The vast expanse of the attic spread out before me. There is furniture, boxes, old fashioned trunks, all very dusty, and some things looked very old. There are cobwebs everywhere. It would be fun to come up here to explore, but I am after a leather trunk for now.

"Frederick, are you alright?" Ingrid called out as she climbed the stairs. "Have you found it?"

"Yes, I am fine."

"You might need this," she said, leaning towards me and handing me a giant feather duster. As I clear a path through the boxes, I come across pictures, more packages and a beautiful oak desk.

*My God, what is it doing up here? I would love it in my study.* I am amazed at the amount of stuff that is up here. *From where did it all come?* Some of it was old, like antique. I couldn't resist running my hand over the desk. It was beautiful.

*I will talk to Raoul and see if we can carry it down.*

There were chests and crates of all sizes, probably from previous centuries when people travelled. They would store their belongings in these. An idea began to form in my mind. The history of the packing chest. *No, too silly.* How about how our ancestors prepared for a holiday? Ladies wore long gowns so they would take up a lot of room. An idea, but for now, I was looking for a chest.

Grandmother said it was ordinary and brown, but I would know it when I found it.

*Trust me, you will know it*, she had said. And I did. It was my boat from when I was little. I remember sitting on it while she sang, 'Row, row your boat.'

How come I remember that now but can't remember my mother's face. I picked up the chest and made my way towards the door. I would take it down to my room and open it. I switched off the light, locked the door and dragged the chest downstairs to the bedroom. After fetching a cloth from the bathroom, I wiped off all the dust before attempting to open it. I had left the keys Mr Abrahams had given me on my bed, so picking them up, trying each one until the lock gave. It squeaked on opening.

What faced me was overwhelming. The chest contained books, more cameras, photo albums and various things I didn't recognise. Then, carefully taking out the cameras and placing them on my bed, I thought, *why father, why*.

Later, when lifting out a leather-bound book, I found it filled with writing. My mothers' journals, perhaps? The albums held photographs of Nanny, my father and me when I was a baby. "Oh, why haven't I seen all this before. Why was it all hidden?"

I didn't realise I had spoken aloud when I heard a response from behind me.

"Because it was too painful to see it all day in and day out."

I turned to the doorway, and there stood my father. I had not realised he had arrived home as I was so engrossed in what I was doing.

"But, why? I want to know why you kept all this from me. Why were you so cruel when I could have grown up knowing about my mother, a woman I know who loved me and loved you? Instead, you had her locked away as if she didn't exist. Why, Father, why?"

My father looked down. "Because it hurt so much having her things around. Reminding me every day that she wouldn't walk through the door, sit at the table for dinner, lie down with me at night. It seemed the best thing to do."

"That is so selfish of you. I had to learn my mother loved me from a letter that her solicitor has held since before she died. Shame on you, all of you. I have missed all these years of knowing her."

"May I?" he asked, entering the room. He sat on the bed. He was still wearing his overcoat.

"I loved your mother."

"Really!!! It's a shame you were so selfish that you couldn't share it with her son."

"The day she died," he went on, "the sun went out, stars stopped shining, life held no

meaning, I wanted to join her forever. But a little boy, so very like his mother, reminded me I needed to love and care for him. You were only just three at the time and did not understand what had happened. So, I took you away, and when we came back, your grandmother and Aunt had packed everything of hers away. I didn't care. I just didn't want to see it. So, the last time she went to the hospital, I locked our bedroom and moved to where I sleep now. Her clothes, jewellery, everything is still as it was that day."

"What?" I didn't understand this power of love a person had for another. Sure, I loved my father, my aunt, my grandparents, and my friends Geordie and Liam, but I had no experience of that kind of love.

"My love had gone where I couldn't go with her. So, I locked my heart and put one foot in front of the other and made some semblance of life."

"Surely, father, that isn't what she would have wanted. She would hope that you would find a different kind of love and happiness again, maybe even marry again. From what my Grandmother Aunt and Mr Abrahams tell me, she didn't appear to be a selfish woman".

"No, she wasn't. She was the most generous, loving person I knew. She spread happiness wherever she went. Life was wonderful. Then an unkind God took her away. You are so like her that my heart aches with the hope that maybe she will walk through the door, but no, it's you every time."

"Do you blame me for her death?'

"God no, Freddie. Evil cancer took her away. If she were alive today and had contracted cancer now, she would still be here. Back then, they didn't know how to treat it. Never, ever think it was your fault. It was no one's."

"Then why was everything put away. I just want to understand."

"Not everything was." My father said.

"I know my grandmother, and my aunt was here, and I have spoken to them. I was so angry, but I want to understand why."

"In this room, your mother is everywhere. The bookcases, some of the books, the Lemur rug and the cover on your bed were all hers. I just couldn't handle trying to explain where she had gone. It was bad enough when you woke at night calling for her, and there was only ever me. I just couldn't cope, which is why your grandmother lived in, as did your Aunt. I am very sorry for not having told you before. Nanny said I should have before you went to high school, but time got in the way. Not an excuse, I know. Do you think we could go and get a drink and some dinner as this truth-telling is very exhausting"?

"Yes, we can do that in the kitchen with my Aunt and Grandmother, a family meal. But, first, I want to ask a question. In the loft, there is a beautiful oak desk. Can I have it for my study?"

"Of course, you can. Your mother would be ashamed that it has not been in use all this time. I will get it brought down for you".

"That's okay. I will help Raoul bring it down. Now let's go inform the

Lionesses that we haven't killed each other but are hungry".

"Lionesses?" my father queried.

"Yes, I had to beard two of them today, then I had to tackle the lion." I said looking at him.

"Oh, I see," he nodded, finally understanding.

On our way down the stairs, father left his overcoat and briefcase in his study, so he looked less severe as we entered the kitchen. The two women each sat with a cup of something in front of them. They both looked as if they had the weight of the world on their shoulders. Then, finally, they looked up and smiled when they saw no blood spilt.

"Everything alright, is it?" they chimed.

"Yes, we are alright, but I think my son is not happy with any of us for keeping him in the dark. So, from today when he asks, we answer truthfully."

Grandmother stood up first and came to each of us, hugging us and kiss. "It is going to be very confusing with two Fredericks in the house," she said.

"Problem solved. When we visit my father in Johannesburg, my son is known as FJ, and I am Frederick," replied my father.

"Can I go ring him and tell him I have a grandmother and an aunt?"

"He knows, but yes, go and ring him. Tell him it's about time he visited," said father.

\*

"Frederick, is everything okay? Freddy was so angry and disappointed when he left me," asked my grandmother.

"Martha, Ingrid, I should never have allowed it to continue for so long, and that is of my doing. He has made me realise that I was wrong and that his mother would have been very disappointed in our actions. I think it will work itself out, but it will take time. At least he is still talking to us. Can we have dinner in here for a change? Yes, I am very aware that when I am not here, he eats in the kitchen. Truth-telling is very hungry work."

Frederick sat down and bowed his head, thanking his lucky stars that the two women still cared enough to want to help and for his son to be talking to him. What he had done was selfish and was of benefit only to him.

Frederick hadn't realised the damage it might have caused his son, although loving people surrounded him. I suppose some of the ways comes down to his friends Geordie and Liam and their families and Grandfather. I have a lot to make up. So, for tonight, we will sit as a family around the kitchen table as a family would.

FJ, as he was now in this house, charged into the kitchen and yelled, "Grandfather will be here next Friday and said I was to tell you it's about time you woke up to yourself".

"Yes, well, let's eat dinner and be thankful for all that we have." "Amen"

# SAMI AND HIS NONNO

## *BERNADETTE WEISS*

Carefully putting the can of Morello beer on the nightstand, Sami sat on Tony's gnarled, wooden, narrow bed with its box-spring mattress. The battered, leather, brown suitcase customarily hidden on the wardrobe now lay open beside him. He had lived with Tony Mozzarella for the last fifteen years. Four years ago, the Italian pensioner suffered a massive heart attack, leaving him with Hemiparesis, muscle weakness on the side of his body. As a result, he had quit his construction job and becoming the man's carer. Today, Sami buried Tony.

Father Bacci, who was taking over from the ageing parish priest, came to give the last rites of the Catholic Church. Tony was lucid at the time and aware that he was dying. Sami knew it and expected it, yet he was in shock when the Nonno gasped his final breath.

Frequent knocks at the door announced the doctor, undertakers, and well-wishers. Mrs Esposito from the Saint Ignazio's Church funeral committee stayed to answer the oaken door with its leadlight panelling. She turned away the parish gossips, overtly bringing meals that needed reheating in an oven. But covertly, they were seeking snippets of information to relay to other newsmongers.

Sami wasn't ready to make the many decisions that were needed. But, guided by the motherly Mrs Esposito, he managed to satisfy the demands made on him as Tony's only living relative.

*

He'd worn his best gun-metal grey suit this morning, with a crisp white shirt straight out of the cellophane packing and his black brogues. No socks. No tie. He'd stood beside Tony's coffin before the altar and from somewhere above looked down on himself and his Nonno. It was a surreal moment. He felt numb all over. The distant bell tinkled from the sacristy announcing that Mass was about to begin. The officious little Mrs Esposito took his hand and pulled him into the front row of pews.

The regulars made the necessary responses and took communion as they did daily at morning Mass. They were not weekly visitors as Sami only came when Tony insisted on going to Sunday services. Mrs Esposito took him up to receive communion. He remembered the touch of her hand as she led him forward. Almost as icy as Tony's were during the last few hours.

*

At Melbourne's General Cemetery, he was fascinated to see a flock of pigeon's wheel across the pale, blue sky marked by the chalk-like smudges of jets travelling in the troposphere. Turning to his left, he watched the two gravediggers laugh at a private joke. They wore Fluro fleecy jumpers over dirty khaki drill pants and steel-toed boots. As the internment ceremony started, they turned their backs away. Sami wondered how many graveside services they'd attended, making them immune to the grief of the final parting with loved ones.

To his right stood the undertaker and his crew. They wore non-descript black suits, pale grey shirts, and black ties. They examined their shiny, black shoes. *They are probably bored*, Sami thought. They didn't want to be here. Father Bacci was clad in his black soutane under a white Alb with its 11-inch lace sleeves and hemline. The purple stole, a symbol of repentance and penance, lay around his neck. Sami was nudged forwards to the left, front corner of the coffin and handed one end of a rope. On the count of three, together with three of the Funeral director's crew, he helped lower the coffin. It broke his heart. But he wanted to do this, for the man he'd known as Nonno, grandfather, for half of his life. He barely heard Father Bacci solemnly pray,

'Ashes to ashes, dust unto dust.' Sami realised that this was his prompt to throw some soil into the grave. He'd thought of throwing himself in as the handful of earth landed with a thud on the wooden coffin with its metallic ivory finish.

Sami walked back to the Fitzroy terrace house he'd shared with Tony for fifteen years. It felt cold and empty despite the warm afternoon sun pouring through the lounge room windows. Slipping off his suit, he washed his face and donned stonewashed jeans, a nondescript dark heather grey T-shirt, and thongs. Then, wandering into the kitchen on autopilot, he reached into the fridge for a beer and found himself in the passage to Tony's room.

The air was still hot and heavy with the summer day's humidity. The battered leather case that always lived above the wardrobe now lay open on the bed beside him. Tucked into a side pocket, Sami found the tattered, black patent leather wallet. Slipped in with the wallet, he'd found a vertically folded A-4 brown business envelope addressed to him. Opening the envelope, he found several pages held together with a giant paperclip. The top page was dated nine months ago..........

*'Sam, when we first met, I was sure that you were not related to me in any way. The hospital staff kept insisting you were Sammy, my grandson. I remembered that we buried him when he was seven. He'd died from a brain tumour. But everyone at the hospital knew better*

*than a grumpy old man recovering from head surgery. To get out of the hospital, we both needed to assure the social workers we'd accept home help in the home we'd shared since I'd become your legal guardian. You needed me as much as I needed you at the time.*

*I do not regret what I did. I did go behind your back and hired a detective in Perth to check out what little you wanted to share about why you had run away to Victoria. The investigator's report shocked me. When the Federal Police came to the door ten months later, I was able to show them the written statements describing your home situation.*

*You came home from high school half an hour later. The police wanted to interview you. And you agreed to speak with them, provided I was allowed to stay in the room. You were candid with the authorities about the homelife issues you'd refused to talk about with me. They advised you that your mother was fatally wounded, and your father was the 'person of interest' in her stabbing death. They warned you that Marco Rocco was on the run, and if he turned up in Victoria and found you, you might well be in danger.*

*The puzzle pieces fit together, and I realised then that fortune was smiling on a lonely man. In a strange quirk of fate, we trusted one another and bonded out of necessity. We were family.*

Sami smiled at the memory of the circumstances which led to their meeting. He had run away from home—a house without love. On a good day, Marco was an opinionated, cantankerous bastard. On a bad day, the barrel-chested man with hands the size of dinner plates would lash out. Lucy, his wife, copping verbal and physical abuse in the bedroom throughout Sami's life. The last time he'd seen his mother, she'd been crawling under the kitchen table, blood streaming from her nose and the stab wound to the arm when she'd tried to deflect the knife away from her face and chest. Marco was standing over her, threatening her with the bloody kitchen knife held high above his head.

'Mummy!' Sami remembered screaming.

Both parents froze and looked at him, standing in the door frame, his eyes bulging from their sockets. He'd been so scared he'd wet his pyjamas, and his naked feet rested in a pool of urine. Dropping the knife, his father rushed over and roughly hoisted him over his shoulder and upstairs to the bathroom. Stripping him, Marco took Sami's face in his hands, promising the child he would not hurt his only child. Then, after testing the water, he pushed Sami under the shower.

'When you're done, put on clean pyjamas and go back to bed.'

Returning to the kitchen, Marco found the discarded, bloodied knife on the table. There were blood spatters on the floor and wall. The kitchen door was ajar, and Lucy was nowhere in the house. Marco dropped into the ornate recliner chair in the front room and cried bitterly.

*

Marco worked hard to curb his drinking habit and temper and become a model father for the first ten to twelve months. His oft-repeated promises that Lucy would return to them became hollow echoes. She did not contact either of them again. Then at Easter, Marco disappeared for a fortnight, coming home with Isabella. He referred to her as his 'live-in squeeze.' She was the first parade of women who stayed weeks or months before fleeing from Marco's drunken abuse.

Eighteen months after Lucy left them, Marco lost his job at the used car yard. His sales dropped off, the length taken for his lunch breaks was out of control, and his sour breath when he returned reeked of alcohol. His physical altercation with his elderly boss Giovanni was the last straw. Giovanni pressed charges after being taken to the hospital with a broken nose and cuts above both eyes. This exchange resulted in a hefty fine and 400-hours of community service, working for the Council parklands division. During this period, Sami became Marco's punching bag to relieve his father's stress levels.

Sami was often shoved out of the way at home, lifted off the ground and held against the walls. His many injuries often landed him in the emergency departments. If they did, Marco was careful to take the boy to a different hospital each time. He was always able to spin a story about the lad's clumsiness.

Sami stopped attending football or swimming classes because he didn't want the black, blue, green, and yellow bruises visible to his mates or the teachers in the change rooms.

Coming home from school, Sami often found Marco passed out on the couch. The stench hinted that the man had soiled himself. Marco allowed the boy to take him to the upstairs bathroom to shower before being helped into the empty double bed.

*

Mrs Romano from the corner milk bar followed Sami home one day, forcing her way inside. She had silently watched the abuse Sami had suffered from his father and decided to get involved. Mrs Romana assessed the state of the house. She organised for Vinnie's to replace the stinking couch and Marco's double bed mattress.

Mrs Romano organised weekly visits by conference volunteers. In theory, they came to deliver food boxes, vacuum clean, wash dishes, and clean the toilet. In practice, they kept an eye on the pair and reported back to the ageing Father Thomasino. Marco would dry out, sober up, be compliant, and be submissive to the ladies from Vinne's who sometimes cooked meals as well as cleaning the house. Many months passed in this way before the cycle would begin again. Marco sought attention, and he always got it.

No one appeared to think Sami's lot in life needed changing. Sami started lifting $50 bills from his father's wallet on Newstart paydays in the months before his fifteenth birthday. The money Sami was taking was building into what he thought of as his emergency fund—adding each $50 note to the stash, hidden in the hem of his tan, fake leather jacket.

Two weeks before his birthday, Marco stumbled into his son's bedroom, clutching a meat cleaver. As the man lurched towards him, Sami kicked him in the undercarriage. Then, grabbing his bomber jacket, he'd jumped out of the bedroom window and began running for his life!

Seeing a bus near the bus stop at the end of his street, he ran faster, finally umping onto the moving vehicle. Out of breath and sweating profusely, Sami stood looking out the back window. Marco was not following him. Whew! He was safe for now. He'd lived in fear for months and vowing to escape. But, having run away, he was scared. Where would he go? What would he do? Would anyone believe a runaway kid?

*

Dark clouds had been rolling in across Fremantle throughout the day, now thunder roared, and the heavy clouds threatened in the night sky. The first fat raindrops splattered onto the bus windows as Sami counted out the bills hidden in the lining of his jacket. There were eleven $50 bills. He closed his eyes, vividly seeing his Dad lunge at him with the meat cleaver. Sami had been scared, silly. He now understood what was meant by the *'fight or flight response.'* He'd done a runner. His mother, Lucy, had too. Now he wanted to get as far away from Fremantle as possible.

As the bus entered West Australia's capital, he'd glanced through the window, seeing a travel agents poster announcing Jet Star Cheap Flights to Melbourne for the Easter holidays. Slowly the plan hatched in Sami's mind. He'd catch a connecting bus to Perth's public airport.

Arriving shortly after 10 o'clock, he went in search of a backpack. He shoved his jacket into the bag in the men's room before strolling over to the JetStar ticket sales counter. Placing the seemingly heavily laden suitcase at his feet, he smiled and asked for on one-way ticket for Melbourne.

'Do you have much luggage?'

'Not really. I only have my backpack. I'm staying with my grandparents as usual, for the school holidays. So, I have lots of clothes in Melbourne.'

'Will you be travelling alone?'

'Yes, dad is away in Karratha, working in the mines, and Mum's on rostered night shift at the Perth hospital and couldn't be here to see me off.'

'The discounted fee for students travelling with limited luggage will be $350, please,' replied the woman wearing the orange and black flight attendant uniform.

'That's what mum told me when she handed me the fare.' Sami counted out seven fifty-dollar bills.

'Mum said she'd be here when I get back in a fortnight. So I generally come back with a suitcase full of gifts,' he laughed.

Smiling, the agent handed the ticket and boarding pass to Sami. 'You are a lucky young man! Your flight leaves from Gate Three in an hour and a half. Enjoy your flight. Thank you for travelling on Jet Star.'

'Always do,' he assured her, striding away, faking confidence he didn't feel.

*

Having never flown before, Sami was scared but convinced himself it was a piece of cake. Besides, there were 90 minutes to get used to the idea. Sitting in the lounge near Gate three, Sami checked the Find My App on his iPhone to track Marco's whereabouts.

On the first check, it revealed his father was at the hospital in Alma Street. Sami was concerned. Was he injured to the extent that his dad needed to go to the hospital? Half an hour later, Marco was at the Bow St Police Station in Mossman. Was he reporting Sami as missing? Perhaps he was picked up for driving under the influence yet again?

'Calling passengers bound for Melbourne. Your flight is now boarding,' the voice-over interrupted his thoughts. Closing the App, Sami lost no time in joining the queue. But, he was not sorry at leaving the responsibility for his father's health and well-being behind.

Settling into his allocated seat at the back of the plane, Sami snapped on the seat belt and waited. His sweaty hands clung to the armrests as the plane taxied towards the departure runway. The jet engines roared louder as the plane tyres raced along the runway until the ground fell away. As his ears popped due to the sudden change in air pressure, Sami looked out of the window as the plane circled above the suburbs below before heading due east.

Wiping the sweat of anxiety from his brow Sami curled up across the two seats and shut his eyes tightly. He felt nauseous and overcome with dizziness but determined not to throw up. Finally, emotionally and physically drained by what had transpired, he fell asleep. As the service cart came past, the hostess didn't bother waking him, clutching a backpack close to his chest, and curled up across the two seats at the back of the plane.

The 'red-eye flight', which left at midnight, hinted that passengers were weary and perhaps red-eyed on arrival at their destinations. Two hours into the flight, Sami roused, becoming aware of the plane's landing. He looked at his watch. It was a tad after 2 am. He remembered the short stopover in Adelaide before the last leg of 75 minutes to reach Melbourne. He'd been reluctant to accept the snacks offered with the Coca-Cola until he realised, they were free. He visited the tiny unisex toilet several times during the last hour of his flight.

'Nerves', he'd explained to the flight attendant, who asked if he was alright. Apart from enjoying the amenities of the pocket-sized bathroom, it distracted him from the unknown that lay ahead.

*

Touching down at Tullamarine on that chilly, miserable Melbourne morning in August, he'd followed the passengers as they de-planed and walked through the eerily quiet airport. He overheard various passengers talking about taking a taxi into the city. Others were being picked up from predetermined places on the concourse out the front of the terminal.

Sami knew he had to go into Melbourne but decided against taking a taxi. Nevertheless, he optimistically set out, hoping that a passing motorist would give him a lift.

After thirty minutes, the sky flashed and crackled. Sami felt the first spots of tepid rain on his face hearing the distant rumble of thunder from somewhere beyond the hills. He'd walked another mile or so before the dark grey clouds burst, dumping a torrent of rain mixed with hail.

Visibility was reduced to 100-feet if that. A truck slowly pulled over onto the shoulder of the freeway up ahead. The driver, Sami thought, must have decided to wait out the rain. Sami approached the truck and clambered underneath the canvas canopy of the vehicle. He was freezing. Hungry. Wet. Sami curled up between a couple of spare canvas tarpaulins on a bed of wooden pallets marked Luciano's Fruit Emporia. Roused from his sleep roughly an hour later, Sami heard many Italian men greeting Angelo. Parking his truck at Queen Victoria Market, the driver jumped down from his cabin. Unseen, Sami leapt from the tailgate and walked away as fast as he could, fully expecting to hear this Angelo guy abusing him for hitching the ride.

Turning several corners, Sami found himself at a bus shelter on Queens Road. A drunk guy lay sleeping it off on the bench. His suit was dishevelled, his tie loosened at the neck, and curly grey chest hairs peeped out from the open shirt collar. The guy was bald with a sallow complexion and had soiled himself. Looking closer, Sami saw blood on his face from a wound at the back of the head. He also noticed the patent, leather, black wallet in the guy's left suit pocket. As he reached for it, the drunkard rallied.

Struggling through layers of confusion, Tony looked at the would-be thief in the eye. Jumping up, the swarthy Italian managed to land a loud smack to the kid's left ear. Then blacking out, he crashed down onto the concrete. Sami's stood over the man shouting,

'Hey, dude! Get up! Man, I'm sorry! I'm not a thief!'

Sami was scared. His left ear hurt like crazy. Then, falling to his knees, he sobbed, 'Shit, mister! Are you okay?'

Sami looked at the open wallet, which now lay between them. He checked for some ID. The guy's pension card said that he was Tony. Tony Mozzarella. There was a faded photo of a younger version of Tony, with a boy of perhaps six, on his shoulder.

As the drunk stirred, he cried out, 'Sammy? Where are you, Sammy? Come to Nonno.'

Sami was shocked. *The drunk guy knew his name?* Looking around, he saw a police patrol car approaching the bus stop. Sami waved them down, yelling the first thing that came into his mind.

'Help! Someone attacked us. My Nonno is hurt bad!'

Tony kept mumbling about Sammy as the police arranged for an ambulance. The officers advised the paramedics Sami was related to the injured man, who took them to the Alfred hospital.

*

In Alfred's emergency department, doctors immediately operated on Tony to relieve pressure caused by a subdural brain haemorrhage inflicted by a blunt instrument.

Sami, who kept up the appearance of being his grandson, signed the permission slips for the procedure, making him responsible for a complete stranger! The nursing staff placed a camp stretcher next to Tony's hospital bed in the private room, enabling the 'grandson' to stay. What no one knew was that Tony was the sole survivor of a horrific head-on collision many years before. The accident had taken his wife and daughter after they'd been visiting his grandson Sammy's graveside. The boy was only seven when he died from an inoperable brain tumour. The pensioner had been alone ever since.

The hospital nurses put two and two together. The child in the faded, creased Polaroid photo in Tony's wallet was the teenager before them.

The lad suffered a perforated eardrum while protecting his grandfather. The police interviewed Sami at the hospital.

Could he describe their assailant?

'Well, he was a big guy, taller than Nonno and me. There was a weird tattoo on his bald head. He stunk of whiskey. It happened so fast. I can't remember anything else.'

*

Tony remained in a medically induced coma for seven days. Sami wandered the hospital corridors whenever the nursing staff suggested leaving the room while treating Tony's needs. That's how he came across the hospital Chapel. It was a calming, quiet place with low-wattage light globes glowing at floor level down the aisles. Dipping his finger into the holy water, Sami made the sign of the cross before moving forward into the front pews. Peace, solace, and serenity crept into his body. Finally, he understood why people spent time in chapels and churches. He felt a sense of tranquillity as if the world had stopped spinning, if only for a moment.

He prayed for his mother, Lucy, wherever she was, forgiving her for running away and failing to return to take him to safety. Hell, he'd run away himself! He prayed for forgiveness, for leaving Marco. He prayed for Marco.

'Please, God, help him? Help him to help himself! I did the best I could, but he's getting bigger, heavier, angrier, and drunker than ever. I'm only a little kid. He's too much for me to handle.'

On one such visit to the chapel, he made a deal with God. Sami would do anything, whatever it took to help the older man. He'd signed the forms to permit the urgently needed operation. He had no legal right to sign off on anything at all as a minor in law. Yet he'd been encouraged into signing off on an operation on a stranger requiring urgent medical assistance! Unfortunately, they didn't have time for another relative to come in to authorise the procedure.

'Please, God,' Sami wailed in desperation, 'forgive me for being a bad son. I want this guy Tony to wake up. To live! I don't want him to die.'

*

Several days passed before Tony awoke slowly. He lay looking at the kid with a dark complexion and jet-black hair sitting next to his bed. The kid sat clutching his left hand. Pulling his hand away, Tony leaned forward. 'Who the hell are you?'

The nurse admonished Tony as she gently but firmly pushed him back onto his pillows. Her platinum grey hair was cut short in a chin-level bob, revealing the silver studs in her ear lobes. Her name was Rosie, and she spoke in Italian to her patient.

'What a silly question! He's your *nipote!* (grandson) One look at the pair of you, and you can tell who he is. He was with you when you got bashed up. The boy has refused to leave your side for over a week now. Fancy asking Sami who he is!'

'You! You're Sammy?'

'Yes,' Sami answered, 'I ran away after Dad came home drunk and threatened me with a meat cleaver. I took off. I used the money I'd pinched from his wallet. It was my emergency fund in case I ever needed it to escape. That's how I paid for the flight from Perth.'

*Shit, now I'm in for it. I've blurted out the truth*, Sami thought. The hospital staff ignored the two of them. They were busy taking temperature and blood pressure and recording the details.

Tony lay processing what the imposter had revealed. He'd run away from Perth.

Something about his father, a meat cleaver, stealing money to escape.

That's how it all started, fifteen years ago.

*

Sami sniffed away his tears as he looked down at the letter in his hand and read on,

*You were a decent sort of a kid, going to Fitzroy high school. You were a big help to me.*

*Together, we got rid of those pesky women who insisted on coming in each day to cook and clean and make sure I took my medicine. You'd left the house daily for school as the women expected you would. You'd wangled your way into high school. Only when the term reports came out did the teaching staff realised that the class's dux wasn't an enrolled student! Fun and games, my dear boy! You worded me up on how and why my grandson had divorced his parents and living in Melbourne with me, his Nonno.*

*You'd proven that you could cook Italian food rather well for your Nonno if I were not up to it. We'd worked together to convince everyone that we were a well-organised family unit. At the end of the school year, your grades were above average. These led to the apprenticeship offer by Grollo Constructions.*

*I was so immensely proud of you during the court case. I'd have done anything for you. So, when you begged me to let you change your name by deed poll to Mozzarella, I couldn't possibly turn you down.*

*

Sami remembered the dark time around the court case once his father was found. The Federal Police came to the doorstep once again. They'd taken another statement from Sami and asked him to be a witness for the prosecution. The summons to attend the court proceedings arrived eight months later. Tony sat in the gallery as the teenager, now aged seventeen swore, to tell the truth, the whole truth.

Having no one to batter or abuse around at home, Marco sobered up once again. One night in a Perth night club he saw Lucy, his estranged wife. He'd followed her to her flat, returning an hour later demanding she open the door. Lucy dialled triple zero instead. Marco battered down the door and baled her up in the kitchenette. He yelled at her, telling her that she needed to come home, not for him but Sami's sake. The neighbours on either side of the East Fremantle unit rang triple zero.

'Yes, we are aware of the disturbance. A patrol car is on its way.'

\*

The constable on the witness stand reported entering the apartment and smelling petrol. He'd found the still blustering Marco splashing petrol over his estranged wife. He'd stabbed her four times. Twice in the chest. The cuts to her forearms suggested they were defensive wounds in that she'd tried to protect herself. But, from the bruising on her neck and throat, it was already evident, Marco attempt to strangle her. Marco was preparing to set Lucy on fire as the two constables wrestled him to the ground. Paramedic treated Lucy for multiple injuries at the scene. On the way to Royal Perth hospital, she suffered a heart attack and died in the ambulance.

\*

Sami's tearful testimony helped establish the violent background from which the slain woman fled. The constable's testimony proved the premeditated murder. The accused, Marco Rocco, had approached the unit a second time that evening, bringing with him a 4litre can of petrol. Thus, he'd known in advance what he intended to do.

As his father was sentenced to life in prison, Sami broke down. With tears streaming down his face, Sami ran into the waiting arms of the one man he loved and trusted, Tony. Sobbing uncontrollably, he'd cried that he didn't want to be the son of the murderer, Marco Rocco.

Later in their hotel room, Sami asked if he could change his name by Deed Poll taking Tony's surname. Tony was delighted.

\*

Knuckling away his tears, Sami read on.

*You've looked after a broken pensioner in his last years of life as if I were your granddad. I'd like to think that my sweet little grandson Sammy would have done as much for his Nonno.*

\*

Sami had been stoic, refusing to show his emotions at the funeral parlour, Mass, and the gravesite with the priest and cemetery attendants standing around him. Now, sitting in Tony's room, the held-in emotions cascaded over him as he dissolved into tears of rage, pain, love, and loneliness.

Finally, wiping his nose and face on his sleeve, he looked down at the open bank statement dated six months earlier. The balance shown was a tad over a hundred thousand dollars at the time. What the? That was a hell of a lot of dough. Where had Tony gotten that sort of money? He read the final page of Tony's letter.

*Enclosed are papers you will need to take care of yourself from now on, son. The detective I'd hired provided me with the enclosed copy of your birth certificate. The Deed Poll papers, when you changed your name, are here too.*

Looking at the cover note attached to official-looking papers further down, Sami read on.

*This is my Last Will and Testament. The witness, Vincenzo Giuliani, is a lawyer and assures me this is perfectly legal. You need to ring him on the company phone number shown on the letterhead. He will help you with the paperwork to finalise my last wishes.*

*I leave you the house and my other earthly possessions, including my Bank of Melbourne bank account balance. I started putting money away for Sammy the day he was born – but stopped when he died.*

*Then ten years ago, when you turned twenty-one, I decided to continue depositing the funds for you. So, it's yours, Sammy Mozzarella. Thank you for being there for me. You gave me years of companionship, love, and respect. More recently, you saved me from entering an Aged Care facility. You enabled me to live at home after the last stroke. You insisted on caring for me. You wanted me to live in dignity, in the house I'd lived in for over forty years.'*

\*

Sami sat on the bed, staring at the photo on the bedside dresser. The one from six months ago. It showed a grey-haired dishevelled man seated awkwardly in his wheelchair with his right arm draped over the shoulders of a man with jet-black hair crouching next to him, intent on helping to blow out the candles. The birthday cake decoration resting on a card table assembled before them proudly declared. *Happy 80th birthday, Nonno*! Both men were smiling.

Sniffing, Sami stood up and, raising his beer, he whispered in a faltering voice,

'Cheers, Tony. You taught me what love, trust, what family should be. I love you so much, Nonno. I'm going to miss you!'

# FINDING PEACE

## *ROBYN KING*

Marjorie found herself staring at the photo of her husband Charlie that adorned the duvet in her bedroom. Next to him was Marjorie's favourite photo of her mother, Grace, holding Marjorie as a toddler. The images, framed by carved wood, Charlie bought back from Thailand when on a peace mission in the fifties.

In 1916, Charlie fought for two years on the ground at Gallipoli. Wounded by gunfire, he fell hard and was eventually medically evacuated out of the war zone.

Charlie was then transferred to England to remove three bullets in the hip and upper leg muscle. Battered, bruised and with an unrelenting infection, his wounds were not healing. Weeping and raw, the puss filled hole in his groin caused Charlie excruciating pain. The doctors were at a crossroads as to what to do. They were contemplating amputation.

The overworked medical staff did the best they could as there were too many casualties. Finally, while showing no improvement, the army decided

459

that Charlie was of no use to the war effort, so they sent him home.

Once in Melbourne. The doctors tried everything to get to the bottom of all the oozing yellow fluid. While carrying out numerous tests and x-rays, a thorough intern decided to x-ray the hip. There they found a bullet fragment embedded in the pectineus muscle.

Once removed, cleaned, and after an extensive amount of antibiotics, Charlie's wound started to heal. The hospital allowed Marjorie overnight visits. They had a private room and could sleep together in a single bed or an upright chair. Nine months later, Marjorie gave birth to a daughter, Grace.

That was over forty years ago.

Thinking of what had happened, a tear ran down her face. Her heartbeat quickened as this week was the hardest she'd ever experienced. She ached for Charlie and thought that her heartbeats were racing to keep her alive. She was indeed a broken woman. It was a week since Charlie's passing, and the visions of him lying on her bedroom floor, not speaking or moving, with just the sound of his laboured breathing caused her tears to flow. The ambulance took him to the hospital, but he was pronounced dead on arrival.

She took out her rosary beads, placing them on her mother's picture frame and looping the end of the chain around Charlie's frame.

Her sadness was overwhelming, but she had to pull herself together, somehow. Marjorie felt empty. She remembered her last meal was when Charlie collapsed when they had sat down to a roast dinner. She walked to the kitchen to investigate what was in the fridge. Then, there was a knock on the door. Long-time friends Betty and Evelyn stood at the doorway with a box of vegetables.

"Come in, ladies, it's lovely to see you", Marjorie said with a surge of relief for the company.

"This is with compliments from the Robianos, the fruiter. They thought you might need some vitamins and couldn't visit. So, they send their love," explained Betty.

Before the war, the Robianos relocated to Australia from Italy. Maria Robiano gave birth to a child every year for seven years. Marjorie assisted, looking after every one of them, and they brought joy to Marjorie.

As her only child, Gracie was jealous and possessive of Marjorie's affections. Gracie would say, "They aren't from here, mum. They eat weird food, and they smell funny." The three girls sat at the kitchen table. Evelyn took out sausages and potatoes and started preparing something to eat.

Betty searched through the box and held out a green vegetable. "What is this?"

"It's a zucchini," cried Marjorie.

"What do you do with it?"

"You cook them. Chop the vegetable into pieces and place them in the frying pan in a bit of butter with the sausages. Not too long though, they cook quickly."

While Evelyn was busy cooking, Betty grabbed some rollers and started setting Marjorie's hair. Marjorie smiled at the lovely friendship she had with her two wonderful friends. She began flicking through the pages of that morning's Sun newspaper when she noticed a photograph of an elderly nun. It was Sister Carmela Mary, Matron of the Good Shepherd Orphanage from 1904 to 1931. She would be devastated to see that her orphanage was left to run down as it has.

"Our orphanage is in the paper, Betty," cried Marjorie.

"There's a photo of it. It looks run down, and the trees in the garden are overgrown. They are blocking the windows of the second floor on the east side, where our room was.

"Betty. Do you remember Sister Carmela Mary?"

"Yes, I do," Betty said. "She used to say, you have two shakes of a dead lamb's tail to finish your work, or you fail."

"Well, she is still alive. She's ninety-seven, and she resides in the convent.

It also says unfortunately that the orphanage will be closed in December due to lack of funds from the government."

"That's awful. The government can't close the orphanage. What will happen to all those poor children?"

"It's all because of money," replied Marjorie despondently.

'How much do they need?' Asked Betty.

"Twenty thousand dollars would help to keep them afloat through next year, 1963. Then they would need to raise money themselves. The building needs repair. Plumbing, electrics, and the fridges are old.

As the girls sat down to a delicious dinner, they continued to discuss the demise of the orphanage.

"Let's visit them, Betty."

"When?"

"What about tomorrow?"

"Ok," said Betty. "I have lovely memories of living at Mayfield's."

"Mayfield's was the girl's section," Betty explained to Evelyn.

"The best thing about that place was that I met you, Marjorie because you looked out for me."

"Oh, Betty. Come here." Marjorie embraced her friend warmly.

"What about me?" cried Evelyn.

"Come in, Evelyn. We love you too."

After finishing their meal and cleaning away the dishes, the girls headed home for a good night's sleep. As Marjorie brushed her hair, her thoughts turned to her friends. Her gaze rested on the photos of Charlie and Grace.

"Charlie, if you are watching over me, keep us safe and help me to go on living without you. I love you, my darling."

Marjorie was ready by 6.30 am when there was a knock on the door. The taxi pulled into the driveway with Betty and Evelyn waving through the window, so she picked up her coat and locked the door.

The three girls laughed and reminisced about their days in the orphanage. Evelyn had met Marjorie and Betty at church. She had two hard-working parents and five brothers and sisters.

Marjorie vaguely remembered her parents. She remembered the shouting, though. Then one day, her mother didn't come home; she was never told why. Marjorie had no information at all about her mother. But her father was seen at the Bendigo races by Father Brendon. Marjorie had eavesdropped on the nuns discussing it.

Then, one day her father visited and brought chocolates. He said he was getting married, and he would return and collect her. But he never did. Marjorie never judged her parents because she loved the nuns dearly.

Betty had a similar story. Her mother was sixteen and too young to raise a child independently, and Betty never knew her father.

It took a couple of hours to drive to Bendigo. The driver dropped them off at the front doors of the orphanage, where they banged the knocker. They could hear the sound echoing from inside.

"I remember these doors. Years ago, I thought they were huge. But now they just look normal." daydreamed Betty.

A little old lady, wiping her hands on a tea towel, answered the door.

"Yes. Can I help you?"

The girls looked at each other for some guidance. Then, finally, Marjorie decided she was going to do all the talking.

"Hello, I'm Marjorie. These two are Betty and Evelyn," Marjorie said, gesturing at the others. "Betty and I were raised in this orphanage, and we came back to reminisce and offer our condolences. But unfortunately, we hear that the orphanage might close," explained Marjorie.

"Yes. Well, Sister Michel is here. Would you like to talk with her? She is about to have some tea in her room, but I'm sure she will accompany you to the main room. Down the passage to the right. I'll let her know you are here."

"Thank you," the women said in unison.

They shivered with the cold while waiting in the main room, filled with old furniture.

"Don't they have any heating?" mumbled Evelyn.

"Maybe that's on the blink also." They all laughed.

Marjorie explained to Betty that she felt like a little girl again, returning to her childhood home. The feeling was mutual. "This place does something to you."

Evelyn didn't like it. "It looks haunted," she exclaimed.

The girls all stood when Sister Michel walked in, holding two folders. The Sister looked well despite her advanced age. She studied each one of them in turn, then gently smiled and gestured for them to sit. Immediately the girls feel welcomed. Then, as they all sat down, the maid entered, carrying a tray with a pot of tea, biscuits, fruit cake, milk, and sugar, which she placed on the table.

"Well, hello, ladies." Sister Michel said in a soft voice. "It's a pleasure meeting you. Now, what can I do for you?"

Once again, Marjorie did the talking. First, she glanced for approval from Betty, then when getting the nod, she started to tell the Sister that they grew up at the orphanage and had learnt that it was going to close.

"Yes, we might have to close," the Sister nodded.

"Might!" Is there a possibility that it might not," questioned Betty?

"Well, you see," explained Sister Michel. "A family has offered to donate their parents' estate to us, so we are in luck. But we must be vigilant. We will still have to fundraise and increase the charge from respective adopters, as we need to raise twenty thousand a year to stay afloat.

The girls felt relieved.

"I have your intro papers here. I thought you might like to read them." Sister Michel said, opening the two folders.

"There we go. Marjorie Grace Mullin and Elizabeth Catherine Mullin."

"No, my name is Post, not Mullin," Betty said.

Sister Michel was quite adamant. "There you are, Betty, it says. Elizabeth Catherine Mullin."

The girls sat forward, trying to make sense of it.

"We can't have the same last name. We have different parents," said Betty, confused.

Sister Michel tapped the paper with her finger. "Well, it says here, Betty. Your mother is Catherine Mary Post. Aged 16. Unmarried. Your father is James Alwen Mullin. Aged 39."

"Really? questioned Marjorie. "Betty's father and my father are the same man?"

"That seems to be the case," replied Sister Michel. "There are notes here. I'll read them out loud."

"Catherine Mary Post presented a female baby to the orphanage. 1st June 1904. Aged fourteen days old. The mother was distraught. "She screamed when I took the baby away. The mother insisted that the baby was named Elizabeth Post, as her father would not take any responsibility."

Sister Michel looked up at them before continuing. "And Miss Post also wished that the child is told who her mother is if she ever asked. But unfortunately, the baby's father was married to someone else and already had a family. So, the father was not present," she added.

Sister Michel saw that all three girls were crying. Tears flowed, and Evelyn sneezed and spilt her tea.

"My Goodness, Holy Mary. Betty, we are sisters," sniffled Marjorie, blowing her runny nose with an old hanky she had in her clutch purse.

The maid brought in some handkerchiefs. "Thank you," dribbled Betty. I thought I was going to have to use my dress." The girls were talking over each other.

Sister flicked through Marjorie's papers. "There you are, Marjorie. You were brought in as an older girl by your father. You were five at the time. James Alwen Mullin. Aged 44. Your mother's name was Grace

Millicent Mullin. Aged 40. Mother not present."

"I knew her name was Grace, but that's all. I named my daughter after her," replied Marjorie.

"The Sister's notes explain what happened," Sister Michel said, reading from the folder. "The father dropped the little girl off. There was no apparent feeling for the child. He was charming and sat quite close to me when I was filling in the paperwork. He had a smooth disposition and tried to charm me. I explained to him that I was a Sister of the Lord. He still tried to touch me. I explained he needed to sit back and keep his mind on the task at hand, or I will stop this adoption. My rejection made him angry, and he told me to hurry up. He had things to do. An unapologetic man."

"That's all of Marjorie's notes," Sister Michel said.

"Is there anything about my mother? Where was she in this equation?" asked Marjorie.

"Sorry, I'm afraid, that's all we have. There are no notes on your mother."

Betty rubbed Marjorie's back. "There, there, Marjorie. I guess we'll never know," sniffed Betty.

Sister Michel handed the girls their paperwork. "You can keep them." We are having a clean-up, and the papers were going to be shredded."

Marjorie looked out the window as the sun was setting. It will be dark soon. We better get a move on as we have some travelling to do," said Betty.

The maid entered the room to collect the dishes. There were thankful smiles all around as the three women wished Sister Michel all the best.

The trip back to Melbourne was long. Marjorie stared out the window most of the way, nodding and agreeing while Betty and Evelyn talked and laughed about the day. Eventually, the taxi pulled into the driveway of Marjorie's house.

All three girls hopped out and hugged each other. "Are you ok, Marjorie?" asked Betty.

"I'm alright, just tired. It's been a long day."

"We are half-sisters." Betty reminded Marjorie with a smile.

The thought made Marjorie feel better. "I love you both, girls. Thank you for today."

"I'll call you sis, from now on," laughed Betty.

"Yes," Marjorie felt her arm. 'My arm feels funny. I think it has fallen asleep while in the taxi."

"Call in tomorrow, and we'll go to church together."

"We will, bye Marjorie."

Marjorie walked inside her dark, cold house. Shivering, she placed newspaper and some briquettes in the fireplace, adding kindling on top and lit it. Soon it was blazing.

"Urgh, that's better," Marjorie spoke out loud, rubbing her hands. Warmed up. She made a cup of tea and sat by the fire."

Her arm wasn't letting up. Now her jaw was aching, so she tipped a Bex powder into a glass of water and gulped it down. As she walked into her bedroom to get ready for bed, there was a knock at the door. Marjorie wasn't in the mood for visitors.

"Gracie."

"Hello, mum."

"Just letting you know Patricia and her boyfriend split up. She is devastated. She wants to end her life. But, of course, she won't. Tomorrow she'll be dating someone else. You know what the young ones are like. Everything is a drama. I can't stay long. I just wanted to see you and let you know I'm going to church tomorrow. I'll pick you, Betty and Evelyn, up, and we'll all go together."

"That's nice, dear."

Suddenly Marjorie felt dizzy. She held her head. Her arm felt twice the size, and her head was throbbing, collapsing to the floor she didn't hear Gracie screaming.

With her hands shaking, Gracie dialled for an ambulance.

Marjorie saw the ambulance light reflecting on the wall and was grateful they had arrived to help her. She was disoriented but felt safe now that the ambulance was here. The next sensation she felt was, floating. There was no pain. Her body wasn't hurting. Her arm was back to normal, and her head stopped thumping.

She opened her eyes to look for Gracie. But instead, she was looking at Charlie. He was looking at her. He was smiling. "Charlie! It's you. What are you doing here? What happened? I'm confused. Where am I?

Charlie cuddled her.

"Marjorie, I've been waiting for you, as I knew you were coming."

"Where am I? What's happening?"

"Let me explain, my darling."

"You are in a place where most people go when they first leave Earth. You are not in human form anymore. You are in the spirit world. And Marjorie, you will love what I have to show you."

"Charlie, I'm scared. Charlie, you're not limping?'

No, I'm cured. Where I'm taking you, there is no pain. There's no worry. You don't have to be scared of anything. The children here are safe. They are free to be themselves. No one hurts anyone here." They walked towards what looked like sunlight. A woman stood in the light, smiling and holding her arms out.

"This is your mother. Grace."

"My mother?"

"I've been watching over you, my darling daughter. I'm so happy to see you again finally. I never stopped loving you, Marjorie."

"What happened to you? Why did you leave me?"

"All I can do, is explain that I had a profound melancholy and took my own life when you were five. I've always regretted leaving you. But I lost my husband to other women, and he told me he didn't love me anymore. I couldn't see past that. I'm so sorry that I did that to you. But I can see that you have had a wonderful life with Charlie. He doesn't stop talking about you."

Marjorie felt a pull. "Where's my father?" asked Marjorie.

"He died twenty-two years ago. His lover's husband shot him dead. He's not here, though. He has gone somewhere else, and we don't know where that somewhere is. We aren't told. No one knows anything about it.

Marjorie wanted to keep talking with them, but she kept feeling herself being pulled back.

"Your time on Earth isn't finished, Marjorie. We'll see you again. I will always watch over you, my daughter."

"Go, Marjorie. I love you. Until we meet again," said Charlie lovingly.

Marjorie felt one more strong, mighty pull, finding herself on a hospital bed with loud voices, bright lights, and bells.

"She back!" exclaimed the doctor who was standing over her.

"Blood pressure is rising."

"Temperature, 98"

"She's stable!"

"Time's Sunday 6.35 am."

Looking around the ward, Marjorie processed her experience with Charlie and Mother. *Did it happen, or did I dream it?* Marjorie thoughts and the knowledge she had seemed so tangible.

"I'm going to be ok", she whispered to herself.

Closing her eyes, she heard a whisper in her ear.

"Now sleep, my dear. We'll always be with you."

Marjorie nodded off, smiling.

# THE GOVERNORS SECRET

### *THIS EXCERPT IS TAKEN FROM A NOVEL WRITTEN DURING THE LOCKDOWNS.*

### *RODERIC GRIGSON*

## *PROLOGUE*

On the island of Sri Lanka, once known as Ceylon, just south of the city of Colombo, there's an imposing colonial structure built on a promontory overlooking the sea. The sprawling building constructed in 1806 as a country mansion for the British Governor-General, the most powerful man on the island, retains an intriguing secret. From its deep cellar, a long, narrow tunnel extends to a disused well in the village that adjoins the property. The tunnel, it's been whispered over the ages, was used to smuggle the young lover of the Governor, a beautiful half-caste Mestizo dancer, the underground passageway allowing them to keep their nightly trysts secret. For several years, the two lovers engaged in a clandestine romance, their deep passion for one another flourishing in secret, away from the disapproving eyes of circumscribed English society in the capital, just 12 miles away. The prestigious Mount Lavinia Hotel now stands in its place, the passage entrance still visible to those who ask to see it. This is their story.

*

The Chief-Steward, dressed in a navy-blue coat with brass buttons, over a tight white shirt and breeches, greeted a dozen members of the troupe at the South Gate to the Colombo Fort. Red-jacketed native soldiers carrying long rifles manning the walls looked down at them as they filed through a side postern into the fort. Torches blazed in their sconces, throwing off shadows that danced with abandon against the dressed walls of thick *kabook* (clay ironstone).

'Follow me,' the thin-faced man barked. 'We don't have much time.'

Two native servants dressed neatly in white shirts and sarongs held torches above their heads as the Chief-Steward impatiently led the way. Banda and the rest of the troupe weighed down by cloth packs on their shoulders with their dance costumes and various musical instruments, followed.

The troupe were guided up a steep, stone staircase, past battlements with iron cannons and reached a long tunnel honeycombed on either side by niches, guardrooms and galleries that sloped upwards through the thick ramparts.

The transition from warm sunlight to cold shadow and the eerie echo under the black vault of the roof served to intensify Lovinia's unease. Suddenly, it seemed to her as though she was entering prison from which she would never be able to escape. It was a new and troubling thought, and she shivered as though with cold.

Aletta walked firmly in her shadow, with her hand grazing Lovinia's lower back as if to remind her she was not alone. Her usually vigilant eyes appeared even more watchful than before.

The tunnel took a sharp turn to the right and came out into a small open courtyard with more soldiers. On the far side, another gateway led into a square quadrangle. Beyond this lay the main bulk of the fort. A fantastic jumble of walls, stone-faced buildings, and warehouses–the more significant part of it screened from the city by the outer battlements.

Finally, out in the open, they walked through a heavy brass-studded wooden door leading to a side entrance of an enormous building with a bell-shaped roof. A door led directly into the eastern antechamber of the central hall. It was a small space marked off with a low false ceiling, plastered pillars and draped with thick curtains. The troupe had used it before as a waiting space during their previous performances. Lovinia could see a lofty, smoke-filled hall illuminated by several tall windows through a gap in the heavy drapes.

Several English officers were smoking pipes and hookahs and drinking from ornate glasses. Many reclined against yellow-and-gold bolsters placed on carpets around an intricately carved wooden chair. The rest of the room was filled with red-coated English soldiers from the garrison, talking, and arguing loudly while drinking directly from large wooden tankards. Several lamps gleamed, creating a festive atmosphere.

Lovinia could feel the Chief-Steward looking at her but pretended to ignore him. The man appeared to be over forty, or even nearer fifty. His sunken cheeks and thin lips spoke of a *ganja* (opium)-smoking habit. His large hawk-like eyes looked as though they filled his entire face. He seemed unable to take his eyes off her.

Lovinia felt Aletta's eyes on her, reminding her what she had to do. Holding the man's gaze, she spoke in the sweetest, most seductive manner possible. 'Sir, how can we make this the best evening you've ever had.

But, please, tell me what else I can do for you?'

The Chief-Steward was dumbstruck. He blinked like a man just woken up from a deep slumber. Lovinia blinked her beautiful deer-like eyes at the official. She smiled and caressed her right cheek with her hand, running her fingers gingerly over her hair. Her lips quivered. Her whole posture changed.

The Chief-Steward's eyes brazenly took Lovinia in. His gaze moved up her body, openly admiring the curve of her hips, the swell of her breasts.

Lovinia saw lust creep into his eyes. *But, just like any other man*, she thought, *it is all they ever want; it is all they ever think about!* Hiding her disgust, she smiled invitingly at the man instead.

'*Mahathaya* (Sir),' a deep voice called out from the doorway. 'The *Aṇḍukāraya* (Governor) is ready.'

The Chief-Steward broke contact with Lovinia's eyes and turned angrily to look at the speaker. The head of the Governor's household pursed his lips in thought, his eyes flickering to Lovinia before turning and walking out.

Lovinia breathed a sigh of relief. She picked up a vial of scented rosewater from her bag and pulled out the glass stopper. The perfume smelled heady and sweet—like a bouquet of ageing blossoms. Intoxicating and mysterious. She absently dabbed the plug on her neck and arms before putting it back.

Banda cleared his throat, breaking the silence. 'Musicians, be ready. Wait for my signal to begin.'

'Hold still!' Aletta commanded. The white linen garment clung to her svelte frame in all the right places. Her eyes were sparkling blue, lined in kohl with the practised hand of an expert. Her lips puckered into a perfect moue, stained pink with carmine and beeswax. She looped a thick silver band around her upper left arm and clutched Lovinia's chin, lifting the tiny, three-haired brush to Lovinia's eyelid. 'Tonight is a night to turn heads. Make them remember you. Make sure they never forget.'

Lovinia lapsed into a sullen silence, and Aletta tapped her cheek. 'Don't pout. I can't do this properly if you make such a face.'

Lovinia tried to relax her brow, but her thoughts made it impossible. So instead, she brooded as Aletta continued to apply creams and colour to her face.

'There,' Aletta said. 'You look lovely.'

Banda, who was watching, nodded his head at the musicians. Upali, a bearded man with a *ravanahatha* (bowed musical instrument), slid the hair of his bow across his device, checking to see if it was in tune by tightening its ivory pegs. At the same time, Anshu adjusted her *horanawa* (temple flute) reed one last time. Juana carried both a *raban* (one-sided drum) she played with her fingers and a *thalampata* (cymbals) which she tapped with her foot.

Mahinda settled his *dawula* (drum) base against his left hip and struck the drum's taut surface with a curved stick called a *kaduppu,* slow, then quick, quick. Finally, he began pounding out a driving rhythm, and the resonating sound of the *hak gediya* (conch shell) played by Samitha joined in before all five musicians were lost to their music, lost to the beat.

The music was rhythmic, layered, and deep. It combined the drum beat with the chink of tiny cymbals and the call of the flute with the crescendo of a strong pair of lungs.

It was time for them to dance. Lovinia stood at the gap by the curtains and searched the faces and every corner of the room for the Chief-Steward, but no—she could not see him. Instead, a British officer dressed in his regimentals lounged on the chair placed in the centre of the room with a second older officer standing behind him.

Lovinia narrowed her eyes, studying the seated man. Could this be the Royal Emissary from the Great King across the sea? His dark hair tied back with a velvet ribbon at the nape of his neck mainly favoured by seaman gave him *a slightly old-fashioned charm,* she thought, but it suited him.

*

A sudden tinkle of stringed instruments, the thud of a drum and clang of cymbals, followed by the squeal of flutes, started from beyond the door.

Then, through the entrance, a troupe of dancers came, swaying in rhythm with the music. Thomas had seen such performances a time or two before in Madras. Such groups travelled about India from the court of one native rajah or nizam to another, were sometimes employed for months to entertain the ruler, his family, and retainers.

Thomas had been reluctant when his Chief-Steward invited him to a party at the Garrison Hall in his honour. But he agreed, only after he realised that he was the Commander-in-Chief after all, and his power came from the troops under his command. Settling the current conflict with the Kandyan kingdom was as crucial as understanding the finances and administration of the colony. To do that, he needed to be seen and respected by his troops.

Thomas guessed that these dancers were creole, beautiful, petite, light-skinned women, bare above their girdles, only flowing skirts with intricate embroidery along the hem below, wearing bracelets about wrists and ankles jangled with each movement of the dance. The mixture of French, Spanish and African natives was a common sight in the West Indian islands where he had spent the last five years of his life.

A sigh went through the room, but there was only one drunken whoop as the dancers went through their movements, keeping time to the music from beyond the door. Thomas sat back, relaxed, and enjoyed the interlude, marking time with his foot. The women went through their repertoire, their dark eyes rimmed with kohl, flashing in the candlelight, the graceful bodies matching in time every nuance of the music. They slipped from one tempo into another and came at last to a flashing crescendo of movement and music, dominated by cymbals and drum; with a final thunderclap, they froze in statuesque attitudes.

Sir Thomas cheered with the rest as the four girls demurely genuflected, then left the room. A native man slipped into view carrying a brazier filled with glowing coals he placed on the floor. He sprinkled a handful of crystals into the red-hot brazier from a pouch at his waist, which burst into flame.

The flames rose into the air with a loud whoosh and died down almost as quickly. Thick clouds of scented smoke rose from the container obscuring the entire area.

The room grew ominously still for a moment, and then the music exploded in a torrent of rhythm, wild and exciting yet unmistakably disciplined by some rigid underlying structure. The rhythm soared in a cycle, returning again and again. After each elaborate interlocking of time and divisions, it cycled back to a forceful crescendo.

Out of the smoke burst a dancer, arms upraised. She whirled in a frenzy to the centre of the room in time to the music. Clad in a skirt sequined with gold and flaring around her, she spun currents of red, purple, and blue, her long slim legs flashing, her toe rings sparkling. She sported a gold spangle on her forehead, her hair arranged in two long plaits secured with ribbons, and her hands decorated with henna. She was wearing a small, fitted top of fiery red silk that left little to the imagination and her flowing skirt with intricate embroidery along the hem.

The woman's plaited hair fell past her waist in spiralling curls of ebony, with hints of gold ribbon set aflame by the torchlight. Her face would have brought a painter to his knees—high cheekbones, flawless skin, arched brows, and a fringe of black lashes that fanned over obscenely large eyes.

She captivated him with unguarded beauty and unassuming grace. Her hair twisted behind her like whips of ebony, her pointed chin turned high and proud. The light gold of her scarf cloaked the deep red of the silk beneath it. Sir Thomas thought this woman unbelievably beautiful. She appeared around twenty years of age.

She danced with her arms gliding above her head as if composing a new melody. Her hair flew in the wind as if drawing a veil over the night, her steps caressing the ground, and her gaze—from which Thomas couldn't take his eyes off for a second—sometimes embarrassed, often mischievous, and occasionally aglow with a naïve flirtatiousness.

The room erupted in a roar when the dance ended. The soldiers clapped and shouted, thumping the ground with their boots, their blood raised by the heady mix of alcohol, opium, soul-wrenching native music and rampant sexual desire. The dancer ended in a tantric pose which Thomas knew meant to heighten sensual awareness of those watching.

She flashed a look at him, and he saw her eyes, blazing like green jewels in her lightly tanned face. There was no submission there and not a trace of fear. On the contrary, as he studied her eyes, they seemed locked into his own and betrayed no notice of anyone else in the hall.

Sir Thomas gestured at the woman to come closer. The room quietened as she approached. Thomas felt Major Staples shift his feet behind him. The woman bowed, sinking gracefully into a submissive pose before him. He grinned down at her involuntarily. He felt an overpowering curiosity— which he had no intention of admitting.

'What is your name?' When the words came out of his mouth, Thomas realised that she would not understand what he had asked.

She lifted her head at the sound of his voice, looking questioningly up into his face, but she replied. 'Lovinia.'

Sir Thomas started at the sound of her voice. *She understood me.* He thought as he felt his heart, beat faster.

'You speak English.' Sir Thomas had to raise his voice as the clamour in the room rose as the soldiers went back to their drinking and talking.

The dancer looked at him for a minute and got slowly to her feet shaking out her skirts. She looked magnificent, her green eyes flaming, her colour heightened, her small, dark nippled breasts heaving with her quickened breath, noticeably clear under the red silk of her tunic. Her skin was fair, with a warm hint of olive, and her high cheekbones stood in stunning relief. Her nose was thin and sculptured, while her lips would have been fuller had they not been drawn tight in response to some unspecified inner determination. Yet her eyes were clear and receptive, even warm, and Thomas asked himself at that moment if this bespoke innocence, or guile.

'No—little Inglish.'

Sir Thomas did not realise that he was staring. The dancer looked at him, blushed on meeting his eye and looked down again. The pulse in her neck quickened. Her breathing grew heavy.

So, she was a natural flirt. Sir Thomas found himself wishing that this woman, this half-caste dancer, did not have to pass so soon out of his life. He felt his cheeks burn and cursed himself for a fool. Not that he was a romantic person. He was known for being ultra-reserved, a hard taskmaster and ruthless when it suited him. He had needed to be because his life had not been easy. He only succeeded by fighting every inch of the way for what he wanted and by being sure of what he did want.

'I have never seen such a dance before. What do you call it?'

Slowly, the woman raised her head. For the second time that evening, her bold, beautiful face mesmerised him. Then, finally, she shook her head, her magnificent black eyes meeting his questioningly.

Sir Thomas felt the colour rising on his face. 'Oh, I forgot. You don't speak English.'

For the first time since she had appeared in the room, the dancer smiled, seeing his reaction. Something stirred in Thomas's heart. Only once before in his life, a woman had been able to hold such power over him.

A sudden commotion at the entrance and a liveried retainer entered the room. The man walked quickly over to where Thomas was sitting.

Major Staples pulled the retainer aside. Then, after listening to what the man said, the Major leant over to Thomas. 'You're wanted up at the residence. Your Excellency.'

Sir Thomas looked over his shoulder. 'Who wants me?' He felt a rise of resentment at being interrupted at such a moment.

'There has been an attack against one of our outposts at the river crossing. As a result, General Wemyss has requested your presence.'

Thomas found himself annoyed and rose to his feet reluctantly. The Kandyan's continuously probed their defences, looking for weak spots, but he did not understand what was so important that General Wemyss could not handle.

Major Staples stared at him quizzically. Thomas studied the Major's face and could see the doubt in his eyes. 'I don't understand what the General wants of me at this time. Is he like this always?'

Thomas had read General Wemyss's reports in the regular dispatches to London, which he found remarkable. Unfortunately, however, he had met him only once when the General had called on him at Government House soon after his arrival in the country.

Major Staples nodded noncommittally. 'I can assure you, your Excellency, that he's very clever indeed. Even his staunchest detractors would agree on that. And he is also resourceful. Not many here are aware he has an intelligence network of his own.'

Sir Thomas pulled himself alert. 'I had no idea. Tell me more ....'

He heard a sudden rustling behind him. He turned to see the dancer had retreated and removed the scarf from her throat. She began twirling with her legs lose, her spine flexible, her movements fluid. The decorative gemstones on her skirt twinkled in the lamplight. A gold ring flashed on her third toe. She flew onto the dance floor, her hands weaving images and emotions, filling the space with her presence, compelling everyone to watch her. She whirled one arm around her head and loosened the coils of braided hair by pulling on the ribbons. Lustrous black hair streamed down her back. The sound of reawakened music and the pounding of drums rose to a crescendo.

The rhythm of her movement almost made Thomas want to rise and join. However, he was spared that embarrassment when she suddenly stopped, bowed gracefully before disappearing behind the curtains to the sound of cheers and catcalls by the intoxicated soldiers.

With a sudden urgency that revived him like a glass of brandy, he knew that he wanted to see the woman again. He must talk to her, to be with her and for the moment, he could think of nothing else.

*

Lovinia had always been a light sleeper and heard the rattle of the doorknob. She was usually up around dawn, but they had got back to the village after midnight, and she had taken a while to fall asleep.

Golden sunshine flooded the room through the gaps in the door as she rolled out from under the thin cotton sheet. She could hear her father's rhythmic snores from the other room. He had been pleased the Chief-Steward had paid them in full for their performance.

'You made an impression,' Banda said, smiling at Lovinia. 'He even paid what he owed us.'

The members of the troupe were excited when Banda handed out their take from the evening. Many of them supported family groups which included their parents and sometimes, even their in-laws.

Lovinia could see that Aletta was anxious to talk to her about what happened during her performance, but they didn't get a chance to speak in private. Instead, the door rattled again, this time a bit louder.

'I'm up.' Lovinia noticed the mosquito bites on her arm as she called out, knowing who was at the door.

Aletta barged in at the moment she heard the door unlock. 'You're still asleep,' she accused Lovinia, who was still wiping the sleep from her eyes. 'We have a lot to talk about.'

'Yes, but I am not ready yet,' Lovinia smiled at her friend, who was always so full of life in the morning. 'Why don't you get the fire going, and I'll join you in a moment.'

Aletta nodded, bouncing out of the room through the back door. Lovinia folded her bedding and put it away, taking a sip of water from the water jug before following her into the back verandah. Aletta had already started the fire.

'I couldn't wait any longer to talk to you,' she said, looking at Lovinia. 'You must tell me what happened.'

Lovinia could remember every single moment. She had played it over and over in her mind several times. When she danced into the room, her focus was totally on the man who sat in the place of prominence. While waiting, it had become evident to her that he was the new emissary from the Great King, and she had focused her attention entirely on him. She had been surprised when he addressed her.

'He spoke to me. Asked me what my name was.'

Aletta looked at Lovinia with a hint of a smile. 'He wanted you.'

Lovinia nodded. She could see that the *Aṇḍukāraya* was attracted to her. She had danced for enough men to recognise their desires.

'He tried to say more, but....' Lovinia had felt a connection to the officer until the messenger abruptly broke it.

'What happened?' Aletta's expression grew grave.

'He received a message. Something important, I think. He was distracted afterwards.'

'Do you know what it was about?' Aletta asked gently.

Lovinia shook her head. 'They were speaking English,' she said quietly. 'I didn't understand a word of it.' She spoke Creole, Cingalese and had a few words of English. A terrible foreboding gripped her senses as she uttered the words. She thought of the Kandyan and what he had asked her to do. How could she have missed such a splendid opportunity? The day had suddenly lost its lustre for her.

Aletta studied Lovinia, her head tilted to one side. 'I heard that he's not married and does not have a companion. You can manipulate such men quite easily as they are lonely.' She reached out and took Lovinia's hand in hers. 'We have to find a way for you to dance for him again.'

'What about the chief-steward?' Lovinia asked. 'Wasn't I supposed to get closer to him? But, of course, the Kandyan is expecting nothing less.'

'What, Kandyan?' The question took them both by surprise. Banda stood by the door, scrutinising them both thoughtfully. 'What's going on?'

Lovinia felt the blood drain from her face. Her throat went dry. She had never hidden anything from her father, and she did not know how he would react.

Aletta acknowledged Banda's presence with a smile. 'You'll have to ask Lovinia,' she said, with a toss of her head. 'She's becoming extremely popular these days.'

Lovinia dug her elbow into Aletta. She hated it when her friend treated her like a child. She took in a big gulp and told her father of her encounter with the Kandyan outside the village.

'You should have come to me right away,' Banda said sympathetically. 'I know whom you are talking about.'

Lovinia looked up in surprise. 'You know him?'

'No, but I have heard of him.' Banda walked over the hearth and poured some boiling water from the kettle into an earthenware mug. 'He's a dangerous man, I've heard.'

'He'll want to know what happened.'

'It will become known around the village very soon about our performance last night. Our people will spend the money they received and talk. It may be enough to satisfy him.'

Banda poured a heaped spoon of coffee grounds into the mug. 'Do you want one too?' he asked them both. They both nodded at him.

'Is he able to do what he threatens?'

'If he is in the employ of the King, he can do whatever he wants. So we can lose all of this,' he said, waving his arm around their home. 'One word from someone like him, and we will have to move. These are dangerous times.'

Banda exchanged a look with Aletta.

'You should stay away from the village for few days,' he said, preparing two mugs. 'You will do well not to leave the compound. Do not go roaming the streets as you do. You must be careful.'

Cold, invisible fingers swept Lovinia's back. She could remember the look the Kandyan gave her. She needed to do something to keep him from harming them.

Aletta had been watching the interplay between them. 'I think you should forget about the Chief-Steward,' she said. 'You should concentrate your attention on the man for whom you danced. He's the important one.'

'You can't be serious.'

'The Kandyan will not bother you if you set your sights higher. Leave the Chief-Steward to me, and you can tell your Kandyan that he now has two of us doing his bidding.'

Banda handed each of them a cup of steaming coffee. 'She is correct. It will buy you some time. But he will not be patient, so we have to come up with a plan.'

His warning rang in Lavinia's head as she stirred her coffee. She felt relieved that she carried the burden with the two people closest to her. Her father would move heaven and earth to protect her.

'Can you come live with us for a while?' Banda asked Aletta. 'I am not always around, and I don't want her to be alone.'

Aletta nodded. 'I will move right away,' she said without hesitation. 'I have wanted to move anyway, and this will be as good a place as any.'

Lovinia knew that her friend rented a room close to the village centre where she carried out various activities.

'You can stay for long as you like.' Banda had always treated Aletta like a daughter and knew the two women together would make a formidable pair. 'I will feel better if you can protect yourself.'

Banda walked back into their hut and emerged a few moments later with something wrapped in a leather cloth. Inside the wrapping was a small, double-edged stabbing knife with an inlaid handle. 'Carry this on you at all times.'

Lovinia took the dagger from him hesitantly. It was smaller than the length of her hand. She understood the danger she found herself in sometimes when intoxicated men, their minds feverish with *ganja*, tried to grab at her. Her father or men he employed as security would take care of the matter, usually dragging the offender away without interrupting the performance.

'Strap it to your thigh.' he said, pointing to a spot on his upper leg. 'Aletta will show you how.'

'Why do I have to wear this,' Lovinia questioned. 'There has never been a reason to use a weapon for defence.' The moment she uttered those words, she remembered the moment the Kandyan had grabbed her arm when she tried to leave him. He could have killed her if she had not agreed to do his bidding.

'We all do.' Aletta pulled back her skirt and showed Lavinia a triangular-shaped dagger strapped to the inside of her slender thigh by a piece of linen. 'It has saved me more than once.'

Lovinia nodded, having witnessed the incident to which Aletta referred. She had always thought that Aletta had taken the knife from the man who had tried to touch her.

'We still have to find a way to bring you to the attention of the English noble.' Banda's forehead wrinkled in thought. 'I will try to arrange a meeting with the Chief-Steward again.'

'She'll also need to learn to talk to the *Aṇḍukāraya*,' Aletta said thoughtfully. 'I know a woman in the village who can speak the language. I'll ask her to teach you.'

Lovinia smiled but did not know what to say. She tried to gather her thoughts. It all seemed so final. She licked her lips which suddenly seemed dry. She had thought what was asked of her, first by her father and then by the Kandyan, would be an impossible task, but with everyone supporting her, it could become a reality.

Lavinia looked up in confusion at the amusement on her father's face.

'Wouldn't you want to become the concubine of one of the two most powerful men on the island?'

Lovinia envisioned a different kind of life opening out before her if she could ever find a way to be placed in such a position.

'I will take lessons', she agreed. 'It's the only way.'

*

The following day Thomas breakfasted early. He had not slept much that night. He had lain awake thinking over what had happened during the evening. He had been tired when he came to bed, but had been unable to sleep. He could not forget the beautiful smiling face of the mestizo woman who had danced for him.

The feel of the cooling salves and the razor sliding over his chin restored a sense of normality to the day, and he was grateful for Johnson's silence, which enabled him to compose himself. Then, as the fragrance of sandalwood from the last lotion rose on the air, Thomas stood up, running a hand over his jaw.

'Johnson, you said you were married to a local woman?'

'Yes, Sah. But not a native Cinghalese, Sah. A mestizo woman!'

'A mestizo? Are they like the creoles in the Caribbean?'

'Yes, Sah. But of Portuguese descent.'

Thomas was familiar with the mixed-race Creoles of French, Spanish or African descent born in the West Indies or French or Spanish America. He had dealt with many of them on his posting as Brigadier-General on the French island of San Domingo.

'Who were the natives who danced for us in the garrison hall last night?' Thomas queried. 'They looked quite different to the locals.'

Johnson considered Thomas, his bushy white eyebrows rising, making his face look elongated. 'They are mestizos, Sah. Like my wife. They are a local dance troupe who are popular with the men.'

'Are they from around here?'

'Not far, Sah. A little village called Galkissa, just a few miles south of the fort.'

'Is that where your wife is from?'

'Yes, Sah.'

'Hmm,' Thomas remarked without responding. He regretted the moment he had to leave the welcome arranged for him by the unreasonable request of General Wemyss, which could have waited at least until the morning. The man wanted to send a battalion of English soldiers reinforced by native troops to attack the pass leading to the city of Kandy. In his mid-forties, the General had forgotten the lesson taught to him by the complete decimation of the previous force sent against the Kandyan kingdom.

'Those were native troops, Sir,' the General had blustered when Thomas questioned him on the wisdom of repeating the same mistake. 'We'll send a battalion of our good English lads and see how they'll like it.'

Thomas sighed in annoyance. He had refused, of course, angrily sending the General away, demanding he not throw away his men's lives needlessly. However, the attack on the river outpost only a dozen or so miles to the north concerned him. Before the General left, Thomas had ordered the officer to recommend three possible small actions against the Kandyan's for him to study.

'We are not going to win this war by playing into the natives' hands, General. 'I think that this matter is resolved given time and by using commerce as a means of pacifying the rebels.'

Looking back at the discussions with the General, they were almost too improbable to be explained. The war was not going well from all accounts and had rendered the treasury nearly empty. Moreover, there were vast leakages of expenditures everywhere. He now faced the difficulty of finding the money to run the colony without borrowing money from the Madras Presidency or the Colonial office in London. Thomas glanced down the neatly inked figures on the account sheet, turned it, and thumbed through the attached inventory when he was interrupted by Major Staples.

'I beg your pardon, Governor. You asked that you not be disturbed, but you have some unexpected visitors who crave your attention.'

Thomas leaned back and looked up at the Major, rubbing his eyes to refocus. Rays of dying light from the setting sun crossed the room, trying to pierce the darkened corners.

'Visitors? At this time?' Thomas' mind was still processing the mass of information he had been reading as he rose to his feet almost in a daze, stretching his arms above his head.

He waved his right hand at the two unequal stacks of documents on his desk. 'I need a distraction to take my mind from all this.' Briefings and meetings with colonial civil servants who ran the island for the Crown had filled the past week. Determined to understand how every department on the island was running, Thomas got buried in an avalanche of paperwork.

Thomas shrugged on the coat hanging on the rack by his desk. 'Who may I ask are these visitors, Major?' he asked, smoothening the lapels with the palms of his hands.

'Representatives of the Dutch East India company, your Excellency.'

Thomas nodded at the Major. He had been expecting some form of contact from them. It bothered him that the formidable Dutch East India Company was still trading in the colony. They arrived in Ceylon earlier than the British East India Company, thus gaining a head start, and successfully built up an intra-Asian trade network in the last half-century, extending as far as Japan. They traded raw silk, saltpetre, spices, opium, and indigo dye, just like the Company. Still, they far surpassed it in Asia with their experience by order of magnitude. Not only did they have more extensive warehouses, but they had also adapted well to the nuances of conducting business here, established several trading stations, and developed an extensive network of trading relationships. The closest Dutch trading post was in Batavia, a little too close for his comfort. Their goal would be to eliminate the English as a competitor as they had done with the Portuguese earlier.

Thomas was entirely unprepared for the four people waiting in the residence's bright and airy downstairs salon. He had expected an administrator or two, with ruddy complexions matching the highly polished mahogany panelling and figures more in keeping with the well-padded chairs and settees.

With effortless grace, Major Staples bowed to the two men and two women. 'May I present the Governor, Sir Thomas Maitland.'

Thomas had time only to glance at the men and notice that one of the women was young before Staples completed the introductions. 'Monsieur and Madame Van Rijn, their daughter Mademoiselle Van Rijn, and Monsieur Maarten.'

'We are honoured,' Van Rijn said as they shook hands, and Thomas kissed the ladies' hands. 'I apologise for disturbing you, your Excellency.'

Thomas waved off the apology. 'It was only a matter of time before we met. What can I do for you?'

Van Rijn seated himself comfortably and waited until the others settled before turning to Thomas.

'Surely you are the man who distinguished himself at the capture of Palicatchery in India.'

As he spoke, in almost perfect English with an accent that only hinted at his Dutch nationality, Thomas tried to think why the names had a curious – even spurious – ring about them.

'That was a long time ago,' Thomas replied. He was still trying to come to terms with his visitors, especially the two women.

The salon was surprisingly comfortable with its large fan slowly flapping under the high ceiling, worked by a footman who had no other function than to pull the rope every few seconds. Everything was on a grander scale than he had imagined - the room was more significant than his office, kept far cleaner, and many more servants bustling around. The furniture was comfortable, well suited for the hot climate.

'You are wondering why we are here, your Excellency.'

'I have expected some representation from the Company, no doubt Meneer, but I must admit that this sudden meeting with the four of you is unexpected.'

'I decided to bring my family with me to help you understand the dire situation we find ourselves in,' Van Rijn said. 'Bram here,' he said, waving at Maartens, 'is my secretary. He will keep a record if you don't mind.' The young man flickered his eyes at Van Rijn but said nothing.

Thomas nodded his agreement at the arrangement.

'My husband is not completely truthful, your Excellency.' Madame Van Rijn interrupted suddenly, looking at her husband with a mixture of compassion and pity. 'I have heard that you have never married, and we wanted to present our daughter.'

'Bernadette?' said Van Rijn, his eyes wide in disbelief. 'What can you be thinking of?'

'Helena is unmarried and has quite a lively talent, Sir Thomas,' said Madame Van Rijn, touching her daughter's arm. She has a fine ear for music and will play for you when your Excellency so desires.'

'I am sure you are right,' said Thomas, anxious now to turn aside from this blatant advertisement of her daughter, a plain girl who looked quite mortified at hearing her mother's words. 'But begging your ladies' pardon, I was hoping that this meeting would lead to something more fruitful.'

'This is not right, your Excellency.' Van Rijn responded with a voice soft with desperation.

Madame Van Rijn was not in the least abashed. She shook a finger at Thomas and replied with a knowing look. 'What you need is a woman's presence, your Excellency.'

Major Staples rose from his settee, taking a step forward. 'Perhaps I could take the two ladies out into the garden?'

Thomas smiled at the Major gratefully. 'Yes, I would be most grateful Major. We don't want to bore them too much.'

Van Rijn looked at his wife with a mixture of shock and pity. 'I too think it will be best if you go with the Major. I insist on it.'

Madame Van Rijn got to her feet haughtily looking like she realised that she had gone too far. 'Come with me, Helena. It is obvious we are not wanted here.'

Thomas watched at the two women were ushered out by the Major, who glanced over his shoulder at Thomas before leaving the room.

'What can I do?' Van Rijn cried, his voice rising with anger. 'She is getting impossible. We must find a way to solve this problem, your Excellency,' he implored, leaning back hopelessly in his chair. 'I must apologise for her attitude.'

Thomas felt sorry for the man. Not only did he have to face the humiliation of handing the Dutch trading interests of the entire colony to the Crown, but he also sat waiting with the rest of his Company for his masters in Batavia and Holland to decide on their fate.

Thomas waved the man's regret away. 'It must be hard for them,' he admitted. Thomas leaned forward, rubbing his hands together. 'Let's discuss what this visit is really about,' he said. 'I know you have been waiting a long time for something to happen, and I would like to understand what it is that is holding up the transfer.'

Van Rijn leaned forward, running a finger around his collar. 'I believe your predecessor did not give it much attention, your Excellency.'

Thomas knew that his predecessor Governor North had promised to repatriate all Dutch prisoners, many of the detainee's officers, to Batavia. However, progress had been slow for several years. The pensions to which they had a right as prisoners of war had become too costly. Thomas seriously mistrusted the Dutch and considered it wise to secure their departure as a matter of security. There was also the possibility of their colluding with

Kandy. But arranging their removal would amount to a heavy expense, Thomas realised.

'It is on my list of matters to be addressed, Meneer Van Rijn. But as you know, finding the money to hire the ships to transport these men to Batavia will take some time.'

'I am aware of that, your Excellency, and unless we do something to help these men, I am afraid that both the long incarceration and rampant disease will take a great toll on their lives.'

Thomas waited for Van Rijn to continue. It was a problem he, too, had considered.

'I have been in correspondence with the Principals of the Vereenigde Oost-Indische Compagnie back in Holland and have a proposition I would like you to consider.'

Sir Thomas turned his head sharply to look at him. 'What proposition is that?'

'If you could send an emissary to Batavia to arrange suitable transport, the principals will be willing to bear all expenses for the repatriation of the men and their families. I have received a letter from Holland which lays out the terms.' he remarked, holding the official letter aloft so he all could see the VOC seal emblazoned into the top of the paper.

'Why wasn't this arranged before?'

Van Rijn cleared his throat, clearly uncomfortable with what he was about to say. 'Governor North was more interested in his war with the Kandyan's. The men were being used to build roads and strengthen your forts. We were waiting for your Excellency to arrive.'

'You had not raised it with him before his departure?'

'Yes, I did,' Van Rijn said ruefully. 'But one did not want to get on the wrong side of the man either, so I didn't insist.'

Thomas nodded understandingly. It pleased him to hear this. Finally, he could strike off the books one of the more significant expenses in the colony.

'I will have to talk to my people, but I don't foresee any issues,' replied Thomas briskly.

Van Rijn sat back in his chair, smiling contentedly.

'How long would it take to conclude this matter?'

'I understand there is a ship being readied for the transfer to take place.' Van Rijn said, glancing across at Maartens, who nodded in agreement. 'It requires your official request for matters to be undertaken.' He paused. 'I would think less than six months at the most.'

Thomas wondered how the Dutch exchanged these messages between Holland, Batavia, and Colombo. But unfortunately, he had not seen anything in his briefing notes about it. So, he made a mental note to find out.

# WRITERS PROFILES

## DALE WALKLEY

Dale is a retired public servant whose life revolves around family and friends. A busy lifestyle sees her often at Balla Balla Community Centre, where she is part of the 'Morning Melodies' Team, a long-time member of the Scribe Tribe and two craft groups. In addition, she is one of the 'Writers of Balla Balla' who published their stories in Anthology Vol I.

## GRACE DE WISSER

Since retiring from Early Childhood Education, Grace spends quality time with her husband and growing family. Grace participated in writing courses at the Balla Balla Community Centre with Rod Grigson, became a member of The Scribe Tribe, and contributed stories and poems to their first book "The Scribe Tribe Volume One." Grace loves reading and poetry and likes working on short stories while researching her Family history with the desire to one day leave a lasting written family history for her family. In addition, Grace loves the outdoors and enjoys sharing her love of learning and nature with her grandchildren.

# MARYANN GRIGSON

Maryann hails from the beautiful island of Sri Lanka and is an ardent admirer of Mother Theresa. She is passionate about writing and has been a member of the Scribe Tribe writing group for many years. She has written and published her first book 'Links In A Memorable Chain', a story of her life journey, and enjoys reading, walking and dancing. Maryann migrated to Australia in 2007 and resides in Melbourne. She has three wonderful children, eight beloved grandchildren and a cute little great-grandson. She is a 'people person' and serves as a volunteer at the 'VINNIES' shop on Glenferrie Road.

# JUDY NEARY

Judy was born Judith Helen Latchford in Melbourne in 1951. She was the fourth child of twelve. She married Thomas Neary in 1972 who are both retired. She loves reading, writing, and travelling. Judy's stories are published in both volume one and volume two of the Scribe Tribe anthologies. Judy has a wonderful family and credits them as her inspiration to write.

# ZOE SKJELLERUP

Hello all readers. Thank you for choosing this book. My name is Zoe and I live in Melbourne. I'm diagnosed with a rare genetic disorder CDG syndrome type 1A. It affects my speech, loss of vision and balance. I also have a slight auditory processing delay. Due to these reasons, I prefer to communicate via writing. I'm very strong willed and have been published in Anthology Vol One in 2019.

# MELISSA SAYERS

Melissa Sayers has been writing for 30 years. She studied Literature for four years at Monash University and took the skills obtained there into a role as a commercial proof-reader, working in this field for 10 years, then moving to editing fiction works. The selection of poems and short stories in this Anthology are tales of life, love, highs and lows, successes and failures. They tell of obstacles she has faced and overcome in her life, and of the things she holds most dear and that lift her up. An insight into a complicated mind.

# DIANE BROWN

Diane is the author of the memoir, "The White Cockatoo", published in 2012 and is one of the Anthology authors, The Scribe Tribe, Volume One, published in 2019. Diane's passion is writing, and she has been a member of the Scribe Tribe for three years. Diane was a member on the Board of the Mental Illness Fellowship Victoria for 14 years and in 2008 was elected as Vice-President of the Board. She also chaired the Directions Committee of that organisation and was a member of the Research and Ethics Committee for Melbourne Health for two years. Before retiring, Diane worked as a Senior Para-legal for an Albury law firm and now lives in Melbourne with her husband. Diane has two adult children.

# REBECCA KENNA

A Dad who told tales of growing up in India and a Mum who read to her every night fostered Rebecca's love of books, words, and language. Real-life and fictional stories fuelled her active imagination, and by six, she was writing her own. Fast forward several decades, and her passion was reignited after completing a creative writing course in lockdown last year. Rebecca's writing journal is never far away these days. She is inspired by observing the behaviour, emotions and interactions of everyday people and discovering the stories that lie behind them. She has written several short pieces and is currently working on her first novel.

## NORMA SAVIGE

Norma is a retired educator, counsellor, and bureaucrat. She is a member of a large family in which story is important. Since her retirement, she has indulged a long-held passion by undertaking creative writing classes and joining two writing groups. She has had a particular interest in the short-story form and contributed to the Scribe Tribe Vol I Anthology published in 2019. Her past careers have fostered a genuine curiosity and appreciation for the vagaries of human behaviour. Currently, she is working on a novel, allowing her to explore this further. She lives in Victoria, is married, and has two adult children. She is a voracious reader, belongs to a book club and an online strength-building group. In her spare time, she studies the French language and is a member of a French Conversation group. You may discover any, or all, of these, creeping into her writings.

## ROBYN KING

Robyn is married with two grown boys. The drama in her writing comes from having a hairdressing salon for eleven years. There she came across many fascinating stories from clients and their experiences. She exaggerates them when writing her tales. Nothing surprises her. 'People are the best source of stories,' she says with a knowing grin. She notices the consequences and how people react to their grief or happiness when listening to their plight. It all makes for a good story. She then took the Creative Writing course at the

Balla Balla CC to learn how to put it all into words. She was the joint winner of the Balla Balla Story Competition for her story 'The Diary' featured in this publication.

## HANNAH SMITH

Hannah Smith is a "hopes to be" best-selling author, "wishes she wasn't" lawyer and "loves to be" mother to a teenage boy and Groodle puppy. The recent superfluous time she has spent stuck at home through COVID has reinvigorated her love of reading, writing stories and blogging. She was the joint winner of the Balla Balla Short Story Competition for her story, "The Boy Next Door", a story of hope and friendship in a time where people are most distanced. Her blog "IVF Got My Journey" documents her trials, tribulations, and rollercoaster journey throughout the IVF. Born and raised in Melbourne, Australia, Hannah has a deep desire to retire to and live out her days in the Disneyland Castle, overlooking the carousel, wearing a tiara and writing stories to convert those who don't believe in wonder and magic.

## ANNA ROBERTS

My name is Anna, and the year is 1960. My family is living in an apartment in Rome, Italy. So, picture this, I'm a tiny three-year-old, and most days, I carry my wooden stool under one arm together with a comic book in the other. I make my way down the corridor to Eva's place. Eva is a seamstress who works from her apartment while also looking after me while my mother, Caterina, worked in a local restaurant. Sitting quietly, I would devour my comic book literally by reading and then carefully tearing out the bad guys and eating them. Even a child can hate cruel people portrayed in books, so to even the score, I ate them. While flicking through a comic one night, my mother wondered why certain characters were missing and noticed only the baddies torn out. With my secret discovered, Eva kept a closer watch over me to make sure I didn't punish any more bad guys. Those comics ignited a passion in me for reading which has never waned. Though these days, I don't feel compelled to tear the bad guys out. Instead, the love of words has come full circle from reading to the love of writing, allowing me to produce stories for others to read and enjoy. I owe a huge debt of gratitude to Roderic Grigson for being my mentor, tutor and giving me honest feedback on my work and encouragement to WRITE, WRITE, WRITE!

## BRUCE HEWETT

After graduating as a pharmacist in Perth, Western Australia, Bruce set off to see the world but fell in love with Fiji. Over the next 10 years, he managed a community pharmacy before establishing his own community pharmacy and representing Fiji in the 1984 Los Angeles Olympic Games in yachting. Following marriage to a local Fiji gal Beverley and the birth of their first child, the family made the difficult decision to leave Fiji, to commence a new life in Sydney, Australia. In Sydney, Bruce joined the pharmaceutical industry where he spent the next 35 years in a variety of senior management roles around the world before establishing his own successful consulting business. Bruce has just published his first book 'Cry In Your Sleep' and is currently working on its sequel. Living in Melbourne, Bruce enjoys writing, keeping fit, performing voluntary charity work, and spending time with his two children, Vanessa, Sean and their families.

## CORINNE KING

Corinne King nèe Pereira was born in Ceylon (Sri Lanka) of European and British descent. Corinne's paternal side was Portuguese and British, and her maternal side was German and Dutch. Corinne was a student at

Methodist College in Colombo and migrated to Melbourne forty-nine years ago. Actively involved in the Past Students Association of her Alma Mater, she served on many Committees and held the position of President from 2003 to 2004. Corinne married her husband, Ian King, in 1975, becoming parents to their only daughter Karen Lisa born in 1981. Corinne and Ian are now grandparents to their granddaughter Ebony Nora who was born in 2015. Corinne has a radio background, having been involved at Radio Ceylon in the late 1960s. Currently, Corinne and Ian have a radio program called 'The King & I' on Friday evenings on Casey Radio 97.7FM from 8 pm to 10 pm. Corinne and Ian enjoy an uncomplicated life, keeping themselves busy travelling overseas when they can and performing many charitable acts behind the scenes. Corinne's ultimate goal is to write a book of her own that she has started, with many anecdotes she has stored from her life experiences.

## BRONWYN VAUGHAN

Bronwyn is an Australian scientist and educator, with specialisations in education intervention and case management. Her career of over 30 years has spanned in teaching across the sciences, gifted education and special needs, researching in State and Commonwealth medical projects and working in business. She is a trained soprano, lover of poetry and you'll often find her reading and volunteering her time in local politics. She spent a year in the office of the current deputy premier and education minister as a campaign assistant. Her love of learning is evident and is committed to keeping up with the latest in medical and educational research, related COVID19 policies and applying her knowledge in business. This short-story entry into the Scribe Tribe Anthology II is an historical fiction piece based on her own research and it's dedicated to the local storytellers who shared their own memories with her since childhood.

# BERNIE WEISS

Becoming a retiree in 2010, Bernie ticked off most of the items on her bucket list within eighteen months. The last item related to her dreams as a teenager, getting an undergraduate degree. Taking a second bite of the proverbial apple, she became a part-time student for seven years. Despite a hip replacement and needing a pacemaker, she qualified for a double degree gaining first-class honours in History in October 2019. Having some success in academic prose, Bernie anticipated an easy transition to creative writing and joined the Scribe Tribe. During the initial COVID months, she undertook two courses to master the challenges of writing short stories with a creative twist. She enjoys the camaraderie of the writer's group and combines her research capabilities with her newfound writing skills. She is currently working on a creative writing version on one area of her history thesis.

# TIFFANY LEONG

Tiffany Leong is an Australian writer and a video game reviewer at *GameNewsAus*. With a double degree in Science and Arts (Honours in Creative Writing), she's often balancing fact with fiction. Besides an interest in dystopias and angsty romances, Tiffany is fascinated by the interwoven elements of scripts, visuals, and acoustics in video game narratives. In her spare time, she enjoys long walks in the wilderness and relaxes with a book under the glow of a scented candle. Tiffany loves engaging with writers and readers alike; you can connect with her online at www.theseventhranger. wordpress.com

# RODERIC GRIGSON

Rod has always had the desire to travel. He was born in Ceylon (Sri Lanka) with a British heritage dating back to the colonial administration of that island. In the early 70s, after completing his formal education in Colombo, he travelled to the US where he found employment at the United Nations Secretariat in New York. During his 14-year tenure at the UN, he was awarded the UN Peace Medal after serving two years with the UN Peacekeeping Forces in Egypt, Israel and Lebanon. Coming back to NY in 1980, Rod worked with the newly formed UN Technology Innovations Programme developing foreign languages on computers, implementing Office Information Systems in UN offices across the world before migrating to Australia with his wife Mena in 1986. After holding several senior executive positions in global multinationals overseeing the Asia Pacific region, Rod retired when he was 60 to a leafy south-eastern suburb in Melbourne, where he became a full-time writer. Rod has successfully published three books since and is currently working on his fourth. When he is not writing, he facilitates the Scribe Tribe Writing Group and runs a Creative Writing Course at the Balla Balla Community Centre. He also teaches seniors and new migrants how to use modern technology.

# MEANING OF
# "BALLA BALLA"

## INDIGENOUS SIGNIFICANCE

The history of the name Balla Balla has links to the Indigenous community as part of their language. While there are no strict interpretations for the word 'Balla', taken in context has two meanings. In one Indigenous language, Balla means 'resting' which is also part of the word and suburb, Ballarat which means 'resting place'. In the second Indigenous language, Balla means 'mud', which is a very significant description of the particular area the facility is located in. Initially, at times throughout the year, this land sat at the 'bottom' of the swamp. This was a precious resource for the indigenous people and was seen as a 'seasonal supermarket'. In winter, they would come to the edge of the swamp to collect birds' eggs, eels, reeds and to harvest bark.

## HISTORICAL SIGNIFICANCE

Interestingly, Balla Balla was also the name of one of the first homesteads to be established in the area and is the name of the council ward in which the centre is now situated. Balla Balla may have different meanings in other languages; however the intent in choosing this name was to reflect the history of the area, as well as the indigenous significance.

The Balla Balla Community Centre is part of the City of Casey's network of fourteen Neighbourhood Houses and Community Learning Centres' in the municipality.

www.ingramcontent.com/pod-product-compliance
Lightning Source LLC
Chambersburg PA
CBHW031024030726
47497CB00004B/989